ARMY RANGER REDEMPTION

BY
CAROL ERICSON

First Published in Great Britain 2016
By Mills & Boon, an imprint of HarperCollins*Publishers*
1 London Bridge Street, London, SE1 9GF

© 2016 Carol Ericson

ISBN: 978-0-263-91919-6

46-1016

Carol Ericson is a bestselling, award-winning author of more than forty books. She has an eerie fascination for true-crime stories, a love of film noir and a weakness for reality TV, all of which fuel her imagination to create her own tales of murder, mayhem and mystery. To find out more about Carol and her current projects, please visit her website at www.carolericson.com, "where romance flirts with danger."

For the water polo moms

Chapter One

Dread thumped against Scarlett's temples as she stepped out onto the porch of her cabin. Clouds rolled across the waxing crescent moon, teasing her as light and shadow played across the trees crowding up to her front door. Holding her breath, she hunched forward and squinted into the darkness until her eyes and muscles ached.

Since she couldn't see a thing beyond the tree line, she tilted her head and listened to the sounds of the forest—a rustle of dried leaves, the snap of a twig, the soft coo of a nighthawk.

Had her mind been playing tricks on her when, from inside the cabin, she'd heard the strangled cry? It could've been a wounded animal who'd moved on in his pain and suffering.

She hadn't been back in Washington one week from her art show in New York and already she was on edge. She no longer had to fear Jordan Young, the man who'd been harassing her. That FBI agent, Duke Harper, had shot him dead to protect Beth St. Regis.

The Timberline Sheriff's Department had done a clean sweep of her property to make sure Young or his cohort hadn't planted any more traps. She had no reason to be afraid in her own cabin, on her own land. But she was.

Even before she'd heard what sounded like a muffled

scream tonight, she'd been uneasy since her return to Timberline. She couldn't put her finger on the reason for the feeling, and had dismissed it as leftover angst from going into a dream state to help Beth sort out her own visions. Any time Scarlett used the extrasensory powers she'd inherited from her Quileute granny, it left her jumpy.

Cupping a hand around her mouth, she called out, "Hello? Anyone there?"

Not that she expected an answer, but it beat cowering on her porch. Only the wind responded as it whistled through the branches of the trees.

She huffed out a breath and backed up to her front door. She turned and glanced over her shoulder before stepping across the threshold and slamming the door behind her. The top dead bolt stuck as she tried to click it into place. After four tries, she gave up.

The dead bolt had been Granny's idea, but Scarlett hadn't used it in years. Now that she needed that extra layer of protection, the darned thing had rusted or jammed or whatever. She'd have to replace it.

She twitched the curtain back into place and returned to her chair in front of the fireplace, where a crackling blaze welcomed her. Five minutes later, with a book open in her lap and her legs curled beneath her, a loud knock on the front door disturbed the peace and set her heart racing again.

This time she went to the front door with a poker clutched in one hand and her cell phone in the other, even though she couldn't get cell reception out here. She jumped as a louder knock resounded through the room. Another thing this door was missing was a peephole. Why hadn't she gotten a peephole installed along with the dead bolt?

She shoved aside the curtain at the window next to the door and peered onto the porch. The light spilling onto the deck illuminated a large man. She swallowed and backed up, but the movement must've caught his eye and he pivoted toward the window.

"Are you okay in there?"

Sweeping aside the curtain, her cell phone prominently displayed, she asked, "Who are you? What do you want?"

"I'm Jim Kennedy. I have a place—" he waved behind him "—up the road. I heard a noise and came out to investigate. Was it you?"

Her muscles coiled. He sounded sincere, but it could all be a ploy to lure her outside and... "Jim Kennedy?"

"Yeah, my folks had this place before...before. The Butlers used to live here. Y-you're not Gracie Butler, are you?"

Kennedy. She knew the name. She'd known the man, or at least the boy—a rough boy, a solitary boy. "The Butlers sold out and moved to Idaho, where Gracie and her husband settled."

"So you're a local?"

They couldn't stand there yelling through the door all night. As she yanked it open, she had the fleeting thought that she'd known Wyatt Carson, too, and he'd turned out to be a psychopath.

The man before her stepped back, his eyes widening as if surprised she'd opened the door. Her gaze raked over his six-foot-something frame. He'd have nothing to fear from wandering around the forest at night.

"I'm Scarlett Easton." She thrust out her hand. "I grew up on the rez, but went to Timberline High. You were in my geometry class."

He blinked and heat rushed to her cheeks. Why in the

world had she brought that up? She only remembered because she used to copy off his paper sometimes—not because she'd been intrigued by the loner who had a shock of black hair always falling in his eyes and rode a motorcycle.

She cleared her throat. "Mr. Stivers? Sophomore year?"

"Scarlett, yeah. You used to copy my answers all the time."

Her lips twisted into a smile. "Once in a while. Do you want to come in? I heard a noise, too. A scream, or…something."

"Sure."

She widened the door and stepped to the side as he limped over the threshold. She averted her gaze. The limp was new unless he'd just injured himself.

"Did you see anything out there?" The wind gusted as she shut the door, snatching it from her hand and slamming it.

Jim took a turn around the room with his halting gait, running his fingers along a table carved from a log, brushing his knuckles across a hand-painted pillow and studying the watercolor landscapes on the wall. "It's like a museum in here."

"Some of the pieces are for sale if you're interested."

Snapping his fingers, he said, "You were into all those art classes at school. You got suspended for painting a Native American mural on the wall outside the gym."

"Some of my best work."

He leaned forward to study a small painting of a storm-swept Washington coast. "Did you go outside right after you heard the noise?"

"I didn't say I went outside." She swallowed and took a step back to the door, curling her fingers around the knob.

"I heard a door slam." He straightened up and shoved his hands in the pockets of his black jeans. "I figured it had to be the door to this cabin since there aren't many others around here, are there?"

"N-no." Did he have to remind her about the isolation of their cabins? And how had he heard her door from a mile away? Since she'd bought this place, the Kennedy cabin had stood empty, but she knew it was a good distance away. She ran her tongue along her lower lip. "Let me get this straight. You heard a scream from inside your cabin, went outside to investigate and then heard my front door slam?"

"No." He moved in front of the fireplace, and a log rolled off the grate, causing a shower of sparks. "Do you have a poker?"

She reached behind her for the weapon she'd brought to the door for protection and grabbed it. If Jim Kennedy tried anything funny, she had no problem using the business end of this poker on him.

What *was* the business end of a poker?

He narrowed his dark eyes and they glittered behind half-mast lids. "I was already outside taking a walk when I heard the noise. I took off in the general direction of it, didn't hear anything else until the sound of a door shutting. I knew the Butler cabin was out this way, so I came over to investigate."

Rolling her shoulders, she strode forward with the poker in front of her and handed it to him—point first.

He took it around the middle and then prodded the log back into place, where it lit up in a quick blaze. "So, did you go outside after you heard the scream or just open your front door?"

"I stepped outside, but I didn't hear anything else, either. I'm thinking it might've been a wounded animal, and either it died or took off."

"Maybe. It sounded—" he shrugged "—familiar."

She thought he was going to say *human*, because that's what it sounded like to her.

"It gave me the chills." She held her hands out to the warmth of the fire, and the flickering flames caught the light from the many rings she wore on her fingers, creating a light show on the wall.

"I'll let you get back to your book." He tipped his chin at the book she'd left open on the recliner. "When I saw the lights on, I just wanted to make sure you were okay in here."

"Thanks." She led him to the front door and opened it wide for him to pass through. As he crossed the threshold, she inhaled his woodsy, masculine scent. On impulse, she touched his arm.

"Where've you been all these years, Jim Kennedy?"

He turned, brushing a lock of black hair from his face, and for the first time she noticed a scar across his forehead.

"Here and there."

She stood at the door watching him as he walked down the two steps with his halting gait. Just as she was about to close the door, a howl rose from the forest, causing a ripple of fear to skim across her flesh.

"It sounds closer here." Jim took off with surprising speed, and Scarlett followed him.

"Wait for me." She grabbed on to his leather jacket, stumbling against his broad back.

"Hey, who's out here?" Jim crashed through the branches of the trees as he illuminated the ground in front of him with a flashlight he'd pulled from his pocket.

He'd obviously come prepared, and then she saw the

gun in his other hand. Prepared for what? She released her hold on him, and he continued forward, thrashing his way through the foliage, off the designated trail.

She staggered backward, twisting her fingers in front of her. What was Jim really doing out here and why did he have a gun? She knew hunting weapons, and that gun wasn't intended for use against some hapless deer.

As Jim called out again, she found her footing on the cleared path. She should make her way to the cabin and lock herself inside. This time she wouldn't open the door for anyone—former high school classmate or not. Jim Kennedy could take his sexy self back to here and there.

Tapping the light for her cell phone, she pivoted on the toes of her sneakers and took a step forward.

Then a hand grabbed her ankle.

Chapter Two

The scream chilled his blood. It was the sound of a terrified woman—Scarlett.

Why had she stopped following him? Why had he let her?

"Scarlett?" He reversed course, staggering and tripping through the underbrush, cursing his bum leg. Cursing the men who'd caused it.

She screamed again, just as loudly but with a little less edge. His flashlight flickered on the path ahead of him as he charged back the way they'd come.

He plowed through the tree branches back onto the trail, which allowed him to move faster. "Scarlett?"

"I'm here, Jim."

His light picked her out, crumpled on the ground at his feet, and he jerked to a halt. He grabbed on to a tree branch to stop himself from falling on top of her.

"What happened?"

She pointed into the underbrush beside her. "There. It's a man. H-he's injured or…"

Jim crouched beside her and aimed his flashlight at the bushes, where it illuminated an outstretched arm, hand fisted into the dirt.

He pushed aside the foliage that covered the man and reached out with two fingers to feel the pulse at his throat.

"He's dead. How did you even see him there without a light?"

She gasped, covering her mouth. "He grabbed my ankle. Are you sure he's dead?"

"What?" He scooped aside more of the underbrush and flattened his palm against the man's chest. Blood seeped through his shirt, moistening Jim's hand with its stickiness. He bent forward, putting his ear close to the man's nose and mouth.

"Call 911."

"I can't get reception out here. I'll have to at least walk down the access road to the front."

He gestured to the man's body. "He's dead. He's not going anywhere. I'll come with you."

"What happened to him?" She clambered to her knees, and he held out the hand that didn't have blood on it.

"He has a chest wound. I can't tell what did it, but he lost a lot of blood. I'm surprised he had the strength to reach out and grab you, or even the wherewithal to realize anyone was passing."

She grabbed his hand, and he pulled her up beside him, where he could smell her musky-sweet scent.

"He must've been the one moaning out here. Maybe he lost consciousness and then came to when we passed him. He reached out to me as a last-ditch effort." She bent her leg at the knee and rubbed her ankle.

"Let's go." He tugged on her hand to get her away from the dead guy in the bushes. "From the looks of the blood pumping out of his chest, he was fast on his way out and wouldn't have survived even if we had discovered him when he was moaning."

As they burst onto the access road, he aimed his light at the ground and hurried across the gravel and dirt, practically dragging Scarlett behind him as she kept trying her phone.

He didn't want to run into whatever...or whoever that man had encountered.

When they reached Scarlett's mailbox on the road, she nudged his arm. "Got it."

"Let me report it." He took the phone from her and spoke to the emergency operator, giving her what he could. When he finished the call, he dropped the phone back into Scarlett's palm.

She asked, "Did you see his face? Do you know him?"

"I didn't get a good look at his face, but I doubt I know him. It's been a while since I've been back to Timberline." He held out his hand in front of him and lit it up with the beam from his flashlight. "I got his blood on my hand, though."

"Ugh. Do you want me to get a towel while we wait for the cops? I have paper towels in my car."

"I'll leave it until the sheriff's department can have a look at it." He jerked his thumb over his shoulder. "What happened back there? Why'd you stop following me?"

"I—" Her eyes darted to his pocket where he'd stashed his weapon. "I didn't want to go any deeper in the forest."

Especially in the company of a man with a gun—a man she'd just met even though they'd been high school classmates years ago. Smart girl.

"And then the guy just grabbed your ankle? Hard?"

"Not that hard but enough to surprise me and trip me up."

"When did you realize he was hurt?"

"I kicked out when I fell, to loosen his hold. I'd already had my cell phone out for the light. When I was on the ground, the little beam of light illuminated his hand, and

I could see that it was limp. His arm wasn't moving, but I screamed again just in case."

"I heard you, loud and clear—both times. You didn't see his face?"

"I wanted to run the hell out of there, but I couldn't move. My muscles froze. I certainly didn't want to look at him. Did you see his face?"

"Nope." He shook his head. "Maybe you know him. Maybe he was a friend on his way to visit you."

"Me?" Her dark brows shot up. "I don't think so. The only people who come out here to visit me are my cousins, Jason and Annie. And that wasn't Jason's hand."

"We'll find out who he is soon enough." He held up one finger. "Sirens."

The revolving lights on top of the emergency vehicles cast an eerie glow in the misty air as they flew down the small road to Scarlett's cabin.

Jim waved the flashlight in the air to flag them down.

The vehicles—one ambulance, one fire truck and a squad car—squealed to a stop in front of Scarlett's mailbox.

Jogging next to the squad car, Jim knocked on the passenger window, and the deputy buzzed it down. "You can go up the access road. The body's in the woods, just off the trail."

The deputy gestured out his window for the ambulance to make the turn onto the access road, and then he followed it.

Jim and Scarlett caught up just as the officer was getting out of his cruiser. "What's going on, Scarlett? More shots fired out here? More bear traps?"

Jim shifted his gaze to Scarlett's face. She hadn't told him about any shots being fired out here or any bear traps. That's all he needed for his other leg—a bear trap.

"Cody, you remember Jim Kennedy, don't you?" She swept her arm in his direction.

With his left hand, Jim shook Cody Unger's hand. Must be Deputy Cody Unger now. He'd been the high school quarterback and an all-around good guy. Jim hadn't known him well—different circles.

"Kennedy." Unger nodded. "Did you find him?"

"Scarlett did." Jim held up his right palm. "But I checked him out. He has a wound to the chest and lost a lot of blood. This way."

As Jim led the way with his flashlight, Scarlett asked Unger, "Where's Sheriff Musgrove?"

"I called him. He's not feeling well, told me to handle it."

Jim stopped and pointed to the arm flung out on the trail. "That's him. The rest of his body is beneath those bushes. I don't know how he got there, but both Scarlett and I heard a scream or a cry earlier. Must've been him."

"I have a couple of other deputies en route. They can canvass this area." Unger squatted down next to the body and pushed the bushes away from it while shining his flashlight on the man's face. "Doesn't look familiar. Let's get out of the way and let the EMTs do their thing."

The EMTs squeezed past them as Jim and Scarlett followed Unger back to the access road.

"Do you mind if we talk inside your cabin, Scarlett?"

"I was hoping you'd ask." She sniffled. "It's cold out here."

They ran into the other two deputies in front of Scarlett's cabin and Unger instructed them to look for evidence in the area and to check for the man's ID.

Once inside the cabin, Unger pulled a kit out of the black bag slung across his body. "I'm going to scrape some of that blood from your hand and get it on a slide. Then you can wash it off."

Jim held out his hand, palm up, and Unger ran a stick over his skin to collect a sampling of the blood. He transferred it to a slide, sealed another slide on top of the first one and dropped it into a plastic bag. "You can clean up now. Thanks for preserving the evidence."

Scarlett tapped his arm. "Bathroom's the first door on your right."

The art gallery spilled over to the bathroom with a border of flowers and cupids painted on the wallpaper and a mirror that looked fit for a wood sprite, with carved leaves and flowers curling around its edges.

Jim soaped up his hand and removed the blood. He didn't want to mess up any of Scarlett's artfully placed towels with residual blood, so he plucked a couple of tissues from the box and wiped off his hands just in case. He dropped them in the toilet and flushed.

He hunched forward, studying his reflection in the mirror, and grimaced. How the hell had he gotten mixed up with a dead body his first week back in Timberline? Not exactly the way to keep a low profile.

When he returned to the front room, he interrupted Scarlett reenacting the moment when the man grabbed her ankle.

"So, I kicked out, fell on the ground and screamed, just not sure of the order of those actions."

Unger turned to him, his notebook in hand. "That's when you returned? When you heard Scarlett scream?"

"I ran back, she pointed out the body and I felt his pulse and his chest." He wiped his damp hand on his jeans. "That's how I got his blood on me. I felt for a pulse first and listened for his breath, too. He was dead."

"You ever had any CPR training, Kennedy?" Unger tapped his pencil against his pad.

"Six years as an army ranger sniper. I know the signs of a dead body when I see 'em, and I know when it's too late to render aid."

As he held Unger's gaze, he heard Scarlett's sharp intake of breath.

A slow smile spread across Unger's face. "I guess you know what you're doing. Did either of you recognize him?"

"I didn't get a good look at his face and Scarlett didn't see his face at all. He had a beard. I felt that when I listened for his breath."

Scarlett asked, "Did you recognize him, Cody? You looked at his face, didn't you?"

"Older guy, beard, long, reddish hair. I haven't seen him around, but the conditions out in the woods are not optimal for identifying a body." He shoved his notebook in his pocket. "I got your stories. If I have any other questions, I'll let you know. It could just be an accident. I don't know yet what caused his wound, but if it turns out to be homicide, we'll call in the boys from county and they might have additional questions for you."

Jim followed Unger to the front door and stepped out onto the porch with him. Scarlett tagged along, slinging her jacket over her shoulders. Did she plan to go out again?

Unger pointed to the trees crowding close to Scarlett's cabin. "You should get those removed, Scarlett. Most cabins out here have some sort of clearing around them. I don't know why the Butlers never did it when they had the place."

"It's one of the features that drew me to the cabin— the privacy. I need it for my work."

Jim crossed his arms. "Don't artists need natural light?"

"Not for the kind of work I do."

He knew nothing about art or artists, except the kind that did tattoos, so he'd keep his mouth shut.

Scarlett gasped and grabbed his arm. "They're bringing him out."

Peering through the trees that ringed Scarlett's property, Jim could make out the EMTs wheeling a gurney from the woods onto the access road.

They all made their way down the path, through the trees, and stopped short of the gurney at the mouth of the ambulance doors. The EMTs had yanked the white sheet over the dead man's face.

One of the guys turned to Unger. "Looks like he succumbed to a stab wound to the chest—multiple stab wounds."

Scarlett swayed beside him, and Jim put a steadying arm around her shoulders. "Did it happen here, on Scarlett's property?"

The EMT shrugged. "I can't tell. That's for those deputies thrashing around out there to figure out."

Unger whistled. "I'll call Sheriff Musgrove right away. We're going to need county out here now."

"Should we wait for the county coroner?"

"Take him to the morgue at the hospital. The county coroner can work there."

Unger turned to go back into the woods and Jim held up his hand to stop him. "Is Scarlett safe here? The guy could've been murdered twenty-five yards from her front door."

Scarlett's body stiffened beside him and he drew her closer.

"I'm calling the county sheriff's department right now.

They'll probably be here the rest of the night. I don't think Scarlett has anything to worry about." Unger charged off toward the crime scene.

As the EMTs adjusted the straps on the body, Scarlett said, "Wait. C-can we see his face? I just want to make sure it's not anyone I know, although if Cody didn't recognize him I doubt I will."

"Sure." The EMT whipped back the sheet from the man's face.

Jim clenched his jaw as sour bile rose from his gut. Scarlett and Unger might not know the murdered man, but Jim did.

And if the man hadn't already been dead, he might've killed him himself.

Chapter Three

Scarlett swallowed as she studied the dead man's face, half obscured by his bushy beard and mustache, some sort of tattoo creeping up his neck with an *L* and a *C* intertwined. She'd never been a portraitist, but if she had been she'd want this guy's likeness on canvas. Even in death, he wore his life story on his face, etched in every line and wrinkle.

She blew out a breath. "I don't know him. Jim?"

"Never saw him before in my life."

The EMT tugged the sheet back over the man's face and loaded him into the ambulance.

Unger returned with his deputies. "The county sheriff's department should be out here shortly, Scarlett. They don't need to disturb you tonight, but the lead detective will probably want to talk to both of you tomorrow. Going anywhere, Kennedy?"

"I'm staying at my…my place."

Scarlett glanced at him out of the corner of her eye. The Kennedy cabin had been the closest residence to hers, but nobody had lived there since she'd bought the Butler place. Apparently, Jim Kennedy, the town enigma, had been off to war with the army rangers all these years.

When the EMT had lifted the covers on the dead man, Jim had moved away from her. She hadn't minded his arm draped over her shoulders or the solid presence of his muscular frame, although she'd never been one to lean on a man. Her own father had died in a car accident along with her mother, and her uncle had been a black sheep, ostracized from the reservation.

She scooped her hair back from her face. "I'm going to call it a night. Tell those county deputies they can talk to me anytime they want, but mornings are best, before I get to work."

Unger smacked the side of the ambulance as its engine started. "I'm going to back out and let these guys out of here, but I'm sticking around to wait for the county guys."

"Okay if I leave, Unger?" Jim shoved his hands into his pockets where he must've still had his weapon stashed.

If the man had been shot instead of stabbed, would Jim have told Unger about his gun? If he had a gun, maybe he had a knife.

Scarlett closed her eyes and dragged in a deep breath. Nothing about Jim screamed cold-blooded killer, but she couldn't shake the coincidence of his appearance followed by the discovery of a dead body on her property.

"You can leave. Again, just be available in case anyone wants to ask you any more questions."

Scarlett pivoted on the gravel. "Hope you can figure out what happened to that poor man."

Jim drew up beside her with his flashlight. "I'll walk you back to your place, if that's okay."

"If you want, but I think I'll be fine with half the Timberline Sheriff's Department on my property and the county sheriffs showing up in a few."

"I can take a look around and check your doors and windows—for when all those deputies leave."

A little chill zapped the back of her neck, and she hunched her shoulders. "That's a creepy thought."

"Not my intention to scare you, but sometimes a little fear is a good thing."

They returned to her cabin and Jim flicked the broken dead bolt. "You can start here by getting this replaced, and you might want a peephole in the door so you don't have to look out that window."

"Funny enough, I noticed those deficiencies myself when you banged on my door."

"Why don't you give me a tour?"

She spread her arms. "This is the great room, perfect for entertaining three guests at one time."

His lips twisted as he checked the front window. Then he moved to the other two. "At least they all have working locks."

"At least?"

"Anyone can smash a window."

"Thanks for that."

"But then you'd wake up and the intruder would lose his advantage, and you could always come at him with this." He strolled to the fireplace and replaced the poker she'd snatched for her defense when he'd first come to her place. "Do you have a gun?"

"A gun? I hate guns."

He pulled his own gun from his pocket and caressed the handle. "You hate guns because you're afraid of them. If you learned how to take care of a gun and all the safety measures associated with gun ownership, you might feel differently."

Shaking her head, she gritted her teeth. "I doubt it. Almost everyone around here has at least a shotgun and spends a lot of their time hunting defenseless animals."

"I agree. You don't have anything to fear from a wild animal." He returned his gun to his pocket. "I spent my time in the army hunting a different kind of animal—definitely not defenseless."

"You used to hunt, though, didn't you?" She snapped her fingers. "That's why you became a sniper. You were a great shot."

"Something like that." He pointed toward the kitchen. "Do you have a back door?"

"Two of them—a side door off the kitchen and then a back door from the addition. That's another thing I liked about this cabin. The Butlers had added a room to the back of the house, which made a perfect studio."

He checked the kitchen door and tapped the wood. "You need a dead bolt on this door, too."

"I'll get someone out to do both doors, same key."

He stood in the middle of her kitchen, dwarfing it. He'd even been buff as a teenager. Instead of playing team sports for the high school, Jim had spent his time working out and lifting weights.

From the way his shoulders filled out his jacket, he hadn't given up the weights.

"You know what you need in this kitchen?"

"Besides a twenty-four-hour chef?"

"A landline telephone. You can't keep running to the end of the road in an emergency."

She hunched over the kitchen counter, planting her elbows on the tile. "I came back here, bought this cabin to get away from it all, to work, not to get all plugged in."

"After what just happened out there—" he jerked his thumb over his shoulder "—you need to think about your safety."

She widened her eyes. "Why? Do you think there's a serial killer on the loose or something? I'm not happy that someone died outside my cabin, but I don't think it has anything to do with me. From the looks of the guy, it could've been a bar fight or drug related."

Jim straightened up so fast from where he'd been bent over looking for a phone jack, he almost hit his head on the bottom of the cabinet.

"Why would you say that?"

"I don't know. He looked a little rough around the edges, could've been using."

"The point is, we don't know his story." He limped from the kitchen and tipped his chin toward the short hallway. "Okay if I take a look in the other rooms?"

"There are just the two bedrooms. You already visited the one bathroom, and then the room at the end of the hall—my studio."

He pushed into the bathroom and placed his palms flat against the small, beveled-glass window. "Someone can slide this up and out. You can buy a rod to put across the top of the slider to prevent that, or you can even use a pencil."

"Good idea. I never realized how unsafe I was before."

"You never found a dead body on your property before—have you?"

"That was a first, although I guess it's not all that rare for Timberline cabins to be housing dead bodies. Did you hear about Jordan Young killing his mistress twenty-five years ago and stuffing her body in the chimney of his cabin?" She sucked in a breath between her teeth and shivered.

"I read about the whole thing online when I got here. So much for peaceful little Timberline."

He checked the windows in the guest bedroom, and then she led him to her own room. As he took a turn around the bedroom, she actually blushed—not out of modesty but because she'd just had a sudden vision of this man spread out on her bed.

"You should keep these closed at night." He yanked the curtains together and she jumped. "Are you still nervous?"

"It's not every day someone is murdered in your neighborhood." She caught her lower lip between her teeth. She should be feeling more anxious about that instead of daydreaming about Jim Kennedy in all his naked glory. She'd put it down to shock.

He tilted his head and that lock of dark hair fell over one eye—just like in high school. "Let's take a look at that back door."

As she led him to her studio, she clasped her hands in front of her, twirling her ring around her middle finger. She usually didn't invite people into her inner sanctum, unless they were other artists. Not even potential clients saw her workspace.

Dragging in a breath, she threw open the door and flicked on the light.

Jim froze at the doorway, his mouth hanging slightly ajar. "I've never seen anything like this before in my life."

"Well—" she waved her arms around "—it's an artist's studio."

"You're very...productive." He swiveled his head from side to side, taking in the work on the walls, canvases stacked in the corner and unfinished pieces languishing on easels stationed around the room. "And kind of schizophrenic."

"I guess that's one way of putting it."

"You've got normal stuff over here—" he flung out his right arm "—and...different kind of stuff over here."

"Landscape watercolors on the right and modern, abstract oils on the left."

"Let me guess." He pointed to a painting comprising of skyscrapers, a pair of eyes and a wolf head. "This is the expensive stuff."

"Good guess." She held her breath waiting for him to ask her to explain the painting.

He studied it for several seconds with his head to one side and then shrugged. "This room isn't secure at all."

She released the breath. "Because of the glass wall."

"It must look incredible during the day, but at night anybody could peer right into this room. If you keep expensive work in here, I'd think you'd want to protect it better."

"This is Timberline. I really didn't expect to move back here and experience a crime wave." She rapped on the glass. "What do you suggest?"

"This is the back door?" He navigated through the easels and stands and yanked on the handle of the sliding glass door. He crouched down and inspected the track. "You can put a rod in here for an extra measure of safety in case someone breaks the lock. A camera wouldn't be a bad idea, either."

Twisting her braid around her hand, she sighed. "I might as well go back to the big city."

"That man who died tonight probably has nothing to do with you."

"Don't try to make me feel better now after you just did a security check on my home...and found it woefully inadequate."

"Problem is, we don't know what he was doing out there, why he was killed or who killed him."

He straightened up, grasping the door handle for support. She would've offered a hand, but Jim didn't seem like the type of man who would accept assistance easily.

"Hopefully the county sheriff's department can figure

that out. I don't need any more people lurking around my cabin, causing trouble."

"Jordan Young was after that TV reporter, not you, right?"

"Jordan turned out to be Beth St. Regis's biological father. He'd murdered her mother, his mistress, twenty-five years ago and sold Beth on the black market when she was a baby. He just turned his attentions toward me because I was helping Beth." She shivered and pressed her hands against her stomach. "Pure evil."

"He figured if anyone noticed his daughter's disappearance, he could pass it off as another Timberline kidnapping?"

"Something like that, but nobody noticed the disappearance of mother and daughter since Beth's mother had moved away after the pregnancy and had just returned to Timberline. Young had kept them hidden away in his cabin until he killed Angie, Beth's mother."

"Makes you wonder." He shoved one hand in his pocket and stared out the wall of windows at the forest lurking in the darkness beyond.

"Wonder what?"

"If there was an active black market for children, maybe that's what happened to the Timberline Trio."

"Not you, too." She shut off the light in the studio. "Ever since Wyatt Carson kidnapped those three children to recreate the Timberline Trio so he could play the hero, everyone and his brother have been snooping around looking into the Timberline Trio case."

"You think that's a bad idea?" He'd turned from the window and his eyes glimmered in the dark room.

"It's over." She'd never admit to him that she had her own reasons for finding out what had happened twenty-five years ago. She'd never admit that to anyone, since curiosity about the case seemed to put a target on your back.

He said, "I suppose it's never over for the families. Look what it did to Wyatt Carson. Losing his younger brother like that must've jarred something loose in his psyche for him to go on and kidnap those children years later."

"You're right." She stepped back into the light from the hallway. "I don't mean to be insensitive, but..."

"You're Quileute."

"What's that supposed to mean?" She jutted out her chin.

"Just that I know your people had some fears and superstitions around the whole Timberline Trio case." He held up his hands. "Hey, they weren't the only ones."

As far as she could recall, Jim never had a problem with the Quileute, but his father was another story— loudmouthed bigot. Members of her tribe had been in a few barroom brawls with Slick Kennedy.

He'd gotten the nickname Slick because of his movie-star handsomeness and pumped-up physique. Her gaze tracked over Jim as he stood in the middle of the room, and she swallowed. The apple hadn't fallen too far from *that* tree.

But Jim had never been in any trouble with her people, although all the guys her age had been wary of him because of his father, his brother and his father's buddies— beer-drinking, bigoted bikers.

She lifted and dropped her shoulders quickly. "Yeah, there were some crazy stories going around at the time."

He crossed the room and joined her at the door. "Anyway, you might want to look into securing this place better—at least until the deputies can figure out why that man dropped dead in the woods outside your cabin."

"I'll do that, thanks." She closed the door to the studio. Halfway down the hallway, she turned suddenly and Jim bumped into her. She placed a palm against his chest where his heart thundered beneath her touch. "Sorry."

His body tensed as he stepped away from her, and she dropped her hand.

"What are you doing back here, Jim?"

His lids lowered over his eyes and he studied her from beneath his thick, dark lashes. "Trying to get away from it all, just like you."

She blinked and turned, calling over her shoulder. "How long have you been out of the army?"

"Over a year."

"Is that...is that what happened to your leg?"

"Long story."

It didn't sound like he had any intention of sharing it with her. Maybe he'd loosen up after a few beers or a shot of whiskey.

When they reached the living room, he made a beeline for the front door. "See you around."

Scarlett blinked. "I was going to offer you something for your trouble tonight and for staying with me. Beer? Coffee?"

"I'm good, thanks."

Now it seemed as if he couldn't get away from her fast enough. Must've thought she was prying into his business. She followed him to the front door, which he'd already opened.

He stepped out onto the dark porch.

"Oops, I turned off my porch light. Be careful. I have some plants..."

As he turned, Jim tripped over one of the pots and stumbled down the two steps, falling to the ground.

He cursed on his way down and landed with a thud in the dirt.

"I'm so sorry." Scarlett switched on the porch light and flew down the steps. As she lowered herself to the bottom step to help Jim, his bare back, exposed by his shirt hiking up, drew her gaze.

Shock tingled through her body as she saw the edge of Jim's tattoo—an *L* and a *C* curled together—just like the tattoo on the dead man.

Chapter Four

"Dammit." If Scarlett touched him or tried to help him, his humiliation would be complete.

She jerked back and pushed to her feet. She must've sensed the vibe coming off him.

"Why'd you turn off the porch light?" He rolled to his back and peered up at her wide eyes. "I'd forgotten those damned potted plants were there."

"Yeah, sorry. It's a habit for me to turn off that light when I come inside for the night." She took another step up, reaching for the door behind her. "You okay?"

"I'm all right." He hoisted up to his feet and brushed the dirt from his jeans.

"Maybe one of the deputies can give you a ride home."

She wasn't offering? He didn't blame her, the way he'd snapped at her. Wasn't her fault he had a gimp leg.

"I think I can make it." He stomped his boots on the ground. "No permanent damage, or at least no *more* permanent damage."

"Okay, then. Good night." She slipped into her cabin and slammed the door.

That spark he'd felt between them had just been extinguished. The fall made her realize he was damaged goods. A woman like that needed a strong man to match her, not some physically weakened, brain-addled vet.

He trudged through the trees toward the deputies canvassing the crime scene, giving them a wide berth to avoid being questioned tonight. He couldn't handle it right now.

Seeing Rusty Kelly's dead body had been a shock. What was Rusty doing back here? That type always rode in packs. Did that mean the rest of them were close on his heels? Was it a coincidence that Rusty had turned up dead a week after Jim had arrived in Timberline?

He edged around the squad cars and took the long way back to his cabin by following the road. When he got back to his place, he withdrew his Glock and checked out the perimeter of the cabin.

Unlike Scarlett's place, this cabin had a wide clearing around it that extended all the way to the road. He believed in having an unobstructed view of whatever was coming at him.

But he hadn't seen Scarlett Easton coming at him. He'd noticed the smoke from her chimney since he'd been back, but he'd figured it was Gracie Butler living in her folks' place. He hadn't been prepared for a dark-haired beauty to hit him like a thunderbolt.

Scarlett had been something of a mystery in high school—a rebel but not a bad girl, lost both of her folks in a car accident. She'd never partied much unless it was on the rez, and she'd traveled with a pack of very protective guys from her tribe. That bunch wouldn't have let him within two feet of Scarlett, but then they'd judged him based on his old man. He didn't blame them.

Satisfied there were no strangers or, worse, people he knew lurking around the cabin, he went inside. He locked the door behind him and faced the room, his breath coming in short spurts.

Squeezing his eyes shut, he massaged his bad leg. It

didn't hurt him anymore, but sometimes it ached in remembrance.

He dragged in a deep breath, but it didn't do any good. Even with his eyes closed, he could feel the room spinning, the darkness closing in on him.

He managed to make it to the couch, dragging his left leg behind him. Collapsing to the cushions, he ripped off his jacket and dropped it to the floor. He sank, his head in his hands, his fingers digging into his scalp.

The heat. He couldn't take the heat. He yanked off his shirt and the T-shirt beneath it. He bunched them both into a ball and pressed it against his face to mop the sweat pouring from his brow.

Falling to his side on the couch, he let out a low moan. Then the images began flashing behind his closed lids. He drove his fists against his eyeballs to make the pictures in his head go away…but they kept coming.

He needed his medication. How had he thought he could do without it, especially in this place?

He needed a drink. He needed to sleep. He needed a warm body.

He needed Scarlett Easton.

"He was killed somewhere else?" Scarlett cupped her hands around her mug of tea and inhaled the fragrant steam as it rose to meet the cool morning air. "I suppose that's…a relief."

Deputy Collins, from the county's homicide division, nodded. "We're thinking maybe someone stabbed him in a car or even before, and then loaded him up and dumped him out on the side of the road. There were some blood spots on the asphalt. Then he dragged himself through the woods. Maybe he was heading toward your cabin to get help."

She shivered. "He didn't have a cell phone on him?"

"No, and he didn't have a wallet."

"You haven't identified him yet?" She laced her fingers around her cup.

"Not yet. The coroner's doing an autopsy this morning, and we'll get his prints and DNA. Nobody's reporting anything yet—no missing persons, no accidents, no barroom fights."

She didn't know why she wasn't telling this nice deputy all about the tattoo the dead man shared with Jim Kennedy. Why hadn't Jim said something? Maybe he hadn't seen the man's tattoo emblazoned on his neck. But why did he have the same one?

How could that possibly be a coincidence? It had an *L* and a *C*. It's not like it was the tattoo of a hula girl. It meant something.

She kicked the toe of her boot against the planter on the corner of her porch, the same one Jim had tripped over in the dark.

What had happened to his leg?

The man was as full of secrets as the boy had been—and just as dangerous. She'd been as drawn to him last night as she'd been in high school, but this time she'd sensed an answering spark of interest.

She hadn't been alone in her feverish daydreams about Jim Kennedy during high school. Lots of the girls at school—even the popular ones—had whispered and giggled about Jim, but none of them, including her, would've been allowed to go out with him. He was every parent's nightmare—long hair, motorcycles and a bad, bad family.

It had just been Jim, his older brother and their father. They all rode motorcycles, and the older brother and Slick had been hard drinkers and hard partyers. She had no idea what had happened to his mother.

Deputy Collins glanced at his notepad. "A Mr. Kennedy was with you when you discovered the body?"

"That's right. He lives in the next cabin up the road."

"Thanks for your help, Ms. Easton. We'll contact you if there's anything else or if we think you might be in some kind of danger."

"Danger?" Her pulse jumped. "You mean if the man's death was some random murder and there's a killer on the loose?"

"I don't think that's the case. He looked like a rough customer, probably ran with a rough crowd. Once we ID him, we might be able to put your mind at ease. You probably don't have anything to worry about."

Yeah, except for her attraction to Jim Kennedy, who had the same tattoo as the dead man. That worried her.

"Well, I'll be here if you have any more information for me."

He tipped his hat, and the copse of trees ringing her property swallowed him up as he made his way to his car.

Through narrowed eyes, she watched him get into his car, the last of the emergency vehicles that had been out here all night.

If this *rough customer* had died in the woods beyond her cabin as a result of a fight, she had nothing to fear. She hadn't seen anything. She couldn't point the finger at his killer, and she didn't know the dead man.

But if someone was running around Timberline stabbing people and dumping them on her property, then she had plenty to fear.

She snorted and took a gulp of lukewarm tea. Why would someone want to do that? She knew nothing about anything—no more dream quests for her, no more psychic mumbo jumbo, as her cousin Jason called it.

Except that she did know something. She knew Jim

Kennedy and the dead man shared the same tattoo, and Jim hadn't said a word about it to anybody.

She retreated to her cabin and slammed the door. She'd come back to Timberline to work, and she planned to keep her head down and do just that.

She didn't have the time or energy to sort out a brooding war vet with trouble in his eyes and sin on his lips.

"Is THIS FOR your granny, Scarlett, or have you taken up knitting, too?"

Scarlett dropped the two skeins of yarn on the counter. "Me? Knit? You've gotta be kidding."

Barbara, the owner of A Stitch in Time, rang up the yarn on her register. "You're so artistic, you could probably do it."

"Totally different kind of art, Barbara."

"I like those pretty landscapes you do." Barbara pursed her lips and stuffed the yarn into a bag.

Scarlett covered her smile with her hand. Barbara didn't have to like her modern art—enough people did.

"Thanks, Barbara."

"You know," Barbara said, and shook her finger at Scarlett, "you should do some local crafts, like Vanessa Love does with those Libby Love frogs. Maybe something… Native American."

"You mean like dream catchers and tom-toms?" Scarlett raised her brows. "Ah, no. I don't do that kind of stuff."

Reaching for her wallet, Scarlett glanced out the window just in time to see her cousin duck into Sutter's Restaurant. "How much do I owe you, Barbara? I just saw Jason go into Sutter's and I'm going to try to catch him."

"That'll be ten dollars and fifty cents. Your cousin is

always at Sutter's." She cleared her throat. "Not that I'm spying out my window, mind you."

"He's dating a waitress there." Scarlett put a ten on the counter and dug in her purse for two quarters. "Thanks, Barbara. You're a lifesaver for finding that purple shade for me."

"Anything for your granny, Scarlett."

Scarlett tucked the bag beneath her arm and charged across the street to Sutter's. Jason had been shirking his duty in checking up on Granny when Scarlett had been out of town and she planned to read him the riot act. He couldn't dump all the responsibility on his sister, Annie.

The lunch crowd from Evergreen Software was thinning out, and Scarlett zeroed in on Jason lounging at the bar adjacent to the dining area. She waved off the hostess. "I'm going to the bar."

She swung around to the side of the restaurant and snuck up behind Jason, tapping him on the shoulder. She grinned as he almost fell off the bar stool.

"Wow, cuz, are you trying to give me a heart attack?"

She shook the yarn bag in his face. "It's gonna be worse than that if you don't start checking up on Granny more regularly."

"She doesn't want to see me. She'd rather see you and Annie."

"That's ridiculous and it doesn't matter. She's getting up there in age, and you need to check on her. You can't leave that up all up to Annie. She's busy with her new cleaning business."

He shrugged, whipping his long hair back from his face. "Heard you found a dead body outside your place last night."

"That's a neat way to change the subject." She perched

on the stool next to him. "Yeah, some older guy—long, reddish-gray hair. I'd never seen him before."

"And I thought your problems were over when that FBI agent killed Jordan Young."

"Problems? The county sheriff's department thinks someone dumped him on the road near my place and he made his way into the woods." She folded her arms on the bar. "It's not my problem."

Chloe, Jason's girlfriend, approached them, tucking a notepad into her apron. "Did they find out who the dead guy is yet?"

Scarlett rolled her eyes. "Does everyone know?"

"Of course." Chloe snapped her gum. "It's Timberline."

Jason pinched Chloe's hip. "I gotta go. Just popped in to say hi and, yes, I'll check up on Granny more, Scarlett."

"I'll see you after work." Chloe's eyes widened as she stared past Jason's shoulder. "Who is that?"

Scarlett jerked her head around just in time to meet Jim's gaze across the dining room.

Jason growled. "He's that racist SOB biker."

Scarlett jabbed her cousin with her elbow. "Jim's not like that. You're talking about his father. What *did* happen to Slick Kennedy, anyway?"

"Someone killed him in Seattle a few years back… and nobody around here gave a damn." He kicked Scarlett's foot. "Shh. He's coming this way."

"Why's he coming over here?" A slow blush spread across Chloe's cheeks, and Jason gave his girlfriend a sharp look.

"H-he was with me last night when I found the body."

Jason transferred his look from Chloe to her.

"I guess he has his dad's place now. It's down the road from mine."

As Jason opened his mouth, Scarlett nudged the leg of his stool to shut him up.

"Are you okay? Did you get any sleep?" Jim studied her through dark-smudged eyes while running a hand through his messy hair.

"Looks like I got more than you." She wanted to ask him if he'd injured himself falling off her porch, but he wouldn't appreciate her concern—especially not in front of Jason and Chloe.

"I have a hard time sleeping in that place, dead body or no dead body."

She tipped her head toward Jason. "This is my cousin, Jason Foster, and his girlfriend Chloe Rayman."

Jim took Chloe's hand and the girl looked ready to faint. Then he shook Jason's hand, despite the once-over her cousin was giving him. "You know anyone interested in some old Harleys?"

Jason's eyes lit up. "You selling?"

"I have a few bikes I'm looking to get rid of. Stop by any time if you want to have a look. I'll give you a deal."

"I'll do that, man. Thanks." Jason kissed Chloe on the side of the head. "Now I really have to get back to work."

They said goodbye and Chloe scooted back to her abandoned tables with a flick of her hand.

"Do you mind?" Jim pushed out the stool next to her with his foot.

"Go ahead." She grabbed a menu from behind the bar as if she'd planned to eat lunch here all along. "Was the rest of your night uneventful?"

His dark gaze drifted away from her face for a few seconds, and then he cleared his throat. "Yeah. You? Were the deputies there all night?"

"I think so. They were there when I went to bed, and a few were there this morning."

"Any news?" He pointed to her menu. "You done with that?"

She slid it across to him. "Autopsy this morning, but I haven't heard anything."

The bartender dropped another menu in front of Scarlett. "Are you two ordering lunch?"

"I am. Give me a minute." Jim ran his finger down the menu and looked at her over the top. "Burgers any good here?"

"You're asking the wrong person. I'm a vegetarian."

He peered down the bar. "They seem popular."

When the bartender returned, Jim ordered a burger and fries, and she stuck to the vegetarian chili, her go-to meal at Sutter's.

"Anything to drink?"

They both ordered water.

When the bartender placed their glasses in front of them, Scarlett followed a bead of moisture running down the outside of her glass with her fingertip. "I wanted to ask you if you were okay after…after your fall last night."

His jaw hardened and a muscle ticked in the corner of his mouth. "The darkness, the excitement, threw me off balance. I usually don't trip over my own feet, believe it or not. Spent enough time in physical therapy to avoid that."

"What happened to your leg?" Taking a sip of water, she avoided his gaze. Would he lash out? Refuse to answer her?

"It broke in a few places and never healed properly."

Okay, so he'd just be vague about it.

"Ouch. Sounds painful. I suppose it happened when you were…over there."

"Uh-huh." He gestured to the bartender. "Can you bring me some ketchup when you get a chance, please?"

She didn't need a brick wall to fall on her to get the hint. Personal stuff—off-limits. "I sure hope the sheriff's department can find out who this guy is and what happened to him—and if he had some kind of beef with his killer."

"I'm sure they'll be able to ID him soon, and most likely it wasn't a random hit. You still need to upgrade the security on your place. Even if you believe you're safe in Timberline, you might want to do a better job protecting your...art."

She narrowed her eyes. "Did I detect a little sarcasm in your tone?"

"What? Not at all." He rolled his water glass between his hands. "I like it."

"The landscape art."

"That, too, but the other stuff..." He shook his head. "Crazy intense."

A warm glow settled in her belly. Usually she didn't care what people thought about her art. She created her work from a personal, imaginative space inside her brain, and if she didn't give expression to those thoughts, her head would explode. It had just been a side bonus that other people, including the art critics, had appreciated her abstract art and paid top dollar for it.

The fact that a man like Jim liked it, got it, made her feel like he got her, that he saw her.

She wanted to get him, too. She felt like she could if he'd let her.

"Veggie chili and Sutter's burger." The bartender dipped beneath the bar and gave them each a silverware setting wrapped in a cloth napkin.

Jim proceeded to drench everything in ketchup.

She pointed a spoon at his fries. "Have some fries with your ketchup."

One corner of his mouth lifted, which was about the closest thing she'd seen to a smile from him.

"One of my many quirks." He bit off the end of a French fry and asked, "Where do you live when you're not spilling your guts on a canvas in Timberline?"

"San Francisco. I have a small place in the city that I share with another artist. When he's gone, I'm usually there and when I'm here, he's in the city."

"Boyfriend?" He took a big bite of his burger.

"What? The artist?" She slipped a spoonful of chili in her mouth to hide her smile, happy that he'd been concerned enough to ask. "Marco is not my boyfriend."

"I was gonna say, tough to have a relationship with someone you hardly see."

"Tough to have a relationship with another artist. Marco and I had a thing once, but it was exhausting— and not in a good way." She winked at him.

He raised one eyebrow and took another bite of his burger.

She zigzagged her spoon through the hot surface of her chili and watched the steam curl up. How had he gotten her to open up while he remained aloof and close-mouthed?

"And you? Are you going to settle in Timberline or do you have a home somewhere else?"

"I don't have a home, and I sure as hell don't plan to stay in Timberline."

"Are you here to sell your father's place? I'm sure you know, ever since Evergreen Software moved in, housing prices have shot up."

"I'll probably sell it. Nothing but bad memories attached to the place."

He offered nothing more. Where had he been since being discharged from the army? What was he doing in Timberline? And why did he have the same tattoo as a murder victim?

Jim dragged a napkin across his mouth and tapped her arm. "Incoming."

She jerked her head to the side. "It's Sheriff Musgrove. I guess he's feeling better."

"Is he new?"

"He's new and lazy. More interested in fund-raising, but he's been keeping a low profile lately, since he was good friends with Jordan Young."

"Well, he's making a beeline for us, so maybe he has some news from homicide."

As the sheriff made a few stops on his way, Scarlett leaned close to Jim and whispered, "Does it look like everyone is reassured at what he's telling them? Because I'm pretty sure they're asking him about the murder."

"Nobody's screaming and fainting."

Musgrove finally made it to them and positioned himself between their two bar stools. "Trouble just seems to follow you around, doesn't it, Ms. Easton?"

"Me and you both." Scarlett pushed away her bowl. "This is Jim Kennedy. He was with me last night when I stumbled across the body."

The two men shook hands and Jim asked, "News about the murder?"

"Yeah, which is why I came over here when one of the deputies said he saw Ms. Easton at the bar. The fact that you're here, too, is convenient, since I don't have to go out to your place."

"What's the news?"

Musgrove smiled and waved at the bartender. "We identified the victim."

Scarlett slid a glance at Jim. "Who is he?"

"Name's Jeff Kelly, goes by the name of Rusty. He's fifty-one years old and a member of the Lords of Chaos motorcycle gang."

"Club."

"Excuse me?" Musgrove cocked his head, his eyebrows colliding over his nose.

"They prefer to be called a club—the Lords of Chaos Motorcycle Club."

"And how exactly do you know that, Kennedy?"

"Because I was a member—and I knew Rusty."

Chapter Five

Scarlett grabbed the edge of the bar—*LC*. So, those letters stood for Lords of Chaos. She vaguely remembered a bunch of motorcycle-riding tough guys hanging around town, usually with Jim's father and brother. She never realized they were an actual motorcycle gang and that Jim had belonged to it. That explained the tattoo. Explained a lot of other things.

At least he'd owned up to it, but why'd he wait? Why didn't he mention the tattoo earlier, even if he didn't recognize Rusty?

Musgrove must've had the same thought since he fished in his front pocket and asked, "You didn't recognize him last night?"

Jim shrugged. "It was dark. It's been over ten years since I last saw him."

"Have you seen any other members of the…club since you've been back in Timberline?"

"Look, Musgrove. If you want to question me further, can we do it more formally at the station?" He jerked his thumb over his shoulder. "We're attracting attention."

"Technically, it's not even our case anymore, but I'll give your name to Deputy Collins. He's heading up the investigation for the county's homicide division."

"You do that." Jim grabbed a cocktail napkin and a

pen and wrote out his phone number. "Have him give me a call. I can't tell him much. I didn't even realize Rusty was still here. As far as I know, the club doesn't operate in this area anymore."

Musgrove hunched forward. "Is it true the Lords of Chaos were involved in the drug trade here in Timberline?"

"Didn't know much about their business, didn't want to know. I was a teenager and got out when I could."

Musgrove tugged on his earlobe. "Didn't Gary Binder hang out with the club?"

"Gary?" Jim pulled his bottom lip between his teeth. "Nah, kind of a hanger-on. I heard he died in a hit-and-run accident recently."

"We've never found the driver." Musgrove shrugged. "Me? I figured it for an accident, but did you have any contact with Binder since returning?"

Jim spread his hands. "Dead before I arrived."

"All right then, Kennedy." Musgrove stuffed the napkin with Jim's number into his pocket. "I think Deputy Unger already gave your number to Collins. He'll probably want to talk to you at some point once I tell him you knew Kelly."

"I'm not going anywhere for a while."

Musgrove saluted and walked back through the dining room, glad-handing when he could. When he walked out the front door, Scarlett turned to Jim. "That's why you have the tattoo."

Jim choked on his water. "How do you know about that?"

"When you…fell last night, your shirt hiked up in the back. I saw it then, and I had seen the same tattoo, or at least the same letters, on the neck of the dead man."

"Thought about getting it removed a few times, but it reminds me where I came from and what I have to battle."

She swirled the ice in her water glass. "Is that why you joined the army? To get away from your family?"

"One reason."

"So why'd you come back here?"

"Settle my dad's stuff."

"Liar. We found a dead body together. You can tell me the truth."

He rubbed his knuckles against his sexy stubble. "I came across a news story online about those kidnappings a few months ago. It brought back some...memories."

Not very good memories from the look in his dark, haunted eyes.

"Sounds like you'd rather forget those memories. Why torture yourself by coming back?"

His lips twisted and he smacked the bar as he emitted a noise that sounded suspiciously like a laugh.

"What's funny about that?"

"I wouldn't call being in Timberline and remembering fond times with my old man and my older brother torture—miserable, but not torture."

"Figure of speech, I guess." She waved at the bartender for the check. "Timberline still has a lot of secrets."

"That's because the mystery of the Timberline Trio was never solved." He jerked his thumb over his shoulder at the dining room. "It doesn't affect the newcomers with their shiny tech jobs and their shiny cars in their shiny homes. But for those of us who were kids here at the time, I think it left its imprint."

"I think you're right."

The bartender dropped two separate checks for them. Jim reached for her check at the same time she did.

"Lunch is on me."

As his warm hand curled around hers, a shock flashed through her body and a sharp pain knifed the back of her skull. She squeezed her eyes closed and fought off the visions before they engulfed her.

"Scarlett. What's wrong?"

Her eyelids flew open. Jim's face, etched with worry, was inches from hers. She'd felt electricity from his touch last night, but nothing like this. This had gone beyond the pleasant sensations of attraction and connection she'd experienced before.

She'd dived straight into his psyche and had been overwhelmed by terror and darkness. His terror and darkness? What had his father done to him?

His nostrils flared as he saw something in her eyes. "What just happened?"

"I—I got dizzy for a minute." She slipped her hand from beneath his. "I'm okay, and you really don't have to buy me lunch."

"I absolutely have to buy you lunch now, since it seems as if my touch made you sick to your stomach." He pulled out a few bills from his wallet and put the ketchup bottle on top of the checks and the money.

She gave a halfhearted laugh. "It wasn't that, probably just low blood sugar."

"Do you need something else to drink? A soda? Orange juice?"

His narrowed eyes told her he wasn't buying any of it, but she could at least make good on the pretense.

"Some orange juice is probably just what I need."

When the bartender placed the tall, skinny bar glass full of orange juice in front of her, she downed it. "Ahh, that's better."

"Did you have a chance to call someone about the security measures I suggested?"

"No time yet. Spoke to the deputies this morning, went out to visit my granny and then came into town to pick up few things for her."

"I'm going to that hardware store in the new shopping center out by Evergreen Software. I can pick up a few locks and window rods for you."

"If you don't mind." She snatched a couple of twenties from her wallet. "Use this and let me know if I owe you more."

He stuffed the money in his pocket. "I can drop by later to set things up for you."

"I work during the daylight hours, so catch me when the sun goes down."

They walked out of Sutter's together with several pairs of eyes following them. Word must've gotten around that they'd found Rusty's body. She preferred keeping a low profile when she was in town working, but she'd been the center of attention on her last visit and this one was shaping up to be the same.

"Thanks for lunch and for offering to get my locks."

"No problem." He lifted a helmet from the backrest of his Harley and straddled the bike. "Thanks for not ratting out my tattoo to the cops."

She parted her lips and then stepped back as he revved the noisy engine of the bike. Of course, he'd realized she had kept that from the sheriff's deputies since she'd admitted she saw the tattoo on Rusty's neck and then had seen a replica on Jim's back.

He revved the Harley's engine again, and then peeled away from the shoulder of the road.

Sighing, she ran her fingers through her hair and tucked the bag of yarn beneath one arm. Time to put

Rusty Kelly and Jim Kennedy out of her head and get back to work.

Rusty? That was easy. Jim? That presented a whole different kind of problem.

JIM LOCKED HIS helmet against his bike and grabbed a basket on his way into the hardware store.

Why had Scarlett kept quiet about his tattoo? When she saw it on his back, she must've realized he'd lied to the cops about knowing the dead man, or at least lied about knowing something about him. Had she believed his story about not seeing Rusty's tattoo? Had Musgrove believed his story about not recognizing Rusty last night?

He didn't even know why he'd lied. Habit? He'd lied so much over the past few years of his life he didn't even know the truth anymore.

He steered his basket down the home security aisle and looked over some sensor lights and cameras. He'd been planning to make a few improvements to Slick's cabin, but security hadn't been one of them—until Rusty turned up dead last night.

Who'd murdered him and why? Could be a barroom fight or some kind of deal gone wrong. But why here in Timberline? As far as he knew, the Lords of Chaos didn't operate in this area anymore, and Rusty didn't have family nearby.

He dropped a few items in his basket and wandered a few aisles over to have a look at the dead bolts. While he was reading the back of a package, a man bumped his arm reaching for a bin of locks.

"Sorry, bro." The man swore and smacked him on the back. "Jim Kennedy. J.T."

Jim's muscles tensed as he drew back. He didn't like people touching him when he didn't see it coming. He really didn't like surprises, and he didn't like being called by his nickname.

The man beside him grinned, his yellowed teeth peeking through a heavy beard. "You don't remember me? It's Chewy. I ran with your old man back in the day."

Jim squeezed the plastic packaging in his hands until the sides cut into his fingers. What the hell was this, some kind of LOC reunion?

He remembered Chewy—mean SOB with a short-fuse temper, used to smack his woman around.

"Chewy. Yeah, I remember you."

"So the army took your sorry ass, huh?" Chewy had dropped the big paw he'd proffered in a shake when Jim ignored it. "Heard you were some hotshot ranger, a sniper. You always were a good shot, son."

"Tell me, Chewy. Are the Lords of Chaos running a club in Timberline again? You heard about Rusty, right?"

Chewy blinked his small, flat eyes. "Rusty? Haven't seen that fat SOB in a couple of months. What happened to him?"

Jim thought he might be able to catch Chewy in a lie since the sheriff's department hadn't released the identity of the dead body yet. Chewy was as dumb as a box of rocks, but not that dumb.

Jim lifted one shoulder. "Just that he's back in town, too. Saw him the other day."

"I'll be damned. Old Rusty. I'll have to look him up."

"You're staying in town?"

"For a while. Had some good times here." He ran his fingers through his graying beard. "Sorry about Slick. That was a tough break. If any of the Lords had been with him that night, whoever killed him would've been dead meat."

"Yeah. Gotta go." Jim tossed two dead bolts into his basket and rolled away.

Should he bring up Chewy's appearance in town when Deputy Collins questioned him about Rusty? Chewy would clam up or run if the cops came down on him... and Jim just might need the old biker for information.

Jim finished shopping for Scarlett's items, as well as his own, and then secured them in the saddlebags on his bike. He checked the time on his phone. Scarlett would still be working.

He headed for Slick's place—his own now. His brother Dax had dropped off the face of the earth since his release from prison. Jim planned to sell it and all of his dad's bikes once he finished his business in Timberline. He'd never feel at home in that cabin.

He rode his motorcycle to the front door and parked it. Standing by the bike, he sorted Scarlett's stuff into one bag and his in the other. Then he crammed her items back into his saddlebag.

Slick's motorcycles had been in the detached garage for years after his death and nobody had touched them, but nobody had known they were there. Once Jim started advertising them for sale, the cat would be out of the bag and he needed to beef up security.

He'd start with the sensor lights. He dumped his purchases on the kitchen table and then bagged up the pieces he needed for the sensor system.

With the bag under his arm, he trudged down the gravel path to the garage. He dug his key ring from his pocket as he reached the double doors.

"Damn." He kicked the door with his boot.

Too late. Someone had broken off the padlock that held the two doors together.

He loosened the broken lock, letting it fall to the

ground. Using his T-shirt to avoid leaving fingerprints, he flicked up the latch and nudged the door open with his foot.

He yanked the chain to turn on the overhead lights and released a sigh. Slick's five Harleys were all where he'd left them when he'd checked them out his first day back.

He entered the garage and scanned the walls, his gaze skimming over the two shotguns mounted in racks and a collection of fishing poles and tackle.

Nothing jumped out at him. Slick had kept plenty of tools in here and God knows what else. He hadn't done an inventory when he'd been in here before. He didn't care if someone robbed Slick blind and Slick wouldn't mind now.

Only the bikes mattered to Jim.

He wandered toward the shotguns and ran a hand down the long barrel of one. That's one thing he owed the old man. Slick had taught him to shoot—and he'd been a crack shot right from the get-go.

He spent the next few hours setting up the sensor lights on the outside of the garage and fixing the padlock latch. He'd have to think of a better way to lock these doors, and he should probably file a report with the sheriff's department.

He peered at the sky as he returned to the house. The cloud cover hid the setting sun, but it had to be dusk and Scarlett would be done working. Should he bring something more than her locks? Dinner?

At least he knew she hadn't cooled off toward him because of his clumsy fall. His tattoo had freaked her out. Had she believed his story about not seeing Rusty's tattoo or recognizing him in the dark? He wouldn't have believed that lame explanation.

He finished showering and dried off in front of the

mirror. Turning his back to the mirror and twisting his head over his shoulder, he could just make out the tail end of the tattoo on his back—the tattoo that ended in the letters *LC*.

Maybe he should've gotten the damned thing removed. At least it had caused some fear among his captors.

He slicked back his wet hair, which almost reached his shoulders. Didn't look much like a ranger these days. He smoothed the pad of his thumb across the thin, white line on his forehead. But he had the battle scars to prove his service.

He shaved and dressed in a pair of jeans and buttoned a red-and-black flannel shirt over his black T-shirt. He grimaced at his reflection in the mirror. "You're dropping off some hardware, Kennedy, not going on a date."

He stuffed his arms into his leather jacket and locked up. He could've walked through the woods to her place, but he was sick of the woods already.

He rode his motorcycle the short mile to Scarlett's place and left it on the edge of the ring of trees sheltering her cabin. He made plenty of noise taking the two steps to the door since he didn't want to startle her and risk getting attacked with a poker.

He used the lion's-head knocker and called out, "Scarlett, it's Jim."

The curtain at the window shifted and he took a step to the side to show himself.

She opened the door. "I thought you'd forgotten about me."

Forget about her? Never.

"You said dusk. I didn't want to disturb your work."

Poking her head outside, she sniffed. "This is night, not dusk."

"Excuse me for missing the nuance." He held up the bag. "These are for you, and I have your change."

She opened the door wider and as the light from the cabin spilled over him, her gaze tracked across his body, igniting a fire in his belly.

Her long, dark lashes fluttered and her chest beneath her tight sweater rose and fell. "C'mon in."

He swung the bag from his fingertips. "Can you install this stuff, or do you know someone who can?"

"I can use a simple screwdriver and hammer, but I draw the line at drills. I don't even think I have a drill."

"I'm sure you can find a handyman to do the job for you."

She shoved her hands in the back pockets of her jeans, which made her sweater fit tighter. "I was kind of hoping you could help me out. I'll pay you...and feed you."

His heart thudded against his chest. All she had to do was look at him like she was doing right now, and he'd hand her the moon on a silver platter.

"Feed me?" He sniffed the air and his mouth watered at the scent of garlic. "Now?"

"I thought it would be more effective to offer you food at the time of the request." Folding her hands in front of her, she batted her eyelashes. "Pretty please?"

He snorted. "You're pulling out all the stops. I'm pretty sure you've never said *pretty please* or batted your eyelashes in your entire life."

She wrinkled her nose. "That bad, huh?"

"Bad, but the food smells great. Is it all vegetarian?"

"Salad, eggplant parmigiana and some penne with meatballs for you. I ordered in from that Italian place in the new shopping center."

"It's a deal."

"Thanks."

She went into the kitchen and he followed, admiring the way her jeans fit her.

She reached into a cupboard and stacked a couple of bowls on top of two plates, and then placed them on the counter. "We'll eat at the counter, if that's okay with you. I rarely use the kitchen table."

"Okay by me." He set the dishes on top of the woven place mats on the counter and pulled out the high chairs beneath it. "Do you want me to put the salad in these bowls?"

"Uh-huh. And…" She spun around, holding a bottle of wine in front of her. "I have wine."

"Just water for me."

She squinted at the label on the bottle. "It's a good year—a cabernet from a Washington winery."

"I don't drink."

"Oh." She hugged the bottle to her chest. "I hope you don't mind if I do."

"Help yourself." He dumped some salad evenly into the two bowls while she opened the wine. He didn't even miss the stuff—except for on nights like the one he'd just had.

After they loaded their plates with food, they sat down at the counter and Jim raised his water glass. "To a drama-free night."

She tapped her glass against his, and the red liquid swirled and caught the light, giving Scarlett's cheeks a rosy glow.

"Did you get much work done this afternoon?" He ripped off a piece of garlic bread and dropped it onto his plate.

"Not really." She waved her fork in the air. "I'd been working on a piece that I'd hoped to finish in the next few weeks, but I started a new project and it distracted me all afternoon. I hate it when that happens."

"You're lucky to have a creative outlet."

"What about you? Now that you're out of the army, what are your plans?"

He stabbed the pasta on his plate and dragged it through the red sauce. She expected an answer. This is how normal people had conversations—give and take. He put down his fork and cleared his throat. "I'd been doing some work with some organizations that help disabled vets."

"Like physical therapy?"

He tapped his head. "The other kind of therapy."

"Wow, that has to be tough."

"For me or for them?"

"For everybody."

"It's no picnic." He hunched forward. "That's why I liked your modern artwork. It looks…therapeutic. I mean, we're looking for all kinds of things to help these guys adjust—pets, music, art."

"Sounds like a great program. Are you going to do that when you're done with…whatever you're doing here?"

"I need more training. I might go back to school. I mean, go to school, since I enlisted in the army after high school."

"Can I give you a piece of advice?" She took a sip of her wine and the ruby liquid stained her lips.

He shifted his gaze from her mouth to her eyes. "Sure."

"You might want to open up a little more."

"I'm supposed to be getting *them* to open up."

She took another swig of wine and tilted her head so that her long hair fell over one shoulder. "You know, you're right. And you're pretty good at that, since you definitely got more out of me than I've gotten out of you."

"I'm not trying to get anything out of you, Scarlett."

"I know, but I've been open with you because…" She ducked her head and stuffed a piece of garlic bread in her mouth.

Garlic or not, he'd kiss her later, anyway. He dragged his gaze from her mouth to her eyes.

"Because?"

"Oh, you know. Because I knew you in high school."

"Yeah, and we were such good friends."

She snorted. "You weren't friends with anyone."

"And you were only friends with the other kids from the rez."

"Couple of social butterflies, I tell ya." She tossed her hair back and laughed.

The knock on Scarlett's door cut across her laugh, and Jim dropped his bread.

"Now what? I guess my toast was a jinx."

She hopped from her stool and stalked toward the front door. He had no intention of letting her open that door by herself, so he dogged her steps and hovered over her shoulder as she peered out the window.

She blew out a noisy breath. "It's Deputy Collins with another officer I don't know."

Jim's muscles tensed, and a rush of adrenaline slammed against his temples. Why would they be out here at this time of night?

Before he could stop her, Scarlett opened the front door. "Do you have any news, Deputy Collins?"

The deputy's eyes widened as he looked past Scarlett and met Jim's gaze. "I thought you might be here, Kennedy."

Jim widened his stance, placing his weight on his good leg. "Here I am."

Collins placed his hand on his service revolver. "James Kennedy, you're under arrest for the murder of Jeff Kelly."

Chapter Six

Darkness rushed in on Jim and he clenched his fists at his sides. He couldn't be confined. He couldn't let them take him.

The blood raced through his veins and his heart almost pumped out of his chest. If he assaulted the officer and took off, it would be all over for him. He had to get a grip. Innocent men didn't run.

Scarlett's hand closed around his, her cool touch soothing the rage within him.

"What are you talking about, Collins? Jim was here with me last night. We discovered Rusty's body together."

"Ma'am, Ms. Easton, you need to step back, please. We have a warrant for Mr. Kennedy's arrest and I need to read him his rights."

She stamped her foot. "What evidence do you have? This is ridiculous."

Jim dragged in a deep breath. She was on his side. He could do this.

"It's okay, Scarlett. They'll tell me what they have when they get me to the station. If I give you a card, can you call my buddy? He can recommend an attorney in the area for me."

"Jim, this is absurd. You didn't kill anyone."

Her cheeks reddened as if she'd suddenly realized the falsity of that statement spoken to an army ranger sniper.

"I mean, you didn't kill Rusty. Tell him."

"It's okay. I'll have my opportunity."

Collins read him his rights and then asked if he had any weapons on him.

"Not on me." He tilted his head back. "My Glock's in the pocket of my jacket, hanging on that hook."

Collins gestured to the other deputy and then tapped Jim on the shoulder. "Turn around."

Turning, Jim gritted his teeth at the sound of the cuffs jangling behind him. He had to hold everything together so the cops wouldn't have him for resisting arrest, even though every fiber in his body was screaming at him to fight. He had to tamp down his rising rage.

Breathe. Think. Reason.

"Can you get my wallet out of my pocket and give it to Scarlett?"

Collins patted him down and removed the wallet. He handed it to Scarlett.

Jim met Scarlett's frantic gaze with his own steady one. "There's a card in there for Ken Stucken. Give him a call and tell him what happened. Tell him I need an attorney."

Scarlett's hands shook as she rifled through his wallet. "I found it."

She held up the card and he nodded, giving her a half smile as Collins and the other deputy marched him away from her house, through the trees to their squad car. They couldn't have much evidence, since he hadn't done it, but they wouldn't tell him anything until they got him to the station. He knew how it worked.

Jim kept his gaze pinned to the passing scenery out the car window and took deep breaths. If he had to spend the night in jail, he had doubts he could handle it. The deputies would probably transfer him to the psych ward before the night was over, giving them even more reason to believe he'd killed Rusty.

They took him to the sheriff's station in town. Cody Unger wasn't on duty when they arrived, but this wasn't the local deputy's rodeo, anyway.

Jim asked, "Is Sheriff Musgrove here?"

"Not here," Collins said, and cleared his throat. "But we notified him of the warrant."

Collins nudged him in the back toward a glass-enclosed interview room. "We're going to question you before we book you, Kennedy. You have a right to have your attorney present during questioning."

"I'll waive that right for now. I'm too curious to find out what you think you have on me."

Collins shoved open the door and pointed to a chair. "Coffee?"

"No, thanks. Let's just get to it."

The other deputy set up a camera as Jim awkwardly sank to a chair, his hands still cuffed behind him.

"Do you need to keep me handcuffed?"

Collins took in Jim's frame and then studied his face. "No."

Free of the cuffs, Jim's heart rate returned to something close to normal. He rubbed his wrists. "Why did you arrest me? What evidence do you have?"

The other deputy reached into a box and pulled out a plastic bag. He tossed it onto the table in front of Jim. "Recognize it?"

Jim peeled his tongue from the roof of his dry mouth. "It's my old man's hunting knife."

"It was also used to stab Rusty Kelly."

"Let me guess. My fingerprints are on the knife."

"Your fingerprints and Rusty's blood."

"That's an incriminating combination." Jim folded his arms across his chest and slumped in the metal chair, stretching his legs in front of him.

Collins smoothed the crinkles from the plastic bag. "One you can explain?"

"My fingerprints are on the knife because it was in my dad's shed. The shed is a detached wooden structure that he used as a garage for his motorcycles. I was in there last week and moved some things around. I remember handling the knife, which was on the tool bench."

"That explains the fingerprints."

"I just discovered today that someone broke into the garage. It has double doors that lock together with a simple padlock."

"Did you file a report?"

"No, but I called the station. I couldn't tell if anything was missing, so the deputy... Stevens, asked if I wanted to make a report but I declined. Deputy Stevens—ask him."

Collins snapped his fingers. "Jenkins, find Deputy Stevens to verify."

"There's also my alibi."

"Alibi?"

"I was with Scarlett Easton when she found the body."

"Kelly was stabbed before you arrived at Ms. Easton's."

"How much earlier before we discovered his body? I have an alibi for that, too."

"What's your timeline?"

"I ate dinner in town at the Miner's Inn and left around eight o'clock. Used a credit card. I had trouble starting my bike, and I talked to a man named Terry while I was trying to get it to work. That was right outside the

Miner's Inn, right in front of the window, so plenty of people saw me. I didn't leave until about eight forty-five or eight fifty. When I got to my place, I thought I heard some noises so I parked my bike and went for a walk in the woods. I got to Scarlett's place around nine fifteen or nine twenty. She can vouch for that."

Collins had been eyeing Jim's face and hands during his narrative without one interruption. Even now, he just nodded.

Jim dragged in a breath. "So, if I stabbed Rusty, I would've had to do it in a short time span, getting the knife, locating him, stabbing him without getting a drop of his blood on my clothes since I wouldn't have had time to change before going to Scarlett's."

"And all this is going to check out?" Collins folded his hands on the table between them.

"It'll all check out." Jim sat up in his chair and faced the camera. "Now if you want to ask me any more questions, you'll have to wait for my attorney."

Jim knew he had a rock-solid alibi. That didn't concern him. What did was the fact that someone had tried to frame him for murder—and he had a feeling it was all related to what happened to him twenty-five years ago.

WHEN THE PHONE RANG, Scarlett pounced on it before the call could drop off, grabbed her purse and ran outside.

She reached the end of her drive and answered, out of breath. "Is Jim going to have to spend the night in jail? What do they have? What can I do to help?"

Wade Lewiston, the attorney Jim's friend had recommended, clicked his tongue. "They haven't even booked him, Scarlett. He's waiting in an interview room while they check out his alibi."

"If they ask me, I can tell them straight out, no way

could he have stabbed someone and then appeared on my doorstep without a smidgen of blood on him."

"From what I understand, his timeline is pretty tight. They're not going to be able to pin this on him. He even phoned in about the garage break-in. He's covered."

"D-do you need to come out?"

"I don't think so. He's not answering any more questions for now. He wanted me to ask you if you can pick him up at the station when they release him."

"Of course I can. I'm on my way right now."

"You might want to wait, Scarlett. The deputies are still looking into his alibi."

"I'm not waiting any longer. This is ridiculous."

"Up to you. If Jim needs anything else, have him give me a call."

"How about a lawsuit? Can he sue the sheriff's department?"

"'Fraid not. His fingerprints were on the murder weapon, and that weapon belonged to him. The deputies had just cause to bring him in."

"Okay, okay." She ran a hand through her hair. "I'm going there now, anyway."

"Good night and good luck. Call me if there's a hitch."

Scarlett hit the key fob and the lights of her car blinked once. "Will do."

"One more thing, Scarlett."

"What?"

"Just be careful."

"Careful?" She slid behind the wheel of her car, glancing in her rearview mirror. "Of what? Jim didn't do it."

"That's not what I meant."

"What did you mean?"

"There's a murderer loose in Timberline, and for whatever reason he dumped the man near your cabin and tried to frame Jim. Be careful."

The hair on the back of her neck quivered. Like she needed reminding. "I'll be careful. Thanks for getting back to me so quickly tonight."

"Anything for a fellow vet—especially one like Jim Kennedy."

Before she had a chance to ask him why Jim was so special, he ended the call.

By the time she pulled into the parking lot of the sheriff's station, her aching muscles were screaming at her. She'd made the drive clutching the steering wheel and sitting on the edge of her seat.

She felt a particular urgency biting at her heels—something telling her that if she didn't get Jim out tonight, he would never get out.

She scrambled from the car and jogged to the station entrance. Deputy Stevens looked up from behind the front desk.

"I'm here to pick up Jim Kennedy. Are you done harassing him?"

Stevens's mouth dropped open. "H-his fingerprints were on the murder weapon, which belonged to his father."

"And he had alibis about a mile long."

Stevens held up his hands. "This was county's arrest. Don't jump on me."

"Well, is he done?" She wedged a hand on her hip and tapped the toe of her boot.

"I think so. They'll bring him up when they're ready. Deputy Collins didn't even book him, so there's no paperwork to process."

Scarlett wheeled around and paced to the other side of the room. After about fifteen minutes of handwringing and peppering Stevens with questions, she froze when she heard a door open down the hall.

The distinctive tone of Jim's low voice carried across the room, and Scarlett rushed to the front desk.

Jim and Deputy Collins, deep in conversation, came down the hallway. Jim jerked his head up, his eyes widening briefly.

"What are you doing here?"

"I'm here to pick you up. I spoke to Wade Lewiston earlier this evening. He said you told him to have me pick you up."

"I was going to call you. Didn't want you hanging around here."

"And I didn't want *you* hanging around here any longer than you had to." Her gaze shifted to Collins and she pursed her lips. "Everything straightened out?"

Jim massaged the back of his neck. "Almost everything. I'd still like to know who stole Slick's knife—a knife that conveniently had my fingerprints on it."

"We want to know the same thing." Deputy Collins shook Jim's hand. "We'll keep you updated. Sorry about the mix-up."

"You were just doing your job."

"Your stuff." Stevens pushed out of his chair and grabbed a box from a credenza. He held out the box to Jim and shook it. "We unloaded your weapon, but your license and permit checked out. You're free to take it."

Jim placed the box on a desk and pocketed his wallet and keys. He shoved the gun into his jacket pocket and dumped the bullets into his palm. "Someone's going to come out tomorrow to dust the garage for prints?"

"Yeah, we'll call first."

Jim held the door open for her and when she stepped outside, the cool air stung her hot cheeks. She rounded on Jim. "How could you be so polite? They arrested you. They handcuffed you and dragged you into the station like some dirtbag criminal."

He put his hands on her shoulders. "They had a murder weapon with my prints on it. What do you want them to do, ignore the evidence?"

His words sounded reasonable, but his hands felt unsteady. He dropped them quickly.

"You're a better person than I am. I would've been livid. You were with me when I stumbled across the body. I wouldn't have noticed if you'd had blood all over you? The cops showed up almost immediately after. They wouldn't have noticed any other blood besides what you had on your hands?"

"It's over, Scarlett, at least this part."

"What does that mean and why is everyone talking in riddles tonight?"

"I wanna know if someone tried to set me up for Rusty's murder."

"Why would someone do that?"

He nudged her back. "Let's get in the car."

As she grabbed the driver's-side handle, he asked, "Are you okay after drinking that wine?"

"Are you kidding? I barely got started on that bottle before we were rudely interrupted." She yanked open the car door. "I plan to finish it off now."

On the way back to her place, Jim told her about the interview and how the deputies had tracked down his alibis.

"I was lucky I hadn't been sitting at home alone the night of Rusty's murder."

"Maybe something drew you to my place last night for a reason."

"Whatever it was, it saved me a lot of trouble."

Turning down the road that led to her place and his,

she slid a glance his way. "Do you want me to drop you off at your cabin or do you want to come back to mine and finish dinner?"

"I thought we finished dinner."

"I bought a cheesecake for dessert."

"I lost my appetite, but I have to pick up my bike."

The car bumped and jostled as she drove up the access road to her cabin. She backed into the spot she'd had cleared for her car when she first bought the place and killed the engine. "Are you sure you don't want to come in? I have the card you gave me inside and your wallet."

"If you're sure. It's late."

"I'm still wired." She shoved open the car door. "And I still have a bottle of wine to polish off."

He followed her down the path through the trees, both of them leading with the lights on their phones.

"You should install some lights along this pathway, too. It's like the blind leading the blind out here."

"I guess I'm used to it now."

She tripped and Jim caught her around the waist.

"You're used to it, huh? Tell you what, you earned more of my services by calling my buddy and contacting that attorney, Lewiston. I'll work on setting up some lights out here, too."

She'd like to earn more of his services than getting a few lights installed.

She cleared her throat. "Do you think there's going to be any more trouble? I was kind of hoping someone targeted Rusty specifically."

"I think he was the target, but I have a funny feeling about that knife. Why my knife and my fingerprints?"

"Where'd they find it?" She opened her front door and left it open for Jim to follow her inside.

"On the road between our two places, a runner found

it. It's probably the same location where the killer dumped Rusty."

"I think I'll have that wine now." She tossed her purse onto a chair and made a beeline for the kitchen. She uncorked the bottle she'd left on the counter and poured a healthy amount into the glass she'd used earlier.

She raised her glass. "Are you sure you don't want some? I have beer in the fridge, too."

"I'm good." He perched on the arm of the sofa. "I saw someone else from the old life today."

"Who?"

"His name's Charles Swanson. We called him Chewy." He rubbed the back of his neck. "I told the deputies about him."

"Do you think he might've had something to do with Rusty's murder?" She took a gulp of wine and welcomed the warm feeling spreading to her chest.

"Seems suspicious that he's in town at the same time as Rusty and then Rusty turns up dead."

"If the Lords of Chaos want to knock each other off, they can have at it—as long as they do it far away from me." She covered her mouth. "Present company excluded, of course."

His dark brows collided over his nose. "I'm not one of them."

"I know. I didn't mean…"

"Were you here when Gary Binder was killed in that hit-and-run?" He pinched the bridge of his nose and squeezed his eyes shut.

"What does that have to do with anything?"

"Were you?"

"I was here. The cops never made an arrest, and it just about destroyed his mother. She stuck with him through all the ups and downs—the drug use, the arrests—and then just when he started getting his life together, it's snuffed out by a hit-and-run driver."

"Binder was cooperating with the police on the Timberline Trio case, wasn't he?"

"Was he? I don't know that I'd call it cooperating. I don't think he had much to offer."

Jim jumped up from the sofa, one hand clutching his hair. "He was on the fringes of the drug trade here in Timberline."

"The drug trade? Is that what Agent Harper was looking into when he was out here investigating the Timberline Trio case?"

"Harper was the FBI agent assigned to the cold case?" Jim stroked the bristle on his chin.

"Yeah. He was going to interview Gary but never got the chance."

"That's convenient. I wonder if Rusty or Chewy was in town then." He took a few steps and then braced one hand against the mantel. "Can I have some water, please?"

Walking into the kitchen, she glanced over her shoulder at his flushed face. "Are you okay?"

"I'm… I'm…" His head fell forward and he sucked in a breath.

"Jim?" Scarlett's heart pounded as she stuck a glass beneath the tap and filled it with water.

He let out a groan and then crashed to the floor.

Chapter Seven

"Jim!" She dropped the water glass in the sink where it shattered and she stumbled into the living room.

She crouched beside Jim, on his side, his knees drawn to his chest. Pressing her hand against his clammy brow, she asked, "Jim, can you hear me?"

His eyeballs rolled behind closed lids, and she brushed his hair back from his face. If he didn't open his eyes in two seconds and talk to her, she'd run outside to call 911. But she didn't want to leave him.

She undid the buttons on his shirt, her hand skimming the hot flesh at his neck. The temperature had to be low sixties in here. Why was he burning up?

His eyelids flickered and she caught the gleam from his dark eyes. "Are you coming around? I'm going to get that water."

She grabbed a pillow from the sofa and tucked it beneath his head.

She took off for the kitchen and filled another glass full of water, ignoring the broken glass in the sink. When she returned to Jim, his breathing was less shallow, his color less pale.

She punched up the pillow behind his head, and held the glass to his dry lips. "Can you take some water? Should I call 911?"

He turned his head, and she put the glass down on the fireplace. As he held up one hand, she grabbed it with her own. Immediately a flow of energy coursed through her body and she jerked back without releasing Jim's hand.

Dread soaked into her skin and it felt as if something was waiting for her just around the corner. Holding her breath, she braced for the terror. She squeezed Jim's hand harder. Her heart thudded in her chest.

Jim ripped his hand from hers and struggled to sit up. "I'm all right."

While she blinked her eyes, Jim grabbed the water and downed it. "I'm fine. It's nothing. Come back."

Her hand snaked up the column of her throat. How had he known? What had he seen in her face?

"I'm here, of course. What just happened?"

"You tell me." He sat up fully, his back against the fireplace, his flannel shirt gaping open, exposing the black T-shirt beneath that clung to the muscles of his broad chest.

"Y-you fell to the floor. You were unresponsive, with shallow breathing and clammy skin. What was that, Jim? You don't seem exactly panicked about it."

"That's because it's happened before. The...attacks or seizures stopped for a while but have started up again since I've been in Timberline."

"Seizures? What causes them? I assume you've been to see a doctor." She crossed her legs beneath her, folding her hands in her lap.

"It's post-traumatic stress. It's been treated. I was on medication for a while—didn't like it."

"Did it help?"

"It reduced the attacks, but I'd rather feel my feelings, not stuff them away."

"You said they stopped?"

"Until I came here." He cradled the glass in his hands, running his thumb along the rim.

"Why? What is it about this place? Is it the stuff you went through with your father?"

"Some of it." He hunched forward. "I'd rather hear about what you feel when you touch me."

Heat washed into her cheeks. "Wh-what do you mean?"

"I'm not talking about the sexual chemistry, although who are we kidding?" He dragged a hand through his hair. "I mean the other stuff—the way you act like I've given you an electric shock when you grab my hand. I've affected different women in different ways, but I've never encountered that response before. What's going on, Scarlett?"

She took a shaky breath and rose to her feet. "I need the rest of my wine for this conversation."

"Let me get it for you." He pushed to his feet and swayed before grabbing the edge of the mantel. He held out his hand as she leaned toward him. "I'm okay. I need to move."

He swept up the empty water glass and walked into the kitchen, his limp more pronounced than usual. "You have broken glass in your sink."

"Yeah, I dropped it when you collapsed in my living room."

"Sorry I scared you." He returned with her wine and more water for himself. "I should've realized I was susceptible after the arrest."

She took the wineglass from his hand and their fingers brushed. She felt nothing but desire this time.

She sank to a chair and he took the chair across from her, resting his forearms on his knees, holding his glass with two hands.

Closing her eyes, she took a sip of wine. "You know about my heritage."

"You're Quileute."

"Yes, but our tribe has shamans, like many others. I'm convinced we don't have greater numbers of people with these sensitivities than the general population, but it's something we identify and foster within our tribe. And I do believe extrasensory perceptions run in families—and it runs in ours."

"Your granny was a shaman. I remember that."

"You do?" A swell of pleasure crested through her body.

"I remember a lot about you, Scarlett Easton."

His dark eyes burned into hers and she felt like that schoolgirl peeking at his geometry test again.

She shook her head. "Anyway, I have these abilities, too."

"And when you touch me...what? You see my future?"

"More like your past."

Jim bolted upright. "You see into my past?"

"Not exactly." She tapped her wineglass with her fingernail. "It's so hard to explain. I'm not really seeing anything real. I have visions, experience feelings, sensations."

"No wonder you recoil every time you grab my hand." He lifted one eyebrow. "It's enough to give a guy a complex."

She stared into the shimmering surface of her wine. "What is it I'm experiencing, Jim? There's so much darkness, so much terror and something else...something unknown."

"Where do I begin?" He rolled the glass of water between his hands.

Leaning forward in her chair, she tapped his bad leg.

"Why don't you start with this? What happened to your leg? Why do you suffer from PTSD?"

"I was captured by the enemy, kept in a confined space, tortured and threatened with beheading on a daily basis."

Gasping, Scarlett folded her arms over her stomach. "Wh-what did they do to your leg?"

"They broke it and never set it. It healed improperly." He shrugged. "I could endure the physical pain more than the psychological. Seeing people I'd grown to like and respect being dragged out and tortured and in some cases beheaded—" his jaw hardened "—was worse than the physical torture."

"How'd you get out?"

"Three of us escaped—me, a Dutch journalist and a German contractor. Just like a prison break, we tunneled out of there. We had help from a few locals who got us across the border."

"I can't even imagine." She collapsed back in her chair. "Was it in the news?"

"My companions were in the news. The U.S. Army kept me out of it, had managed to keep my capture out of the headlines, too. I'd been in Syria on a classified mission. Technically, I was never there."

"You'd worked through the PTSD until you came back here to Timberline?"

"Pretty much."

"Then why come back here? Your memories of home, of family, are hardly healing material."

"I want to deal with everything in my past, put it to rest so it can't come up and sabotage me later." He stretched his legs in front of him, almost touching the toes of her boots. "When I saw the Wyatt Carson copycat kidnappings in the news and then read that the TV show *Cold Case Chronicles* was going to do a segment on the Timberline Trio, I took it as a sign."

"I helped the host of *Cold Case Chronicles*, Beth St. Regis. She thought she was one of the Timberline Trio, which turned out not to be the case. I know you don't think you were one of the Timberline Trio, so what's your connection to the case?"

"I wasn't one of the Timberline Trio, but I could've been."

"What are you talking about? Three kids were kidnapped—Kayla Rush, Heather Brice and Stevie Carson, the only boy and Wyatt's brother."

"During that same time, a man appeared in my bedroom and tried to put a foul-smelling rag over my mouth. I fought him off and made enough of a commotion that it woke up my old man from his drunken stupor in the living room."

"Oh, my God. I never heard about any of that. Did he run away when your father got there?"

"No." Jim massaged his temples. "That's just it. Slick stopped him, but then they moved to the other room and Slick told me to go back to bed. Of course, I didn't. I listened at my bedroom door while the two of them argued. It's like they knew each other and Slick was trying to weasel his way out of something."

"That's crazy, Jim." She picked up her wineglass and took another sip. She could use a shot of whiskey about now, but Jim obviously didn't drink and she didn't want to scare him off.

"After he left, Slick came into my room and I pretended to be asleep, but he caught up with me the next day. Told me if I ever told anyone about what happened, he'd give me a beating I'd never forget. I believed him."

Her heart hurt for the boy Jim had been, and she placed her hand on her chest. "Was that the end of it?"

"No. Kayla Rush was kidnapped a week later, and then Stevie Carson and finally Heather Brice."

She swallowed. "Do you think the Timberline Trio kidnappings were related to your botched kidnapping?"

"Yes. I don't know how or why, but I've always felt it—" he pounded a fist against his chest "—here. That means Slick had something to do with the Timberline case or he knew something about it."

"What about your older brother?"

"He was fifteen at the time. I'm not sure he'd know anything."

"Have you ever spoken to him about it?"

"Until recently, he was in prison for drug trafficking as part of the Lords of Chaos. I know he's out of the joint because he dropped me a line through the army, but we haven't been in touch since."

"That might be a place to start."

"I'm hoping Slick's cabin turns up some clues."

"Or…"

"No." He pushed up from the chair and grabbed her empty wineglass from the table next to her. "You're not going to help me by reading my mind or getting me into some sort of hypnotic dream state. I don't need that. I remember exactly what happened twenty-five years ago."

"If not me, how about help from a therapist?" She waved her hands. "I don't mean with repressed memories, but getting treatment for your PTSD."

"I had some of that before. I figured I'd kicked those spells—or whatever you want to call them—for good, only to have them crashing back on me in good old Timberline."

"I know a good therapist. Her name's Dr. Shipman,

and she practices in Port Angeles. I can give you her number."

"I'll take it."

Yawning, Jim stretched his arms over his head and she got a full view of his muscles flexing beneath his T-shirt. But the man had more than sexy packaging.

His life story had given her a whole new appreciation for his fortitude and bravery. He'd faced enough demons to last most people a hundred lifetimes and yet here he was back in Timberline to confront another.

He rubbed a hand across his mouth. "That's the most I've talked since my debriefing. I don't expect you to care or want to get involved with any of this."

"I kind of didn't have a choice, did I? For whatever reason, Rusty decided to make his way to my cabin after someone stabbed him and dumped him on the road."

"I hope to God it was just a coincidence that led him to you. The Lords of Chaos?" He sliced one finger across his throat. "Not anyone you want to be involved with."

"You survived."

"Only by enlisting in the army. Otherwise, I'd be dead like Slick or an ex-con like Dax."

"I didn't even realize you were a member of a motorcycle gang. How far were you into it?"

"Further than I wanted to be. It's like a legacy—club membership is handed down from generation to generation. To escape is to turn your back on your family and your friends. I had to do both."

"You never regretted it?"

"Never. In the army, with my unit, I found another family." He flicked the card he'd given her earlier, which listed the name she'd called to get to the attorney in Seattle. "This guy's someone I can count on in any crisis."

"You're lucky."

Twisting his wrist, he glanced at his watch. "It's late. You've done more than enough tonight. At this rate, I owe you a remodel."

"I might take you up on that." She stood up beside him and shoved her hands in her pockets to keep from touching him. "Are you sure you're okay? That seizure was pretty scary."

"It's more like a blackout, and the medical doctors tell me it's all in my head and there's nothing physically wrong with me…except my messed-up leg. I'm all right, but I will take Dr. Shipman's number if you have it handy."

"Give me your cell number and I'll send it to you that way."

He recited his cell phone number to her and she forwarded Dr. Shipman's number to him in a text.

She held up her phone. "Not sure that text is going through, but it will eventually."

"When are you going to get that landline?"

"I'll get to it."

"You can't keep running outside down to the road to make calls in case of emergencies."

"Funny thing is?" She tossed her phone on the kitchen counter. "I never had any emergencies before people started digging into the old Timberline case."

"Wyatt Carson started it all by kidnapping those three kids in an attempt to duplicate the original crime, and then positioning himself as the hero by rescuing them."

"You're right. That put Timberline back in the news and prompted Beth St. Regis to make a pilgrimage out here, and now you. I'm glad Beth got her answers and I hope you do, too, but digging into all this old stuff is stirring up trouble."

Jim reached her front door and grabbed the handle.

Without turning around, he said, "Maybe you should go back to San Francisco, Scarlett."

"Maybe I have a stake in this myself."

He leaned his back against the door, facing her. "What would that be?"

"The Timberline Trio kidnappings affected me, too."

"I think they affected all of us who grew up here."

"It's more than that. I'm sure you've heard the rumors about the Quileute legends and how some of the elders believed it was a creature from our own myths who kidnapped those children."

"I remember a little about that."

"Well, I remember a lot. We were forbidden from discussing the case. It was all hush-hush."

"Maybe the elders didn't want to frighten the kids on the reservation."

She snorted. "They scared us all the time with those old stories, mostly to keep us in line. This was different. Any time the older kids talked about the kidnappings, they were shushed. The parents wouldn't even discuss it. It was all strange, and Granny wanted no part of it."

"What do you mean by that?"

"Granny is a more powerful shaman than I am, or at least she was. With children missing, I would've thought she'd offer her services to the sheriff's department, even if they ended up scoffing at her, but she wanted to distance herself from that case."

"What are you saying?"

"I don't even know, but I'd be happy if the case were solved and everyone could put their demons to rest."

"I don't know if I'm going to solve the case, Scarlett. I just want to understand my part in it, my father's part in it."

As she hung on the door, he stepped into the glow of

light on the porch. "Just be careful. I'll stop by tomorrow to install those new locks for you."

"After lunch is a good time for me."

"See you then, and thanks for...everything."

She watched him disappear into the trees surrounding her cabin and listened for the growl of his Harley's engine. Then she closed the door and rested her forehead against it.

What was it about this damned case that it kept haunting her, insinuating itself into her life? Now she had an even greater reason for seeing it solved—because Jim Kennedy would never be available until it was.

She banged her head against the door—not that she needed him to be available. She didn't need a complicated man like Jim in her life. She didn't need to take care of him or rescue him. She was done rescuing men— most didn't want it and ended up dragging her down with them, anyway.

She returned to the kitchen, corked the rest of the wine and washed out her glass. If Jim abstained from drinking, maybe he was an alcoholic. Even if he was in recovery, she didn't want to go down that road again.

After cleaning up, she lay in bed staring at the ceiling. Despite that second glass of wine, she couldn't get to sleep. Jim's story haunted her. How did anyone survive something like that without cracking up? Death had been hanging over his head on a daily basis. No wonder peeling back the bandage on his painful childhood didn't scare him. What would?

A relationship with someone. She could see that in his eyes, too. She didn't even need her special powers for that.

A yellow glow peeped in from the curtains, and she looked at the clock radio beside her bed. How long had she been lying awake? The sun did not rise at three in the morning. Even if it did, the cloudy sky rarely allowed it to shine through like this.

She caught her breath and stumbled out of bed, yanking the curtains back from the window.

Her eyes widened at the view—flames danced among the trees outside her cabin, sending a cloud of black smoke into the air.

With her heart pounding, she ran into the living room and grabbed her purse and yanked her phone off the charger. Jim had been right. She needed to make this call now but had to run out to the road to call 911.

She rushed to the front door and threw it open. Tripping to a stop, she smacked a hand over her mouth.

The blaze had spread to the trees in front of the cabin, too. She jumped off the porch and turned in a circle. Fire licked at the entire copse of trees surrounding her place.

She was trapped—and someone had made sure of it.

Chapter Eight

The pounding in his head drove Jim outside. He should've never spilled his guts to Scarlett. He needed to keep his demons to himself. He'd seen the horror and the pity in her eyes…and something else. Maybe it was that something else that kept drawing him to her.

As he headed into the clearing around his cabin, he sniffed the air. The acrid smell of smoke permeated the mist.

Tilting his head back, he scanned the dark sky. An orange glow appeared over the top of the tree line—in the direction of Scarlett's cabin.

He scrambled back inside, grabbed his jacket and keys and jumped onto his bike. The smoke grew thicker and he could see dark clouds of it billowing up to the sky the closer he got to Scarlett's place.

He roared past her mailbox onto the access road leading to her cabin and stopped well behind the ring of trees that encircled her property. The ring of trees that was burning up like kindling in a fireplace.

The flames could easily jump from the trees to her cabin given their proximity to each other.

Was she even awakc? Hc called 911 on his phone for the second time in three days. The emergency operator assured him that the fire engines would be on their way in minutes.

Scarlett didn't have minutes.

He edged around the fire to see if he could get in around the side, but the wall of flames continued around her entire property.

How the hell had that happened?

He scoured the ground and found a long stick. Then he covered his head with his leather jacket and beat a path through the fire.

He stumbled into the clearing and dragged in a smoky breath.

As he peered at the front door of the cabin, it burst open and Scarlett appeared on the porch like a ghost, a white T-shirt floating around her.

He yelled, "Scarlett, you need to get out of here."

"Oh, my God. The fire's everywhere. I couldn't breathe outside anymore. How did you get through?"

"Very carefully." He charged past her into the cabin. "We could use some wet towels. The fire department is on its way."

She grabbed three towels from the floor and held them up as they dripped water. "I already thought of that. I was going to put these against the doors."

"We're going to use them to get through the burning copse instead. As the tree branches burn and break away, it's actually creating some space." He grabbed one of the sopping wet towels from her. "Put this over your head. Wrap the other one around your arms. I'll lead you out."

"What about you?"

"This wet towel is more than I had coming in. I'll be fine."

When they got to the line of fire, Jim draped the towels over Scarlett's head and face. "Just hang on to me and I'll get you through the fire."

He tucked the other towel around her arms and hands and created a tent over his head with the third towel.

Using his stick again, he beat out a swath through the smoldering areas of brush with Scarlett clinging to his back.

They broke free to the clearing just as the fire engines came wailing up the road.

"Move to the road, Scarlett. I'm going to back my bike out of here."

"What about my car?"

"Leave it. You won't be able to get it past the fire trucks."

Scarlett ran toward her mailbox as the first fire truck careened to a stop. It backed up and then rolled up the access road, stirring up the gravel and breaking branches as it squeezed through.

Jim pushed his bike up the road, and Scarlett followed him. A second fire engine rolled onto the scene, followed by a cop car.

Deputy Stevens jumped from the car almost before he parked it.

"Everyone okay? Ambulance on the way."

Jim squeezed the back of Scarlett's neck. "How's your breathing, Scarlett?"

She coughed. "It's been better."

"I'm fine. EMTs should see to her first."

Scarlett pointed to his arm. "You got burned."

"It's nothing. Just a few embers hit me. You?"

She brushed her hand down her bare leg below her knee. "Same. Feels like a few hot spots, but nothing major."

"We'll let the EMTs decide that." Stevens jerked his chin toward the oncoming ambulance.

Jim asked, "Is Sheriff Musgrove coming?"

Stevens shook his head. "The sheriff's out of town today—on business. Let's get Scarlett to the ambulance."

Taking Scarlett's hand, Jim led her to the ambulance and waved at the EMT exiting the vehicle. "She needs assistance. Possible smoke inhalation and burns."

The EMT opened the back of the ambulance. "Anyone else injured?"

"No."

Scarlett tugged on his shirt. "Check him out, too."

"Have a seat, ma'am."

Scarlett sat inside the van on the edge, while the other EMT pulled out some equipment.

Jim eyed Scarlett's flimsy T-shirt, now soaking wet from the towels. "Can you get her a blanket?"

Once Scarlett had a blanket draped around her shoulders, Jim touched her knee. "Are you okay here? I'm going to have a look at the fire."

"Go. Let me know if it reached the cabin. All my work is in there."

As Jim loped back to the fire engines, he tilted his head back. A helicopter had swooped into the area and dumped its flame retardant material onto the tree line behind Scarlett's cabin. They wouldn't want this fire to spread to the rest of the forest.

He approached the firefighter giving orders. "How's it going? Is the residence safe?"

The fireman tipped back his helmet. "Cabin is safe. We have the fire mostly contained in the front here and the helicopter should take care of the back. We'll be here for another few hours, though, and investigators are going to want to come in the morning. Do you live in the cabin?"

"My friend does—the woman."

"Is she okay?"

"Getting treatment now."

"She should find another place to bunk tonight—or at least for the rest of the morning. She's not getting back inside for the time being."

"She can stay at my place down the road. Do you need us for anything?"

"You can leave." He pointed to Deputy Stevens standing by his patrol car. "Check with the deputy over there so he can get your name and number. The investigators will want to talk to you tomorrow."

Jim dipped his head and waited until Stevens got off the phone. "I'm going to take Scarlett to my cabin. She doesn't have her phone or anything, so you can send the arson investigators to me tomorrow when they want to talk to her."

"Arson?" Stevens pocketed his phone. "Who said anything about arson?"

"I just did. Did you see that fire? It didn't hop over from the forest. It didn't start on one side of the cabin and burn in a line. Somebody set fire along the line of trees ringing Scarlett's cabin. I don't know if that person wanted this to look like a natural occurrence, but he failed."

"If that's true, the investigators will figure it out." Stevens jerked his thumb over his shoulder. "Is Scarlett okay?"

"I'm gonna go find out right now."

Scarlett hopped off the back of the ambulance when he approached, tugging the blanket around her body. "Did my cabin burn?"

"Nope. Did you notice that helicopter? It's keeping the flames at bay in the back. The fire chief told me your cabin was safe."

"Thank God." She covered her eyes with one hand. "Can I go back inside? I'm assuming I can't stay."

"You can't stay and you can't go back inside."

"My purse. I left my purse, my phone—" she plucked the wet T-shirt away from her body "—my clothes."

"It's not safe, Scarlett. What did the EMT say?"

"I'm fine. They want to have a look at you." She held out her arms and the blanket slid to the ground. "They put some ointment on my burns, but they're not serious."

One of the EMTs came around from the front of his vehicle. "Sir, we'd like to test your lung capacity and treat your burns."

Jim shrugged out of his leather jacket. "Here, Scarlett. Put this on and wrap that blanket around your waist."

Not that he didn't enjoy the view through the wet T-shirt clinging to her body, but the fire had done nothing to heat up the gray skies and cool temps of the early morning.

Jim followed the EMT's instructions but stopped short of allowing him to dab ointment on his burns. "I can do that."

The EMT dropped a sample tube of the burn ointment into Jim's palm. "You two are lucky you got through the fire line, but you probably could've waited it out in the cabin until the fire department arrived."

Jim jumped off the ambulance. "I don't like leaving my fate in the hands of others. Any follow-up treatment recommended for Scarlett?"

"Just watch those burns for any signs of infection, take some ibuprofen for the pain, if necessary, and report any breathing problems immediately."

"That sounds easy enough." Scarlett joined them, hugging his leather jacket around her body.

Looked a lot better on her than it did on him.

Jim held up the ointment. "Did you get one of these?"

She shook her head, and Jim tossed the tube to her. "Stick that in the pocket of the jacket and let's get out of here."

"Not many places I can go looking like this." She spread her arms wide and the jacket opened. He kept his gaze pinned to her face, even though the wet T-shirt molded to her breasts.

"My place. Didn't I make that clear before? I'll take you back to my cabin—as long as you're not expecting some kind of art gallery like you have."

She dropped the blanket back inside the ambulance. "I'm expecting a quick shower and a warm bed."

He couldn't tell if her red cheeks were a result of embarrassment at what she'd just implied or the lights still spinning on top of the emergency vehicles.

"I've got both." He dragged the keys to his bike out of the pocket of his jeans. "I came over here without a helmet, so hold on tight."

He swung one leg over his motorcycle and cranked on the engine. Then he tipped the bike to the side for Scarlett to climb on.

She placed one bare foot on the footrest and hoisted herself on top of the bike behind him.

From his position, he had no idea what she looked like on the back of his bike wearing nothing but a knee-length T-shirt and a motorcycle jacket, but the vision he conjured in his head made him hard.

Twisting his head over his shoulder, he shouted, "Hang on."

Then, as she curled her arms around his waist and pressed her body against his back, he got even harder.

This was gonna be the longest mile of his life.

He aimed his bike down the road, taking it slow, assuring himself it was for safety reasons and not to prolong the sensation of Scarlett wrapped around him, cheek against his back, knees digging into his hips.

He rolled up at his cabin and took the bike around the side. Before he parked it, he leaned it to the left. "Can you get off okay?"

"Yeah."

The leather of his jacket creaked as she peeled herself away from him and then managed a little hop onto the ground. Her T-shirt hiked up, exposing a flash of her shapely thigh.

He parked the motorcycle and jingled the keys in his hand as he walked to the porch of the cabin. "Shower first?"

"Please." She fluffed her hair with her hands. "I smell like smoke."

"Excuse the mess." He pushed open the front door. "I haven't done much cleaning up since I got here."

Folding her arms, she edged into the room, turning her head from side to side. "It's not too bad."

"Yeah, biker chic." He strode to the hallway and plucked a clean towel from the stack in the cupboard. Then he pushed open the bathroom door and hung the towel over the rack. "Do you want a washcloth?"

She came up behind him, framed by the bathroom door. "No, as long as you have some shampoo in there."

"Generic."

"I'm not picky." She tugged at the hem of the still-damp T-shirt.

He made a gun with his fingers, pointing at her. "I can

get you a clean T-shirt, maybe a pair of sweats. Anything else of mine you'd be swimming in it."

"A T-shirt's fine."

"Okay, then. I'll leave you to it." They did a little dance as he squeezed past her at the door. She did smell smoky...but still sweet.

He closed the door and as she cranked on the shower, he headed for the bedroom. She'd have to sleep in the bedroom he'd been occupying. The other bedroom still had a bunch of junk in it and no sheets on the bed. At least he'd washed his sheets two days ago.

He'd crash on the couch in the living room. He didn't sleep much, anyway.

His gaze darted around the room, making sure he hadn't left anything embarrassing out in the open. He smoothed a hand over the bedspread and fluffed the pillow as if he was a preparing a hotel bed for a guest.

He pawed through the T-shirts hanging in his closet and grabbed an extra-long black one so she wouldn't suspect him of wanting to see any more of her body—which is exactly what he did want.

He shook out the shirt and placed it on the bed. Leaving the bedroom door open, he grabbed a blanket from the closet and dumped it onto the couch.

"Jim?"

"Yeah?" He looked down the short hall.

She'd poked her towel-wrapped head out of the bathroom door. "Do you have that T-shirt?"

"Comin' right up." He returned to the bedroom and snatched the shirt from the bed. He tapped on the bathroom door. "Got it."

She stuck her hand out the door. "Thanks. Can I use the hair dryer in here?"

"Yeah, of course, if it still works. It was my old man's."

He backed up from the door. "You can sleep in the room across the hall. Bed's all ready for you."

The roar of the hair dryer drowned out his words, and he shrugged.

He sat on the edge of the couch and pulled off his boots and then his socks. Had he really been at the sheriff's station tonight suspected of murdering Rusty? It seemed like a hundred years ago.

Why had someone set that fire? And why not set the whole cabin on fire with Scarlett in it? The singed hair on his arms stood up. He had to convince her to go back to San Francisco, even if that meant moving back in with her ex-boyfriend.

He took off his flannel shirt and pulled his T-shirt over his head. He smelled like smoke, too. He yanked off his jeans and tossed everything in a pile near the fireplace.

As he shook out the blanket, Scarlett exclaimed behind him, "Oh, sorry."

He turned, wearing only his boxers, raising his eyebrows. "Do you need something?"

"I wasn't sure where I was supposed to go." She plucked at the neckline of the shirt, which was so baggy it slid off one of her shoulders, dipping to expose the swell of her breast.

What made him think she'd look any less sexy in an oversize T-shirt than a tighter one?

Her gaze wandered over his body, and his flesh prickled with heat.

"I left the bedroom door open for you. The other room isn't habitable."

"I can sleep here on the couch. I don't want to kick you out of your bed."

"Don't worry about it. I've spent a few nights on

this couch already." He pointed to the TV in the corner. "Sometimes I just fall asleep in front of the TV."

"Sounds like insomnia to me."

"The least of my current troubles."

She sucked in a breath and reached forward so quickly he couldn't avoid her touch, didn't want to avoid her touch.

Tracing a fingertip over the scar on his chest, she asked, "Is this a souvenir from your captors?"

"One of many."

She flattened her hand against his skin. "I'm sorry. I shouldn't have…"

He swallowed hard, unable to shift his gaze from her plump lips. With a voice rough around the edges, he said, "You don't have to keep being sorry, Scarlett."

"I know." Her long lashes fluttered. "I'll just… Good night."

"Good night."

She spun around and almost ran to the bedroom. When the door clicked shut, Jim let out a long breath.

How the hell was he supposed to let that woman go anywhere?

SCARLETT PRACTICALLY DOVE into the bed. She dragged the pillow against her chest, burying her face in it.

Bad move. The pillowcase had Jim's scent on it—clean, masculine, totally irresistible. She tossed it aside.

When she'd touched the scar on his chest, she hadn't wanted to stop there. She could've run her hands all over his hard body and died a happy woman.

She'd put her momentary lapse in sanity down to smoke inhalation. She didn't need a complicated man like Jim in her life, didn't need to fix him, didn't need to help him solve his problems.

She *could* allow herself one little taste, a little autumn fling. He'd made it pretty clear he wouldn't kick her out of bed or off his couch if she made that move. But who was she kidding?

Flings and shallow affairs were reserved for shallow men—not guys like Jim. If she succumbed to her physical desire for him, she'd be jumping into the deep end without a life jacket.

She rolled to her side, bringing her knees up to her chest, trying not to think about how much warmer she'd be curled up next to Jim. Closing her eyes, she relaxed her muscles and began to drift off.

Minutes or maybe hours later, a crash from the other room had her bolting upright in bed. Had Jim just had another seizure?

Bumps and thumps resounded from the living room, and Scarlett scrambled from the bed. Her gaze darted around the dark room and settled on the shotgun mounted on the wall. She stood on her tiptoes and lifted the gun from its brackets as the cacophony from the other room continued.

Raising the gun to her shoulder, she crept from the bedroom into the living room. Two dark shapes scuffled and scrabbled on the floor, rocking this way and that. Her heart skipped a beat. Someone had broken in and attacked Jim.

She primed the shotgun, pointed the barrel at the ceiling and pulled the trigger. The blast rang in her ears and plaster showered down around her.

The fighting stopped and one of the men staggered to his feet and turned on the light.

Jim, still wearing just his boxers, sporting a trickle of blood beneath his nose, stared at her, and then jerked his head toward the man moaning and sputtering on the floor.

Jim let out a string of curses.

Scarlett turned the gun on the intruder, whose curses had turned into a laugh.

Was he crazy? She leveled the gun at the man's head. "Jim, are you okay? My God, did this man break in?"

"He didn't have to break in. I imagine he still has a key."

"What? You know him?"

"He's my brother."

Chapter Nine

Still cackling, the man sat up and rested his back against the couch. "You still got it, little brother. Always were tougher than me."

Scarlett's mouth dropped open, but she kept the gun trained on Jim's brother.

"What the hell are you doing here, Dax?"

Dax Kennedy wiped a hand across his mouth as his gaze traveled to Scarlett. "You didn't tell me you had a little honey with you, bro."

Jim stepped between her and Dax's gaze. "You can put the gun down, Scarlett."

"Sorry about that." She lowered the shotgun and brushed some plaster from her arm. "But what were you guys rolling around the floor for? I thought someone was going to get killed. I thought Dax was a stranger."

"That's Dax's idea of a joke. He let himself in with his key and jumped me. I didn't know who the hell he was and he didn't bother telling me."

"What would be the fun in that?" Dax pushed up from the floor and adjusted his leather jacket, which sported a patch with the letters *LOC* and a skull with handlebars through it.

"Wanted you to give me your best, J.T." He lifted his

chin to look at his taller younger brother. "And your best is pretty damned good."

"What are you doing back here, Dax?" Jim folded his arms and nodded to Scarlett. "Scarlett, you can go back to bed."

"And miss all the drama? No, thanks."

Jim crossed the room in two steps and dragged the blanket from the couch. "You might as well keep warm."

Standing in front of her, he draped the blanket around her shoulders and bunched it together under her chin.

She shuffled to a chair and sat down, curling her legs beneath her, looking from Jim to his brother. Those dark good looks ran in the family, but Dax was a paler, smaller version of Jim—like a poor copy.

"Why are you here and when did you get out of the joint?"

"I've been out for over a year, keeping out of trouble."

Jim tapped the left side of his chest. "You're still riding with the club."

"It's in my blood, bro. I'm an OG now."

"Are you sure you're staying out of trouble?" Jim bent over to snag his jeans, flashing his back and the tattoo of the motorcycle club he'd escaped. He pulled on his pants.

"The club ain't what it used to be, J.T."

Scarlett asked, "J.T.?"

"My initials, James Thomas, my nickname from the old days." Jim pointed at his brother. "How long have you been here? Did you hear Rusty's dead?"

Dax's head snapped up. "Are you kidding me?"

"Someone offed him two days ago. Stabbed him and left him for dead. Tried to pin it on me."

Dax's dark eyes narrowed and he stroked his goatee. "You're serious."

"I'm serious. The killer used one of Slick's hunting knives—stole it from the garage."

"The SOB didn't touch the bikes, did he?"

"Didn't touch the bikes." Jim hooked his thumbs in his front pockets, and his unbuttoned jeans dipped lower. "And I saw Chewy in town. What is this, some kinda Lords reunion?"

"Chewy, huh?" Dax pushed his long hair out of his face. "Are you going to introduce me to your friend, or just stand here and give me the third degree?"

"This is Scarlett Easton. Scarlett, my brother, Dax Kennedy."

Scarlett poked her hand from the blanket and waved.

"Scarlett? You're that pretty little Indian girl from J.T.'s class."

Jim rolled his eyes.

Scarlett stuck two fingers behind her head and wiggled them. "That's me...the little Indian girl."

Dax threw back his head and barked out a laugh. "I like you. I like her, J.T. She your woman?"

She wished.

"I live up the road, and someone set fire to the trees around my property tonight. You wouldn't know anything about that, would you?"

"Me? What the hell has this guy been telling you about his older brother? Why would I want to set fire to your place? And what the hell is going on around here? Murders, fires, setups."

Jim folded his arms and widened his stance. "You never answered my question. What brings you back to Timberline?"

"You. Heard you were back."

"Who told you that?"

"Does it matter? Thought we could settle some of the

old man's stuff." He held up his hands. "You can have the cabin, but I might want a couple of those bikes."

"I don't have a problem with that. You plan to stay here? In this cabin?"

"Bro, I've been riding all night. I need a place to crash."

Scarlett hopped up from the chair. "Dax, you take the couch. Jim, you can have your bed back. I mean, uh, share it with me."

Winking, Dax slapped Jim on the back. "Sounds like a good deal for you, J.T."

Jim shot her a glance. "I don't want... If you..."

"I'm fine with it." She shrugged out of the blanket and dropped it back on the couch. "Now I really need to get a few hours of sleep."

She left the two brothers talking in low voices and crawled beneath the covers, keeping to one side of the king-size bed. When life gave you lemons, make the whole dang lemon meringue pie and stuff your face.

Jim tapped on the door. "Scarlett?"

"C'mon in."

He slipped into the room and clicked the door behind him. "Are you sure you're okay with this?"

"Your brother's a pretty rough character. Honestly, I figured I'd feel safer with you in here, anyway."

"Dax? Yeah, he has his issues, but harassing women isn't one of them." Jim sat on the edge of the bed and fell back onto his side, his feet still planted on the floor.

"Whoa, mister." She placed her hands on his back and gave him a shove.

"Change your mind already?"

"You're not climbing into this bed wearing those jeans. They still smell like smoke."

He got off the bed and, with his back turned to her,

he yanked off his pants. He turned back the covers and slipped in beside her. "Good night, Scarlett."

Poking his shoulder, she asked, "Are you going to find out what Dax is doing here? He didn't exactly give you a straight answer."

"Dax isn't too good at straight answers, but I'll get it out of him—one way or another. Good night."

She turned her back to him and closed her eyes with a smile on her face. His body heat was warming up the bed already. The two of them could warm it up a lot faster, but his brother in the next room was saving her from making a big mistake.

Or keeping her from the time of her life.

THE NEXT MORNING, Scarlett peeled open one eye and followed a shaft of light beaming through a hitch in the blinds. She rolled toward Jim's now-empty side of the bed and inhaled the scent he'd left behind—slightly smoky and woodsy.

Another smell floated through the air, replacing it. This one made her mouth water almost as much as the other—and she didn't even eat bacon.

She scooted out of the bed and landed in front of Jim's closet, where a row of T-shirts swayed on their hangers. She pulled another black T from the bunch and swapped it with the huge one Jim had picked out for her last night. Had he given her that one just so that it would fall off her?

A girl could hope.

"Hello?" She poked her head into the hallway. "Everyone decent?"

Dax yelled back. "I'm never decent, sweetheart."

She tiptoed into the living room and raised her brows at Dax in the kitchen, spatula in one hand and oven mitt on the other. "You cook?"

"Nothing fancy. Went to the store and picked up some eggs and bacon, potatoes, bread." He waved the spatula at the counter. "Dig in."

"Where's Jim?" She hunched over the counter and picked up a piece of toast.

"In the shower, I think."

Scarlett bit into the toast and dropped it on a plate. She scooped some scrambled eggs onto her dish and added some potatoes. After several bites, she said, "Not bad. Where'd you learn how to cook?"

"From my mom. She taught me a few things before she ran off, and then I cooked for my dad and brother when she did. J.T. was just a little guy when Wendy, our mom abandoned us—maybe four, and I was thirteen."

She wrinkled her nose as she did the calculations in her head. Jim's mom must've left right before the kidnappings. When Jim had told his story of almost being snatched from his bed, he hadn't mentioned his mother. She must've been gone by then.

"You really stepped up." She crunched into her toast, her assessment of Dax Kennedy shifting by the minute.

"I thought you were a vegetarian." Jim came up behind her, toweling off his dark hair, the muscles across his chest and shoulders bunching and flexing.

"I eat eggs." She held up a forkful of scrambled egg.

"Yeah, but these potatoes?" He snatched one from her plate. "Cooked in bacon grease."

"Oh." She shoved the potatoes to the side of her plate. "Thanks for warning me."

"You didn't have to cook breakfast, Dax." Jim took a plate from the stack and loaded it with everything.

"I figured I wouldn't get anything to eat if I left it up to you, unless you learned how to cook in the army." He jerked his thumb at Jim. "This guy never stepped one foot in the kitchen."

"Are you going to tell me what you're doing in Timberline?"

Dax paused, a piece of bacon dangling from a pair of tongs over the sizzling frying pan. He dropped the bacon onto a plate covered with a paper towel. "Thought I told you, bro. Wanted to check out the old man's place."

Jim grunted and then dug into his food.

Scarlett planted her elbows on the counter. "Do you mind if I ask you a question, Dax?"

"Shoot."

"What were you in prison for?"

"A few things. I don't even remember anymore."

Jim raised his fork in the air. "Try armed robbery, possession of narcotics with the intent to sell."

"Oh, yeah. Never intended to use that gun."

"Because you led such a peaceful existence otherwise."

Dax ducked his head in the fridge. "Motorcycle club business."

"Doesn't excuse it."

"Okay, sorry I asked. I didn't mean to stir up trouble." Scarlett aimed her fork at Jim. "Have the investigators from the fire department been around yet?"

"No." Jim glanced at his brother. "Have they?"

"I wasn't up much earlier than you, but I didn't hear anything."

Scarlett plucked at the T-shirt. "I'd really like to get back into my place and at least pick up some clothes if they won't let me stay there."

"I think they'll let you back in." Jim broke a piece of bacon in two and popped one half in his mouth. "The fire didn't reach the cabin. The fire department may have soaked your roof and if you had any leaks, you might be in trouble, but I didn't see any damage to your cabin."

"It's been raining on and off since I've been back. I know I don't have any leaks." She spread her arms. "Not like the Kennedy brothers haven't offered me first-class hospitality."

Dax chuckled and then whistled an unidentifiable tune as he piled his plate with food. He brought it to the small kitchen table, stationed near a sliding door that led to a small patio decorated with a rusted barbecue and a dead plant.

"If Scarlett's going back to her place, can I bunk here, J.T.?"

"Are you into anything illegal? Weapons? Drugs? Pimping?"

Scarlett swallowed her orange juice the wrong way and coughed. Her rising opinion of Dax had just taken a nosedive.

"Hey, hey." Dax leveled his fork at Jim. "I never ran the girls."

"Whatever. If you're running anything, hit the road. You can't stay here."

"Scout's honor." Dax held up two fingers. "I'm clean. Even gave up the drugs and booze."

"You're kidding."

"I gave up the drugs and the hard drinking. I can handle a beer or two. I got a woman in Seattle now. Belinda won't put up with that stuff."

A knock on the door interrupted their conversation, and Jim strode to the door. He peered through the peephole. "Looks like the arson investigators."

He opened the door to two men in suits, and Scarlett tugged her T-shirt below her knees.

How much more uncomfortable could this get?

Jim shook hands with them and invited them inside. "This is Scarlett Easton. The fire was at her place. Scarlett, this is Investigator Young and Investigator Elgin."

"Excuse me for not getting up, but I ran outside in my pajamas last night and all my clothes are at my house."

"We just have a few questions, Ms. Easton."

Jim gestured toward Dax, still stuffing his face. "This is my brother and he was just leaving."

Jim grabbed a key chain from a hook in the kitchen and tossed it to Dax. "Have a look at those bikes in the garage. Let me know what you want to keep and what we can sell, and be on the lookout for the cops. They're coming to dust for prints around the garage—had a break-in earlier."

"Great, cops." Dax stacked up all their dishes and dumped them into the sink. "I'm outta here."

Scarlett stayed where she was at the counter, while Jim sat at the kitchen table with the two investigators.

They asked questions about any noises she may have heard—none—and any other unusual activity around her place.

"You mean like a dead body in the woods?"

Neither Young nor Elgin batted an eyelash. They must've already been briefed about Rusty Kelly.

Jim asked, "Did you confirm it was arson?"

"Preliminary findings point to arson. We discovered some accelerant at the base of several trees in different areas."

Scarlett rubbed the goose bumps from her arms, even though the findings didn't surprise her. Did someone want to kill her or just drive her away? And why?

Jim shot her a glance and asked, "Can you track down who did it? Will it be easy?"

"Depends on what else we discover. If this is a serial arsonist, he'll probably strike again."

Scarlett exchanged another glance with Jim. They both knew this was no serial arsonist. She'd been targeted.

"When can Ms. Easton go home?"

"You can go home now, Ms. Easton. Just stay out of the areas cordoned off with yellow tape. We'll be sifting through the remains. When we're done, you can clean the place."

She blew out a breath. "There goes my privacy."

"I can't say that bothers me much." Jim pushed away from the table and joined her at the counter, squeezing her hand. "You're too isolated back there. Maybe it'll even improve your cell reception."

The investigators stood up. "That's all we have for now. If we discover anything else or need to ask you any more questions, we'll contact you."

Jim walked them to the door. When he shut it behind them, he turned and said, "You wanna go home?"

"Yes, it would be nice to put some pants on. And shoes—shoes would be good."

"You want to put on a pair of my sweatpants for the ride back?"

"Absolutely. That Lady Godiva stuff is okay for the wee hours of the morning, but I could get arrested for that this time of day."

He quirked an eyebrow at her, and she could feel a surge of warmth in her cheeks. She'd never blushed so much in her entire life than she had these past few days with Jim—must be her heightened sense of awareness… or how he looked in a pair of jeans.

"I have a clean pair of sweats in the bottom drawer of the dresser in the bedroom."

"I'll find them." She made for the bedroom and

crouched in front of the dresser, pulling open the last drawer. She plunged her hands into the soft material and her fingers stumbled across some hard, metal objects.

She parted the sweats and sweatshirts and closed her hand around one of the objects, pulling it out of the drawer. She held it up, the dull gold of the medal glinting in the light.

She ran her thumb along the raised lettering on the disc. It was some kind of medal for bravery. She peered into the drawer at the other medals. If he wore every one of them at once, he'd be bowed over from the weight.

These couldn't all be recognition for surviving and escaping his capture. He'd been a sniper. He must've gotten medals for killing people—lots of people.

His imprisonment and torture must've gone a long way toward alleviating any guilt he'd felt about that. She stuffed the medals back into the drawer. Somehow she didn't think Jim would feel guilty about doing his job, about killing the enemy and saving his brothers in arms.

"You ready?"

"Just about." She snatched up a pair of dark blue sweats and pulled them on. She pushed up the elastic to her calves and cinched the waist as much as she could.

"Ready." She stepped into the hallway and Jim met her with a helmet.

"I do have this for you."

She took it from him, tucking it under her arm. As they walked out the front door, Dax revved the engine of a Harley parked next to Jim's.

"This one's a beauty. Mind if I keep it for myself?"

"Take what you like, Dax, but leave a couple since I promised Scarlett's cousin he could buy one."

Jim flipped up the kickstand on his bike and mounted it. He dipped it to one side. "Hop on."

With a lot more confidence than this morning, Scarlett hitched one leg over the seat of the bike and settled behind Jim. She even leaned against the backrest, hooking her fingers in Jim's belt loops, but when he started the bike and rolled onto the road, she grabbed him around the waist.

When he pulled up in front of her mailbox, she dug her fingers into his side. Her cabin stood in the center of a ring of blackened and charred trees and foliage. Soggy, yellow tape stirred in the breeze, waving a sorry welcome.

Jim steered his bike up to her front porch and cut the engine. "Looks like a war zone."

She lifted the helmet from her head and shook out her hair. "There goes my little hideaway. The cabin is completely visible from the road now."

"You can replant, but give yourself a clear view of the road this time."

"I hope everything doesn't smell like smoke in there." She slid from the bike.

"You'll probably have to air it out and clean up."

She jogged up the two steps to the front door and tried the handle. "Great. It's unlocked."

She pushed open the front door and hovered on the threshold, sniffing the air. "It doesn't smell too bad and I don't see any damage from the fire hoses or flame retardant."

"You should check your studio. You're probably going to have to clean all those windows in there."

Jim left the door open, and she edged down the hallway toward the studio. The door had been left open. Had the firefighters come inside her place? She never left that door open.

Pushing the door back, she scanned the room. Her

current canvas was in place and undamaged, but Jim had been right. Streaks of flame retardant and rivulets of water clouded the glass walls of the studio, practically blocking the view to the outside world.

"I'm going to have to get a professional window cleaner in here to take care of this mess, unless my cousin Annie can do it."

"Add a professional landscaper to clean up the mess outside."

Scarlett wandered around the room, unease tickling the back of her neck. She flipped through some canvases and took a step back to scan one wall covered with her landscape paintings.

"What's wrong?"

"I'm not sure. Something feels off."

"Something missing? You do have an inventory, don't you?"

She tapped her head. "The inventory is up here."

"And?"

"Can't put my finger on it yet."

"Make sure you check all your stuff, and if there's anything missing, make a report."

Scarlett paused in front of an easel with her current project clipped onto it, the smell of paint tickling her nose. Glancing at the tray, she noticed a pot of open black paint and a dirty brush.

Her pulse thrummed in her throat as she ran a fingertip across the damp ends of the brush. "This is weird."

"What?" Jim joined her at the easel.

"There's an open pot of paint and a used brush. I always clean up when I'm done."

"You mean someone broke into your place, came in here and painted a picture?" He scratched his head.

She dabbed her fingers across the painting on the

easel. "Maybe someone just wanted to be helpful and finish this work for me."

She barked out a short, dry laugh and licked her lips. She turned toward the wall of paintings again, her gaze scanning each row.

"Does the second row from the bottom look crooked to you?"

Jim squeezed past her, and his head swung from side to side. "Yeah, it's this bunch here on the right."

He shuffled to the right and reached up to adjust the frames on the wall. "Scarlett!"

She jumped at the sharpness of his tone. "What's wrong?"

"You might want to have a look at this forest painting."

She tripped forward, grabbing onto Jim's arm as she leaned toward the painting.

She gasped, her fingers digging into his biceps. Someone had altered one of her landscapes—adding three stick figures at the edge of the forest, holding hands.

Chapter Ten

A chill snaked down Scarlett's spine, and she took a step back, dropping her hold on Jim.

Jim leaned in for a closer look. "You know what that's supposed to be, don't you?"

Scarlett swore and pushed past him. She grabbed the painting from the wall. "Some crude representation of the Timberline Trio. It's sick. Who would do this?"

"Put the frame down and don't touch the paintbrush or paint."

She dropped the painting on the floor. "You really think the sheriff's department is going to come out here and fingerprint over what amounts to a bad paint job?"

"When we tell them what was painted, they will. They're investigating this fire as arson. They'll be interested."

She flicked her fingers at the painting. "What do you think it means? Who is it that won't let this case die?"

"Maybe it's a warning to do just that—let it die. There's been a lot of attention focused on the case these past few months. The kidnapper or kidnappers were never caught and the children never found—dead or alive. This spotlight on the case must be making someone nervous."

"I get that, but why me? I haven't opened an investigation into the Timberline Trio. And what does it all have to do with Rusty?"

"Or my brother."

"So you don't believe he's here looking at your dad's bikes?"

"Too coincidental—him, Rusty, Chewy. What are they all doing here at the same time?"

"A biker reunion?"

"Right." He put his hand on the small of her back and steered her out of the studio. "Let's go outside and call the police to report this."

A deputy came out faster than Scarlett expected but found only one set of prints on the paint and the frame, which had to be hers.

The deputy took it more seriously because of the fire, but he didn't know what to make of it any more than she and Jim did. He took pictures and notes, but there wasn't much else he could do.

When he left, Scarlett collapsed in a chair and crossed her arms behind her head. "I don't get it. What do I have to do with the Timberline Trio? I was just a kid when it happened."

"Have you ever questioned your granny or any of the elders about why they wouldn't discuss the case?"

"They shut me down every time I tried."

He nodded toward the studio. "Maybe it's time to try again now that you're involved."

"I never did drop off that yarn I picked up for Granny." She pushed out of the chair. "How about it? Feel like a trip to the reservation?"

"Don't think I'm welcome."

"The Quileute had an issue with your dad and Dax, never you."

"Guilt by association."

"Well, you'll be with me."

Jim glanced at his watch. "What time are we taking this field trip?"

"Do you mind?"

"No. I want to know as much as you do, but I want to talk to Dax, too."

"Do you think you can get him to admit what he's really doing here?"

"Nobody can get Dax to do anything he doesn't want to do—the only one who could was the old man and he used threats of violence."

"Okay, you talk to Dax." She held up her dead cell phone. "I'm going to charge up my phone and call a few landscapers. I'm also going to buy a landline phone and hook up my service."

"Good idea." He hesitated by the front door. "Are you going to be okay here by yourself?"

"I'll be fine. Besides, my cabin is fully visible from the road now."

"That's not a bad thing, Scarlett." He raised his hand and slipped out the door.

WHEN JIM PULLED up to his cabin, Dax looked up from tinkering with a motorcycle and wiped his hands on a rag hanging over the handlebars of the bike.

Jim parked his Harley and joined his brother. "You need any help?"

"You can hand me that wrench by your right foot."

Crouching down, Jim swept up the tool and handed it to Dax.

"Took you long enough to get back. Did you and that feisty chick finally get it on?" Dax loosened a spark plug with the wrench.

"No, and if we had, I wouldn't be telling you about

it. Someone broke into Scarlett's place and defaced one of her paintings."

"That sucks. You think it's the same person who set the fire?" Dax squinted at the spark plug he was trying to remove.

"Probably. You know what the person put on her painting?"

"Something obscene?"

"Kind of. Someone painted three stick figures at the edge of a forest scene, holding hands."

Dax dropped the wrench and swore. "What's that supposed to mean?"

"It's obviously the Timberline Trio."

"Obviously? How'd you get that out of three stick figures?"

"Holding hands?"

"Maybe it's supposed to be like a threesome or something—I told you, something obscene, although…"

Jim kicked his brother's booted foot. "It wasn't supposed to be a threesome, Dax. It was a representation of the Timberline Trio."

"Bro, you're obsessed with that case." Dax threw his ponytail over his shoulder.

"You know why I am." Jim picked up the wrench and tossed it from hand to hand. "What do you know about that night? The night someone tried to abduct me?"

"I don't know nothin', J.T. I was sleeping, remember?"

"What are you doing in Timberline, Dax?" Jim rose to his feet and crossed his arms over his chest as he loomed over his brother.

"This is gettin' old. If you don't want me to have any of Slick's bikes, just say so."

"It's not about the…forget it." Jim dropped the wrench onto the ground and went to the house.

Dax had tried to cover it, but he'd been rattled when Jim told him about the stick figures. Why?

The sudden appearance of Rusty, Chewy and Dax meant something, and Jim had a sick feeling that their presence in Timberline was related to the fire at Scarlett's.

Jim cleaned up the rest of the breakfast dishes and went into the bedroom for his laundry basket. He fingered the T-shirt Scarlett had folded on top of his bed and then pressed it to his face.

The sweet, clean scent triggered all kinds of memories of the early morning hours he'd spent with her. He tossed the shirt into the basket. He couldn't believe he'd had that woman in his bed, right beside him and had been able to resist her.

Not that falling asleep next to her warm, soft body had been easy. He'd felt every breath from her parted lips, every shift in movement, every touch as her hand or leg brushed against his body.

It had been torture.

He threw his laundry in the washer and wandered back outside to help his brother, who eyed him with suspicion.

Jim held up his hands. "No more questions. I'm just here to help you."

The brothers worked side by side for over an hour until a call from Scarlett came through on Jim's cell phone. He wiped his hands on the rag and answered the call.

"What's up, Scarlett?" He ignored Dax's raised eyebrows.

"I'm picking up a phone today and my service should be turned on by tomorrow. I also got two estimates from a couple of landscapers, and I'm going with the one my cousin Jason knows. Are you ready?"

"I've been helping Dax work on a bike. I need to

shower and change. Do you want to go over on my motorcycle?"

"Sure. My car is filthy from the fire."

"I'll be kind of conspicuous on the bike. Are you sure you don't want to keep my visit a secret?"

"Kind of hard to keep a guy your size a secret."

"Let's just try not to draw attention to ourselves. Nobody needs to know why we're there."

"I have every right to visit Granny and bring an old high school friend. Is a half an hour enough time for you?"

"Sure. Tell you what. You bring your dirty car over here and I'll have Dax wash it for you."

"If you think he won't mind."

Jim watched his brother through narrowed eyes. "He likes anything having to do with cars. Bring it over."

Scarlett ended the call, and Jim tucked his phone into his front pocket.

"Hot date?" Dax pushed a lock of hair from his forehead with a dirty thumb, leaving a smudge of grease.

"We're going to the reservation."

Dax narrowed his eyes. "What for?"

"Scarlett is going to drop off something for her grandmother."

"And she needs your help, why?"

"She just wants the company." If Dax could be close-mouthed about his motivations, so could he. He'd told his brother plenty and had gotten nothing in return. "You mind washing her car if she leaves it here?"

"No problem."

By the time Jim had showered and changed, Scarlett had pulled up to the cabin. He charged outside before she could get into conversation with Dax. He didn't want her telling his brother about their mission.

As she greeted Dax, Jim tried to catch her eye, but she ignored him.

"Is that one of the bikes you're going to take?"

Dax stood up, shoving the rag in his back pocket. "If I can get it running. Why are you taking my brother to the rez?"

"My grandmother wanted to meet him after I told her he rescued me from the fire."

Jim let out a measured breath. He didn't have to worry about Scarlett.

"Yeah, that's our J.T." Dax pounded Jim on the back. "Hero material."

"I hope you're not being sarcastic, because he really was heroic when he barged through that fire to get to me."

"I totally mean it. He was always the good brother—" Dax quirked his eyebrows up and down "—and I was the bad boy."

"You didn't have to be, Dax. You let Slick influence you too much."

He squeezed the back of Jim's neck in a vise. "Some of us are just born that way."

"We'd better get going." Jim shrugged him off.

"Are you sure you're okay with washing my car?"

"It'll be the best damned car wash you ever had." Dax winked. "Have fun, you two."

Jim wheeled his bike toward the road, away from Dax. He handed her the helmet and swung his leg over the bike, straddling it.

As Scarlett pulled the helmet on her head, she asked, "Did you get anything out of him today?"

"Nope. That's why I'm glad you didn't say anything to him about why we were going to see your grandmother." Jim started the engine of the Harley. "If he's not going to be straight with me, I'm not going to be straight with him—not until I know what he's doing here."

"I agree. Did you tell him about the painting?"

"Yeah, and it rattled him, as much as anything can rattle Dax."

"But he didn't say anything about it?"

"He made jokes about it."

She puffed out a breath. "Has Dax seen the other guy, yet? Chewy?"

"I don't think so, but I don't expect him to tell me about it."

Scarlett climbed onto the bike behind him, and her arms around his waist gave him a thrill like he hadn't felt for a woman in a long time.

He liked Scarlett. He'd always liked her, even way back in high school. She'd been different from the other teenage girls—always had a purpose. But just because their attraction seemed mutual, it didn't mean he had to act on that attraction. He wasn't ready for a relationship, and Scarlett wasn't the type of woman you loved and left.

He drove north to the Quileute reservation, following a road that meandered next to a river, bordered by lush forest on either side. The reservation came into view, the small houses dotting the landscape, the roadside vendors selling their wares.

When his bike came into view of an old woman and a young girl on the side of the road, the girl jumped up and down and waved. Jim held up his hand.

Slowing down, he steered his motorcycle onto the Quileute land until Scarlett tapped his arm. He pulled up to a small, brown-and-green house.

When he cut the engine, Scarlett said, "Thanks for waving to Prudence back there. You probably made her day."

"Prudence? The girl with the old woman?"

Scarlett took off the helmet and handed it to him. "She goes to the reservation school but wants to transfer to the public school next year. I'm trying to make that happen by convincing her grandmother that Pru will blossom in the public school environment."

"You did."

She jerked her head to the side and her hair fell over one eye. "I don't know about that. It did introduce me to Mrs. Rooney, my art teacher, and she's the one who encouraged me to go to art school instead of regular college."

He nodded. "Blossomed."

A little smile lifted one corner of her mouth as she pointed to the low-slung brown-and-green house that looked like it grew up out of the forest. "Granny really does want to meet you. I wasn't lying to Dax about that."

"You told her about me?"

"Of course. I told her the whole story about finding the body and the fire."

"Did you tell her about the stick figures?"

"No. I'd rather see her reaction."

He got off the bike and planted one booted foot on the ground, cranking his head to the side. "Nobody's going to come after me with pitchforks, are they?"

"At least you didn't say tomahawks." She nudged his shoulder. "What are you so worried about? Nobody remembers what a bigot your dad was."

"And Dax. Don't forget him."

"He seems to have reformed and mellowed. Besides, Granny always was one to make her own judgments of people."

"My kind of woman."

She squeezed his biceps. "You're her kind of man, too. Don't let her sexually harass you."

Jim laughed, but Scarlett just raised her eyebrows before turning and striding toward her granny's house. She tapped on the front door and called out, "Granny?"

A strong voice answered. "I'm here, Scarlett."

Jim followed Scarlett into the house, already warmed by a blaze in the fireplace. Scarlett's grandmother waved them over. "C'mon over here. I don't bite, but I might make an exception in your case."

As she laughed, her thin shoulders shook.

"Granny, behave yourself or you're going to scare off Jim."

The old woman gripped the arms of her chair and sized him up through large, dark eyes that took up half her face. "He doesn't look like a man who scares easily."

"Yeah, well, he's never met someone like you before." Scarlett crossed the small room and dipped down to kiss her grandmother's cheek. "Granny, this is Jim Kennedy. Jim, my grandmother."

Jim joined Scarlett and took her grandmother's thin hand in his. "Nice to meet you, ma'am."

"Nice to meet you, too, young man and you can call me Evelyn. Granny this, granny that—makes me feel ancient."

"I brought you the yarn." Scarlett waved it in the air.

"Drop it in the basket. Would you two like something to drink? Tea? Coffee?" Evelyn winked. "Something a little stronger?"

"Jim doesn't drink, Granny, and it's a little early for me."

"Nothing like Slick, are you?"

"No, ma'am, and some water would be fine."

"Go make us some tea, Scarlett, and bring Jim a glass of water."

"Okay." Scarlett rolled her eyes at him before she headed for the kitchen.

Evelyn patted the cushion beside her. "Have a seat, Jim."

He sat down, turning his body slightly to face her and her penetrating stare.

"War hero, huh?"

"I just survived is all."

"Did you?" She curved her bony fingers around his wrist with surprising strength and closed her eyes. Her frail body bolted upright and her eyelashes fluttered.

"You did more than survive. You helped the others, but—" she squeezed harder "—you have guilt. So much guilt. They took the other three but left you."

"The other three?" Jim licked his lips. She couldn't be talking about the cell in Afghanistan anymore. He'd been held there with more than three people.

"Do you mean the Timberline Trio?"

Evelyn's eyes flew open. "Is that why you're here?"

"Granny, are you reading him?" Scarlett walked into the room with a tray in front of her.

Evelyn released his wrist. "Why are you back in Timberline, Jim?"

"Going through my father's things."

Evelyn narrowed her eyes as she took her cup from Scarlett. "Don't try to fool an old woman, Jim."

"Especially an old woman who has the gift." Scarlett sat down next to him and put his water and her tea on the table in front of them. "Why don't you tell Granny what happened to you as a child?"

"I thought—" Jim pinged the water glass with his fingernail "—that topic was off-limits here."

Evelyn's dark eyes focused on Scarlett over the rim of her cup. "Is that what you told him?"

"Come on, Granny. How many times did you tell me to stop asking questions about the kidnappings? How many times was I shushed by the elders?"

Evelyn lifted her narrow shoulders. "Most of those elders are dead."

"You mean you're ready to talk now?" Scarlett hunched forward, her thigh bumping his.

"I don't know what you imagine I know, Scarlett, but I want to hear from Jim first. What happened to you? You still carry it with you even after everything else you went through during the war, your captivity."

"My cap— How did you know about that?"

"I felt it, Jim. Tell me what happened in Timberline."

He launched into the story about his attempted kidnapping and how his father had threatened him with bodily harm if he dared tell another soul about it.

Evelyn listened with her eyes closed and through occasional sips of tea, nodding calmly as if his story didn't surprise her one bit.

When he finished, the silence hung heavy over the room, and Evelyn appeared to be sleeping. Jim raised his brows at Scarlett, who put a finger against her lips.

Evelyn drew in a breath and inhaled the steam from her hot tea. "You probably believe there was bad blood between the Quileute and the Lords of Chaos, don't you do?"

"I know my father for what he was—a bigot. He held ugly stereotypes about the Quileute and wasn't shy about voicing them."

"There was that side of him. Do you think our tribe was completely blameless?"

"I know there were fights."

"There were fights. We had our own troublemakers. Did you know that?"

"Young men with not a lot to do?" Jim swirled the water in his glass. He'd been one of those. "I can believe that."

"They managed to keep busy with…other activities—illegal activities."

"Are you telling me that the Lords of Chaos and the Quileute were working together?"

"They had business that crossed paths."

"Granny, what does this all have to do with the Timberline Trio?"

"Drugs." Jim placed his glass on the table with a click. "The Lords of Chaos moved drugs through the Washington peninsula and they got them from suppliers."

"Some of our tribe members were suppliers of drugs?" Scarlett's gaze darted between him and Evelyn.

He'd let Evelyn give her the bad news.

The old woman dropped her chin to her chest. "They were bad apples, Scarlett. Even as a child you must've been aware of your uncle Danny and his feud with your father. Of course, Danny's influence never spread to the entire tribe, despite his best efforts."

"But the elders must've known about it, known about Danny." Scarlett jumped up from the sofa and took a turn around the room, her arms folded across her chest. "Why else would they try to protect these *bad apples*?"

"Nothing was known for sure. There was no proof."

"Wait, wait, wait." Scarlett pressed two fingers against her temple. "I still don't understand what this all has to do with the Timberline Trio kidnappings."

Evelyn laced her fingers together in her lap. "I can't tell you that. I only know the Lords of Chaos and that gang of Quileute were in business together, and I believe that business involved the kidnapping of those children. Now that I've heard Jim's story, I'm more convinced than ever."

Jim ran his knuckles across his jaw. "Did the elders tell you to keep quiet, Evelyn?"

"They did." She held up her hand at Scarlett, who had begun to speak. "I didn't have any proof I could take to the police, anyway, Scarlett, so don't give me that look. I was never allowed to get that proof."

"Was there any evidence?" Scarlett sat on the edge of the coffee table and clasped her grandmother's hand.

"There was the pink ribbon."

"Pink ribbon?" Jim and Scarlett said the words in unison.

"You found it. Don't you remember, Scarlett? You picked it up off the ground. You brought it to me and complained that it felt hot in your hands. You didn't understand your gift yet, so you didn't realize what the ribbon's warmth meant."

Jim interrupted her. "But you did."

"I couldn't get a read on it." Evelyn wrapped her hands around her cup as if to warm them. "And then it was stolen from me."

"I stole it."

The cup in Evelyn's hands jerked, sloshing the tea inside. "You took the ribbon?"

"I couldn't understand why you wouldn't let me keep the ribbon, so I snuck into your knitting basket and took it back."

"How do you know this—" Jim twirled his finger in the air "—pink ribbon had something to do with the Timberline Trio case?"

Evelyn wrinkled her nose and screwed up her eyes as if looking into the past. "I didn't at first. I just wanted to protect Scarlett from any visions she wouldn't know how to handle. But then the gossip started up about the kidnappings. I'd heard from someone who'd heard from someone else that a pink ribbon was taken from one of the little kidnapped girls—Kayla Rush. When I heard that, I went to retrieve the ribbon, but someone had taken it."

Scarlett raised her hand. "That would be me."

"I suppose it's too much to hope for that you still have it somewhere." Jim blew out a breath.

"Yeah. I mean, I have some trinkets and mementos from my childhood, but I can't imagine I still have a ribbon."

"You never showed it to anyone, did you?" Evelyn struggled to sit forward, and Jim reached over the table to take her hand.

"Maybe a few friends. I don't remember." Scarlett dipped next to the table and gathered Jim's glass and her own mug. "Do you think that's why I'm involved now? Somebody thinks I know something?"

"Perhaps." Evelyn reached for her knitting in the basket at her feet. "A few of that bunch have returned to the reservation recently, including Danny."

"That's interesting." Jim moved the basket within Evelyn's reach. "A few of the Lords of Chaos have returned to Timberline, too. Is someone or something calling them home?"

Evelyn's hand trembled slightly as she picked up her needles. "I hope not."

"We'll get out of your hair, Granny. If you think of anything else, let us know." Scarlett stroked her grandmother's head.

"Thanks, Evelyn."

She aimed one of her knitting needles at Jim. "You have nothing to feel guilty about, young man."

He winked at her and followed Scarlett from the house. "That was enlightening but not useful."

"Oh, I don't know. I could look for that pink ribbon and try to get something out of it."

"That's a long shot." As he approached his bike parked outside Evelyn's house, his spine stiffened and then he cursed.

"What's wrong?"

Jim strode to his bike and dropped to his knees. "Someone slashed my tires."

Chapter Eleven

Goose bumps raced up Scarlett's arms, and she jerked her head to the side to scan the road. Was this malicious mischief because someone didn't want Jim Kennedy here or was it because someone didn't want them talking to Granny about the Timberline Trio?

"I'm pretty sure someone did this with a knife." Jim ran his hands along the shredded pieces of his tire.

Crouching beside Jim, her shoulder bumping his, she asked, "Who would do something like this here?"

"Either it's someone on the reservation with an old grudge against Slick or someone with a new grudge against me."

A truck rolled up, spewing exhaust, and Scarlett rose to her feet and covered her nose and mouth with one hand.

Her cousin Jason waved through the window. He parked next to Jim's bike and hopped out of his truck. "I thought it was my turn to look in on Granny."

"I had something to drop off."

Jason's eyes widened as he took in Jim examining his bike's tires. "What happened?"

Jim cranked his head around. "I guess someone wanted to keep me on the reservation."

"Someone here did that?" Jason scratched his head beneath his black beanie.

"Did you just get here? Did you see anything?" Scarlett studied her cousin's face.

"Me?" He stabbed his chest with his thumb. "You think I did this?"

"Did I say that? I just asked if you saw anything... or anyone."

Jason took a step back toward his truck. "I just drove onto the rez. I didn't see anyone running away or burning rubber or anything like that if that's what you mean."

Jim brushed his hands together and pushed to his feet. "Resentment of the Lords still run high around here?"

"Not that I know of. That was a long time ago, man. This isn't going to hurt my chances of buying one of those sweet bikes, is it?"

"Not if you give your cousin, me and my bike a ride back to my place."

"Yeah, sure. No problem." He pointed to Granny's house. "Should I stop in to see her?"

"I'm sure she'll want to see you, but—" Scarlett grabbed Jason's arm as he started to move toward the house "—don't tell her what happened out here. I don't want her to worry."

"Whatever, but I don't think Granny's going to be worried about Jim's tires getting slashed."

"Just keep it to yourself. Shh."

"Okay if I load my bike into your truck bed?"

"Go ahead, or you can wait for me and I'll help you." Jason continued up the steps and disappeared inside the house.

"Do you think he knows anything?" Jim lowered the back of Jason's truck and shoved a hand in his pocket as he scoured the landscape through narrowed eyes.

"No. What are you looking for?"

"Something I can use as a ramp."

"Granny has some old construction materials in the back of her house. I keep telling her to toss the stuff, but she hates to throw anything away."

"Lead the way."

She crooked her finger, and Jim followed her around the side of the house. "Wood?"

"That'll work."

Together, they hauled a two-by-four to the front of the house. Jim wedged it against the back of Jason's truck just as Jason exited the house.

"I can help you with that." He jogged over and took Scarlett's place on the other side of the ramp. "I'll secure it while you roll the bike up."

Jim wheeled his bike up the makeshift ramp and put it on its side. "I appreciate it."

She asked her cousin, "You didn't mention this to Granny, did you?"

"Said Jim was having problems with his bike and I was giving you two a ride back."

"Thanks." She hopped into the truck after Jason and Jim squeezed in beside her.

On the ride back to Timberline, the three of them discussed who could be behind the vandalism of Jim's bike, but she and Jim kept mum about their true suspicions.

When they arrived at Jim's cabin, he and Jason unloaded the bike, and Jim invited him into the garage to look at the other motorcycles.

While Jim and Jason were in the garage, Scarlett sat on Jim's front porch, stretching her legs in front of her and tapping the toes of her boots together. Dax and his bike were gone, but she figured he'd be back. He had business in Timberline, and Jim was convinced that business involved more than looking over Slick's motorcycles.

Jason emerged from the garage with a big smile on his face.

She called out, "You see something you like?"

"Oh, yeah. Do you want a ride back to your cabin? I drove by earlier and it's still a mess."

"I left my car here." She pointed to her now-clean car parked at the side of the house. "And I have someone coming out tomorrow to start the cleanup and landscaping—your friend, Tony."

"He told me." Jason raised a hand to Jim, who was locking up the garage. "Thanks, man. I'll be back later when I have the cash."

Jingling the keys in his palm, Jim joined her at the porch as Jason turned his truck around.

"You gave him a deal, didn't you?"

"He's a nice kid, really appreciative."

"Is your brother going to mind that you're selling one of the bikes for a steal?"

"Dax won't care as long as I leave him a few. He doesn't care about material things."

"Then why the crime?"

"Beats me. Excitement? A big snub to authority?"

She traced a crack in the wood handrail with her fingertip. "I wonder if it was the same for that gang of Quileute who was involved in drugs."

"Could be, not that I'm discounting money as a motivator for most criminals. It just never motivated Dax."

"So, the Quileute gang manufactured or procured drugs and sold them to the Lords of Chaos who turned around and sold them on the streets."

"Or distributed them elsewhere."

"And somehow the drugs and money are tied to the

kidnapping of three young children. How?" She picked at a piece of chipped paint.

"Trafficking maybe."

She clenched her teeth against the chill racing up her spine. "That's horrible."

"Sometimes the world is a horrible place." He covered her fidgeting hand with his own and his warmth seeped into her flesh. "Are you okay to go home by yourself?"

She flung out her other arm. "It's daytime. I'll be fine."

"I never did get the chance to install your new locks."

"Not that those locks would've protected me against the fire last night, and since the firefighters just left my place unsecured, the locks wouldn't have prevented the break-in, either."

"True, but that's no reason to ignore basic security measures. That was an extraordinary event last night."

"Funny thing about those extraordinary events."

"What?"

"They seem to be happening to me on an ordinary basis."

"Ever since the Timberline Trio case was unearthed."

"Pretty much." She disentangled her hand from his and pulled herself up by grasping the porch's handrail. "My cousin Annie is coming by to help me clean up this afternoon, so I won't be alone. I'm going to have a look for those childhood mementos."

"Looking for a pink ribbon?" He stood on the step above her, towering over her even more than usual.

"Yep."

"Be careful, Scarlett." He smoothed a hand down her arm. "Don't tell anyone about it."

"I'm not going to run around town blabbing it. I'm

convinced there's not one person in Timberline who can keep a secret."

"Not even the sheriff's department."

She leaned back to look into his face. "Why do you say that?"

"How else did that story of the pink ribbon get out? If the kidnapper took something from one of the children, you'd think the police and the FBI would want to keep that quiet."

"It's the Quileute. We hear things. I'm pretty sure that info wasn't available to the other citizens of Timberline."

He bent forward and touched his forehead to hers. "Just be careful. We don't know who's watching and listening."

Her fingers dabbled against his jaw, and she felt his warm breath caress her cheek.

Then he wedged a finger beneath her chin and, tilting her head back, brushed his lips against hers.

The roar of a motorcycle engine broke them apart, and Scarlett glanced over her shoulder at Dax, his long hair blowing behind him.

"What are you going to tell your brother about the tires?"

"I can't hide that the tires were slashed, but he doesn't have to know anything about what we discussed with your grandmother."

Dax parked his bike next to Jim's and circled the damaged motorcycle. Then he pulled off his helmet and shoved his sunglasses to the top of his head as he trudged to the porch.

"What the hell happened?"

"Someone took a knife or a box cutter to my tires at the reservation."

Whistling through his teeth, Dax shook his head. "Old resentments die hard, don't they?"

"Could've been teenagers." Jim shrugged his broad shoulders. "Reminded me of something you'd do."

"Guess so. How'd you get back here?"

Scarlett waved her hand in the direction of the road. "My cousin gave us a ride in his truck."

Jim descended the porch steps and buried his hands in his pockets. "I'm selling him one of Slick's bikes."

"That's cool, man."

"I'll give you half the proceeds."

"As long as you didn't sell him the two I was eyeing, I'm good." Dax rubbed his bloodshot eyes, the deep lines on his face making him look more like Jim's father than his older brother. "I'm gonna head inside and get some shut-eye. I'm beat."

Jim raised one eyebrow. "What've you been doing today?"

"Ridin'."

"Not using again?"

Dax chuckled. "I'm just old, brother. See you around, Scarlett."

"Thanks for washing my car."

He nodded and then tromped past them, his boots heavy on the steps. He closed the front door behind him with a slam.

Biting the side of his thumb, Jim stared at the door. "Something's not right with him."

"That applies to a lot of people around here." Scarlett dug her keys from her purse. "I'm going back to my place."

"When I get my tires changed, I'll come over and install those locks for you."

"I'll be there. Sorry about your bike, sorry it happened on the rez."

"Not your fault. I'm just wondering if we'd taken your car if the same thing would've happened."

"Something tells me it would have."

She slid into her car with her lips still tingling from Jim's soft kiss. She'd wondered what would've happened to her car if they'd taken it to the reservation, but even more, she was wondering what would've happened if Dax hadn't interrupted that kiss.

HER COUSIN ANNIE aimed the hose at the last window in the front, spraying water against the glass streaked with flame retardant. "They make a bigger mess putting out the fire than the fire itself."

"Not quite." When the water stopped, Scarlett scrubbed the window with a cloth and then sluiced the water off with a squeegee. "I really appreciate your help, Annie."

"I'm just glad you weren't hurt. Who would do something so stupid? This is just not your year."

"It's gotta get better, right?" She traced her bottom lip with her finger. Running into Jim this trip had just about made everything a little better.

Annie turned off the water and wound up the hose. "I think getting rid of all those trees in front of your place is a blessing in disguise. I never liked parking beyond the copse of trees and then walking through them on that path—creepy."

"But very private."

"Too private if you ask me. When's Tony coming out to clear the land?"

"Tomorrow. I'm hiring him to do some landscaping, too."

"Do you need me to do anything else? I'm meeting some friends in Port Angeles tonight and need to get going."

"No. I can do the rest. Thanks again."

She helped Annie pack up some of her cleaning supplies and load them into the van she used for her cleaning business. When she pulled onto the road, Scarlett turned toward the house. She'd skipped lunch, so she popped open a carton of yogurt and carried it to the hall closet, which she used for storage.

The cabin didn't have a garage, just a shed out back, but Scarlett didn't store much beyond paint supplies there. Any photos or newspaper clippings or cards she'd boxed and stashed on the top shelves of this closet.

She dragged a chair in front of the closet and pulled two boxes from the top shelf. Would she have kept something as inconsequential as a ribbon?

Once Granny brought it up, Scarlett remembered filching it from Granny's knitting basket. It had been important enough for her to steal back because of the way it had made her feel.

It was sort of like when she and her girlfriends would go out to the woods and spin around and around just to feel dizzy. Stroking the ribbon had given her the same sensation.

When Granny had sat her down and explained to her about the gift of the shamans, it had never occurred to Scarlett that the pink ribbon was momentous in that way.

Tucking one box under each arm, she returned to the living room and sat cross-legged on the floor in front of the fireplace. She pulled the first box toward her and rummaged through its contents.

She smiled at the photos and the cards she'd saved from friends and even tried jamming the promise ring she'd gotten from Tommy Whitecotton onto her pinky finger. But no pink ribbon was nestled among the memories.

She popped the lid from box number two and fished around inside. These photos and keepsakes were from her high school years. She thumbed through a stack of senior pictures, collected from her friends, and stopped at one of a serious, dark-haired boy.

She traced her finger over Jim's young face. She must've gotten up the courage to ask him for a picture. She flipped the photo over, but he hadn't signed it. Maybe she'd stolen it from him.

Giggling like a high school girl, she plucked the photo from the bunch and dropped it on the coffee table. He'd been such a hottie back then and had only gotten better with age.

She shuffled through the rest of the photos and keepsakes but didn't find a pink ribbon, or any ribbon. She replaced the lid on the second box and stacked one box on top of the other on the kitchen counter.

As she scraped up the last bit of yogurt with her spoon, a horn began to blare outside. She dropped the carton in the sink and flew to the front window. Sweeping the curtain aside, she peered through the glass at her own car sitting just beyond the burned logs and scorched trees.

Must be her horn, but it didn't sound like her car alarm. She grabbed her keys from her purse and, aiming the key fob in front of her, she jabbed the button to unlock the car door as she stepped outside and walked toward her wailing car.

She opened the door and blinked at the block of wood propped up on the seat and wedged against her horn.

"What the hell is this?" She hunched forward to knock the wood loose.

She sensed a whisper of movement, but before she could turn around someone shoved her face-first onto the passenger seat.

She screamed and struggled to turn her head.

A hand gripped the back of her neck, the thumb pressing close to her windpipe.

She tried to kick out behind her, but a body fell heavily on her back and the point of a knife pricked her throat just beneath her jawline.

She froze, her next scream turning into a whimper.

Hot breath and a hoarse whisper in her ear. "You've been warned. Leave it alone."

Chapter Twelve

Jim rolled up to Scarlett's cabin on a set of tires borrowed from another bike, enjoying the view. She'd be so much safer once the landscaper cleared the burned mess and passersby could see her cabin from the road.

His eyebrows collided over his nose as he took in Scarlett's car with the car door open wide. Then his heart started pumping double time when he saw her pointy-toed boots hanging out the door.

He parked behind her car and jumped off the bike. "Scarlett?"

As he reached the car door, she rolled over on her back and choked.

He took one look at her tear-streaked face, pale with fear, and grabbed her hands, yanking her out of the car and into his arms. Her body trembled against his.

"What in God's name happened? Are you hurt?"

Sniffling, she hauled in a couple of shaky breaths. "Someone just threatened me, held a knife to my throat."

His pulse jumped and he scooped her into a tighter hug. "How long ago? Why were you just lying in the car? Did he hurt you?"

"He didn't hurt me, but he told me to stay where I was. That was about five minutes ago. I'm sure he's long gone, but I was too afraid to move."

"Did you get a look at him?" Resting his chin on the top of Scarlett's head, he scanned the woods at the edge of her property. "What direction did he go?"

"I didn't hear a vehicle, so he must've come and gone on foot, which probably means through the forest. He wouldn't want to chance being seen from the road."

"You didn't get a look at him?"

"He approached me from behind and smashed my face into the car seat."

"How'd he do all that without revealing himself?"

"It…it was a trap." She kicked at a piece of wood on the ground. "He rigged this up to honk my horn. When I came out to investigate, he came up behind me. The horn was blaring and my ears were ringing, so I didn't hear him approach."

He combed his fingers through her long hair. "What did he want? Did he say anything?"

"He told me I'd been warned and to leave it alone. He obviously meant the Timberline Trio case."

He took her by the shoulders. "Do you want me to try to go after him?"

"No." She grabbed his jacket. "He had a head start, and he might…"

"I'm not afraid of him, Scarlett. He's a coward."

"You're not going to find him, Jim. Don't leave me here."

Cupping her face with one hand, he drew his thumb across her cheek. "I'm not going anywhere, but we need to call the sheriff's department."

"The man was wearing gloves. The cops aren't going to find anything."

"Let them worry about that. If he took off through the woods, he might've left evidence behind. Besides, didn't I tell you it's important to document all of these incidents?"

"The sheriff's department is going to deem me a public nuisance."

"Let 'em. They don't seem to be doing their jobs—murder, arson, vandalism. Where does it stop?"

"It stops when people give up on investigating the Timberline Trio."

He lifted the piece of wood on the ground with the toe of his boot and let it fall. "How does this person or people know you're looking into the case? I'm thinking it has to do with your association with me."

"My association with you? How do they know we're not just old friends, or…?"

"Something more?" His blood stirred at the thought of something more with Scarlett.

"Probably because we found a dead body together and visited your grandmother together."

"Maybe—" she twirled a strand of hair around her finger "—we should make people believe we're not just together to investigate the Timberline Trio."

He snapped his fingers. "Dinner tonight? In public?"

"That might do it. Of course," she said, and looked up at him through her dark lashes, "we have to make it look like more than just a business meeting."

He swallowed. "I can do that, but first let's get the cops out here."

Deputy Stevens came out to investigate and he and another deputy canvassed the woods but came up empty-handed.

They seemed to dismiss the connection to the Timberline Trio case and asked Scarlett a lot of questions about her known enemies—the hunters in the area, as she'd been known to sabotage their traps and protest expanded hunting areas.

When they left, she rolled her eyes at Jim. "Law enforcement in this town seems to think I deserve these attacks because of my stance against hunting. I don't like hunters, but even I'll admit they're not violent types—against humans, anyway. We've exchanged words and heated arguments, but not one of them has ever attacked me."

"Could be a first."

"I've been too busy to protest much lately. Why would they turn violent on me now? No, this all started happening when I stepped in to help that reporter, Beth St. Regis, who was planning to do a segment on the Timberline Trio for her *Cold Case Chronicles* show."

"I thought you told me that was a cover for her own investigation into her past."

"It was, but nobody else knew that, except the FBI agent who was out here—Duke Harper."

Folding his arms, Jim wedged his hip against the post on the porch. "Do you think he'd talk to me about his findings when he was out here? Did you make that kind of connection with him?"

"I got friendly with him and Beth. They knew each other from before and are still together, as far as I know."

"Would you mind calling him for me or giving me his number?"

"Sure. I'll do that." She rubbed her throat, where an angry red mark remained as the only evidence of the attack she'd suffered. "Do you want to install those locks now?"

"Yeah, but I think you should upgrade to security cameras. If you'd had one, right now we'd be looking at the tape of the guy who assaulted you."

While he worked on the new locks, Scarlett retreated to her studio. When he poked his head into the room, she looked up from a laptop.

"Working?"

"Working, not creating. I'm doing an inventory of some pieces for my upcoming show."

"When's the show?" He weaved his way through the explosion of colors and textures in the room to reach the sliding door in the back.

"It's in a few weeks, in West Hollywood."

He pretended to concentrate on the sliding door. She had art shows all over the world. He'd looked her up on the internet. Critics raved about her modern art and high-end buyers snapped it up.

"What do you do with your cabin when you're away?"

"My cousins check in on it, and sometimes Jason stays here." She tapped her keyboard and closed the laptop. "Are you going home before we have dinner?"

"Yeah." He plucked his black T-shirt away from his chest. "I was wearing these clothes when I changed the tires on the bike. I won't be long. You hungry?"

Her eyes flicked over his body like a hot lash that he felt to his core. "Starving."

He finished his work in record speed as Scarlett wandered around the studio, assessing her work for the show. When he packed up his tools, he was more than ready to call it a day and spend some time with Scarlett—time where they wouldn't have to be looking over their shoulders every two minutes. Precious time before she left Timberline.

Hovering by the front door, he asked, "Do you want another spin on the bike, or do you want to drive?"

"I've had enough excitement for the day. I'll pick you up around seven."

He hesitated and then marched back to her. "Don't open the door for anyone, and don't go outside—not for a horn, not for an animal in distress."

"Thanks, you just made me scared to be in my own house." She bit her lip and glanced out the window.

"A little fear isn't a bad thing right now. Someone set fire to your property and someone physically threatened you." He folded his arms so he wouldn't be tempted to pull her against his chest again. There was no telling where that would end. "In fact, maybe you should think about heading down to California early for your show. Stop off in San Francisco on the way."

"Are you trying to get rid of me?"

"I'm trying to protect you, Scarlett. Let the sheriff's department handle Rusty's murder. Let me handle my own memories. I may not ever find out what happened that night, and maybe I'm not supposed to."

"I don't believe you'd be okay with that. It's the reason you returned to Timberline—you need to face all your demons."

He shook his head. "That could take years."

"Oh, wait." She held up her index finger. "I texted Dr. Shipman's number to you earlier. Did you get it?"

"I'm not sure. Do you want to give it to me again at dinner tonight?"

She rolled her eyes. "Lucky for you, I also wrote it down and stuck it to my fridge." She spun around and went into the kitchen, plucking a sticky note from the refrigerator.

With the yellow note stuck to her fingertip, she waved it at him as she returned. "Here you go."

"Thanks." He peeled the note from her finger and shoved it into his pocket. "See you at seven."

When Jim got back to his place, Dax was stretched out on the couch watching a fishing show.

Jim glanced at him out of the corner of his eye as he

tossed his keys on the kitchen table. "You been like that all afternoon?"

"I'm tired."

"Did you happen to run into Chewy when you were out today?"

"Matter of fact, I did drop in on him."

"So was it the stars aligning that brought the two of you back to Timberline at the same time? Rusty, too?"

"His woman's mother lives in Port Angeles. She's there visiting. Not much of a stretch for Chewy to come this way to check out his old stomping grounds. And I told you I don't know nothing about Rusty."

"Did you and Chewy talk about Rusty?"

"Uh-huh." Dax sat up. "Look at that fish. I need to do some fishing while I'm here…maybe some hunting."

Jim stopped at the entrance to the hallway, hooking a thumb in his front pocket. "You were never much for hunting."

Dax looked up, his hand buried in a bag of microwave popcorn. "That was you and Slick, wasn't it? He taught you to use a rifle like a pro. You put that knowledge to good use and started hunting another kind of animal."

Jim flinched. "I saved more lives than I took."

"I know that, J.T." Dax crammed a fistful of popcorn into his mouth. "Does that Scarlett feel the same way? She's out here in Timberline trying to save a few turkeys from their final resting place on the Thanksgiving dinner table. And you were over there…"

Jim banged his fist on the wall and shut out the rest of Dax's words by closing the bedroom door. As if he needed any more proof that Scarlett wouldn't want to start something with him.

Even if she *had* saved his high school senior picture.

SCARLETT VENTURED ONTO the porch, looking from left to right. She'd been spooked enough without Jim driving it home for her that someone had her in his crosshairs— just like prey.

She crept to her car and then slammed the door and locked it, releasing a long breath. She hated that someone had made her fear her own shadow, on her own property.

Pulling the car in front of Jim's cabin, she beeped the horn once. A rectangle of light appeared with the silhouette of Jim's body framed in the center.

As he descended the steps, she held her breath but didn't know why. His gait was more unsteady on steps, but he seemed to be able to navigate them with ease. He certainly didn't need her worrying about him.

She popped the locks as he approached, grabbed her purse from the passenger seat and shoved it on the floor of the backseat. As he slid in next to her, she breathed in the scent of soap and leather. The smell would always remind her of Jim forever after.

She blinked and forced a smile to her lips. "Sutter's? It's the place to see and be seen in town."

"That's the purpose behind this date."

"Date? Does that mean you're picking up the tab?" She tried to keep her tone light. Was showing others they were more than just investigative partners really the only purpose behind their dinner?

"I will absolutely pick up the tab. How'd it look otherwise?" He snapped on his seat belt.

"Like you're a cheapskate, so I'm glad we settled that."

"How much can rabbit food possibly cost? I'm guessing you're a cheap date."

She snorted. "You've obviously never shopped at health food stores."

She turned onto the main road to town and they drove

in silence as Jim poked the radio buttons, never staying on a song for more than a few seconds. When they reached town, she parked in the public lot across from the restaurant.

Jim jumped from the car before she cut the engine and came around to the driver's side and opened the door. "Just getting into character."

She slid from the car and hooked her hand around his arm. "Me, too."

He opened the door of the restaurant for her, and several heads turned their way. That was the thing about small towns—everybody got up in your business. Maybe word would get around that they were dating and not together because they were poking their noses into kidnappings.

The hostess tapped her pencil on her notebook. "There's about a ten-minute wait right now unless you want to sit at the bar."

"We'll wait." Jim steered Scarlett toward the wall across from the hostess stand and gestured to the paintings decorating it. "Do you ever display your work here? Too lowbrow?"

"Not at all. I'll hang my landscapes of the area here occasionally. People like local art."

"But you wouldn't place your modern art here?"

"And scare everyone away? Nope."

They studied the artwork together until the hostess called them over.

"Your table is ready. Do you mind? It's kind of the center of the dining room. If you wait another ten minutes or so, I can probably seat you someplace more private."

"That's okay." Scarlett charged ahead to the only empty table in the place.

Jim pulled out a chair for her, and they both thanked the hostess.

Leaning forward, Jim asked, "Is Jason's girlfriend working tonight?"

"I have no idea." She looked around the room. "Doesn't look like it."

"Even though we're supposed to look like we're not talking about the Timberline Trio case," he said as he took her hand across the table, "doesn't mean we can't talk about it."

"Did your brother open up to you any more today?"

"No, but he did say he met with Chewy."

Her fingers toyed with his. "Your brother, Chewy and Rusty were all in town at around the same time and one of them ends up dead. Then Granny tells us that a couple of members of the old Q-gang show up out of the blue, including my uncle."

"I think they're all here for the same reason, and it has something to do with their association years ago at the time of the kidnappings."

"I think you're right, but nobody's talking."

The waiter approached their table and took their drink orders.

"You don't mind if I have a beer, do you?"

"No, but if you have more than one, I'll take the wheel on the way home."

"That's a deal. I'll probably need about five after the day I had." She held up her hands. "Just kidding."

"Go ahead and have five, Scarlett, if you want. I'm not a leading member of the temperance movement or anything."

"When did you give up drinking?"

"When I was in the army."

"Helluva time to swear off booze."

"You're telling me."

"Did you call Dr. Shipman this afternoon?"

"By the time I thought about it, she'd left for the day. I'll try again tomorrow."

The waiter returned with her beer and Jim's soda. "Are you ready to order?"

When they'd placed their orders and the waiter left, Jim asked, "You don't mind that I ordered pork chops, do you?"

"I'm not the leader of the vegetarian movement, either." She clinked her glass against his and took a sip of her beer.

Jim hunched forward and touched his finger to her upper lip. "Foam."

"Smooth move, Kennedy."

"That wasn't for show. You really did have some foam on your mouth."

She licked her lips. "What if you just gave it up? What if you just let that particular sleeping dog lie? Something unexplainable happened to you as a child. Can you let it go?"

"Not sure." He stirred his ice with his straw. "It haunted me when I was…imprisoned. Funny, all the things they did to me in captivity and my constant nightmare was the attempted kidnapping."

"Maybe because it happened to you as a child, it holds a special terror. I'm not sure we ever get over our childhood fears."

"And what was yours? All I ever saw was a confident, pretty girl who knew what she wanted in life and went out to get it."

"I put up a good front." She took a long pull from her beer, savoring the warmth in her belly. "You know I lost my parents and my baby brother in a car accident. I was supposed to be in that car."

"I didn't know you had a brother. I'm sorry."

"He wasn't even a year old. I should've stopped all of them that day."

"How old were you?"

"Six, and before you start in with the 'you were too young' business, I believe that was my first experience with my special gift, only it wasn't so special."

"What do you mean?"

"I was supposed to be on that trip, but I faked a stomachache so I wouldn't have to go. I had a feeling, even back then."

He brushed his knuckles along her forearm. "And Evelyn was telling me to deal with my guilt. I hope she told you the same."

"I've worked through it. How do you think I know Dr. Shipman?"

"This is supposed to be a date. We're way too serious over here. People are going to have their suspicions confirmed that we're working on something together." He hunched forward on the table and kissed her mouth. "Do you think that'll convince them otherwise?"

"It's a start."

She wouldn't have minded practicing a little more convincing, but the waiter showed up with their food.

During their meal, they caught up on what they'd been doing since high school, and Jim's eyes lit up when he talked about his work with vets.

"You had a great idea before." She placed her fork on the edge of her plate. "Art."

"Sculpture?"

"Any kind of art—painting, sculpture, ceramics. Is

there anything like that in any of the centers where you worked?"

"Not that I noticed, but I think that could work."

"I could probably get a fair number of my artist friends to volunteer some of their time."

"That would be incredible if you could provide the volunteers."

Smiling, Scarlett picked up her fork. Jim's approval gave her a warm feeling inside. She cut off a corner of her spinach lasagna. His approval was coming to mean a lot to her—maybe too much. He had demons to slay and she had an art show in West Hollywood.

"Hey there, Scarlett."

She dropped her fork as she met the dark gaze of her uncle, a little frisson of fear glancing the back of her neck. He'd appeared out of nowhere, just like he always did, stealthy as a cat.

"Uncle Danny. Are you back in town?"

He spread his arms, his eyes flickering toward Jim. "I'm here, aren't I?"

"I—I just didn't hear anything about your return." She gritted her teeth at the way her voice wavered, but she had no intention of admitting she and Granny had talked about him. Her uncle could reduce her to a stammering child with one look from his cold eyes—even when she wasn't lying to him.

"You shouldn't depend on the reservation grapevine." He formed his fingers into a gun and aimed it at her. "It's usually wrong."

"I'm sorry." She tipped her head toward Jim. "This is Jim Kennedy. He's a local. I went to high school with him. Jim, this is Danny Easton, my uncle."

"I remember the Kennedy family—Slick and your brother. You a bigot, too?"

Scarlett drew in a quick breath, her eyes darting to Jim's face.

Jim pushed his plate away and crossed his arms over his chest. "I guess they weren't too bigoted for you and your boys to do some business with them."

Scarlett held her breath as Danny's lips formed a thin line and his black eyes glittered.

"Sounds like you've been listening to gossip from the rez, too." He drummed his long fingers on the table. "I'd join you, Scar, but I'm meeting someone at the bar."

"Are you going to drop in on Granny while you're here?"

"Why? She never liked me. Never thought our family was good enough for your mother."

Scarlett dropped her gaze to her plate and twirled the tines of her fork around a string of melted cheese. "She never had a problem with Dad."

Danny released a soft snort, and the heels of his boots clicked away from the table.

"No family love there, huh?"

"Uncle Danny is no friend to the Quileute. He's always been bad news. When my mom and dad started dating, Granny was concerned about her marrying into the Easton family, but like I said, she judges everyone individually. When she met my dad, she could tell he was one of the good guys—Danny, not so much."

"I don't remember Danny, and I sure don't remember that he had some gang of his own."

"That surprised me, too, but I do know that he was persona non grata around the reservation. After the accident that killed my parents, I never saw him."

"So, another piece of the puzzle moves into position. We have Rusty, Chewy and my brother all converging on Timberline and now Danny Easton shows up. It's like a dark cloud hovering over the town." He shook the ice in his glass. "I suppose you'd have known if it was your own uncle holding a knife to your neck, wouldn't you?"

"I would, but you know what's unsettling?"

"Let's see." He held up his hand and ticked off his fingers. "Finding a dead body, arson, a defaced painting and a knife attack?"

"Besides all that." She picked up her butter knife and ran her thumb along the dull, serrated edge. "The man who attacked me was wearing gloves."

"*That* was the most unnerving aspect of the whole event?"

"Gloves, so he avoided skin-to-skin contact with me."

"It wouldn't be unusual for someone planning an attack like that to include gloves in his kit. And if he's the same one who killed Rusty and broke into your place, we already know he doesn't leave fingerprints."

"I know that, but there's another reason why he'd wear gloves in an attack on me—there's always the chance that I'll flash on him. You know, feel his touch and be able to determine something about him."

"So you think it's someone who knows you or knows about your special gifts."

"Uncle Danny knows all about that—and how those gifts work."

Jim jerked his thumb over his shoulder. "Can you see who he's meeting at the bar?"

"He's behind the wall that separates that half of the bar from the dining room. I can't see him."

"Trip to the ladies' room? Men's room is on the other side."

"Good idea." Scarlett swept her napkin from her lap and dropped it beside her plate. She didn't even have to be obvious about spying on Danny, since she could walk to the ladies' room through the dining room without passing through the bar. She turned left into the passageway to the restroom, without looking into the bar.

While she washed her hands, she peered into the mirror to make sure she didn't have any spinach in her teeth. She was still treating this as a date, even though it had veered off its intended course with the appearance of Uncle Danny.

She tossed a paper towel into the trash and then hit the swinging door with her hip to open it. She meant to glance quickly to her right just to check out Danny and his companions, but what she saw halted her in her tracks and made her blood boil.

She swerved into the bar and poked her cousin Jason in the back. "What are you doing with him?"

Danny's lips curled into a half smile and Jason jumped. "Scarlett. What are you doing here?"

"I'm having dinner with Jim. More to the point, what are *you* doing here and what are you doing with Danny?"

"I—I just came in to pick up a check for Chloe, who's not feeling well, and I ran into your uncle."

"Really? Because he just got through telling me he was meeting someone here."

Danny patted her shoulder. "I am, Scarlett, and it's not Jason. Relax. I'm not corrupting your cousin. Besides, shouldn't you be more worried about J.T. and Dax Kennedy corrupting him? At least I'm not an ex-con."

"Doesn't mean you shouldn't be." She shook her finger in Jason's face. "Whatever he's offering, it's sure to have a high price down the road. It's not worth it. Just keep doing what you're doing, Jason."

She spun around as Danny called after her. "Always nice to see you, Scar."

She flounced back to the table and dropped into her chair.

"What happened? Who's Danny meeting?"

"My cousin Jason."

"Is Danny his uncle, too?"

"No, Jason and Annie are my mom's brother's kids—Fosters, not Eastons."

"You don't want Jason associating with Danny?"

"Danny doesn't show interest in family unless he thinks he can get something out of it. I'm just worried he's filling Jason's head with all kinds of get-rich-quick schemes—illegal get-rich-quick schemes."

Jim shifted forward, his knees bumping hers beneath the table. "Jason seems like he's got his head on straight."

"Yeah, but construction work has been slowing down for him, and Chloe's still trying to finish school, but she had to drop out last semester. Money's tight for them, and I know how persuasive Uncle Danny can be."

"Do you want me to talk to Jason?" Jim's lips twisted. "I have some experience in resisting the dark forces around me."

"Would you?" She grabbed his hand. "That would be awesome."

"He's coming by to look at his bike tomorrow. I'll give him an earful then." He raised her hand to his lips and kissed her knuckles. "This hasn't been much of a romantic date, has it?"

"Honestly?" She brushed her fingertips across his dark stubble. "This has been one of the best dates I've had in a long time."

"Those artist types must be a dull bunch, but just to amp up the romance—I paid the check while you were sleuthing in the bar."

"Positively makes my heart flutter."

"Imagine what I could do if I really tried."

As she met his smoldering gaze, her heart really did flutter.

She grabbed her purse. "I'm ready to get out of here."

"Me, too."

As Scarlett rose from her chair and squeezed past a table on her way to the exit, Darcy Kiesling, an old friend from high school, stopped her. "I heard someone attacked you today. Are you all right?"

"I'm okay. It was a threat, not exactly an attack."

"I don't care what you call it. Someone held a knife to your throat." Darcy pressed a hand to her own throat. "Did the guy really warn you about looking into the Timberline Trio case?"

"Maybe." Scarlett shrugged. "I don't know why he's warning me. I'm not looking into anything."

"Hmm, I wish that whole thing would go away." Darcy's gaze tracked to Jim and she gave him a head-to-toe.

"Darcy, do you remember Jim Kennedy?"

"I do, and do you remember Renée Meyers?"

After they said hello to Renée, Darcy introduced them to the other two women at the table. Only Renée was a local. The other two were recent transplants, but from the way all of them were eyeing Jim, it was clear the man was just as sexy as the boy had been—more so.

Darcy flipped her hair over her shoulder. "What happened to your leg, Jim?"

"It's a long story, Darcy, and I don't want to ruin your dinner. Enjoy your evening."

He limped away from the table and Scarlett smiled sweetly. "Good night."

She caught Jim by the arm as they stepped onto the sidewalk. "I think you just *did* ruin their dinner."

"Was I too harsh?"

"Just a little." She held her thumb and forefinger about a half an inch apart. "Does it bother you when people ask about your leg?"

"I can understand the curiosity, especially from people who knew me before. It's just not a subject for polite discussion. Do you really think Darcy and her tipsy friends want to hear what happened to me in that hole?"

Scarlett stopped walking and tugged on Jim's back pocket to slow him down. "They probably don't want to hear, but I'm all ears if you ever want to unburden yourself."

Stepping toward her, he put his hands on either side of her waist. "I'd never do that to you, Scarlett. It's bad enough that you experience snatches of it whenever I touch you."

He dropped his hands as if he was in danger of having his mind read right then and there.

"It's not whenever you touch me." She laced her fingers through his and put his hand back on her hip. "I can assure you, when you touch me I'm not thinking about prisoner of war camps and torture."

"What are you thinking of?" He drew her into the circle of his arm, so close that strands of her hair caught on the stubble of his beard.

She whispered, "Sometimes I can't think at all."

When he kissed her, she melted against him, her knees weakening and her bones turning to jelly. She curled her hands around the leather of his jacket to keep from sliding to the ground while returning his kiss.

He murmured against her mouth, "Let's go back to your place."

She nodded once, and they practically ran to her car.

He stopped her at the driver's side and held out his hand. "I'll drive."

"It was just one beer."

He snapped his fingers and she dropped the keys into his palm. He followed her to the other side of the car and opened the door for her.

She'd never been with such a take-charge guy before. When Jim had landed on her porch a few days ago, she'd actually had the thought that he'd be just another man for her to prop up and nurture.

He couldn't have proved her more wrong.

Yeah, he still had those demons, but he seemed completely capable of battling them without any help from her.

That didn't mean she couldn't offer.

As he turned off the main road, he said, "I'm going to swing by my place first, if that's okay. I want to make sure Dax locked up the garage when he finished working on his bike."

"Okay, but you don't need to bring your toothbrush. I have extras."

"Is that a dig at me because I didn't have any extras when you stayed here?"

"Actually, I was happy to see that you weren't prepared for overnight…guests."

He pulled into his drive and leaned over and pinched her chin. "I wish I had been more prepared for you—in every way."

"If you'd been prepared, that would've ruined all the excitement."

"You like excitement? I think we've had more than enough of that around here."

"Isn't that what you signed up for when you decided to come back and find out what happened to you twenty-five years ago?"

"I didn't realize there would be people today hell-bent on keeping that truth from me."

"Makes you wonder what they're hiding."

He tapped on the windshield. "Good thing we swung by here. I can see already that Dax left that garage door wide open...unless he's still working out there."

"Let's find out." She hopped out of the car, which rocked as Jim slammed his door.

"Dax?" Jim strode toward the garage, while she hung back.

Drops of rain started hitting the ground and pinging the top of her head. Head down, she jogged toward the covered porch. As she reached the top step, the wind gusted and rattled the screen door.

She jerked her head to the side, noticing the open front door. Taking one step down on the porch, she yelled, "Jim! I think he's inside."

She studied the entrance to the garage, but Jim didn't answer or appear.

She returned to the front door, made a half turn and grabbed the screen door handle, her hand closing around a sticky substance. She snatched her hand back and spread her fingers in front of her face.

The sight of the blood smeared across her palm made her gag. She ignored the faint voice in her head urging her to turn and run.

As if on autopilot, she reached for the screen door again with the same hand. She yanked it open and almost tripped over the booted feet of Jim's brother—lying on the floor in a pool of blood.

Chapter Thirteen

For the second time that week, a bloodcurdling scream from Scarlett made the hair on the back of his neck stand at attention.

Jim dropped the shredded tire he'd been inspecting and spun around, keeping his bum leg stiff so he wouldn't trip over it.

He ran toward the house, where he could see Scarlett's back at the door. With his heart pounding out of his chest, he raced up the drive and took both steps in a single bound.

He grabbed Scarlett's shoulders and yanked her back against his chest.

His gut heaved when he saw Dax laid out on the floor, blood meandering in a slick trail leading from his body. He shoved his phone into Scarlett's hand.

"Call 911."

He crouched beside his brother and felt for his pulse, weak but ticking. "He's still alive."

He rolled Dax onto his back and ripped off his shirt, already slashed open with a knife.

"Get me a towel."

Still speaking into the phone, Scarlett stepped over Dax's inert form and returned seconds later with several towels.

She thrust one toward Jim. "An ambulance is on the way."

Jim folded the towel and pressed it against the wound that zigzagged from his brother's chest to his belly. If the knife had hit an artery, Dax didn't stand a chance.

Jim applied as much pressure as he safely could while whispering to his brother, "Hang on, man. You've come too far to let go."

"Can I do anything? He has some cuts on his hands. Should I put pressure on those?"

Sirens called from down the road and Jim said, "Go out and direct the ambulance into the driveway."

She sprang to her feet and stumbled outside.

A minute later, two EMTs bustled through the front door and nudged Jim away from Dax. "Good job. We'll take it from here."

Jim backed up, leaving the towel in place. He gazed at his hands, stained with Dax's blood.

"Any other wounds? Any allergies? Preexisting conditions?" The EMT in charge rattled off the series of questions in staccato.

"Some cuts on his hands. No allergies. No preexisting conditions, unless you count drug and alcohol addictions."

"Current?"

"Recovering—about a year sober."

More sirens followed and Jim staggered out the front door and down the steps, his bloody hands in front of him.

Scarlett left the deputy's side to rush to his. "Is he still…?"

"He's still alive but unconscious."

One of the EMTs blew past him on his way to the ambulance and Jim watched as he rolled a gurney out the back doors.

Just like for Rusty, but Jim prayed for a different outcome this time.

The deputy was mouthing words at him, but Jim couldn't make sense out of anything he was saying.

As the EMTs loaded Dax into the ambulance, Jim broke away from Scarlett.

"I'm coming with."

"We need to work on him in the back. Follow us to the emergency room."

Scarlett joined him and pressed a fresh towel into his hands. "You take my car. I'll finish talking to the deputy and we'll meet you at the hospital."

Wiping his hands on the towel, he nodded and returned to the car where he and Scarlett had just shared some moments of closeness.

He gulped as he threw the car into Reverse. She had to get out of here, away from Timberline. She had to demonstrate to the perpetrator of this mayhem that she had no interest in the Timberline Trio case. But for him?

This had just gotten personal, and he'd go to hell and back to find out who'd tried to murder Dax. He'd already been to hell and back once. What was one more trip?

He followed the revolving lights of the ambulance, mumbling the same prayers he'd recited each time his captors had dragged another prisoner from the cells, prayers that hadn't done a lot of good back then. He couldn't do anything else for Dax at this point, but the attack on his brother had just amped up his resolve to get to the bottom of this mystery.

The ambulance pulled up to the entrance of the emergency room, and Jim swung around it to find a parking space in the lot to the left of the hospital.

By the time he had parked and returned to the entrance, the EMTs had already unloaded Dax and wheeled him into the building.

He hunched over the reception desk. "That ambulance just brought my brother in—Dax Kennedy. Can you tell the doctor in charge I'm here and will be waiting for news?"

The nurse took down his info and went back to her computer.

Jim wandered around the waiting room, studying the vending machine, getting a cup of water and shuffling through a few golf and hunting magazines.

He tapped on the counter. "Any news yet?"

"No, sir." This time she didn't even look up from her computer.

Heaving out a breath, he slumped in a plastic chair next to a woman flipping through a fishing magazine, her face tight and her knuckles white.

The door of the emergency room burst open and Scarlett rushed through with Deputy Stevens on her heels. She flung herself into the chair next to him, bringing the damp, cold air in with her.

"Have you heard anything? Is Dax okay?"

"Nope, and I haven't talked to anyone yet, either."

She tipped her head toward the deputy talking to the nurse at the front desk. "Maybe he'll have better luck. He wants to talk to the doctor."

"Did Dax say anything to you, or was he already unconscious?"

"He was already unconscious."

"You didn't see or notice anything?"

"No. Was there anything in the garage?"

"Dax had left his tools and a motorcycle part on the floor, sort of like he'd been called away suddenly. I figured he'd gone in the house to get something to drink or answer the phone. Thought you'd find him inside."

"I did." Her jaw tightened.

"Scarlett, you need to—"

"Mr. Kennedy?"

Jim jerked his head around and answered the doctor who'd stepped into the waiting room. "Yeah, that's me."

He crossed the room with Scarlett beside him and the deputy tagging along behind them.

"I'm Dr. Verona." He pushed up his glasses and rubbed his eyes. "It's bad. Your brother lost a lot of blood."

"Is he going to make it?"

"Can't say right now. He's in a coma. We're going to transfer him to a bed in the intensive care unit in the hospital next door."

"Can you tell me his chances at this point?"

"Fifty-fifty, maybe less. I've seen worse survive, and I've seen better succumb."

"So, you're telling me it's pretty much a crapshoot at this point."

"I'm afraid so. No major organs involved, so that's a plus."

The doc went on to explain Dax's condition in greater detail, but all Jim heard was fifty-fifty. His brother had beaten those odds before, and Jim had faith that he could do it again.

Although he hadn't seen Dax in years, he wasn't ready to lose him now. "His girlfriend. He has a girlfriend who's in Seattle right now. I should call her. Do you have his personal effects?"

"The nurse can help you with that. I'll transition your brother to the ICU tomorrow morning and have his doctor there give you a call."

"I appreciate it, Dr. Verona. Can I look in on him here?"

"Of course. I'll have the nurse bring you back."

As the doctor turned, Deputy Stevens held up his hand. "Can I ask you a few questions, Dr. Verona? We're treating this as an attempted homicide."

The doctor pointed to the left. "We can go in that office, but I just have a few minutes."

When they disappeared into the office, Jim leaned against the counter and addressed the nurse. "Dr. Verona said I could go back and see my brother."

She held up her finger, and then picked up the phone. "Tell Tiana the brother wants to see five twenty-eight."

Jim lifted his eyebrows and Scarlett said, "His name is Dax."

"Sorry." The nurse spread her hands. "It's just a shortcut. He received excellent care. Dr. Verona's the best trauma doc around."

The door to the exam and operating rooms swung open and a nurse in pink scrubs poked her head out. "Are you Dax's brother? This way."

Jim grabbed Scarlett's hand. "She's my wife, and she's coming with me."

The nurse rolled her eyes. "No, she's not. She's Scarlett Easton, and I know for a fact she's not married, but she can come, anyway."

"Tiana…" Scarlett snapped her fingers. "Your grandmother and mine were friends for years."

"That's right—Gokey. Tiana Gokey. I didn't grow up here because my parents left the reservation, but I moved back here when my grandmother was ill and I stayed."

"Thanks for letting me check in on Jim's brother. I—I'm the one who found him."

"It's a good thing you two acted quickly. If he lives, it's

because you stanched that flow of blood." Tiana pulled aside a curtain and Jim's eye twitched at the sight of his brother with tubes running in and out of him, hooked up to machines.

"The doc said Dax had a fifty-fifty chance."

"If that's what Dr. Verona said, it's probably close. He's the best." She stuck a chart in a holder at the foot of the bed. "We'll be moving him out of the emergency wing to the main hospital in the morning. Take your time."

"Thanks, Tiana." Jim dragged a plastic chair next to his brother's bed, his gaze tracking along the tubes and monitors crisscrossing Dax's body. "He looks bad."

Scarlett stood beside him and squeezed his shoulder. "Shh. He may be able to hear us. Be positive."

Jim leaned close to his brother's pale face and murmured a few words of encouragement, talked to him the way he might talk to one of the vets he worked with.

"God, I hope he pulls out of this."

"We just have to have some faith and think positive thoughts." Scarlett reached past him and twitched Dax's sheet into place, her hand skimming his arm.

She jerked back with a gasp.

"What's wrong?" Jim narrowed his eyes. "You felt something, didn't you?"

Scarlett stared at her fingers, which trembled in front of her face. "I flashed on something."

"Hopefully, the face of my brother's assailant."

"Not quite. Just…something." She wiggled her fingers. "I could try again."

"Not if it's going to upset you." He held his breath, torn between wanting any information Scarlett could glean and wanting to protect her from harm.

Scarlett nudged the sheet aside and curled her fingers around Dax's hand, over the tubes stuck in his flesh.

Closing her eyes, she exhaled a long breath. Her chin dropped to her chest and her breath quickened. Her lashes fluttered.

The curtain across the doorway whipped back, and Scarlett yanked her hand back.

"I'm sorry." Tiana smiled brightly as she grasped the curtain. "We have to run a few tests on Dax before we send him over tomorrow morning."

Jim scooted his chair back, blocking Tiana's view of the bed. "Sure, sure. Thanks for letting me see him."

Out of the corner of his eye, he glanced at Scarlett, blinking and pushing her hair back from her damp forehead.

She patted Dax's hand and straightened the sheet. "Hang in there, Dax."

They walked silently out to the reception area where Deputy Stevens was waiting for them.

"Do you need anything else from us, Quentin?"

"Kennedy, can you come into the station tomorrow? I just want to ask you a few more questions about your brother. Another Lord was spotted around town— Charles Swanson—Chewy. You know him?"

"Yeah."

"He and your brother on good terms?"

"I have no idea, Stevens. Can we leave this for tomorrow like you said?"

"Yeah. You two going to be okay? It's like a mini crime wave between your properties out there."

"You're telling me. I'm assuming my cabin is an active crime scene right now?"

"That's right."

Scarlett tugged on the sleeve of his jacket. "You can stay at my place tonight."

That had been their original plan, and it sounded even

better now. If Stevens was surprised at Scarlett's easy invitation, his stoic face didn't show it.

"That's probably a good idea, since we still don't have a lead on the arsonist, and he might very well be the same person who threatened you the other night and then stabbed Dax today."

Jim scratched his chin. "Busy...busy and desperate."

"For what? I can't believe a twenty-five-year-old cold case is still causing this much havoc." Stevens clapped his hat on his head.

"If the perpetrators of the kidnapping are still here and have something to lose, they're going to want to shut up everyone involved."

"Are you saying your brother was involved? Scarlett? She was just a kid, and so were you."

"Yeah, well, kids sometimes know more than adults give them credit for."

"All right. I'll let you go. I notified Sheriff Musgrove, so check in with us tomorrow, Kennedy."

"Will do." Jim propelled Scarlett out the main entrance and toward her car. When they were both ensconced inside, he turned to her. "Did you see anything when you touched Dax?"

"Nothing. I was just getting started when Tiana interrupted me." She drummed her fingers against her chin. "Hadn't she just told you to take your time?"

"You know how hospitals are." He paused. "What are you saying? Do you think Tiana stopped you on purpose?"

"She's Quileute. She knows what I am."

"So, she might be trying to protect someone."

"Like I told you before, there's something about this case that always had my people on edge."

"Doesn't seem to have your uncle Danny on edge."

"I'm going to have to pay a visit to Jason tomorrow to find out what Danny was up to tonight."

"Do you think he'll tell you?"

"I have my ways." Scarlett cracked her knuckles and winked. "Now, let's get going. You must be exhausted."

"I'm still doing better than Dax."

As Jim cranked on the engine and then pulled out of the hospital's driveway, Scarlett tipped her head back against the headrest. How had their evening gone from delicious to deadly?

And how could she get it back to delicious?

She sighed, and Jim bumped her shoulder with his. "Would you rather I stay at a hotel tonight and leave you in peace?"

"Peace? What's that?"

"I'd do it, except I don't think you should be alone in that cabin—not with everything that's going on right now."

"I don't want to be alone, Jim." She turned to him and traced a finger along the seam of his jeans running along his thigh. "I have an idea."

She'd lowered her voice to almost a whisper, and he dipped his head to the side to catch her words. "Tell me."

"There's a nice, shiny hotel in the new area of town near Evergreen. It has a hot tub, a bar—for me—king-size beds, and the best thing of all? No dead bodies outside and no fire circling the building."

He paused at the intersection, the *tick-tick* of the turn signal breaking the silence. "Would you feel safe at this hotel?"

"With you, yes."

He bumped the indicator down with his fist and made the left turn instead of the right. "Take me there."

She called out directions to the hotel until he pulled into the parking lot.

"Looks nice."

"It's a little pricey, but much better than the dumps near the center of town."

Jim used his credit card to check in and, after Scarlett made sure the hot tub was still open and the bar was still serving, they made their way to their room on the third floor.

Jim shrugged out of his jacket and hooked his thumb through his belt loop. "You keep mentioning this hot tub, but as far as I can tell neither one of us has a swim suit."

"Shh." She put her finger to her lips. "I think we can sneak down there and wear our underwear. There won't be anyone there at this time of night."

"I always knew you were a rebel." He sat on the edge of the bed and wasted no time pulling off his boots.

Scarlett grabbed two thick towels from the bathroom, slung one over her shoulder and tossed the other to Jim. "Just in case there aren't any at the pool."

Barefoot, in their jeans and T-shirts, they made their way to the lobby on the first floor and turned the corner for the gym and indoor pool, and for the first time in a long time, Scarlett really did feel like a rebel.

She cupped her hand above her eyes and pressed her nose to the glass, peering into the pool area. "Empty— just the way I like it."

Jim swiped his card key at the door and pushed it open when the green light blinked at them.

The moist air settled on Scarlett's skin, and she dipped a toe in the pool as she walked along its edge. "The water's warm."

"That water's warmer." Jim pointed to the hot tub, in the corner, steam rising from its surface.

Scarlett rested her hand on the tile and poked her head inside the hot tub enclosure. "Nice and private, too."

"Let's keep the towels close by, just in case." He dropped his towel on the edge of the hot tub and glanced over his shoulder before peeling off his T-shirt.

The steam from the hot tub warmed her cheeks, or maybe it was just the sight of Jim's muscled torso—battered and scarred, but still beautiful.

"Let's get this party started." He twisted a dial on the wall and the jets churned the water in the tub.

Jim yanked off his jeans and slid onto the top step in one fluid motion, his boxers floating above his thighs.

"You're fast." She slipped her arms from the sleeves of her T-shirt and then tugged it over her head. Her bra, nothing fancy, actually covered more than a bikini top would. So why did she feel so bare beneath Jim's hungry gaze?

"Here goes nothin'." She pulled off her jeans and stepped into the hot tub, the thin material of her underwear clinging and molding to her body as she submerged herself in the water.

Her knees bobbed against his, and he reached for her hands. "Join me on this side. This way we can both keep an eye on the door."

Her body floated in the bubbling water as he pulled her to the other side. She settled on the step beside him, resting the back of her head against the edge of the hot tub.

The jets pummeled her lower back and she stretched her legs and wiggled her toes against the bubbles across the tub.

"This feels heavenly. I can almost forget everything that's happened the past few days."

"Everything?" He draped an arm across her shoulders, the tips of his fingers dabbling a pattern on her arm. "Even this...electricity between us?"

"If we give in to this—" she flicked some water at his chest "—thing between us, how's it going to end?"

"It's gonna end with me making mad, passionate love to you."

The hot water got hotter and she wriggled in closer to him on the step, her thigh brushing his. "Not that I have any objection at all to making love—especially the mad, passionate kind—but what happens when you get your answers? When you sell your dad's place? When you go to school somewhere?"

"When you take off for your next art show?"

She nodded and then wedged her chin on his shoulder, the steam rising from his skin making her blink—it couldn't be tears.

"I don't know. I can only give you the here and now. I don't even know what's going to happen in a day or two, but I do know that I want you." He growled softly in her ear. "I know that I want to be inside you."

She gave a little shiver and slipped farther beneath the water, her fingers digging into his thigh for leverage.

"But I understand if you don't want to go there with me if I can't promise you anything more. Hell, maybe that's the answer you're looking for. Maybe you don't want to be saddled with a beat-up vet like me for the long haul, anyway."

With a quick glance at the door to the pool area, she swung around to face him, straddling his lap with her legs. She put a finger to his lips and then replaced it with a wet kiss.

"You couldn't be more wrong, and it makes me wonder how you can possibly make mad, passionate love to me when you don't seem to understand the first thing about me or what I want."

He cinched her waist with his hands. "So, you're looking for something long-term, or you don't care if this is a fling?"

"For a guy, you're analyzing this way too much." She scooted against him and felt his erection swell against her inner thigh. "Or maybe not."

Slipping his hands beneath the elastic waistband of her panties, he smoothed his palms across her bottom, his fingers kneading her flesh.

She dipped her head to his chest and ran the tip of her tongue along the jagged scar that marred his smooth skin, as she rocked her hips against him.

He groaned and dragged his fingers over her hip to pull aside the skimpy material of her underwear. Sighing, she fell forward and lodged her head in the hollow between his neck and shoulder.

Closing her eyes, she held her breath as the warm, bubbling water coursed over her sensitive flesh now laid bare. Then he took two fingers and drew them across her skin, leaving a trail of fire that she felt even under the hot water.

She took a quick peak over her right shoulder. "Do you think it's safe?"

"I'll keep my eyes on the door and my hands on your body. How's that?" He caressed her again and then slipped his fingers inside her.

She collapsed against him again, curling her arms around his neck. Jim really was a bad boy. This was exactly the sort of behavior all the girls' parents had been worried about—and rightly so.

As his fingers explored her, his thumb swept back and forth across her throbbing flesh, stoking the flame in her belly. She pressed her lips against his throat, where a pulse hammered wildly.

She dropped her hand between their bodies to where his fingers were toying with her, teasing her, driving her mad.

He captured her fingers. "Do you want to feel how hot you are?"

Before she could peel her tongue from the roof of her mouth to answer, he replaced his fingers with hers and she could feel her own burgeoning desire. With his hand driving her own, she stroked herself. Then he brought her hand to his lips and kissed her palm.

He continued to wind her up as she trailed her fingers along the length of his erection. He might be a broken-down vet as he liked to call himself, but he had a lot of full-functioning parts.

Her muscles tensed, she gripped his hips with her thighs and then the wave of passion cresting in her body broke and she fell apart. As she rocked against him, riding out her orgasm, the water lapped between their bodies.

Cupping her face with his hands, he kissed the tremulous sighs from her lips. When the last spasm of pleasure slipped away and melted in the water, she dragged her fingernails lightly across the tight flesh of his erection.

He wrapped his fingers around her wrist. "Let's finish this party on the bed, in the room, behind a locked door. Once I start with you, I don't think I'm going to be able to stop—interruption, or no interruption."

With the tip of her tongue, she caught a droplet of water meandering down his chest. "Is what we just did illegal?"

"If there had been anyone in the pool area, I'm sure it would've been, but if you don't tell, I won't." He ran his hands across the silky material of her underwear, smoothing it into place. Then he flicked up the straps of her bra.

"Don't bother." She stilled his hands with her own. "I'm not going to put my nice, dry clothes on over these sopping wet undergarments."

He lifted one eyebrow. "You plan to wear those sopping wet undergarments through the lobby, or pull off another Lady Godiva?"

"We'll take them off, dry off and put on our dry clothes." She brushed her thumb across his lower lip. "We'll wrap up our undies in the towels and nobody will notice a thing."

"You've done this before?" Lifting his backside from the step, he peeled off his boxers and balled them in his fist.

She coughed as her gaze swept over his nakedness beneath the water. "Have you?"

"You seem to be the expert."

"Just using my common sense." She tapped the side of her head.

"Might as well get it over with." Hunching forward, he reached for his towel, steam rising from his back and buttocks, water coursing over the intricate design of his tattoo and his hardened muscles.

Scarlett's lashes fluttered and butterflies claimed her belly. However things turned out with his man, she'd have no regrets about this night.

Jim toweled off his upper torso and then stepped from the hot tub to finish the job. He wrapped the towel around his waist and pulled on his jeans beneath the towel.

"You're right." He dropped the towel and shook out his T-shirt. "This feels a lot better than wearing wet boxers."

"Looks a lot better, too." She winked.

He held out her towel. "You going to float in there all night ogling me, or are you going to get dressed?"

"I could do just that, Jim Kennedy, but I'm going to do more than ogle when we get up to the room." She shimmied out of her underwear and stood up on the top step.

Jim stepped between her and the door to the pool area. "Just in case someone decides on a late-night swim."

"Oh, is that what people do in here?" She snorted and dried off her body.

Jim came up behind her and yanked her T-shirt over her head.

She copied him by wrapping the towel around her waist and putting on her jeans. She squeezed out her wet underclothes and rolled them up in the towel. "There. Now we won't have our wet stuff seeping into our dry stuff."

"It won't take us long to get back to the room, anyway."

"I'm going to make a stop at the bar for a glass of wine, if that's okay with you."

"As long as you get it to go." He flipped the ends of her damp hair over her shoulder. "Because I'm not waiting another minute for you, Scarlett Easton."

Leaning forward on her tiptoes, she pressed her damp bundle into his arms and kissed his lips. "Do you mind taking my clothes to the room? I'd hate to have them fall out of the towel in the middle of the bar."

"That could definitely be awkward."

When they stepped into the hallway, leaving the humid atmosphere of the indoor pool, Scarlett shivered. She'd felt safe and protected in the hot tub with Jim, and the cool air in the hallway was like a cold dose of reality. She hugged herself. Soon they'd be wrapped in each other's arms making love…and she'd feel safe again.

They paused at the elevator bank and Jim stabbed the button. "Do you have money?"

"I'm going to put it on the room—three eighty-two, right?"

"That's the one. Are you sure you don't want me to go with you or wait here? You know I can be in a bar and not go crazy?"

"I know that. You can lay out our clothes so they'll be dry by tomorrow morning, and maybe get a hot shower going." The elevator dinged as it settled at the lobby level. "I'll be right up."

She waved to him as the doors closed and then spun around toward the lobby. She crossed the room, making a beeline for the dark bar in the corner, which was emitting live folk music.

Who knew Timberline had an actual nightlife? Evergreen Software really had changed the town.

She walked to the entrance of the bar, her bare feet sinking into the carpet. A couple deep in conversation didn't even look up when she entered. The lone guy at the bar gave her a quick glance before turning his attention back to the silent TV screen, and a woman seated in front of the musician gave Scarlett a dirty look and put her finger to her lips—must be the folk singer's girlfriend. So much for Timberline nightlife.

Scarlett ordered a glass of red wine from the bartender and then stuffed a pretzel in her mouth while tapping her foot to the beat of the song.

The bartender delivered her wine. "Do you want me to open a tab?"

"No, I'm taking this to my room. You can give me the check now."

Once he delivered the bill, she scribbled her signature on it and then raised her glass. "Thanks."

As she left the bar, a group of people in front of the

elevator exploded in laughter. Suddenly self-conscious about her lack of underwear, her bare feet and the glass of wine in her hand, Scarlett pivoted toward the stairwell. She could handle three flights.

She slipped through the fire door and had started climbing the first set of stairs when the fire door behind her swung open. Looked like she couldn't avoid people even if she wanted to.

A whisper floated through the stairwell, and she slowed her steps. Had she stumbled upon another couple looking for a private spot for an intimate encounter?

The whisper turned into a lowered male voice. "We can't do it again, not with those two snooping around."

"I'll make it worth your while, just like last time."

The other speaker snorted softly. "Didn't work out that great twenty-five years ago."

Scarlett's muscles froze and she held her breath.

"Not my problem. I can take care of her, but you gotta get rid of him—and it all has to look like an accident."

"Shouldn't be too hard. He's got that gimpy leg and I heard he's kinda messed up in the head."

She backed up one step, the hand holding her wineglass, trembling.

The fire door above her burst open and Jim called down. "Hello?"

Terrified Jim would say her name, she spun around, taking the first step. Her toe hit the edge and she dropped her wineglass.

It shattered into a million pieces and broadcast her presence in the stairwell—loud and clear.

Chapter Fourteen

Jim jumped when he heard the crash of broken glass echo in the stairwell. Taking a step forward, he drew in a breath to call out to Scarlett. A split second later she appeared before him, her face white, a finger held to her lips.

Then he heard it. Heavy footsteps from the floors above.

Jim widened the door and grabbed Scarlett's arm when she reached him and pulled her into the lobby.

She gasped out one word: "Run."

If they were running from the people coming down those stairs, they wouldn't get very far. Jim pulled Scarlett in his wake as he careened down the hallway, looking for an out.

A supply room door stood open and Jim pushed Scarlett into the small room and yanked the door closed behind them. He braced his shoulder against the door in case it didn't lock and shoved his hand in his pocket and withdrew his Glock.

With his other arm, he held Scarlett against his chest where her heart pounded in rhythm with his.

His muscles coiled when the door to the stairwell crashed open, and Scarlett's body stiffened in his arms.

He put his lips close to her ear, the damp tendrils of her hair tickling his nose. "Shh."

The carpet in the hallway muffled the footsteps heading their way, but to his ears they sounded like a herd of elephants.

He didn't know what the hell Scarlett had been running from, but the panic on her face told him everything he needed to know.

As the footsteps drew near, Jim licked his lips, his trigger finger tensing. The door handle went down and stopped with a click.

A bead of sweat traced Jim's hairline and dripped off his jaw.

Scarlett's warm breath permeated his T-shirt, but she didn't let out one sound.

The footsteps moved away, and Jim wedged his finger beneath Scarlett's chin and shook his head.

Would the men be waiting for them in the hallway? Did they know he and Scarlett had ducked into this closet? He pressed his ear against the door, barely discerning a murmur of voices. He and Scarlett would camp out in this little room all night if they had to—not the end to the evening he'd been anticipating.

With his back to the door, he slid to the floor, taking Scarlett with him. The maid's cart and the shelves stacked with towels gave him just enough room to sit with his knees bent.

He pulled Scarlett between his legs, and she rested her back against his chest, her head falling onto his shoulder. He kissed her temple and whispered, "Are you okay?"

She nodded.

He tightened his arms around her. He wanted the whole story, but he wanted to keep her safe more. They had time and he was patient. Hadn't he waited for his death in a filthy prison for nine months?

Over an hour later, Jim nudged Scarlett. "Are you sleeping?"

"Dozing. Can we talk now?"

"I think it's safe to leave our self-imposed captivity."

Twisting around, she placed her hands on either side of his face. "How are you doing? No flashbacks? No seizures?"

"Not even a twinge." Bracing one hand against the door, he rose to his feet and stretched as much as he could. He helped Scarlett up and rubbed her back.

"Just stay behind me while I open the door." He pulled out his gun and leveled it in front of him.

"Do you think they could still be out there? Waiting? Watching?"

"I think they went out the side door, so maybe they think we ran outside. I haven't heard any noises on this end of the hallway, but keep yourself hidden behind me."

He pushed down on the door handle, holding his breath. Then he eased it open a crack and peered through it.

"I think we're good." He widened the door and stepped into the hallway, gripping his gun at his side. "We're taking the elevator. Just keep moving and run if I tell you to run."

He jabbed the elevator button to call the car and let out a breath when the doors opened immediately on the lobby floor. He urged Scarlett into the elevator ahead of him and crowded her into the corner until the doors closed.

For several more tense minutes, they rode the elevator to their floor and Jim didn't take another breath until he slammed the door to their room behind them.

Scarlett collapsed, throwing herself across the bed, one arm flung over her face.

He sat on the edge of the mattress and rubbed her foot. "What happened in the stairwell?"

She took a few more shaky breaths and hoisted herself up on her elbows. "Two men are planning to get rid of us."

Jim hardened his jaw but didn't stop massaging Scarlett's cold, bare foot. "What men? Did you recognize them?"

"I couldn't see them. They were whispering and talking so softly, I couldn't distinguish their voices. The only reason I heard what they were saying was because of the acoustics in the stairwell."

"Why do they want to get rid of us? What else did they say?"

"Because we're meddling." She sat up and dug her fingers into his biceps. "They're planning more kidnappings."

"What?"

"They said something about repeating what they did twenty-five years ago. We have to tell Sheriff Musgrove. We have to warn everyone."

His hand moved up her leg and stroked her calf. "If they just put a target on your back, you're getting out of Timberline. Maybe I should've let them catch up to us so we could've identified them."

"They may know who I am, anyway." She fell back on the bed and hugged a pillow to her chest. "I dropped that glass of wine. They don't have to be rocket scientists to trace that back to the bar."

"Did you know the bartender?"

"No."

"So, if he tells them anything at all, he's going to say

a woman with dark hair bought a glass of wine? Not a lot to go on."

"We don't have a lot to go on either, do we? Have you heard anything about Dax's condition?"

"I called the hospital when I was waiting for you to get your wine, and he's the same."

"Why did you come downstairs to find me?"

"You know, it's funny. I had a feeling something wasn't right, or maybe I wasn't happy with the idea of you wandering around on your own after everything that happened."

"Maybe I'm rubbing off on you. I'm the one with the ESP. How'd you even know I was in the stairwell?"

"I had just stepped off the elevator and saw you go through the door. There were a bunch of people waiting for the elevator, so I couldn't get your attention." His hand slipped up to her thigh. "And you're definitely rubbing off on me."

"I—I think one of the men was my uncle."

"How are we going to prove that? How are we going to prove anything?" He stretched out beside her. "Maybe it's time to call that FBI agent and tell him what we know."

"Which isn't a whole lot."

"Maybe he knows something that can make sense of what we've been grasping at. He's the one that made the connection between the Lords of Chaos and the drug trafficking."

"I'll call him tomorrow." She yawned. "This was supposed to be a relaxing getaway. I don't even have my glass of wine."

He trailed his hand up her body and slipped it beneath her T-shirt. He cupped one of her bare breasts in his hand, swiping the pad of his thumb across her peaked nipple. "I have ways of relaxing you that don't involve hot tubs or alcohol."

She sighed and her eyelashes fluttered. "We do have some unfinished business, don't we?"

"The thought of that unfinished business is the only thing that kept me sane in that supply closet." He rolled up her T-shirt and flicked his tongue inside her navel.

She combed her fingers through his hair. "Do you know what would relax me right now?"

Rolling his head to the side, he looked up at her through narrowed eyes. "Don't tell me watching TV."

She scooted out from beneath him and pushed him onto his back. Then she straddled him, yanked up his T-shirt and dragged her fingernails along his chest.

As she rocked against his erection, she whispered, "Forget TV. I have all the entertainment I need right at my fingertips."

He closed his eyes and let her entertain him.

SCARLETT KICKED THE tangled covers from her legs and rubbed her eyes. Through the closed bathroom door, she heard the shower running.

She scrambled from the bed. If Jim planned to boot her out of Timberline, she planned to get her fill of him first.

She crept into the bathroom, filled with citrus-scented steam, and whipped aside the shower curtain.

Jim grabbed her and pulled her under the stream of warm water.

She let out a yelp, and he laughed. "If you thought you could surprise an army ranger sniper, you've got another think coming, woman."

She kissed away a rivulet of water sliding down the flat planes of his chest. "Why did you sneak away?"

"Sneak?" He ran soapy hands down her back. "I got

a call from the hospital about Dax and figured I'd better get ready."

"Is it bad news?" She dug her fingers into his sides.

"No. Not good news, either. He's still unconscious. They just called to tell me he's been moved to the main hospital."

"Are you going to visit him today?"

"Yeah. Like you said last night, he might be aware of what's going on around him." He kissed her. "I'll leave the shower to you."

She finished showering by herself, but it had gotten a lot cooler without Jim…and a lot less interesting.

By the time she got out, he was dressed and looking at his phone with his eyebrows drawn over his nose.

"Is it Dax?"

He looked up. "A strange text from an unknown number."

"Really?" She tucked her towel around her body. Coming up behind him, she stood on her tiptoes and peered over his shoulder. "What's it say?"

Find the drugs, stop the kidnappings. Begin at the beginning.

"What?" She dropped to her heels. "Who sent that? What does it mean?"

He pulled out a chair and sat on the edge, tapping his phone against his chin. "Let's think about it for a minute. The Lords of Chaos were selling drugs back then. Even Gary Binder was involved at a low level and he was eliminated."

"And that drug trade had something to do with the kidnappings."

"The Lords had to be getting the drugs from somewhere because they weren't producers, and they had to be getting the money to buy the drugs from somewhere."

"Other criminal activities?" She massaged her temples. "How do the kidnappings fit in?"

Jim snapped his fingers. "Or the Lords paid in trade."

"What does that mean?"

"The Lords were doing something for the drug providers in exchange for product."

"Like what? Fixing their bikes?"

"Like kidnapping."

Scarlett clutched the towel around her waist. "Do you think the Lords of Chaos kidnapped those kids in exchange for the drugs?"

"Yeah, I do."

"A-and who supplied the drugs?"

"Think about it."

"My uncle."

"Bingo." Jim pressed the tip of his index finger in the middle of her forehead.

"But that would mean he ordered the kidnappings. Why? Why would Uncle Danny want to kidnap three children?"

"I don't know, but the conversation you heard in the stairwell last night indicates that he wants to do it again."

"Oh, no." She shook her head, the wet ends of her hair flicking droplets of water here and there. "This town can't go through something like that again. When Wyatt Carson kidnapped those kids, it just about tore Timberline apart at the seams."

"So, back to the text." He drummed his fingers on the credenza. "It sounds like there are some drugs missing."

"Once those drugs are found, they can be payoff for another round of kidnappings, but what's the purpose of the kidnappings? Where are those three—Kayla, Stevie and Heather?"

"I know you don't want to hear this, but I'm thinking it had to be some child-trafficking ring."

"My uncle?" She twisted the corner of her towel between two fingers. "I know he's not a good guy, but that?"

"What else? If some sicko was just murdering kids, he'd do it himself. Why go through some elaborate scheme of using drugs to compensate a bunch of bikers to kidnap the children?"

"And why those bikers?" Shivering, she crossed her arms.

Jim tucked her towel around her body. "Go get dressed and dry your hair. You're getting chilled."

"This conversation isn't helping." She turned and scurried back to the bathroom. "And I'm going with you to see Dax."

An hour later, after checking out via the TV, they slipped out of the hotel.

Scarlett watched the hotel entrance in her rearview mirror as she drove out of the parking lot. "If that was Danny in the stairwell, he can't know for sure that I was the one listening to him. I'm so glad you didn't call out my name."

"Me, too, but you need to watch your back."

"We both do." She tugged on the sleeve of his flannel shirt. "Do you think anyone's going to notice we're wearing the same clothes as yesterday?"

"I don't think it matters unless you want to go home and change."

"That's okay. I at least had a shower."

"I remember." He brushed one knuckle down her thigh.

"Jim, about last night…" She bit her bottom lip.

He squeezed her leg above her knee. "A night to remember."

Her nose tingled and she nodded. "I'll never forget it."

And maybe that's all she'd ever have of Jim Kennedy—the memories. Would they be enough?

SCARLETT PULLED INTO the parking lot of the main hospital, which was around the corner from the emergency entrance. Jim checked in at the reception desk on the ICU floor, and the nurse gave him Dax's room number and the go-ahead to visit him.

When Jim pushed open the door, he froze and Scarlett bumped into him.

Jim asked, "Who are you?"

Scarlett peered around Jim's large frame and met the heated gaze of a redhead sitting next to Dax's bed.

"Who the hell are you? If you take one more step into this room, I'm going to scream bloody murder for the nurse."

"Whoa." Jim held up one hand. "I'm Dax's brother, Jim Kennedy."

The redhead gave Jim the once-over and the deep lines around her mouth softened. "You're J.T. I see it now. You look just like my man—maybe a little softer around the edges."

"You're Belinda?"

"I drove here as soon as I got the call from that Deputy Stevens." She jerked her head toward Scarlett.

"Who are you?"

"I'm Scarlett Easton, a friend of Jim's."

"You're the one who found him." Belinda tossed her mane of hair over her shoulder. "I'm grateful to you."

Scarlett brushed past Jim and approached the bed. "How's he doing?"

"Not great, but he's a fighter. He'll pull through, but then he's got another problem."

Jim edged into the small room and took a spot at the foot of Dax's bed. "What would that be?"

"Didn't you get my text? If you don't find those drugs and stop the kidnappers, they're going to come after Dax again—and this time they'll kill him."

Chapter Fifteen

Jim gripped the metal bar at the end of Dax's hospital bed. "You sent the text?"

"Dax told me to send it to you if anything happened to him." She flung her hand out toward Dax's still form. "Something happened to him."

Jim hunched forward, bracing his hands on the bed. "What do you know, Belinda? What did Dax tell you?"

She raised one eyebrow. "I'm not telling you anything here."

"Have you had breakfast yet?"

"A cup of coffee and a candy bar."

"Scarlett and I will buy you breakfast."

Pushing to her feet, she slung her leather jacket over one shoulder. "Dax said you were a hotshot sniper. You packing heat?"

Jim's hand moved to his pocket.

"Good, because I'm not going anywhere in this hick town without protection."

Scarlett put her hand on his arm. "Let's go to one of the restaurants in the new shopping center. Nobody needs to see us with Belinda at Sutter's."

"I like the way this girl thinks." Belinda shrugged into her jacket, covering the sleeve of tattoos that decorated her left arm.

Jim raised one finger and then leaned over his brother. "Hang in there, Dax. We're going to figure this out."

On their way to the elevator, Belinda stopped at the reception desk and rapped her knuckles on the surface as she hunched forward. "You're going to call me if there's any change, right?"

The nurse scooted her chair back an inch. "Yes, ma'am."

They stepped into the elevator, and Jim leaned toward Belinda, the smell of her heavy perfume tickling his nose. "Are they afraid of you?"

"They'd better be."

Belinda wanted to leave her car at the hospital, so Scarlett drove the three of them to the new shopping center, not far from the hotel where they'd stayed last night.

Jim swallowed. That hotel would always bring a smile to his face—wherever Scarlett wound up in the world. She only thought she wanted something more with him, but she was the same bright girl she'd been in high school and she'd made good on the promise of her youth.

He still had a long way to go, and she didn't need to be along for his journey.

"This place is open for breakfast." Scarlett pulled into a parking space and cut the engine. "Hopefully, we won't see anyone we know here."

"And if we do?" Belinda took the gum out of her mouth and stuck it in a wrapper.

"Why lie?" Jim shrugged. "You're Dax's girlfriend. You're here because he's injured and we're having breakfast with you."

Jim scanned the mostly empty restaurant and blew out a breath when he didn't recognize one person.

They settled in a booth in the corner, and the waitress poured them some coffee.

Jim planted his elbows on the table. "Tell us what you know, Belinda. If Dax had confided in me instead of you sending me cryptic messages *after* someone stabbed him, maybe he wouldn't be lying in that hospital bed right now."

"I don't know much." Belinda swirled some cream in her coffee. "Dax got out of the joint and came to me in Seattle. We had a good thing going. He was off the pills and the booze, and then he got a phone call that sent him over the edge."

"Dax? Nothing sends Dax over the edge."

"I know, right? This did."

Scarlett asked, "Did he tell you about the phone call?"

"He didn't say much. It had something to do with his past. He'd planned to ignore the whole thing until he found out you were in Timberline, J.T."

"Me? He went back to Timberline because of me?"

Belinda traced the rim of her coffee cup with the tip of her finger as she gazed into the caramel-colored liquid. "He was damned proud of you, J.T., of your service. He always bragged about his medaled-up little brother."

A knot formed in Jim's chest. "I didn't… We haven't had much contact."

Belinda lifted one narrow shoulder. "Dax is an ex-con. Just figured you didn't want him around."

Jim opened his mouth to ask a question and then snapped it shut when the waitress showed up. They ordered, and then Jim crossed his arms on the table, hunching forward.

"What did he think he was going to protect me from in Timberline?"

"He wouldn't tell me and he wouldn't let me come with him. All I know is the phone call had something to with whatever he'd been involved in here before with his old man. I got the feeling that the person on the other end of the line wanted him to pick up where the Lords had left off."

Scarlett tapped her water glass. "Rusty and Chewy must've been called back, too, and it looks like Chewy's the only one who was game—unless he turns up dead like Rusty."

"What the hell is going on in this town?" Belinda cradled her coffee cup as if warming her hands. "Who's inviting the Lords back and for what purpose?"

Scarlett shot Jim a glance. "We're not sure and it's best you don't know anything more. What we think is that someone hired the Lords to kidnap children twenty-five years ago in exchange for a piece of the drug trade on the Washington peninsula."

Belinda's heavily lined eyes widened. "Dax kidnapping kids? I don't believe it."

"I'm not excusing him, Belinda, but he was just a teenager himself and influenced by our father. It was always hard to defy our old man. Dax was also using. Who knows what kind of pressure the Lords put on him."

"And the important thing?" Scarlett tapped Belinda's tattooed wrist. "He said no this time. That's why he's in that hospital bed fighting for his life."

The waitress brought their plates of food, but even after she left nobody started eating.

Belinda chased a potato around her plate with a fork. "I think Dax pretended to go along with it to buy time… and to protect you. I think he took a delivery of those drugs."

"I think you're right." Jim nodded and grabbed the ketchup bottle. "He took the drugs, hid them and then reneged on the deal."

"So, that's the text he had you send to Jim, Belinda, but what does it mean?"

"He didn't tell me. He texted me yesterday morning and asked me to send those words to his brother if anything happened to him. When I tried to call him to ask him what the hell was going on, he wouldn't respond." Belinda dabbed at her nose with a napkin.

"It has to mean something to me and to Dax—where it all started." Jim scratched the stubble on his chin. "Just wish he hadn't been so vague. Where what started? The whole Timberline Trio case?"

"Whatever happened to those kids?" Belinda finally sawed off an edge of her omelet and took a bite.

"Nobody knows. Poof." Scarlett flicked her fingers in the air. "They disappeared—no bodies, no trace."

Belinda's fork clattered against her plate where she dropped it. "That's horrible. I have a little boy and I can't even imagine. Dax is like a father to him. I still can't stomach the thought of him being involved in snatching children."

"And whoever was behind it twenty-five years ago wants to do it again. That's what I can't fathom. Why?" Scarlett shoved her full plate away.

Jim said, "As long as those drugs stay hidden, they're not going to get another chance. Whoever Danny has lined up to kidnap children this time is not going to do it without payment in the form of those drugs."

"Danny?" Belinda looked up from her coffee cup. "You *do* know?"

Scarlett kicked him under the table. "W-we have a good idea but no proof."

"Maybe that's where we start—with Danny. If he launched this whole plot years ago, maybe that's what

Dax means. We need to start with him. We need to start at the reservation."

"Reservation?" Belinda's gaze darted between them. "This Danny, he's Native American like you?"

"Unfortunately, we're related, but forget everything we told you about his involvement. You did your part by sending that text to Jim. Now you just need to make sure Dax gets better." Scarlett aimed her fork at Belinda's plate. "And you can't do that on an empty stomach."

Jim dragged Scarlett's plate back in front of her. "And you can't investigate on an empty stomach."

"You're not sending me away?"

"How am I going to get on the reservation without you?"

"Granny has pretty much adopted you. I'm sure she'd be happy to entertain you."

Did she want to go back to San Francisco? He should be insisting instead of dragging her into this any further.

He tucked an errant strand of silky hair behind Scarlett's ear. "Then I'll go on my own."

"Oh, no." She jabbed a potato with her fork. "Granny might be ready to adopt you, but the rest of them still hate you. I'll be tagging along."

The three of them managed to finish their breakfasts and leave the restaurant without running into anyone they knew. The sooner Belinda could get Dax out of this town, the better.

When they dropped her off, Jim turned to Scarlett. "Can we go by the sheriff's station first? Stevens wanted me to check in today when Musgrove was there."

Their visit to the sheriff's station was a waste of time. The Timberline deputies didn't know much of anything about his brother's case, and Musgrove wasn't even at the station.

As they walked out, Jim mumbled, "How much golf can one guy play?"

"Especially at the tail of autumn on the Washington peninsula." Scarlett tipped her head back to take in the gray sky.

Jim joined her in the car and put his hand over hers. "One more stop? I'd like to drop by my place for a change of clothes."

"Of course." Her gaze flicked over her body. "Although you look fine to me."

"At least my boxers are dry."

As she started the car, her shoulders dropped and a smile touched her lips.

He'd never been much of a comedian, but someone had to lighten the mood. Scarlett had been so tense he was afraid she was ready to crack.

Hunching forward, he smacked the dashboard. "I think we're going to get to the bottom of this, Scarlett. Bit by bit, we're piecing things together."

She pulled onto the highway, back to the center of town. "Begin at the beginning. So, you think the beginning is with Danny and the reservation?"

"If he's the one who ordered the kidnappings or was part of the ring that originally ordered them twenty-five years ago, and it looks like he was. Unless…" Jim massaged the back of his neck as a shaft of pain shot through his skull.

She twisted her head to the side. "Unless what?"

"Maybe the beginning was with me. The kidnappings started after someone tried to snatch me, and instead of turning the guy in, my dad had a long talk with him. Maybe that's where it all started."

Scarlett's eyes got wide. "D-do you think your dad made some kind of deal with the kidnappers that night?"

"Maybe."

"Do you have any reason to suspect that it was Danny in your room that night?"

"I don't remember enough about him to make that call."

"I can see it for you."

"No."

"If a Quileute was involved, I'm sure I'll be able to sense that. The reason my vision worked so well with Beth St. Regis, that TV host, is because it turns out Beth was Quileute herself. It might tell us what we want to know, Jim."

"I think I already know it. I don't need further confirmation, especially at the risk of harming you."

Slicing her hand through the air, she said, "It doesn't harm me."

"It's not a bed of roses for you, either."

"Beds of roses are highly overrated. Look at you."

His brows shot up. "Me?"

"Your life hasn't been easy."

"That's an understatement. You don't think I wanted it otherwise?"

"Sometimes we don't get to choose. What you went through—all of it—made you the man you are today."

"A wreck?" His lips twisted.

"Jim Kennedy, you are the strongest man I've ever met. Sure, you're battered, bloodied, beaten up—but not defeated."

"So, you're saying you're *glad* I went through hell?"

She smacked his arm. "Of course not. You know what I mean. I'm saying, if you can endure, I can endure. It's not a big deal."

"Let's see what your grandmother has to say first. If

we spill everything we suspect, she might be able to fill in some details."

"But we won't find any drugs at the reservation. There's no way your brother could've hidden them there, and he wouldn't have wanted to."

"You're right about that." Jim drummed his fingers on his knee. "If the beginning was the attempt to kidnap me, maybe he hid them on our property."

"And maybe that's why he was stabbed. One of Danny's guys came looking for the drugs and Dax wouldn't tell him where they were."

When Scarlett pulled up to the cabin, the yellow police tape crisscrossed over the porch was a stark reminder of his brother's condition and the seriousness of their quest. Who would've guessed Dax Kennedy would turn out to be one of the good guys?

Jim opened the car door and turned to Scarlett. "Wait here. I'm going through the back and it'll take me two minutes to change."

"I hope you don't mind if I leave the engine running... just in case."

"You mean you'd leave me behind?"

"I mean in case someone approaches the house, so I can shift into gear and run him over."

"Oh, in that case." He flashed her a quick smile, but somehow he had the feeling she was dead serious.

It probably took him less than two minutes to exchange one pair of jeans and a T-shirt for another set and glance at the bloodstained entryway. If only Dax had confided in him. They could've handled this together. Dax still had the mind-set that he needed to protect his baby brother—just like he'd tried to protect him from their father during their childhood. Dax had played the role of the bad boy to allow Jim to be the good boy because the old man had needed—no, demanded—one son to follow in his criminal footsteps. Dax had sacrificed himself to spare him.

Jim swiped the back of his hand across his tingling nose.

He went out the back way and hopped in the running car. "You didn't see anything unusual?"

"No." She backed the car out of the driveway. "Unless you count stillness as unusual. The forest seems hushed today, like it's holding its breath."

"That's your hypersensitivity kicking in. Let's just hope you're off base this time and there's no impending tragedy waiting for Timberline."

"If there is, we're on the path to divert it."

Scarlett drove to the reservation as if the answer was waiting for them there, but Jim didn't think it was going to be that easy.

He tapped her thigh. "Slow down, lead foot."

"I actually have my foot on the brake. It's speeding up downhill."

Scarlett waved to Prudence and her grandmother on the way into the reservation and then pulled up in front of Granny's house.

Scarlett called out as she opened the unlocked front door. Sitting in the same chair as before, Evelyn raised her head from her knitting, her dark eyes glowing in her lined face.

Scarlett crossed the room and dropped to her knees at her grandmother's side. "Are you okay, Granny? You look tired."

The old woman rested her hand on top of Scarlett's head as her gaze met Jim's. "Your brother was attacked."

"He was. The news spread already?"

"Is he going to live?"

"The doctors don't know yet. Fifty-fifty, they're telling me."

"Get him out of Timberline as soon as you can."

Scarlett touched Evelyn's knee. "What do you know, Granny? We think more kidnappings are planned, and there are drugs—missing drugs. As soon as those drugs get into the hands of the wrong people, the kidnappings will start."

Her knitting needles paused and she closed her eyes. "I don't know why he kidnapped those children."

"But you know who? Was it Uncle Danny?"

"Not then." Evelyn combed the yarn in her lap with trembling fingers. "Danny wasn't the leader, but he followed him and did his bidding as part of the Q-gang."

"Who, Evelyn? Who ordered the kidnappings and why?"

"Do you remember him, Scarlett? Rocky Whitecotton?"

A furrow formed between Scarlett's eyebrows. "Whitecotton? Tommy's family?"

"Yes, a cousin or something, a big man, a force in the tribe, but one that fomented dissent and hatred. He tried to recruit your father, but he had better luck with Danny."

"Are you saying Rocky Whitecotton was behind the kidnappings, Granny?"

"Everyone thought so."

"But nobody told the sheriff's department or the FBI?" Jim ground his teeth together. The Quileute were no better than the Lords of Chaos—protecting their own at the expense of others.

"We didn't know for sure, Jim. He terrified the rest of us, threatened us. Nobody ever had any proof, just our suspicions."

Scarlett hopped to her feet, running a hand through her hair. "Rocky's been gone for years."

Evelyn nodded. "Just about twenty-five years."

"Why?" Scarlett flung her arms out to her sides like wings. "Why would Rocky Whitecotton kidnap three children from Timberline?"

"That I can't tell you, Scarlett. I can only give you the long-held suspicions of an old woman, but I know Rocky had some criminal organization going and he recruited Danny and tried to recruit your father."

A sharp pain lanced her temple and Scarlett sucked in a breath. "The accident that snatched away my family happened before the kidnappings."

"Yes." Granny's eyes dropped to the discarded knitting in her lap.

"Do you think...?" Scarlett took a turn around the room, the pain in her head turning into a dull throbbing. "Could my father have been punished for refusing to go along with Rocky?"

Granny placed a thin hand to her forehead. "You don't think that didn't occur to me all these years?"

Jim put his arm around her waist and drew her close. "And now Danny is back to do more of Rocky's bidding. I think it's time we call Agent Harper and tell him everything we know."

"But if Chewy or any of the other Lords get their hands on those drugs, they'll be ready and willing to carry out Danny's plans."

"We won't stop looking for the drugs, but we need the full resources of law enforcement to stop Danny, and there's no way we can count on Sheriff Musgrove."

Granny shook her head. "Danny may already have Musgrove in his back pocket. Don't trust him."

Her lips touched Jim's ear and she whispered, "Should we tell her about the clue?"

"Maybe she can help."

"Granny, Jim's brother left him a clue about the location of the drugs before he was attacked. It was, 'Find the drugs, stop the kidnappings. Begin at the beginning.' Does that mean anything to you?"

"If your brother knows about Rocky, it could mean here at the reservation, since Rocky seems to be the start of all of this, but Danny would know that, too."

Jim snapped his fingers. "Dax would leave me a clue that only the two of us would understand."

"Which brings us back to your father's cabin. That's where someone tried to kidnap you."

"Maybe Dax didn't mean the beginning of the Timberline Trio case or the Lords involvement in it. Dax had no way of knowing how much Scarlett and I had figured out."

Scarlett rubbed a circle on Jim's back. "The beginning of something between the two of you."

"We were never close, Dax and I. There was a big age gap between us, and he started following in Dad's footsteps pretty early on."

"So, it wouldn't be the beginning of the Lords of Chaos, since that wouldn't mean much to you."

Granny tapped her needles together. "The beginning—every birth is a beginning."

"We were even born in different hospitals."

"Even before that, then. The beginning for the two of you. The beginning of the Kennedy family. Something just the brothers would know."

Jim's body stiffened.

"You know? You remember something?"

"Dax was older than I was when our mom left. He always had a soft spot for her, never blamed her for leaving. He used to tell me that Mom said the only happy memory she had of our father was the day he proposed."

"The beginning." Scarlett squeezed his hand. "Was there someplace special he proposed?"

"Under the Kennedy Christmas tree."

"In the cabin?" Scarlett tilted her head.

"In the forest, by the old mine, where Carson stashed the kids he kidnapped a few months ago. My parents used to hang out at that mine—smoke cigarettes, do whatever teenagers do. There's a pine tree there and that's where my father proposed to her. For some reason, Dax loved that story, probably because it was the only softness in his life and reminded him of Mom."

"Do you think he'd bury the drugs there?"

"It's a place only he and I would know about."

"Then let's go. If we have some concrete proof in the form of drugs, the FBI is going to have to take a closer look."

"Let's go back to my place to get some shovels and tools. I'm going to call Duke Harper on the way."

Scarlett broke away from Jim and kissed Granny on the cheek. "Thanks for the information, Granny. Don't worry. We'll be okay."

Jim squeezed Granny's hands. "I'll take care of her, Evelyn."

When they got outside, Jim held out his hand. "Do you want me to drive?"

"I got this. I'm the one with the lead foot, remember?" She pulled away from Granny's house and made the right turn out of the reservation just as the skies opened and rain hit the windshield faster than the wipers could keep up.

The car crested the hill and started its descent, and

Scarlett hunched forward in her seat to peer through the water sloshing across her windshield. The car picked up speed.

"I wasn't joking about the lead foot, Scarlett. Slow down."

"I—I can't." Scarlett pumped the brakes again and heard the sickening sound of metal on metal as the car lurched to the right.

Her entire family had died in a car crash on this road, and it looked like she was about to meet the same fate.

Chapter Sixteen

Jim gripped the edge of his seat as the car skimmed the shoulder of the road, wet leaves and branches slapping his window. The greenery flew past him in a blur, and his heart thundered in his chest.

Scarlett had both hands on the steering wheel in a life-and-death struggle with the car, her knuckles white.

He shouted, "The parking brake. Put on the parking brake."

Scarlett stomped her left foot on the parking brake and the car shuddered and weaved. The back wheels fish-tailed on the slick surface of the road and they started traveling sideways.

The car bucked and slowed down, but the tires were moving independently of anything Scarlett was doing with the steering wheel. The forest on the right side of the road was rushing at them as the car shook and coughed. A large tree trunk loomed out his window, and Jim yelled, "Step on the gas."

Scarlett didn't hesitate. The car jumped forward one last time before the back end hit the tree so hard his teeth rattled.

It heaved to a stop, and this time Jim didn't hesitate. "Open your door, Scarlett. We're getting out."

A tree was blocking his exit, so Jim clambered over

the console almost into Scarlett's lap. The airbag hadn't deployed, which eased their escape from the car. Scarlett had opened the driver's-side door, and he pushed and prodded her ahead of him and out of the car.

He grabbed her hand and pulled her across the road just as the demolished car started emitting black puffs of smoke.

He parked Scarlett safely next to a tree on the other side of the burning car, shielding her body. He held his breath, waiting for an explosion.

Instead, the fire burned itself out on the metal of the car with the help of the pounding rain, leaving a smoking hulk at the side of the road.

Jim brushed a wisp of hair from Scarlett's wet cheek. "Are you okay? Your back? Your neck?"

She blinked. "I think so. You?"

"Rattled but not broken."

"Oh, my God." She covered her face with her hands. "Danny tried to do the same thing to us as he did to my family."

"He must've tampered with your car at the hospital or when it was at the reservation."

"He's serious, Jim. He wants to get rid of us so we'll stop meddling in his business."

"Once we find the drugs and get Harper involved, we can put a stop to this insanity. There's no way Chewy or any other Lord is going to do Danny's dirty work without getting paid in drugs first. Dax knew this."

A big rig loaded with lumber rumbled into view at the top of the hill. As the truck descended, the driver honked and slowed down. He yelled out his window. "You folks okay?"

"We're fine, but the car's totaled."

"Do you need me to make a phone call?"

Jim held up his cell. "I got it, thanks."

As the truck started moving, Jim called 911 to report the accident. Then he draped his jacket over Scarlett's head to protect her from the rain—at least he could protect her from that. She should've been back in San Francisco by now.

While he wrapped her in his arms, the familiar sound of sirens cut through the late-afternoon air. A squad car and a fire engine came over the hill, the fire truck pulling up behind Scarlett's car.

As soon as Deputy Unger got out of his car, Scarlett descended on him.

"Someone tampered with the brakes on my car. I'm almost sure of it, Cody."

The deputy scratched his chin. "You seem to be having a run of bad luck, that's for sure."

Scarlett choked. "A run of bad luck? Is that what you'd call it?"

"Are you accusing anyone, Scarlett? Do you know who's behind the attacks? Because if you do, we'd sure like to talk to him about Rusty Kelly's murder and the attempted murder of Dax Kennedy."

Jim shifted his weight to his other foot, just enough to touch Scarlett's shoulder. As much as Unger didn't respect his boss, Sheriff Musgrove was still his boss and Evelyn had just warned them against Musgrove. Jim would feel safer spilling his guts to a third party like Agent Harper.

"I—I don't know, but this," she said, and waved her arm at the smoldering car, "was no accident."

The firefighters had made short work of the flames licking at the underbrush around the car, and Jim watched as they put out any remaining live sparks on the car.

Unger gestured to Scarlett's car. "You're lucky that thing didn't blow."

"Jim got us out quickly, just in case." She put her hand through his arm.

The fire chief approached them, asked a few questions and confirmed that the car had been totaled—as if they didn't already know that.

"Did the inside of the car burn up? My purse is still in there, my cell phone. Can I get them?"

"Give it some time. There's still some hot metal on the car, and you don't want to get burned." The fire-fighters wrapped up and took off for an accident scene with injuries.

"What now?" Scarlett tapped the toe of her boot.

"The tow service is on its way, and we'll have an accident investigator from the county go over the car at the tow yard. If it's foul play, he'll spot it." Unger tucked his notepad into his front pocket. "Do you want me to wait for the tow truck driver with you?"

"How long is he going to be?" Jim peered at the setting sun. He had some digging to do.

"This rain wreaked havoc with more than a few motorists this afternoon. When I called in, the operator said he'd be out within the hour. I can give you two a ride."

Scarlett checked her watch. "We'll wait. I still want to get my purse and phone. Maybe the tow truck driver can help me get it."

"Suit yourself."

As Unger drove away, Jim dug his own phone out of his jacket pocket. "I'm calling Harper."

"Let me, and then I'll hand the phone over to you."

He dropped his cell into her open palm.

She tapped in the number and paused. Then she shook her head. "Hello, Agent Harper, Duke. This is Scarlett

Easton. Some new information has surfaced regarding the Timberline Trio case and the connection between the Lords of Chaos and…and certain members of the Quileute tribe. Can you give me a call when you get the chance?"

"Do you think he'll bite?"

"The FBI pulled Harper off the cold case just when he was starting to get somewhere. I think he'd like the chance to see it through."

She handed the phone back to him and he wrapped his fingers around her wrist and pulled her close. "Are you sure you're okay? We can take a trip to the emergency room."

"I'm going to be feeling the pain in my neck and back tomorrow, no doubt, but I'm not injured. Besides, we have someplace to be."

"Now that your car is out of commission." He jerked his thumb over his shoulder. "Do you think you can carry a couple of shovels while you're on the back of the bike?"

"I'm an expert biker bitch now." She pulled back her shoulders and tossed her head.

"If you say so." He rolled his eyes. "While we're waiting for this driver, I'm going to check up on Dax."

He called the hospital first and left a message with Dax's doctor. Then he called Belinda.

"How's Dax doing?"

"He's the same—no better but no worse. I had to set a couple of people here straight."

"What do you mean, Belinda?"

"Some nurse tried to kick me out of his room earlier, but I wouldn't budge. Came to find out that witch doesn't even work over here."

"What?" Jim tugged on the sleeve of Scarlett's jacket and set his phone to speaker. "What nurse?"

"Some little bitch who barged in here and told me Dax couldn't have any visitors right now."

"She wasn't an ICU nurse?"

"Nope."

"How'd you discover that?"

"When I wouldn't leave, she took off in a huff and I went to the nurses' station to complain about her. Those nurses told me it was still visiting hours and asked me about the nurse who told me to get out. I didn't get her name, but when I described her to them, she told me there was no ICU nurse like that."

Scarlett grabbed his arm. "Belinda, this is Scarlett. What did the nurse look like, the one who told you to get out?"

"Tall, black hair, big, pretty eyes, but cold as hell."

"Belinda, do not leave Dax's side, do you hear me?"

"Oh, I hear you, sister, and you don't have to tell me twice. I'm watching over him like a hawk."

When Jim ended the call, Scarlett kicked at the gravel on the shoulder of the road. "It's Tiana Gokey. It has to be. Danny is telling her to keep an eye on Dax. Who knows what else he's telling her?"

"My God. Would she go as far as killing him?"

"I don't know. I don't know what she owes Danny or thinks she owes him. This has to stop, Jim."

"As soon as we have some proof for Harper, it will." He spotted the tow truck and waved his arms in the air.

Forty minutes later, Scarlett had retrieved her belongings from the car and the charred vehicle was sitting on the flatbed of the tow truck.

"Can you give us a lift back to my place? It's on your way."

The driver nodded. "Sure, hop in."

They squeezed into the front seat next to the driver and he dropped them off at Jim's cabin.

As they collected a couple of shovels, a coil of rope and a pickax from the garage, Jim placed his hand on the small of Scarlett's back. "You don't have to go, Scarlett. I can do this by myself. I can tell you how it all turns out while you're having a glass of wine at a bar overlooking the city."

"I know you *can* do it by yourself, Jim." She turned toward him and cupped his chin with her hand. "But I want to be there with you. It's one of my people who caused this whole mess."

"Danny is no more your people than Slick is mine. We're not responsible for their actions. You don't have to put yourself in danger to prove anything or to redeem the Quileute."

"What danger? Nobody but us and Dax knows the location of those drugs, and we may be way off base."

"Don't downplay it. You've been targeted from the get-go."

"And that's why I need to see this through."

He handed her a shovel. "Then let's get busy."

He stuffed two flashlights and the rope in one saddlebag and tucked the head of the pickax in the other.

Once on the bike, Jim rested the two shovels across his lap and Scarlett grasped the handle of the pickax, holding it in place.

"Hang on with one arm. I'll go slowly. I had wanted to go out earlier while it was still light, but going under cover of the darkness might work out better."

As he started the bike, Scarlett's arm wound around his waist and he shoved off. They met only two cars on the way to the area of the forest that contained the abandoned mine where Wyatt Carson had stashed three children in an attempt to recreate the Timberline Trio case.

He cut the engine well before the entrance to the trail and rolled up silently. There were too many low-hanging branches for Jim to attempt to take his bike any farther into the woods, so he parked it off the road, concealing it behind some bushes. No need to advertise their presence here.

He handed Scarlett a flashlight and a shovel, and he took the other shovel and the pickax. He wound the rope around his body.

"Ready?"

She nodded, her eyes wide but her mouth determined.

They ducked into the woods, Jim leading the way with Scarlett close behind him. When they reached the clearing with the entrance to the mine and the tall pine where Slick had proposed to Wendy about a hundred years ago, Jim slowed and held out his hand.

He wanted to check the area first, but Scarlett charged past him. He made a futile grab for her jacket.

"If Dax just buried the drugs, there should be some signs of fresh dirt, even with the rainstorm coming through this afternoon. Hopefully, that rain made the ground soggy enough for some easy digging, and maybe Dax marked the spot somehow." Scarlett marched toward the pine, her flashlight sweeping the ground in front of her.

Jim choked out a harsh whisper as he staggered into the clearing after her. "Scarlett, hold on."

Then he heard it—the click of a gun's safety.

Scarlett yelped as Jim's flashlight illuminated her pale face, an arm around her throat and a gun to her head.

Her uncle growled. "Drop the tools, Kennedy, and you might as well give up your gun right now."

"We called the sheriff's department, Danny." Scarlett squirmed in her captor's grasp. "They're on their way to meet us."

"Nice try, Scar, but I already know Granny warned you off Musgrove. You wouldn't have called him."

Chewy stepped from the shadows and waved his weapon at Jim. "Drop your stuff, Kennedy, and step toward the mine."

Jim hesitated only for a second before Danny placed the muzzle of his gun against Scarlett's temple. He tossed his shovel and the pickax in front of him, dug his gun out of his pocket and dropped it on the pile.

"How do you know what Granny told us? How did you know we'd be here?"

Jim licked his lips. Maybe if Scarlett could keep her uncle talking, he could get his weapon back. Chewy wasn't the brightest biker he knew.

"I had Jason bug her place."

Scarlett gasped.

"Don't worry about your little cuz. He didn't know he was doing it. He just thought he was delivering a gift to her from me—a sentimental gift that had belonged to my brother."

"Y-you killed my father, didn't you? Or Rocky had it done."

"Chewy, get Kennedy over by the mine."

"Move it, Kennedy." Chewy stepped forward, his gun gleaming in the low light, a shovel in his left hand.

Jim shuffled toward the mine entrance and glanced down. Someone had removed the boards from the top, leaving a gaping hole.

Chewy came at him, and Jim's muscles tensed, ready for the attack...or the bullet.

"Hate to do this to a Lord, but you were never one of us, were you?"

Chewy swung the shovel and hit him in the midsection, sending him into the dark abyss—again.

Chapter Seventeen

Scarlett screamed and broke away from Danny, but he grabbed her arm and yanked her back.

"Leave him, Scar. With any luck, he messed up his other leg. He's not your concern anymore. Your concern is finding those drugs."

Chewy rose to his feet from where he'd been crouching beside the mine entrance, aiming his flashlight into the depths. "J.T.'s at the bottom of the mine—probably dead."

Scarlett sobbed and then red, hot fury coursed through her veins and she clawed at Danny's face.

He smacked her cheek and she stumbled backward, catching a tree branch to stop her fall.

"Start digging. Once I get the drugs back and hand them over to Chewy and his guy, we'll be on our way. We'll go to another area, find other kids."

Chewy brushed his hair away from his small, dumb eyes. "But Rocky…?"

"Rocky doesn't have to know where the kids came from. He hasn't been in Timberline for years."

Scarlett touched her throbbing cheek. "What does Rocky Whitecotton want with these children? What did he do with them twenty-five years ago?"

"You don't need to know, Scar. Just start digging. I'll even let you live."

Scarlett snorted. She didn't believe that for a minute, but she had to hang on to the hope. If Danny and Chewy took the drugs and left her alive, she might be able to save Jim. She refused to believe he was dead. Refused to believe that fall had killed him.

She picked up a shovel, and Danny leveled his gun at her.

"Don't try anything stupid. Just start digging."

Chewy joined them and shined his flashlight at the ground under the tree.

A pattern of rocks emerged under the pine, and Danny must've spotted it the same time she did.

"There. Dax must've lined up those rocks like that. You should've warned me Dax's loyalties were with his brother, Chewy. I never would've handed the stash over to him."

"Prison must've changed him. He was always loyal to the Lords first."

Scarlett sniffed. Her guess was that Dax was only loyal to the Lords so his younger brother wouldn't have to be. Had Jim realized that too before…? She squeezed her eyes shut. He couldn't be gone. She'd know. She'd feel it now if he were.

Danny poked his gun in her back. "Start digging, girl. You're going to do all the work, and we're going to make sure you do it."

Scarlett grabbed the shovel and drove it into the damp ground. She drew it out and tossed a shovelful of dirt to the side.

"That's not so hard, is it?"

After five minutes of digging, she wiped a drop of

rain—or was it sweat—from her forehead. "Did you kill Gary Binder?"

"That loser didn't know much, but he knew enough to give that FBI agent some ideas. The agent was already looking into the Lords of Chaos. Gary could've given him the final link between the Quileute and the Lords."

"But why? Why did Rocky kidnap those children?"

Danny smacked the back of her head. "I told you. Don't worry about it. He gives his orders, and I follow them. If your father would've done the same, he'd be alive today and living the good life."

Tears burned behind Scarlett's eye and the dirt below her blurred. "And Rusty?"

"He wouldn't play along." Chewy cleared his throat and spit. "Just like Dax. If Slick were alive, he would've been all in."

"Who tried to kidnap Jim?" She stomped her boot on the shovel to drive it into the ground again.

"That was me." Danny coughed. "I was no good at it, but I struck a deal with Slick Kennedy that night—the Lords would help us and we'd help the Lords."

"A match made in hell." She threw another mound of dirt at Danny's feet, hitting his silver-tipped boots.

"Why didn't you read Kennedy, Scar? That's what I was worried about with the two of you. He had the knowledge buried in his psyche and you had the ability to tap into it."

"We didn't need to go there. Granny knew your character. She knew you were involved, and then I heard your voice in the stairwell that night at the hotel."

"So, that *was* you." He kicked at the dirt. "But you never had any proof until Dax hid the drugs I gave him in good faith. One way or the other, we'll take care of him just like we did his brother."

Scarlett clenched her teeth. If Jim was really gone, she'd make sure there was no way in hell Danny ever got close to Dax. If he didn't kill her.

Her shovel hit something pliant but not as pliant as the mud she'd been shoveling. "There's something here."

"Keep digging." Chewy aimed his flashlight into the pit, highlighting the corner of a canvas bag.

Scarlett scraped her shovel across the top of it, revealing more of the canvas.

Danny shoved her aside. "Get that out, Chewy."

The big man hunched over the hole in the ground and grabbed the sack. He tugged and pulled until he freed it from its grave. Then he swung it onto the ground.

"This is it, Danny. Now I can have it all and I'll get you your kids. I'll get Rocky his new kids."

Danny swung his weapon from Scarlett to Chewy and shot him in the head.

Blood sprayed her cheek and she gagged as Chewy dropped to the ground, next to the drugs.

Danny laughed. "As if I'd trust that oaf to snatch some kids for Rocky. I guess it's back to the drawing board for me, but at least I have my incentive to get someone to do it."

Scarlett took a step back from the madness in her uncle's eyes. He'd never let her live and nobody would ever find Jim in time, even if he had survived the fall into the mine.

But she'd be damned if she'd die without a fight.

She had pivoted to face Danny, her fists raised, when a shot rang out.

For a split second she thought he'd shot her, but then she noticed the surprise on his face.

Danny's mouth dropped open as his chin hit his chest. Another bullet tore his torso and his head snapped back.

As he crumpled to the ground, Scarlett's gaze zeroed in on the entrance to the mine, where Jim's head was just visible over the edge.

Crying and laughing at the same time, Scarlett ran to him where he was dangling from a rope, a gun stinking of gun powder clutched in his right hand.

She dropped to the ground and flattened to her belly. Grabbing the rope tied under his arms and looped over a rock at the edge of the mine, she pulled him over the edge. With a grunt, she hoisted him up and over, and he collapsed beside her.

Smoothing a hand across his mud-caked cheek, she sighed. "You made it."

He grinned and pulled her down for a dirty kiss. "I've made it through worse and never has the reward been so great."

"WE CAN SEND you to a specialist in Seattle, Jim. I think that leg can be broken and reset." Dr. Harrison tapped his clipboard.

Jim shrugged and took Scarlett's hand. "It's just a limp. I don't mind if she doesn't."

"Me?" She leaned over and kissed his chin.

He'd never get tired of those lips.

"If you took away his limp, he might stop trying so hard."

"Give up? Never, not J.T." Dax beamed from his wheelchair, pride etched in every line of his face.

"It's an option. Just let me know if you're interested and I can make the recommendation." The doctor pointed at Dax. "And you—not too long in here. You need your rest."

Belinda curled her fingers around the handles of Dax's

wheelchair. "Don't worry, Doc. I'll make sure he does everything he's supposed to."

Dax shrugged as she wheeled him out of the room. "I'll catch up with you later, J.T.—Jim."

Jim held up a clenched fist. "Proud of you, bro."

When Dr. Harris followed Belinda and Dax out of the room, Scarlett rested her head on his chest.

He'd never get tired of that, either.

"Will it be hard for Dax to leave the Lords? It was hard for you."

"Different time. The Lords are pretty much done in this area. Nobody's going to be coming after Dax."

"I still can't believe you made it out of that mine and were able to get to the gun strapped to your leg."

"Chewy didn't check me for any more weapons. Snipers always carry a spare. And I had that rope wrapped across my body. I guess he missed that, too."

"Or maybe he figured the fall would incapacitate or kill you."

"He figured wrong." He traced a line from her earlobe along her jaw. "Agent Harper dropped by. Did you see him?"

"No. He was here earlier?"

"The FBI was able to trace the drugs to Danny, but they still don't have any idea where Rocky Whitecotton is. It's like he fell off the face of the earth twenty-five years ago."

"So, the FBI doesn't know why he wanted those children and what he did with them?"

"The Timberline Trio is still a mystery. If they can't find Whitecotton, maybe we'll never know what happened to those kids and why."

"I feel for those families, but I'm done. I'm done with Timberline for a while, except for Granny."

"Did you tell Jason what he'd done?"

"He feels bad. He figured Danny was up to no good, but he needed the money he was offering."

"I'm sure he wouldn't have done it if he thought it was going to put you in danger."

"That's his problem." She tapped her head. "He doesn't think."

"And you? What do you think?"

"About what?" She wedged her chin on his chest and gazed into his eyes.

"Seattle."

"I've always liked Seattle."

"There's a training program for counselors there that sounds good. I can even start working at the VA center right away."

"That would be great for you, Jim."

"And maybe for you? I talked to the VA about that art therapy. The folks there are interested…if you are."

"Us? Working together?"

"I think we make a good team—that is if you're willing to throw in with a battered and bruised vet."

"Battered and bruised, but not broken."

She pressed her lips against his and he smiled beneath her kiss. Not broken, not broken at all.

* * * * *

Carol Ericson's series
Target: Timberline *comes to a*
gripping conclusion next month when
IN THE ARMS OF THE ENEMY goes on sale.

You'll find it wherever
Intrigue books are sold!

Resourceful, he thought. That was Risa.

He felt a familiar tug low in his gut, a pull of attraction and admiration and awe, all wrapped up in one small, brilliant woman. And then, like a slow-rolling detonation, the delayed impact of the reality he'd been tamping down beneath his game face finally hit him with devastating force.

She's alive.

Shock waves of pent-up emotion blew through him, and he ended up dropping to the cold bus stop bench before his knees buckled.

He took several deep breaths, his heart hammering as if he'd run for miles. Risa sat beside him, her compact body warm, and she put her hand on his arm.

"What's wrong?"

How could he tell her what he was feeling when he couldn't trust the emotions? Yes, he was thrilled beyond words that she was alive. He had mourned her deeply, longed for her when she was no longer within his reach, but those feelings seemed to belong to another person.

A person who couldn't have imagined that his wife would let him believe she was dead when she was very much alive.

And carrying his child.

KENTUCKY CONFIDENTIAL

BY
PAULA GRAVES

First Published in Great Britain 2016
By Mills & Boon, an imprint of HarperCollins*Publishers*
1 London Bridge Street, London, SE1 9GF

© 2016 Paula Graves

ISBN: 978-0-263-91919-6

46-1016

Our policy is to use papers that are natural, renewable and recyclable products and made from wood grown in sustainable forests. The logging and manufacturing processes conform to the legal environmental regulations of the country of origin.

Printed and bound in Spain
by CPI, Barcelona

Paula Graves, an Alabama native, wrote her first book at the age of six. A voracious reader, Paula loves books that pair tantalizing mystery with compelling romance. When she's not reading or writing, she works as a creative director for a Birmingham advertising agency and spends time with her family and friends. Paula invites readers to visit her website, www.paulagraves.com.

For my editor, Allison, whose Raylan Givens
love led to this series.

Chapter One

"She's dead," Connor McGinnis whispered, though his eyes declared the words a lie.

On the street below his window, the woman he was surveilling tugged her faded coat more tightly around her swollen belly and waited for the chance to cross the street. A light wind swept snow flurries in small white eddies down the street and threatened to whip the gauzy *roosari* from her head. Grabbing the scarf as it slid down to reveal the dark luster of her wavy hair, she tugged it back into place, but not before he got a look at her face.

Her intimately familiar face.

She looked tired and careworn, but there were no signs that she'd been injured. Of course, the crash had happened months earlier. She might have had time to heal from even a serious injury.

Though how she'd survived the blast in the first place...

He tamped down a maelstrom of conflicting emotions. Not yet. Emotions on the battlefield could be deadly. And if Risa was still alive, he was already engaged in a war he hadn't known about only a few days ago.

If Risa was still alive. He couldn't quite bring himself to believe it yet, no matter what his eyes were telling him.

He'd seen news footage of the wreckage found floating in the water off the coast of Japan. Even if someone had survived the bomb blast that sent the jet hurtling into the Pacific Ocean, no one would have come out of that crash unscathed. And Risa's name was on the passenger manifest, which meant she'd gotten on the plane.

He didn't know how this woman could be Risa, no matter how much she looked like her.

Except there were ways to fake passenger manifests, weren't there? Ways to fool transportation security. It was one of the biggest nightmares facing national security agencies worldwide.

Traffic cleared momentarily, and the woman started across the street. Her gaze darted around, right and left, in front and behind, as she made the short transit from one corner to another.

Hypervigilant, he thought.

Reasonable, he supposed, for a refugee from war-torn Kaziristan.

Or for a woman hiding from her past.

Stop. It's not Risa. It can't be.

He was grasping at straws. Letting what he wanted get in the way of what actually was.

That was a good way to drive himself insane. He had to keep his emotions out of the equation. Think logically. Deal in facts.

If Risa had survived the crash, she'd have found a way to let him know.

Wouldn't she?

He lost sight of the woman—the woman who couldn't possibly be Risa—as she turned at the corner and walked under the narrow awnings of the storefronts below the shabby apartment he'd rented earlier that morning. He resisted the urge to run to the ground floor and follow her down the street. It wasn't time to make that particular move.

Not yet.

If ten years of combat had taught Connor McGinnis nothing else, it had shown him the value of patience.

SHE WAS BEING WATCHED.

Inside her apartment, the woman known as Yasmin Hamani locked the door behind her and paused in the entryway to listen. The apartment building was old, prone to settling with creaks and groans of aged wood and plaster, but she didn't sense the presence of another living being within the walls of the small one-bedroom apartment. Still, she unlocked the drawer of the table by the door and withdrew her compact Glock 23, feeling instantly safer.

These days, it was harder to carry a weapon than rely on her disguise to keep her safe. None of her shoulder-carry holsters fit comfortably anymore, thanks to the swell of her pregnant belly. And forget trying to work with any sort of waistband holster.

She made a circuit of the empty apartment with the Glock in hand before she finally relaxed and put the weapon on the side table where she could easily reach it. She removed the *roosari* covering her hair, relieved to be shed of it for a while. She wasn't Muslim, but the majority of the Kaziri refugees who lived in this section of Over-the-Rhine were, and she donned the head scarf as both protection and concealment.

It was unlikely she'd run across anyone she'd dealt with during her years in Kaziristan, but a dead woman couldn't be too careful. She couldn't afford to stand out.

The baby was fussy this afternoon, turning flips in her womb. Impatient, perhaps, to greet the world outside. Yasmin rubbed her bulging belly, smiling a little at the thumps of the baby's kicks against her palms, strong and reassuring.

The baby was her reason for everything she did these days.

She eased into her desk chair, now used to the dull pain in the small of her back from carrying the tiny burden inside her. She typed in the complex password to her laptop computer and checked her email for any message from her former handler.

Nothing.

She sighed, leaning against the back of the chair. If someone had seen through her cover, apparently Martin Dalrymple didn't know about it.

Which meant what? That she was imagining things?

Working in covert operations had a way of making a person see shadows where none existed. Operatives got used to paranoia. Expecting the worst, seeing threats everywhere you looked, kept you vigilant. And vigilance kept you alive. But she'd thought she was done with that life. She had started a new life, one that wouldn't include dead drops and secret identities. One that included stability and trust. Love.

She should have known better.

The baby kicked again, reminding her that she hadn't lost everything. The pregnancy had come as a shock, a complication her analytical mind had deemed an unacceptable risk.

But her heart had wrapped itself around the tiny life growing inside her like a coat of armor, determined to keep the baby safe from danger.

She would give her baby the life he or she deserved, no matter what it took. Somehow, she'd figure out a way to do it.

But she didn't think it could be here in Cincinnati.

She sent a coded email message to Dalrymple, trying to be as oblique as possible so that even if someone managed to break the cipher, he'd still have to figure out what the hell she was talking about. While Dalrymple knew her well enough to understand what she was trying to tell him, there wasn't anyone else in the world who knew her that well.

Not anymore, anyway.

The baby gave another kick. She was only four weeks away from her due date, though her obstetrician seemed to think she might deliver late. First babies often took their own sweet time.

Rubbing her belly, she logged off and closed the laptop, hoping Dalrymple would respond soon. The last thing she needed in the final days of her pregnancy was this kind of stress.

Come on, Dal. Tell me I'm imagining things.

She settled in the rocking chair she'd picked up at a thrift store. Most of her furniture was secondhand. Her clothes as well.

She'd never been wealthy, and she could remember plenty of lean times in her life, both as a child and later as an adult. But life as a pregnant Kaziri refugee was proving to be a whole other level of needy. And there was no hope of ever going back to the life she'd once lived.

From down the hall, faint strains of an old Kaziri folk song added a discordant counterpoint to the Bing Crosby tune playing on the radio in the apartment next door. Refugees had taken over several of the empty apartments in the building, but there were a few native Cincinnatians who'd been living in Over-the-Rhine for decades, through bad times and good. Some of them eyed the newcomers with suspicion and even fear, at times signaling their defiance by shows of blatant patriotism in case the refugees forgot where they were living now.

Yasmin felt strangely caught in the middle, someone who knew all the words to both songs clamoring for attention. Her mother had sung "Nazanin" to her as a lullaby for as long as she could remember. And Bing's "White Christmas" had always been one of her father's favorite songs.

It would have been easier if Dal had placed her in the Raleigh, North Carolina, area, where another group of Kaziri immigrants had started to form their own small cultural enclave. Those Kaziris came from the small Christian community, with its more westernized habits and customs. She could have fit in there quite easily, given her mother's background.

But she wasn't going to find what Dalrymple was seeking in North Carolina. So there would be no Christmas lights this year. No holly wreath on her door or stockings on the mantel. Not if she wanted to fit in with the rest of the Kaziri community here in Cincy.

Still, as she rocked slowly in the chair, making herself wait a little longer before she checked for Dal's return email, she found herself humming along with Bing, feeling a little melancholy.

Christmas was only a couple of weeks away. And this year, she'd be spending it alone.

"Is it her?" Maddox Heller's drawl rumbled through the phone receiver, bracingly familiar.

Connor stepped away from the window. "I'll admit, it looks like her."

"But you're not certain." Heller's voice was tinged with sympathy. A former marine, like Connor, he'd gotten in touch after the plane crash and Risa's death, first to offer his condolences, and later, the new job that had eventually brought Connor to Cincinnati.

"No, I'm not certain." Connor had come to terms with the fact that he wanted to believe the woman he'd seen was Risa. But self-deception during a mission was a great way to end up dead or captured. "The woman is definitely pregnant."

"How far along?"

"How the hell would I know?" He heard a tinge of bitterness in his voice and quelled it. Stick to the facts. "Big. Probably last trimester."

"If it's Risa," Heller said quietly, "then..."

Then the baby could be his. "I know."

"Quinn has feelers out to some of his old contacts at the agency, but if she's part of an ongoing operation, they're not going to tell him anything."

"Do you think..." Connor swallowed and started again. "Do you think she could have planned it all along?"

"What? Faking her death?"

"Yeah."

"I don't know. CIA folks can be a little squirrelly, but..."

But she loved me, he thought. *She loved me, and we didn't have secrets.*

Self-deception, he reminded himself. Always dangerous.

"I think she must live in this area. The Kaziri refugee community seems to be centered here near the new mosque on Dublin Street," he told Heller. The mosque had once been a Methodist church, according to some of the locals he'd talked to earlier that morning. With the exodus of locals and the advent of the refugees, a lot was changing in the neighborhood. Longtime diners had become halal markets and restaurants. A boutique down the street from the mosque now sold hijab coverings for women.

"That's what our intel says," Heller agreed.

By intel, he suspected Heller meant an undercover asset. Maybe more than one. Connor was new to Campbell Cove Security and the academy the company ran. He had a feeling there was a lot about the company he had yet to discover. And other things, he suspected, he might never discover unless there was a pressing need to know.

Heller broke the silence that had fallen between them. "What's your gut on this?"

How the hell was Connor supposed to answer that question? He'd spent the past three days since spotting the pregnant woman in the surveillance photos trying not to feel anything at all, in his gut or anywhere else. If he let himself feel, then he'd lose any chance of dealing with the situation with reason and logic.

"I don't know," he answered. "I can't let my gut lead here."

He wanted to believe way too much to trust his gut about anything where Risa was concerned.

"What are you going to do next?" Heller asked.

Connor checked his watch. Nearly two thirty. "The operative says she works the dinner shift at The Jewel of Tablis, right?"

"Not every night, but yeah."

"So I guess I'll wait a couple of hours and then go have myself a nice halal dinner."

By THE TIME Yasmin had to leave the apartment to get to her job at the restaurant, she still hadn't heard from Dalrymple. Going on twelve hours since their last contact. Dal had always been the kind of man who lived on his own timetable, but he'd never taken this long to get back to her.

Unless something had gone wrong.

As she tied her apron above the swell of the baby, she glanced around the restaurant, trying to remember the feeling she'd had before while walking home from the doctor's office. A tingle on the back of her neck that said, "Someone is watching."

She supposed it was possible a lot of people were watching her. Pregnant women living alone weren't the norm in a culture like Kaziristan's. She had lived there with her mother for three years while her father was doing a tour of duty overseas. At least, that's what her mother had told her, though she sometimes wondered if the Kaziristan years had come during a rough patch in her parents' marriage.

They'd stayed with her mother's brother and his family, and the experience had been eye-opening, not always in a good way. But during those years, she'd learned a lot about being a Kaziri woman. While a large swath of Kaziristan was cosmopolitan and culturally advanced, some of the rural areas were still deeply tribal, including the part where her mother's brother lived. Those areas were patriarchal in a way people in the West couldn't really comprehend.

But even in those parts of Kaziristan, women had ways

of getting things done beneath the veil. It was a lesson she'd never forgotten, and she was banking on that lesson to get her through the next few months of her life.

"Yasmin?" The sharp voice of the restaurant manager, Farid Rahimi, jerked her back to attention. She turned to look at him, trying not to let her dislike show.

He was a short man, and lean, but she knew from observation that he was strong and fast. He was also mean, keeping his employees in line with threats and derision. He was a US citizen, which put him in a far more stable position than most of the people in the community, including all of his employees. Most were here on temporary visas or provisional refugee status, and he made sure they understood just how perilous their lives in the States really were.

"There are a couple of special guests coming tonight. They want the prettiest of the serving girls to wait on them exclusively." He flashed her a bright smile before adding, "So Darya will be serving them. You'll have to pick up her tables."

"Yes, sir," she answered in Kaziri, trying to ignore the flash of cruelty in his smile. One of the hardest things about pretending to be a Kaziri refugee was behaving as if she was resigned to being at the mercy of others.

In another life, she would have cut him in half with her words. And he'd be lucky if she'd stopped there.

"Speak English," Farid added in a harsh tone. He waved one sinewy hand at her head. "And cover yourself."

She reached up and straightened her *roosari*, tugging it up to cover her hair. *It's all part of the assignment*, she reminded herself as she picked up her order pad and went to work, her teeth grinding with frustration.

The conversations she overheard as she worked were unremarkable. Despite its location in the heart of the Kaziri refugee community, The Jewel of Tablis was beginning to draw patrons from all over Cincinnati. In fact, most of the refugees Yasmin knew were too impoverished to eat out, though most of them shopped in the small halal food market attached to the restaurant. So far tonight, all of her diners were English-speaking Americans. Not one of them said anything that might have piqued Dalrymple's interest.

She was beginning to wonder why he'd wanted her to move here to Cincinnati rather than simply relocating her somewhere out West, where she could live in solitude and see trouble coming for miles before it arrived.

"Darya!" Farid's voice rose over the ambient noise of conversing diners, drawing Yasmin's gaze toward the door where he stood. There were two dark-featured men, each wearing an expensive *payraan tumbaan*, the traditional long shirt and pants typical in Afghanistan, Pakistan and, these days, the Kaziri moneyed class. The intricately embroidered silk vests the two men wore over their shirts were definitely products of Kaziristan, adorned as they were with the brilliant-hued fire hawk of Kaziri folklore.

She didn't recognize either man, though the taller man on the right looked oddly familiar, even though she was certain they'd never met. Maybe she'd run across one of his relatives during her time on assignment in Tablis, the Kaziri capital city.

She'd kept a low profile while she was there, playing a similar role blending in with the native Kaziris in order to keep an ear close to the ground during a volatile time in the country's downward spiral toward another civil war. Strange—and alarming—that she'd been afforded more autonomy and respect as a woman in Kaziristan than she was as a woman in the insular Kaziri community in Cincinnati.

On the upside, being pregnant and makeup-free was working in her favor here. People saw the round belly first and never bothered letting their gazes rise to her face, especially with more nubile, exotic-looking beauties like Darya and her bevy of young, unmarried friends to draw the attention of Kaziri men. And the Americans as well, she noted with secret amusement, as the middle-aged male patrons she was currently serving kept slanting intrigued glances at Darya as she walked with sinuous femininity to the VIP table to take their orders.

Out of the corner of her eye, she noticed another customer enter the restaurant and take a seat at a table near the window. She delivered her most recent order to the kitchen and returned to the dining hall, grabbing a menu and pouring a glass of water before heading to the newcomer's table.

A burst of laughter from the VIP table drew her attention in that direction. One of the men was flirting outrageously with Darya, who was eating up the attention with the confidence of a woman who knew her appeal.

Swallowing a sigh, Yasmin turned her attention back to her new customer. He lifted his head, pinning her with his blue-eyed gaze.

Her stomach gave a lurch.

The glass slipped from her hand, but the man whipped his hand out and caught it on the way down. Only a few drops of water splashed across the dark hair on the back of his hand.

He set the glass on the table, still looking at her.

"Hello, Risa," Connor McGinnis said.

Chapter Two

Connor focused his gaze on Risa's pale face, trying to read the snippets of emotion that flashed like lightning across her expression. Within a couple of seconds, her pretty features became a mask that hid everything from him.

"Yasmin," she said quietly as she mopped up the spilled drops of water from the table using a rag she pulled from her apron pocket. Her voice, almost as familiar as his own, came out in a heavy, convincing Kaziri accent. "My name is Yasmin and I will be your server tonight. Would you like to try the mint tea?"

So it wasn't amnesia. There had been a part of him that almost prayed it had been memory loss from the plane crash that had kept her away for so long, but those hopes had been dashed the second her eyes met his. They'd widened, the pupils dilating with shock, before she'd lowered her gaze and set about hiding everything she'd briefly revealed.

He knew what that Kaziri accent hid—a South Georgia drawl as warm and slow as a night in Savannah, where Risa had been born and her parents still lived.

They'd mourned her, too, he thought.

How could she have chosen to disappear the way she

had, letting everyone who knew and loved her think she was dead?

He struggled to keep the anger burning in his gut in check, careful not to let it show in his expression. He, too, was good at wearing masks.

"When does your shift end?" he asked quietly.

She pretended not to hear the question. "The special tonight is lamb kebabs with rice."

"We have to talk, Yasmin." He put extra emphasis on her alias.

"No." Her hazel eyes lifted to meet his gaze before she added, "Sir."

"You don't think I have a right to ask a few questions?"

For a second, her mask faltered, fierce emotion burning in her eyes. But she looked away quickly. "Take your time to study the menu. I will return in a few minutes. Would you like something to drink while you are waiting?"

"Mint tea," he said finally.

She gave a nod and walked away. Her gait was subtly different, her back arched from the weight of her pregnant belly. He realized with some surprise that he'd never before imagined what she'd look like pregnant.

How could that be? Why had they never thought about children, about a family?

A few tables away, a slender young woman in a simple, shape-hugging dress and a matching peacock-blue *roosari* was taking orders from two middle-aged men. The one nearest was dressed in an elaborately embroidered *payraan tumbaan*. Connor couldn't get a good look at his face. His companion, however, sat facing Connor, though his gaze was lifted upward to smile at the pretty server. Connor didn't recognize him.

But there was something about the shape of the other man's head, the slight wave of his silver-flecked black hair, that tugged at Connor's memory.

How did he know the man? Was it from those years he'd spent in Kaziristan? Or was the acquaintance more recent?

He sensed more than saw Risa's approach and turned his gaze toward her, watching her walk to his table. She carried a small tray with a glass of iced mint tea, even though he hadn't indicated whether he wanted it hot or cold. She placed the glass of tea on the table in front of him and started to turn away.

"I didn't ask for my tea to be iced," he murmured. But of course, she'd given him ice because she knew that's how he liked it.

She froze in place for a second before she turned and lowered her gaze. "I am sorry. I will bring you another cup."

He closed his hand over hers as she reached for the glass. "Washington Park. Are you familiar with it?"

For a moment, her fingers flexed beneath his grip. But she gave a tiny nod.

He dropped his hand away before they drew unwanted attention. "I will be on a bench near the bandstand by the water park. Tomorrow morning at ten. If you want to talk." He handed her the menu. "Tea will be all. Thank you."

She lifted her gaze to meet his. "The table will be needed once the dinner crowd picks up."

"Understood." He took a couple of drinks of the cold mint tea and realized she'd added a packet of sweetener, the way he liked it. "Thank you for the tea. It's perfect."

She averted her gaze but didn't move right away. He

thought he saw a hint of moisture glimmering in her eyes before she finally walked back to the kitchen area.

He released his pent-up breath and glanced at the table nearby where the two Kaziri men continued flirting with the young waitress. It was at that exact moment that the second man turned his head, giving Connor a good look at his profile.

A ripple of unease darted through him. He didn't recognize the man, but something was ringing alarm bells in his head. He felt as if he should recognize him somehow. But why?

He looked at the phone lying on the table in front of him. Unhurriedly, he picked it up and swiped the screen to unlock it. Glancing toward the other table, he pushed the camera application button, bringing up the viewing screen, and slowly angled it toward the men at the other table.

Pretending to send a text, he snapped a quick shot of the man facing him. He waited for the other man to turn again, but he was looking up at the flirtatious waitress, who seemed to be regaling them with a story in rapid-fire Kaziri.

The clatter of silverware nearby drew his attention away for a moment, until he spotted the toddler at a table near the door who had thrown his spoon on the floor. As the mother shot a look of apology toward the approaching server, Connor looked back at the table where the two Kaziri men sat. The second man had turned in his chair to watch the young mother and child, his expression harsh with disapproval.

He was perfectly framed in the phone's viewer screen. Connor snapped a couple of photos before the man turned his back again. While he was at it, he took a few other shots, one of the dark-haired man who seemed to be the restaurant manager, another of the pretty young waitress attending to the table where the Kaziri men sat, and finally, carefully, a shot of Risa as she served a nearby table, her *roosari* sliding backward to reveal her dusky hair and delicate profile.

After one more shot, he pocketed his phone and retrieved his wallet. He put a twenty on the table next to the half-empty tea glass before he walked out the door, careful to keep his face averted from the two Kaziri men.

Outside the restaurant, the night had turned bitterly cold, the last fluttering of snow drifting silently from the winter sky. Tugging up his collar to guard his neck from the icy wind, he hurried down the block to a coffee shop angled across the street from The Jewel of Tablis.

A blast of heat welcomed him as he entered. A freckled waitress with straw-blond hair and bright red lipstick greeted him from the counter. "Take a seat, sir. I'll be with you in just a sec."

Connor sat at one of the tables by the window, not entirely happy with the view through the plate glass. The bright interior of the diner reflected back at him, making it difficult to see much of the street outside, though the colorful lights of The Jewel of Tablis were just visible through the reflection.

He pulled out his phone and opened the photo gallery, studying the images he'd snapped at the other restaurant. He'd gotten a good shot of the younger man who had sat facing Connor's table. He texted Maddox Heller a quick message and attached the photo. Then he picked out the best shot he had of the older man and sent the image to Heller as well. Does this man look familiar?

As the waitress arrived with a pot of coffee and a

menu, his phone hummed. He took the menu and checked his messages. There was a text from Heller.

Not sure, Heller had written. The image isn't clear. Can you track? Get a better shot?

Will try, he texted back and set his phone on the table in front of him, peering through his reflection at the door of the restaurant down the street.

PANIC BURNED IN her chest, stealing her breath. She forced herself to slow her breathing, to concentrate on staying calm. Thanks to the pregnancy, her blood pressure was a little higher than normal, so she had to deal with the stress for the baby's sake as well as her own.

Don't think about Connor. Don't think about anything but the job.

"Are you okay?" Darya's voice startled her, setting her nerves rattling. Darya had been born in Cincinnati and spoke Kaziri with an American accent.

"I'm feeling a little tired," Yasmin answered, her own Kaziri as authentic as a native's, thanks to her mother and those years spent in Kaziristan, first with her mother's brother and his family, and then undercover with the agency.

Her gaze drifted toward the VIP table. Maybe that's why she'd thought one of those men looked familiar? Had she seen him before in Kaziristan?

Darya followed her gaze and lowered her voice to a soft hiss. "Pigs," she said with a viciousness that caught Yasmin by surprise.

The younger woman's parents put great stock in tradition and they had raised their daughter to observe their customs, but perhaps Darya had a rebellious side. Despite her flirtations with the VIPs earlier, Yasmin now noticed a pinched look around the girl's eyes and mouth that suggested she had found her role vexing.

Not worth the tips they would leave when they departed?

"I think that handsome customer you served earlier liked you," Darya added, her voice back to its normal, teasing tone. "The one with the leather jacket? Very manly."

"I am pregnant and hardly looking my best," she countered, trying to forget the look of betrayal in Connor's eyes. A pain began to throb behind her forehead. "You were right. I am not feeling well."

She had to get out of here. Go somewhere to think. Figure out what to do next. Try to reach Dal again.

"Go. Your shift is nearly over. I will tell Farid you became ill and left."

Yasmin glanced at her watch. It was eight forty-five. The restaurant closed at nine. "I'll tell him," she said, already heading toward the kitchen. Farid would probably dock her the final hour of her pay, but money was the least of her problems at the moment.

How had Connor located her? What kind of game was he playing?

She found Farid in his cluttered office behind the kitchen and told him she was feeling unwell.

"You'll get an hour less in your paycheck this week," he warned her. "Unless you can pick up an hour later this week."

"I will do that," she said, not at all certain she'd be back to the restaurant at all.

Instead of going out the back door into the darkened alley behind the restaurant, she chose the relative safety of the well-lit front exit. As she left, she spared another glance at the two men sitting at the VIP table. They leaned toward each other over the table, deep in conversation. The older man's demeanor seemed angry, while the younger man looked tense and worried. From her vantage point, she couldn't see the older man's face, but there was something vaguely familiar about the way he held himself erect, about the shape of his head and his slim but masculine build.

Flicking her gaze toward the front exit, she realized she could see the older man's reflection quite clearly in the window. Clearly enough that she was now certain she'd seen him before. But not in person.

Where had she seen him?

It might have been on Dalrymple's office wall, she realized a few moments later. There had been several surveillance shots tacked up on a corkboard behind Dal's desk in his Washington office. She'd asked about the photos once, but Dal had brushed her questions aside. "They're wins," he'd said with grim satisfaction. She'd assumed that Dal meant they were bad actors who'd been killed or captured by the agency.

One of the photos on the wall had looked a little bit like one of the two men Darya had been serving earlier, hadn't it?

But those men on Dal's wall of wins were dead or locked up somewhere they'd never escape.

So how could one of them be sitting at table six in The Jewel of Tablis?

And was it a coincidence that Connor had shown up at this restaurant at the same time as the mystery man? Maybe he hadn't come to Cincinnati looking for her at all.

Maybe he was here looking for the mystery man.

She exited the warmth of the restaurant, the shock of

frigid air sucking the breath from her lungs. Pulling her coat more tightly around her, she started walking down the street toward the bus stop on the corner. The restaurant was close enough to her apartment to walk there most days, but she was cold, tired and feeling hunted. She could splurge on the bus fare after the evening she'd just had.

Light from the storefronts across the street illuminated her way between the circles of light sporadically shed by streetlamps. On a Wednesday night, the crowd of pedestrians was lighter than it would be on the weekends, but there were enough people to make her feel safer as she walked to the corner. A few of them gave her curious glances, their gazes directed either at her head scarf or her swollen belly. A couple of the women flashed her sympathetic smiles. One of the people sitting on the bus stop bench rose to let her take his place.

She took the seat gratefully and sat to wait for the bus, letting her gaze take in the people walking past. Finally, the bus appeared amid the light traffic moving toward the corner, and she reached into her purse to make sure she had exact change. As she gathered the coins in her hand, she heard a deep voice speaking Kaziri.

"The serving girl was beautiful, no?"

Looking up, Yasmin spotted the two VIPs from the restaurant, walking together alone. She looked away as they neared her, covering her surprise so that no one around her would notice and remember. Then, as the men passed by, the bus arrived, and the people waiting with her at the bus stop moved at once to board.

Yasmin remained where she was until everyone else had started toward the bus. She rose, too, but turned to follow the men instead.

She was far enough away that they weren't likely to hear her footsteps following them. They were certainly showing no signs of stealth themselves, the older of them walking with a confident swagger, his colorful *payraan tumbaan* rippling in the cold breeze with each step.

The men walked two more blocks before turning onto a cross street. The lights here were fewer and spaced farther apart. While she'd been on the main drag, she had been accompanied by a scattering of fellow pedestrians, but once she took the turn to follow the Kaziri men, she was alone, and her sense of vulnerability increased.

In her prime, the prospect of following a couple of men down a dark side street wouldn't have given her much pause. But in her prime, she had never been over eight months pregnant and unarmed.

She slowed her gait, let them move a little farther ahead of her but still close enough that she wasn't likely to lose them unless they tried to shake her tail. Her clothing was dark, and her olive skin and dark hair wouldn't be easily visible as long as she stayed in the shadows.

Cincinnati was still a relatively new place to her, but she'd taken care to study the street maps and familiarize herself with the area for just such a situation as this. When she'd come to town seven months ago, shortly after her previous life had all but ended, she hadn't known she was pregnant. She had intended to be much more useful to Dal than she'd turned out to be.

But the job was still the job, and one of the two Kaziri men she'd spotted at The Jewel of Tablis had pinged her radar, big-time. Maybe she was wrong about seeing him before. Maybe his reason for being in Cincinnati was completely innocent.

Or maybe they were planning to bring al Adar terror attacks to the United States, hiding themselves among the poor immigrants who'd fled Kaziristan to escape unrest and persecution back home.

Near the next cross street, the two men slowed their pace as they reached the side door of a four-story brick building. It was hard to tell much about the place until the door opened, spilling light into the darkened street and revealing a quick glimpse of the dingy redbrick facade. Then the door closed, plunging the street into darkness again.

Yasmin peered at the darkened streetlamp overhead. Was it dark from normal wear and tear, or had someone deliberately disabled the bulb? And if so, was it to hide what was inside the building the two men had entered?

The longer she stayed here in the open, the more danger she put herself in, she realized. She'd wandered away from the safety of foot traffic on the main thoroughfare, leaving her vulnerable. And maybe if she had only herself to worry about, it would have been a risk worth taking.

But the gentle kicks of the baby in her womb reminded her that she wasn't the only person in danger if she lingered here much longer.

She reversed course, walking as briskly as a heavily pregnant woman could, keeping her eye on the bright strip of lights just two blocks ahead. Not much farther to go now.

"You!" a deep, accented voice called out from behind her.

She couldn't keep herself from taking a look.

The door at the end of the block was open, and three men stood in the doorway, staring toward her.

She turned around and started to run.

THE SOUND OF a man's voice calling out, followed by the thud of running footfalls, drew Connor's attention as he paused in the middle of the narrow alley he'd used as a shortcut in hopes of catching up to his quarry.

The footsteps seemed to be coming closer, spurring him into a sprint, his rubber-soled boots quiet on the uneven concrete breezeway. As he neared the opening into the street, he heard the sound of hard breathing. A woman's breathing, he thought. The sound was harsh with fear and desperation.

It was her. He could feel it like a shiver in his bones.

His body reacted on pure instinct, his arms reaching out to catch her as she ran past the narrow opening of the alley. He pulled her into the dark recess, closing his arms around her as she flailed to escape.

"It's me," he whispered in her ear.

She stopped struggling, but he could feel the pounding of her heart where her slender back pressed against his chest. Underneath one arm, something in her abdomen fluttered against his wrist, then thumped solidly against his grasp, making him swallow a gasp of surprise.

He urged her toward the other end of the alley and out of the line of sight. Around the corner of the building was a large trash receptacle. The smells from inside were ripely unpleasant, but it offered a decent hiding place until he could be certain the men who'd apparently been chasing her down the sidewalk had given up.

She huddled close to him, as if seeking his warmth, though she was furnace-hot against his chest. When she spoke, it was barely a whisper. "What are you doing here?"

"Saving you," he answered.

Chapter Three

Her name was not Yasmin Hamani, though every piece of identification she possessed proclaimed her to be so. She was not a widowed immigrant from Kaziristan, though over the past few months she had almost convinced herself she was.

But burrowed into the solid strength of Connor Mc-Ginnis's arms, breathing in his familiar scent, hearing the steadying beat of his heart beneath her ear, she allowed herself the truth.

She was Parisa DeVille McGinnis, Risa for short. Her mother was a Kaziri woman who'd married the strapping young US marine who'd saved her from death in a terrorist attack in her war-torn homeland. Risa herself had married a marine, a smart, brave and loyal man she'd met in the mountains of Kaziristan many years later. Like her parents, they'd been on track for their own happily-ever-after.

Until Risa McGinnis had died in a bomb attack on a commercial flight from Kaziristan to the US almost seven months ago. The plane had disappeared from radar over the Pacific and only a few pieces of debris had been found floating in the ocean near the plane's last coordinates on the radar.

All souls lost.

Well, all the souls who'd actually made it aboard the plane.

"We need to get moving." Connor's voice rumbled in her ear. "Lose the *roosari*."

She tugged the scarf from her head and shoved it into the pocket of her coat. She allowed herself a quick look at him, though the sight of his face, so close, so achingly familiar, left her feeling breathless and light-headed.

"How far away do you live?" he asked quietly.

"You can't go there. I live alone, unprotected." The words came out so easily, as if she truly was the woman whose life she'd lived for months now.

"I'm your husband, Risa."

Something inside her chest melted and began to warm her from the inside out. "But they think I'm a widow."

"I hope I died a heroic death." His dry tone should have made her laugh, but her heart ached too much.

"Where are you staying?" she asked. "We could go there."

"It's not far from here." He draped his arm around her shoulder and pulled her closer. "Remember, you're not Yasmin now. You're Parisa. Sexy and smart. You take no prisoners. And you're with me."

She looked at him, her heart breaking. "I'm sorry."

"We'll worry about apologies later." He nodded toward the trash-strewn alley stretching out in front of them. "Ready?"

Risa nodded, ignored the ache in her back and legs, and wrapped her arm around his waist.

Huddled together against the cold, they hurried down the darkened alley until they reached the main drag, where streetlamps lent a twilight glow to the nightlife tableau. It was past ten now, but even on a weeknight, the traffic flow, both vehicular and pedestrian, would continue past midnight.

By the time Connor led her to a shabby-looking walk-up just a couple of blocks east of Vine Street, Risa's back was starting to cramp. To her relief, there was just one flight of stairs to climb before he stopped and led her down the hall to a door marked 201. He unlocked the door and let her inside.

Compared to his place, hers looked almost homey. His living room consisted of a couple of mismatched wooden chairs around a table, and a third chair sat facing the window. A laptop computer lay closed on the table next to a take-out box.

"Have you eaten?" he asked, tossing his keys on the table.

She eyed him warily. His calm, businesslike demeanor wasn't what she'd expected from her husband upon learning she hadn't actually died.

She'd spent the past seven months letting him believe she was dead. If the situation had been reversed, she'd have been furious.

Except he didn't seem furious, either. He seemed... distant.

"Food?" he asked again. "I don't have much here, but I can run across the road to the all-night diner."

"I'm not hungry." She shrugged off her coat and looked around the bare apartment. "But I could use a bathroom."

His gaze dropped to her round belly. "Right." He nodded toward the narrow hallway just off the main room. "It's the door on the right."

The door on the left was open, revealing a darkened

bedroom. In the low ambient light seeping into the hallway from the living room, she saw that his bed was little more than a bunk, wide enough to accommodate—barely—a man Connor's size.

This was a mission, she realized as she closed the bathroom door behind her. Not a man looking for his missing wife, but a soldier on assignment. That was why he was so distant.

He was looking at her as his job, not his wife.

Shaking from a combination of cold and delayed reaction, she stared into the wide hazel eyes of the pregnant woman in the cabinet mirror and realized she'd never felt so alone in her life.

No emotions. Emotions are messy and unreliable.

Connor gazed out the window at the street below. The snow had started again, coming down in light flurries. He was glad they were out of the cold for the night.

"Am I staying?"

Risa's soft alto sent a shiver rippling down his spine. He turned to find her standing in the doorway, one shoulder leaning against the frame. The docile young Kaziri widow was gone, and the clear-eyed CIA agent he'd fallen for three years ago had taken her place.

"I don't think you should risk going back to your apartment."

"I don't have a change of clothes."

"I have a shirt you can borrow." He regretted the words even as they slipped between his lips, for they reminded him of long, sweet nights of lovemaking, followed by lazy mornings with Risa wandering around their apartment in his shirt and little else.

She ran her hand over the large bulge of her stomach. "Make it a big shirt."

He wasn't going to ask. He wasn't. If she had something to tell him about the baby, she would.

Wouldn't she?

The Risa he'd known would have played it straight with him. Always.

But the Risa he'd known wouldn't have let him believe she was dead when she wasn't.

"You must have so many questions," she murmured, walking slowly toward him. She was trying to play it cool and sophisticated, the sexy spy in control, but carrying around a baby inside her was apparently hell on the femme fatale act. She still looked sexy, but in an earth-mother sort of way, all fecund beauty and softness.

He couldn't hold back a smile. "You can drop the act, Risa. You just can't sell it with that beach ball you're carrying under that dress."

She stopped, looking uneasy. "Why aren't you asking the obvious questions?"

He played dumb. "What are the obvious questions?"

"How did you survive the plane crash, Risa?"

"How *did* you survive the plane crash, Risa?"

"I never got on the plane." She took another step.

"Why didn't you call me, Risa?"

He stayed quiet that time, struggling to control a potent storm of anger and hurt churning in his chest.

"Dalrymple pulled me off the flight. He told me there was a price on my head and I needed to lie low. Then we heard the plane crashed."

He looked at her through narrowed eyes, wondering if he could trust what she was saying. It was so pat. So obvious. Hell, maybe she even believed the story herself. Maybe Martin Dalrymple really had pulled her off the plane and told her about a price on her head. The plane crash immediately after his warning was a convincing touch.

A little too convincing, maybe.

"You think I haven't wondered the same thing?" she asked softly, moving another step closer. If he reached out now, he could touch her. Pull her close to him the way he had out in the cold alley. Feel her heart beating against his chest once more, something he'd thought he would never experience again. "You think I didn't wonder if Dal was pulling a scam on me?"

But he kept his hands by his side. "Dalrymple isn't known for his truthfulness."

"I know." She put her hand on her belly. "But if he wasn't lying—I couldn't take the chance. There was too much at stake. Not just me."

His gaze fell to where her hand cupped her round belly, despite his determination to remain unaffected. "You mean the baby?"

"I didn't know I was pregnant when I agreed to play dead." Her voice was soft, her tone sincere. "I found out almost a month later. But you'd already held the memorial service. You'd left the Marine Corps."

"So, what? You decided that what I didn't know wouldn't hurt me?"

"No, of course not—"

"Because it did." His grasp on his emotions broke, and a flood of anger and old grief poured into his throat, threatening to choke him. "It hurt like all hell. It still does. Every damn day."

Her face crumpled. "I'm sorry."

"Sorry you let me believe you were dead?" He closed

the distance between them in one furious step. "Or sorry that I found out you weren't?"

She put her hand on his chest. His brain told him to shake off the touch, but the feel of her palm warm against his sternum, so damn familiar and longed for, nearly unmoored him.

He closed his hand over hers, holding it against his chest. "Do you have any idea what it was like, hearing you'd died on that plane?"

"I'm sorry." Tears spilled down her cheeks, unchecked. "I wanted to let you know, but Dal said you were in danger—"

"Dal said." He spat the man's name with contempt, his anger finding an easier target. "I don't give a damn what Dal said. *You* told me you were quitting, Risa. We agreed. We were done. It's why you were on your way home from Kaziristan in the first place."

"I know, but—"

"We had a life planned, Risa! You and me and a house of our own in a place we both loved instead of living out of suitcases and passing in the airport, remember?"

She wiped her eyes with her knuckles. "I remember."

He raked his fingers through his hair, trying not to let his emotions get the best of him. *Focus, Marine.* "Who were the men you were following?"

"I don't know," she answered. She sounded as if she was telling the truth, but he realized he just couldn't be certain. Not anymore.

"So why were you following them?" he asked.

She moved toward the window, standing just a little short of it, as if she worried she might be seen from the street. "I shouldn't have come here. People will notice if I don't go home. In some ways, living in an immigrant community can be like living in a small town. Everybody keeps an eye out for everybody else."

He noticed that she had formed a habit of rubbing her belly when she spoke, as if she was soothing the child inside. He didn't want to ask the next question, but he had to.

"Am I the father, Risa?"

RISA HAD BEEN expecting the question. Dreading it, because of what it would mean. But she hadn't realized how much his show of distrust would hurt, even as she understood why he harbored it.

"You're the father," she said simply, because anything else would only exacerbate his doubts.

"And you weren't ever going to tell me I had a child?"

"Honestly, Connor, I hadn't thought that far ahead." She turned back to the window. "I was supposed to be on the plane. But Dal had heard chatter that al Adar had put a target on my back. We knew they had people placed in the airports and other means of transportation."

"So he took you off the plane and sent two hundred and twelve other people to their deaths to fake yours?"

"God, no!" She turned to look at him. "I would never have allowed that. You know that."

"But it's what happened, isn't it?"

He looked so angry, she thought, her own chest tightening in response. Was anger the only feeling he had left for her now?

"He seemed genuinely shocked by the bomb on the plane. Connor, he sent another agent on that plane to take my place so al Adar would think I was going to be landing in San Diego as we planned."

Pain flashed across his expression. "I was waiting

there. For hours. They didn't tell us right away that something had gone wrong. I got a call from Jason Ridgeway. He'd seen it on the news. A Russian airliner had disappeared somewhere over the Pacific."

"I'm sorry. It wasn't supposed to happen that way."

He took a deep breath and let it out slowly, raking his hand through his already-tousled hair. "Okay. You didn't expect the crash. But what about after that? You couldn't let me know you were alive?"

"Dal said—"

"I don't care what Dal said!" His voice came out in a pained roar. He turned his back to her, visibly trying to regain control. She waited silently, giving him time and space to do so.

Finally, he faced her. "I'm sorry. What did Dal say?"

"It doesn't matter. I should have contacted you. I was just—it was one thing to think I was being targeted. But to know that they'd kill over two hundred people just to kill me—"

"Pretty shattering, huh?" For the first time, Connor sounded sympathetic.

"Very shattering." She pressed her palm against the curve of her belly, taking comfort in the gentle wriggling of the baby inside her. He—or she—could probably sense her tension. Not for the first time, she wondered whether she was carrying a girl or a boy. Her ob-gyn had offered her the chance to find out the baby's sex, but she'd wanted to wait until birth.

Until this moment, she hadn't known why she'd wanted to wait. But watching Connor's gaze follow the movement of her hand, she realized she had always hoped that somehow, against all odds, she'd be able to share the birth of this child with her husband.

He might never forgive her for letting him believe she was dead so long, but she had no doubt whatsoever that he'd love their child.

"Why are you here in Cincinnati, pretending to be a Kaziri widow?"

She sighed. "Sometimes, I wonder that myself."

Connor looked at her through narrowed eyes. "You look tired."

"I had to walk eight blocks for my doctor's appointment this morning, and then I was on my feet for hours at work."

"And then you followed a couple of men down a dark street."

"Yeah. Not my finest moment."

He pulled a chair away from the table. "Take a load off."

She took a seat, swallowing a sigh of pure relief. She looked down at her feet and saw that her ankles were looking a little puffy. "Ugh, whoever said women glow when they're pregnant was probably blind or demented. I've just inflated."

Connor smiled, giving her the first glimpse of his dimples in forever. Her heart turned a couple of flips in her chest at the sight, just as it had the first time he'd smiled at her. "You look beautiful. You always do."

The kindness in his voice, the sincerity of the sentiment, drew hot tears to her eyes. "I shouldn't be glad you're here, because you've probably put yourself in terrible danger. But I am. I'm so, so glad you're here."

He started to reach out his hand toward her, but he stopped midmovement and let his hand drop to his lap. "Are you?"

She swallowed her disappointment. "Yes, of course. But how did you find me?"

He reached down and pulled a battered-looking brief-case up to the table, unfastened the buckle and pulled a tablet computer from inside. He swiped his finger across the screen, then tapped a couple of times before he handed the tablet to her.

She looked down and saw a photo of a Free Kaziristan rally that several people in the community had held a couple of weeks earlier. She hadn't attended the rally herself, not wanting to put herself in the spotlight of ref-ugee politics in any way, but the rally had taken place on the street in front of the restaurant. She'd had to pass through the throngs to get to work.

She looked lifeless in the photo. Was that how she always looked?

"I kept telling myself it couldn't be you." Connor's voice rumbled low and soft, like thunder in the distance. "You wouldn't have let me think you were dead. But there you were."

"Connor—"

A loud trio of raps on the door cut her short, the sound sending a hard jolt of alarm down her spine.

"Go to the bedroom," Connor said softly, already on his feet. He pulled a large Ruger pistol from his bag and tucked it in his waistband behind his back, letting his jacket drop to cover it.

Risa hurried down the hallway into the bedroom, her heart fluttering with fear. If someone from the commu-nity had seen her come into this apartment with Connor, everything she'd spent the past few months trying to set up would be destroyed.

And she and Connor would be in the worst danger of their lives.

CONNOR LOOKED THROUGH the security lens and saw a familiar face staring back at him. He turned the dead bolt and disengaged the security chain, then opened the door to a bearded man wearing a high-collared shirt and plain khaki pants. His visitor's hazel gaze swept the room quickly.

"Where is she?" he asked.

"Nice seeing you, too, Quinn."

Alexander Quinn didn't wait for an invitation, entering and nodding for Connor to close the door behind him. As Connor reengaged the locks, Quinn crossed to both of the street-facing windows and shut the blinds.

"Heller says it's her. So I tried her apartment. She wasn't home. Then I tried her workplace, and she wasn't there, either."

"I told you I'd handle things my own way." Connor heard the tight annoyance in his own voice but couldn't seem to care. "So why *are* you here, anyway?"

"Because Martin Dalrymple has been murdered."

Chapter Four

Though Alexander Quinn spoke quietly, the apartment was small enough that his voice carried down the hall to Risa's hiding place. She had reached the hallway when she heard his words about Martin Dalrymple.

"Dal's dead?"

Connor and Quinn both turned to look at her.

"You look well," Quinn said.

"Yeah, well, you're a pathological liar," she answered, hoping he was lying about Dal as well. "I talked to Dal not long ago."

Except it hadn't really been that recent, had it? He hadn't responded to her last message, which was highly unusual. He might already have been dead by then, she realized, trying to remember the last time she'd actually connected with her boss. It had been early this morning. He'd sent an email, asking her for an update. She hadn't had a chance to respond before her trip to the doctor. And then, afterward, she'd started to feel as if she were being watched.

Had that been Connor's scrutiny she'd been sensing? Or was it something else?

"Dalrymple's body was found this afternoon in Rock Creek Park."

She shook her head. "He wasn't in DC. He said he'd left the city a couple of weeks ago for a more secluded place."

"All I can tell you is what I know. It's Dalrymple. And he's dead."

"You're sure it's murder?" Connor asked.

"Two gunshots to the head. Double tap."

"Execution style," Risa murmured.

"Considering his line of work, most likely."

She pressed her fingertips to her throbbing temples. "I sent him an email earlier today. He never got back to me. I guess now I know why."

"Was it encrypted?" Quinn asked.

"Of course. Agency-level cipher, plus electronic encryption." Her legs felt wobbly. She crossed to one of the chairs at the table, bending forward and taking a couple of deep breaths.

Connor reached her within a second, crouching by her side to look up at her. He rested his hand on her knee. "You okay?"

"I'm fine." She covered his hand with hers. "It's just been a long, stressful day. And now Dal…"

"If the person or persons who killed Dalrymple managed to get their hands on his communications, Risa could be in grave danger," Quinn warned. He'd stayed where he was, near the door. "You should both come back with me to Campbell Cove."

Risa looked up at Quinn. "Where's Campbell Cove?"

"Eastern Kentucky," Connor said quietly. "I work for Campbell Cove Security Services now."

"Your husband signed on with me not long after the plane crash," Quinn added.

"I thought you were running some place called The

Gates," she said to Quinn. "Down in Tennessee or some-where."

"I was," Quinn said. "I still own the place. But I've trained people there to run The Gates without my day-to-day input. You can say that my country called me back into service."

"So, this is a government agency?" Risa looked at Connor. "I thought you wanted out of that kind of work."

"Technically, it's a government contractor."

"Close enough," she said. "So you changed your mind."

"Circumstances changed my mind." His gaze settled on her face. "You can understand that, can't you?"

She tightened her grip on his hand, wondering how she'd ever thought she could leave him behind, even if it was for his own protection. She'd been miserable without him. Not even the joy of carrying his child had been able to overcome how much she'd missed him.

She'd tried to put him out of her mind, tried to tell herself she had lived most of her life without him, so surely she could live the rest of it without him as well.

But she'd never been able to let him go. Not really. And now that he was here with her again, touching her, gazing at her with those sharp blue eyes that always made her feel deliciously naked and exposed—she couldn't go back. She couldn't walk away again, even for his own safety.

Of course, it was possible that he didn't want her back in his life, after the way she'd betrayed him by letting him believe she was dead.

He stood, pulling his hand away from her grasp. "So, what now?" he asked Quinn.

Quinn looked at Risa. "Is there anything in your apartment you need?"

"My gun and my computer. A couple of changes of clothes would be good, too. Everything else is in my purse." She nodded toward the shoulder bag sitting on the table next to her.

"I'll go get her things," Connor volunteered.

"No. You'd raise too many eyebrows. I'll go get what I need." She pushed to her feet, trying not to grimace at the ache in her back and thighs.

"You've been on your feet all day," Connor protested.

"Let her do this," Quinn said quietly. "She's the one who's been here for months. This is her territory. We're strangers."

"She's not going alone."

"You can wait in the alley behind my apartment building," Risa suggested, grabbing her purse. She pulled a pen and a small notepad from inside and jotted something on one of the pages, tore it out and handed it to Connor. "This is my address. There's a fire escape just outside my window. If anything goes wrong, I'll come down that way. Okay?"

Connor looked from her to Quinn, then back to her again before he nodded. "Okay. Let me at least call you a taxi."

"No." She grabbed the coat she'd draped over one of the chairs and picked up her purse. "People in my neighborhood know I don't make enough money to take taxis. There's a bus that runs past this street in ten minutes. I'll catch it. You can catch it with me, but we have to act like strangers. You can't sit with me or talk to me."

Connor's brow furrowed and his mouth tightened, but he nodded.

"I'll wait here," Quinn said, settling in the chair by the window. He tilted it back on two legs and tapped his watch. "Nine minutes now. Better get a move on."

"I'll go first." Risa finished buttoning her coat and started toward the door. "Wait a couple of minutes, then you come down after me. I'll be waiting at the bus stop. And you should get off at the stop before my street. It's the one on Vine, near Washington Park. I assume you can find my place from there."

"Of course," he agreed.

She slipped out the front door, her heart already starting to race. Logically, she knew that she was probably as safe now as she had been before she'd learned the news of Dal's death. He had been a target long before he'd sent her to Cincinnati, and the people who killed him probably had no idea how many different missions he had running at any given time. He could have been killed for one of those other missions, not hers.

But as she reached the street and walked the half block to the bus stop, she couldn't help feeling as if she had an enormous neon target on her back. Those Kaziri men had seen her outside the building they'd entered. From a distance, yes, on a dark street, but had they seen enough to make it easy for them to recognize her if they saw her again?

What if they were already asking questions around the neighborhood, trying to figure out who the pregnant woman in the dark *roosari* might be?

Stop it, she admonished herself. They probably hadn't gotten a good look at her at all. And she'd been wearing her coat, which might have hidden her pregnant belly well enough in the dark at that distance.

She would go home the way she normally did. If she'd

worked her full shift, and maybe stayed behind to help with the after-hours cleanup, she wouldn't be home much earlier than now anyway.

Everything was going to be fine.

"YOU MUST FEEL as if you're in some sort of surreal dream," Quinn commented in an offhand tone that Connor knew was anything *but* offhand.

"You're not seriously going to try to shrink me now, are you?" Connor zipped his jacket and turned to look at his boss. "Because you would surely know that trying to handle me that way would just royally piss me off."

"You just found out your dead wife is alive and carrying your baby. That's not something you can train for."

"I've got five minutes to get down to the bus stop before I miss my ride. Let's not talk about this now. Or ever."

Quinn lifted his hands with a shrug of surrender. "Don't stay out too late, McGinnis. Time isn't on your side."

Quelling the urge to throw something at the man, Connor opened his door. "I'll be back soon. Don't touch any of my stuff. I *will* know if you do."

The night had managed to grow even more bitterly cold, making him wish he'd added another layer of clothing beneath his leather jacket before he left the apartment. He spotted Risa sitting on the concrete bench situated near the bus-stop sign on the corner, her slender arms wrapped around herself as if to ward off the cold. Her wool coat looked as if it had come out of a charity bin, the material thin in places and appearing ill-equipped to protect her from the cold wind. She'd donned the *roosari* again, he saw. Playing the part of the Kaziri widow.

He kept his distance, as they'd agreed, not even sharing more than a glance with her. But the forced separation only served to make him more aware of her than ever.

And with the awareness came a gut-twisting sense of anxiety that if he turned his head too far and lost sight of her even in the corner of his eye, she'd disappear from his life again, gone forever.

The sight of the blue-and-white Metro bus came as a relief. With a faint squeal of brakes, the bus lumbered to a stop and idled with a low grumble as Risa put her money in the fare box and took a seat near the exit door in the middle of the bus.

Connor paid his own fare and sat on the opposite side of the bus, a few seats back from her. They were among only a handful of riders on the bus at this time of night, most of them young. The pretty African American girl who sat across the aisle from him appeared to be a student, her well-used backpack sitting on the seat beside her while she pored through a large history book spread out on her lap.

Two olive-skinned men in their early twenties sat together a couple of seats ahead of Risa. The one on the aisle turned to look at her, his expression full of disdain.

When he spoke, it was in Kaziri, his tone low and mean. "Are you a whore?"

Risa's back stiffened, but she didn't respond.

The man who sat with him turned to see who his friend was talking to. His brow furrowed, though more in concern than disdain. "Does your father allow you to travel at night alone?" he asked in English.

"I am here alone," Risa answered in heavily accented English. "I have no father to protect me. Please, leave me be."

"Your child has no father?" the first man asked.

"Leave her alone." The studious girl had put down her book and now stood, glaring at the two men across the column of seats. "Those questions aren't your business."

The young man who'd spoken to Risa with concern looked embarrassed and turned quickly toward the front of the bus, but the other man glared at the student for a moment before he turned around and started speaking in low tones with his friend.

Risa turned to the young woman. "Thank you," she said softly.

The student moved her backpack to the floor of the bus and patted the seat beside her. "You can come sit with me if you want."

Risa glanced across at Connor for a brief second before she rose and joined the student across the aisle.

"I'm Kyla," the girl said with a friendly smile.

"Yasmin."

"Nice to meet you."

Though Connor tried to look relaxed and uninterested, he kept one ear open to their small talk while he kept both eyes on the young men at the front of the bus. Fortunately, they exited at the next stop and he was able to drop his guard a little until he reached his own stop.

He wished now he hadn't agreed to get off first. He should have let her exit the bus first, and then get off at the following stop. But the plan was already under way, so he got off the bus when it pulled to a halt and started down the block toward the address Risa had given him.

He'd entered the location on his phone before he left his place. Now he followed the directions, moving at a brisk jog along the mostly deserted sidewalks. As he neared the corner of her block and made the turn, he saw the bus pulling away from the curb.

Risa was walking toward him, her head lowered against the wind. She slowed when she reached the front stoop of a shabby three-story brownstone building in the middle of the block. As she opened the front door, she lifted her gaze to meet his. She didn't show any sign of recognition, only moved a little more quickly into the building.

She'd told him there was an alley between her apartment building and the next. He found the darkened breezeway, which was little more than a footpath between the buildings. Overhead, alternating fire escapes created an open-air canopy that offered no shelter but some small measure of concealment in the darkness.

Her apartment was on the second floor, in the corner facing the alley. Leaning against the cold brick of the opposite building, he fixed his gaze on the dark window, waiting for light as he counted the seconds. Ten. Twenty. Thirty.

There. A light appeared in the window.

He let himself breathe again.

RISA HAD NO idea where she was supposed to sleep in Connor's half-empty apartment, but she didn't particularly care. She was tired enough to curl up in a corner on a spare towel and sleep for a week.

But first, she had to grab anything that a nosy landlord might find that would suggest she was anyone but the pregnant widow she'd portrayed for the past seven months. Her disappearance was going to raise enough eyebrows as it was.

Dal had supplied her with a backpack in which to hide

the laptop and other communications equipment he'd provided for her. The exterior of the pack looked old and well-used, concealing all signs of the expensive equipment inside. She stuffed a few changes of clothing and all of her toiletries in a gym bag she'd picked up on her own at a discount store. Anything she didn't think she'd need, she left behind, along with the cash she'd saved up to pay the next month's rent.

Going from room to room, she checked behind doors and under furniture to make sure she hadn't forgotten anything that might give someone any clues to her real identity. The apartment was small, but over the past seven months, she realized, she'd turned it into something of a home.

But her life here had never been anything more than a facade. Yasmin Hamani was a mask she'd worn to protect herself and her child.

And to protect Connor as well, though she didn't think he could see her choice that way. Not yet.

Maybe not ever.

Finally satisfied she'd left nothing of importance behind, she shouldered the heavy backpack, gripped the duffel bag in one hand and unlocked her front door. After one last backward glance, she turned out the lights and shut the door behind her.

She had made it only a few steps into the stairwell when she heard a man speaking Kaziri. His words drifted up from the first floor. "You are sure this is the place?"

Daring a quick glance over the railing to the floor below, she saw a flash of bright embroidery as the wearer headed up the steps.

It was one of the Kaziri men she'd followed from the restaurant. What was he doing here, of all places?

A second voice, even more familiar, answered her question as well as the Kaziri man's. "This is the address she gave when she took the job," Farid Rahimi answered, his tone surprisingly reluctant. "Why do you want to see her? She is nobody. A poor widow."

Damn it. They were talking about her.

There was another set of stairs at the far end of the hall, but she'd never reach them before the men arrived on her floor. Instead, she scurried back into her apartment and locked the door behind her.

She left the lights off, hoping they might think she was still out. But the person who knocked on the door wasn't Farid or the Kaziri customer.

"Mrs. Hamani? Are you home?"

The voice on the other side of the door was Joe Trammel, her landlord.

And he had a key.

Tamping down a burst of adrenaline, she backed deeper into the small apartment, toward the bedroom. She could hide in the closet or under the bed. Surely they wouldn't do a thorough search of the place with Mr. Trammel there watching.

She heard the rattle of keys in the front door and hunkered down by the bed, ready to slide under it. But the bulge of her belly, pressing hard against her chest, caught her by surprise.

Damn it. No way could she get her pregnant belly under that bed.

She stood and moved toward the closet, listening for a voice in the front room. Joe Trammel spoke first, his voice loud and a little impatient. "Maybe she didn't realize she was supposed to work tonight, ever think of that?"

Farid must have lied to the landlord, told him she hadn't shown up for work. Damn it.

"She is one of my best workers," Farid answered. "She would not miss work. Something may be terribly wrong with her. Maybe her baby has come?"

Trammel sounded faintly horrified. "You think?"

"We will check now, yes?" That was the other man, the one who'd looked familiar to Risa. He spoke with a flawless British accent, as if he'd been schooled there. Which, she supposed, wasn't at all unusual in the world of terrorism these days.

"It's just—I was just about to run out and pick up my wife from work," Trammel said. "I don't want to leave her out there in the cold waiting—"

"You go pick up your wife." Farid spoke in his most appeasing "the customer is always right" tone of voice. "I will stay here until you get back. Perhaps Yasmin will return and all will be well. But if she doesn't, and I find anything troubling, we can decide if we should call the police when you get back. It's a good plan, yes?"

"All right," Trammel said, although Risa heard a hint of unease in his tone. But apparently he overcame the doubt, his heavy footsteps moving away from the apartment.

Risa's heart sank. Now she was alone with Farid and the mystery man. Not good odds. Not good at all.

She had to get out of here.

Hearing them moving around out in the front room, she made her move, easing the lower sash of the window silently upward. One of the first things she'd done upon moving into the apartment was make sure the window sash that opened onto the fire escape could be raised without effort—or sound. She'd just hoped she'd never have reason to make a quiet escape.

She should have known better.

Icy air poured into the room as she lifted her duffel and backpack over the sill and out onto the fire escape outside. As she started to follow, she heard Farid and the other man approaching the bedroom and froze. The men conversed in Kaziri, their voices almost too quiet to make out. She heard words more than sentences— "strange woman" and "surveillance" made it to where she waited by the window.

Their voices came nearer, moving down the hallway. This time, a full sentence came through, loud and clear, from the Kaziri man she'd tried to follow earlier in the evening. "Could she be a spy?"

"Yasmin? No. She is a meek little mouse," Farid answered.

"Mice can do great damage," the other man said grimly.

Risa heard footsteps just outside her bedroom door. She didn't wait for them to enter, stepping out onto the fire escape, her heart in her throat.

Chapter Five

The light in the apartment had gone out a couple of minutes ago, and Connor had breathed a sigh of relief, expecting Risa to appear in the alley any minute. But the light in the window had appeared again moments later.

Had she forgotten something?

Or had she planned all along to ditch him?

As he pushed himself away from the wall, the faint creak of metal scraping against metal made him freeze in place. Moving only his eyes, he looked up at Risa's window and saw a shadowy figure silhouetted briefly against the light in the window. Then, with a soft rattle of iron, the figure dropped the fire escape ladder and began to descend.

It was Risa.

Connor hurried over to the lowered ladder, holding his breath as she started climbing down, her descent encumbered by the small duffel bag and backpack dangling from her arms.

She looked down at him, fear glinting in her eyes. "Take the bags," she hissed, letting them drop into his outstretched hands one at a time.

He caught the bags and put them on the ground, then reached up to help her the rest of the way down. Even carrying the extra weight of the baby, she felt fragile and light.

Breakable.

He'd never thought of her as breakable before.

"My boss and one of those two men from the diner tricked my landlord into letting them in my apartment." Her voice was barely a breath in his ear. "Let's get out of here. Fast, before they spot us."

He pushed her ahead of him and grabbed the bags. The backpack was as heavy as it had felt when he caught it, making him wonder what it contained. Her laptop? Other equipment?

What kind of operation had she and Dal been running?

At the end of the alley, he dared a glance back. Spotting a man's head lean forward to look out the window, he hurried around the corner of the building, hoping they'd made it out of sight in time.

"What excuse did they give the landlord to get inside?" he asked Risa as he caught up to her. She was walking ahead of him, moving at a surprisingly quick clip after the stressful, tiring day she'd just lived.

"Welfare check, from what I heard. My boss must have lied and said I didn't show for work. I guess, since I'm pregnant, it was enough to make my landlord worry that I might be in trouble." She darted a look behind them. "There's a bus stop two blocks this way."

She started across the empty street, leaving him to follow.

They reached the bus stop in five minutes. "There should be one more bus scheduled tonight," she told him.

"Are you sure?"

She slanted a look up at him, a slight smile curving her lips. "I checked the bus schedule online before

I packed up my computer. In case we needed to make a fast getaway."

Resourceful, he thought. That was Risa.

He felt a familiar tug low in his gut, a pull of attraction and admiration and awe, all wrapped up in one small, brilliant woman. And then, like a slow rolling detonation, the delayed impact of the reality he'd been tamping down beneath his game face finally hit him with devastating force.

She's alive.

Shock waves of pent-up emotion blew through him, and he ended up dropping to the cold bus-stop bench before his knees buckled.

He took several deep breaths, his heart hammering as if he'd run for miles. Risa sat, her compact body warm beside him, and she put her hand on his arm.

"What's wrong?"

How could he tell her what he was feeling when he couldn't trust the emotions? Yes, he was thrilled beyond words that she was alive. He had mourned her deeply, longed for her when she was no longer within his reach, but those feelings seemed to belong to another person.

A person who couldn't have imagined that his wife would let him believe she was dead when she was very much alive.

And carrying his child.

He forced himself to leash those dangerous feelings again, pack them away in the rucksack of his self-control. "Nothing," he answered, already feeling his body coming back under control, his heart rate subsiding and his breathing resuming a normal cadence.

Risa's eyes narrowed as if she knew better, but she

didn't push. She just turned her face back toward the street. "There's the bus."

There was little point in sitting apart on the nearly empty bus. In retrieving her things from her apartment, Risa had closed the door on the pregnant Kaziri widow named Yasmin Hamani. She sat close to Connor one row back from the side door of the bus, where they could keep an eye on anyone entering or exiting the bus until they'd reached his apartment.

"I guess we need to discuss sleeping arrangements," Risa murmured. Now that she'd stopped using the Kaziri accent she'd affected for her undercover work, her Georgia drawl was back, all sweet honeysuckle and sultry humidity.

Desire gnawed low in his belly, but he made himself ignore it. "I have a sleeping bag I can use until we can arrange something else."

She slanted a narrow-eyed look at him but said nothing more, and they passed the next few minutes in silence.

They exited the Metro bus about two blocks from the walk-up he was renting. Risa released a soft sigh as she looked up the stairs, but she trudged upward without complaint, waiting for him to catch up.

Quinn was still there when they entered the apartment, waiting in the chair by the window. He sat facing the door, watching calmly as they entered. "I take it the op went well?" His tone was dry and slightly amused.

"Not exactly." Risa sank onto one of the chairs by the table and stretched her legs out in front of her. She rolled her neck side to side and flexed her back, her eyes closing with concentration, as if she could somehow will away the tiredness.

Connor took two strides toward her before he caught

himself, remembering that seven long, painful months
had passed since he'd last given her a foot rub. They
weren't the same people anymore.

He didn't know if they ever could be again.

He changed course, walking to the window. "Risa's
boss at the restaurant and one of the men she followed
tonight talked their way into searching her apartment."

Quinn rose in alarm. "While she was there? Did he
see her?"

"She was in the apartment, but she went out the bedroom window. Took the fire escape down to the alley
and we left that way. I'm not sure if the guy saw us or
not. It was dark. At most, he might have gotten a glimpse
of me."

Quinn's gaze moved to where Risa sat slumped in
her chair. "You need to get out of Cincinnati," he said
to Connor.

"But the assignment—"

"Can be covered by another operative," Quinn finished firmly. "You need to get Risa out of here and to
one of our safe houses in the hills."

By hills, Connor knew, Quinn meant the mountains of
eastern Kentucky, where the security company was located. There were hollows and coves in those hills where
a man could get lost forever, by accident or by choice.

"I don't think anyone here has figured out who I really am," Risa said. Even her honeysuckle drawl sounded
bone-tired. "And if you think I'm going to go anywhere
else tonight after the day I've had—"

"It's a four-hour drive in a comfortable Chevy Tahoe.
Heated reclining seats, satellite radio—" Quinn pulled
a set of keys from his pocket. "I'll stay here tonight, in

case anyone comes calling. Leave me your car keys, Mc-Ginnis."

Risa looked at Connor, as if asking his opinion.

"I think we should go tonight," he told her. "If those guys are suspicious of you, they're going to keep looking into who you are. And if they find out you're still alive—"

"Dal was trying to figure out who had put the hit on me." A flicker of pain passed through her weary expression. "Now he's dead. And I don't know what he found out."

"We have people looking into that homicide investigation," Quinn said. "I can keep you apprised."

"This safe house—are we going to have armed guards there?"

"No. We'll just provide you with extra weapons." Quinn's eyes sparked with wry amusement. "You're both capable of protecting yourselves, and the smaller the footprint, the better."

"So we'll be all alone. Just the two of us." Risa's gaze met Connor's. Tension coiled low in his belly at the thought.

"Weren't you going to be alone together here tonight anyway? At least there, you'll actually have furniture." Quinn traded keys with Connor. If he was aware of the sudden rise of tension in the room, he didn't comment. "We'll have a regular schedule of check-ins. Don't worry. Just get there tonight. Settle in. Someone will be in touch."

RISA WOKE TO the sound of windshield wiper blades swishing in a steady rhythm. Otherwise, the cab of the large black SUV was quiet. As she pulled her reclined seat upright, Connor glanced her way. "Started snowing again about an hour ago. It's going to add some time to the drive."

She rubbed her gritty eyes and looked through the windshield, where the Tahoe's headlights illuminated a thick flurry of falling snow that had already begun sticking to the road in slick patches. "How far out are we now?"

"Maybe an hour."

The clock on the dashboard read four thirty. They had already been on the road for more than the four promised hours. "You sure we can drive up a mountain in this weather?"

"Four-wheel drive. Quinn says we'll make it."

Quinn says, she thought, *and people believe*. The man had never been part of her unit when they were both in the CIA, but she knew enough of his reputation to recognize he'd earned at least some of the belief people placed in his wisdom and knowledge.

But she also knew enough about life in the CIA to know that he'd speak with authority on subjects he knew little about if he thought it would get the job done.

"You don't like Quinn," Connor commented, as if reading her thoughts. He used to be ridiculously good at reading her, she remembered. It had been terrifying on one level, and deeply comforting on another. To be known so well, to be understood—

How could she have let Dal convince her she had to let go of Connor after the plane crash? Was he in any less danger if people thought she was dead? Connor had been a marine. He faced death daily in his work, and even now that he was out of the Corps, he still seemed to be working a job that came with its own share of danger.

She hadn't spared him anything at all. And she could imagine the pain she'd inflicted on him by letting him believe she was dead.

If she'd thought he was dead, she'd have been utterly devastated.

"I'm sorry, Connor."

He slanted a quick look her way before concentrating on the deteriorating weather conditions outside the SUV. "For what?"

"I made a terrible decision. I get it now."

"Hindsight and all that," he said, his tone free of emotion.

"You're never going to forgive me, are you?"

"Risa, we're tired. We're driving in snow and we're going to a strange place so that people we don't know can't find us. It's taking every ounce of my remaining consciousness to keep this behemoth of a vehicle on this slick road. Let's just get to the safe house and get some sleep. We can hang out all our dirty laundry tomorrow, okay?"

"Fine." She swallowed the anger that rose in her chest at his weary tone, reminding herself that she was the one who'd made the mistake, not Connor. She owed him a little patience and forgiveness of her own, even when his unemotional handling of this crazy situation made her wonder if he'd ever really loved her at all.

The safe house turned out to be a small farmhouse of clapboard and river stone in the mountains northeast of Cumberland, Kentucky. The narrow, winding road to the safe house was paved with gravel, and while by the time they reached the road, snow had hidden most of the loose stones from view, the *snap-pop* of the Tahoe's tires on the loosely packed gravel gave away their presence.

The house itself was hidden from view for most of the journey, appearing suddenly as the road took a bend along the banks of a large creek. A narrow iron bridge spanned the creek, acting as a driveway for the house, which lay not far from the bridge's end.

"Quinn says there's a key to the house hidden in one of the foundation stones near the back stoop," Connor said as they parked the SUV out of sight behind the house.

Risa eyed the hundreds of stones that made up the house's foundation. "That's helpful."

"Stay in here where it's warm and dry. I'll see if I can find it." Connor stepped out of the SUV, leaving the engine running for heat. Risa might normally have insisted on joining him in the key search, two sets of eyes being better than one, but she was tired, her back was aching, and going out in the snow probably wouldn't be good for the baby.

Connor turned around, finally, holding up something shiny. She thought he even cracked a smile before he climbed the three low steps of the back stoop and unlocked the door, but that might have been wishful thinking, for when he came back to the vehicle, his deadpan expression was firmly back in place.

"Quinn must have called someone to let them know we were coming," he told her as he helped her out of the passenger seat. "The heat and electricity are on, and there's a fire laid in the hearth just waiting for a match."

"I need a bathroom and a half gallon of water, in that order," she said as he grabbed their bags from the back of the Tahoe. As she started up the short path to the house, he hurried to her side, cupping one hand under her elbow.

"Careful, it's slick out here." He helped her up the

stairs and into the house, then went back out to get the rest of their bags.

The back door opened into a small, clean kitchen. Connor had turned on the lights, which shed a warm glow over the Formica countertops and steel appliances. This part of the house, at least, was blessedly warm.

"Any chance the fridge is stocked?" she wondered aloud as Connor brought the rest of the bags inside.

His gaze dropped to her round belly. "You and the munchkin are hungry, huh?"

"Yes, but mostly I'm thinking about later this morning when it's time for breakfast."

"Well, let's check." He opened the refrigerator, revealing that it was partially stocked. There were a couple of cartons of eggs, both with expiration dates several days away. The gallon of milk was also new, and in the freezer, there were several frozen dinners, frozen fruit, a couple of fish fillets wrapped in butcher paper and cellophane, and a pint of chocolate ice cream.

It was the ice cream that made Risa's stomach growl. As if in response to the rumbling sound, the baby started to kick wildly against her abdomen.

On impulse, she shut the freezer door and grabbed Connor's hand, placing it on the swell of her belly. "Feel that?"

His hand went tense beneath her touch and he frowned. Then the baby gave another hefty kick and Connor's gaze snapped up to meet hers. "Was that the baby?"

She smiled at his thunderstruck expression. "Yeah. That's him. Or her."

"How far along are you?" He moved his hand lightly over her belly, as if willing the baby to kick again.

"A little over eight months. About thirty-seven weeks. Not long now."

Connor dropped his hand from her belly and looked around the small kitchen, his brow knotting with dismay. "And you're stuck out here in the middle of nowhere."

"We have a vehicle. We're not that far from civilization, are we?"

He shook his head, though his expression showed no sign of relaxing. "I think we're maybe ten minutes northeast of Cumberland."

"So we just get online in the morning and figure out where the closest ob-gyn can be found."

"Assuming there's a way we can get online here," he muttered.

"We have phones." She put her hand on his arm. "It's all right, Connor. Women have been having babies for years, and some of them do it without a doctor in sight. Plus, I'm still nearly four weeks away from my due date, and since it's my first baby, I might even be a week late. We don't have to worry about this tonight. Okay?"

He looked at her hand on his arm. "And you've been going through this all by yourself for seven months?"

"I had Dal to talk to." She dropped her hand away, not wanting him to feel sorry for her. She had made the decision to handle the danger hanging over her head the way she had, hidden and alone.

Her choice. Her consequences.

WHEN RISA EMERGED from the bathroom, her hair was wet. She'd taken a bag into the bathroom with her and had changed into soft cotton pajamas obviously cut to accommodate her pregnancy.

Connor watched, mesmerized, as she entered the den where he'd started a blazing fire to ward off the cold. Outside, snow had begun to fall in earnest, already covering the ground outside with a fluffy blanket of white. He'd tried checking the weather on his phone, but he could barely get a signal, and certainly not one strong enough to sustain an internet connection.

He'd made only a cursory exploration of the rest of the house, enough to see that they seemed to have cable TV, which he hoped might mean there was some sort of cable or DSL connection available for the internet. But he'd worry about that later. He and Risa both needed sleep.

"Feel better?" he asked as she crossed to where he sat in front of the fire.

"Cleaner, anyway." She reached her hands toward the fire, flexing her fingers. "Lovely fire."

Pregnancy suited her, he thought. It softened the angular edges of her face and gave her skin a warm glow that even her weariness couldn't quite extinguish.

And he'd missed most of it, damn it. "I wish I'd known."

He hadn't meant to say the words aloud, but he didn't have to explain what he meant. Risa followed his gaze to her pregnant belly and gave him a regretful look. "I should have told you. I shouldn't have let Dal talk me into trying to handle everything by myself. But it's just—"

"It's how you've always done it. I know. I remember."

She drew her hands away from the fire's heat and twined them together on what was left of her lap. "It wasn't anything to do with us. With you or the way I feel about you. I need you to understand that."

"I do." He knew she loved him. Love had never been an issue between them. "But you can't let go of even a tiny piece of your autonomy, can you?"

"I've had to take care of myself all by myself for a

long time. Letting someone else take care of me, take risks for me—"

"Doesn't come naturally."

She leaned her head back against the chair cushion. "I know I've been a disappointment to you."

"Don't do that."

Her eyes, which had drifted shut, snapped open to look at him. "Do what?"

"Turn this around on me. Don't try to make me feel guilty about the way I'm feeling. You're the one who left. You're the one who lied." As the anger and pain he'd been bottling up started to bubble to the surface, he rose from the chair and walked away, needing the distance to get his emotions back under control.

"You're feeling something?" she shot back at him. "That's new. I thought you never let yourself feel anything on a mission."

Her comeback hit painfully close to home. "So this is my mission? And you're what, the client I'm charged to protect? Is that how you want this to go, Risa? Because I'm trained to handle it."

She closed her eyes again, slumping deeper in her chair. "I don't want to dive headfirst into the mess I've made of our marriage right now. Okay? I just want to get some sleep. In the morning, we can rip what's left of it to shreds if you want. But not tonight." She staggered to her feet and headed down the narrow hall, opening the door to one of the two bedrooms and disappearing inside.

Connor stared after her long after the door clicked shut behind her. His gut was burning with restrained emotions, love, anger and pain all wrapped up in a writhing knot in the pit of his stomach.

"You didn't make the mess alone, sweetheart," he whispered.

Chapter Six

Risa woke to the mouthwatering aroma of eggs and toast, but the bedroom was cold enough to give her pause before she finally crawled out from beneath a pile of warm blankets. She dressed quickly in maternity jeans, thick socks and a long-sleeved sweater, and wandered down the hall to the kitchen to find Connor.

"Good. You're up." Connor was at the counter, spreading butter onto a couple of pieces of toast. He waved toward the stools on the other side of the breakfast bar. "Can you drink coffee?"

"I've given it up for now," she said with regret. "The doctor said I could probably have a cup a day, but you know me and coffee. I can't stop at a cup a day."

He gave her a sympathetic wince. "Had to go cold turkey, huh?"

"Yeah." She found herself eyeing him warily as he spooned scrambled eggs onto two plates and added a slice of toast to each. Considering the tension still roiling between them the previous night when she went to bed, Connor seemed awfully chipper. "Did you get any sleep?"

"A couple of hours. I didn't want to sleep too long, though. We have a lot to do today."

She scooped up a forkful of eggs. "We have an agenda for the day, I take it?"

"Well, I do. And I could use your help if you feel up to it. But I can do it alone, at least for a while. If you want to catch up on your sleep."

She glanced at her watch. It was only nine thirty. She'd managed about four hours of sleep. It would have to do. "No, I'm good. What are we doing today?"

"A little mission analysis, I guess you could call it. You and I have been working what seems to me to be two angles of the same investigation. Plus, there's Dal's death and the plane crash earlier this year."

She chewed a bite of toast and thought about what he was saying before she spoke. "For you, it started with that surveillance photo, right? You saw the pregnant Kaziri woman and realized it looked like your dead wife."

"Right." His earlier bright facade slipped a bit.

Imagining what that must have been like for him, she barely kept herself from reaching out to touch him. "That had to have been a real shock."

He ignored the comment. "We think al Adar or some other foreign group—maybe al Qaeda, maybe ISIS—is planning some sort of mass casualty attack. Maybe for the Christmas holidays. But we don't know if it's specifically for Cincinnati, or if they're using Cincinnati as their base of operations."

"Cincinnati doesn't seem as if it would be a big enough target," she said. "They'd want to make a bigger impact, wouldn't they?"

"Maybe. Or maybe they're looking to spread terror out of the bigger cities and into the heartland."

He had a point, she supposed. In the past few years, lower-casualty strikes had already taken place in locations such as an Army base in Texas, a processing plant in Oklahoma and a Navy reserve center in Tennessee. And there was that Christmas party shooting out in California...

Connor picked up his empty plate and took it to the sink. "Those two men from the restaurant—what made you decide to follow them?"

"A couple of things," she said after giving it a thought. "Their flamboyance, for one thing. Most of the people in the Kaziri community try to keep a low profile just out of habit. They came here because of the danger and persecution from al Adar and other jihadi groups, so nobody in the neighborhood likes to stand out. Then here come those two guys, dressed up in their Kaziri finest, throwing their weight around—it was just something out of the ordinary."

"You said there were a couple of things. What was the other?"

"There was something so familiar-looking about one of the men at the diner, and I finally realized why," she said. "Dal used to keep a wall of photos in his office, stuck up on a corkboard. Sort of like most-wanted posters, but in his case, he called them wins. Terrorists who'd been killed or captured."

"And he was one of the people on that wall?"

"I think so. Maybe. It was a glance at a wall months and months ago. And I don't even know his name or anything about him."

"If you're right, this guy clearly wasn't killed. And if he was captured he escaped. Do you know anything about an escaped terrorist?"

"No."

"Neither do I." He leaned back in his chair. "I'll say

this about those guys, though. If they're part of a sleeper cell, they're not doing a very good job of blending in."

Also a good point, she had to concede. "What if they're the diversion?"

"To make us keep an eye on the shiny baubles while the real sleepers make their move?"

"Maybe. They sure weren't happy to see me following them, though."

"They were worried enough to get your boss to help them take a look around your apartment."

She rubbed her chin. "Maybe we shouldn't have left Cincinnati. It makes me look as if I have something to hide."

"You do."

"But now I'm in no position to find out who the real sleepers are, if our theory is correct."

"I don't think you were in any position to find out at all." Connor nodded at her mostly empty plate. "You done?"

"Yeah." She handed over the plate. "You think that being a woman automatically puts me in no position to find out anything that might be going on behind the scenes. That's what you meant, right?"

"You weren't just a woman. You were a pregnant woman with no husband, no family, no money and no standing in the community. I don't know what the hell Dal was thinking putting you in that position."

"I think the idea was that, as a woman, I'd be almost invisible. Able to move around without attracting any real concern."

"Maybe if you were a married woman. Or part of an influential family. But nobody was going to talk freely in front of you."

She hated to admit he was right. But he was.

What had Martin Dalrymple been hoping to accomplish by putting her in the middle of the Kaziri community in southern Ohio? Had he had a secret agenda he hadn't lived long enough to reveal?

"What are you thinking?" Connor asked from where he stood at the sink, washing their breakfast dishes.

"I was thinking about Dal," she admitted. "Everything you're saying is true. I wasn't at all the best choice to go undercover in that community if he was looking for information on jihadis. Unless…"

"Unless what?"

She turned in her chair to face him. "What if he thought there was a terrorist threat coming from the female side of the Kaziri community?"

He leaned against the counter. "You mean female jihadis?"

"We know more and more females are getting involved in terrorism."

"Usually as a sidekick to males."

"If we're right about those two obnoxiously chauvinistic Kaziri men being decoys to hide a sleeper cell, what better place to hide their plot than among the women they openly disdain?" She stood up, stretching her back. She had been in the habit of taking a long morning walk since she'd learned she was pregnant, but there was at least four inches of snow on the ground outside, and none of the clothes she currently owned were very practical for tromping around in the snow. "Don't suppose your company has a home gym hidden in this safe house somewhere?"

"Carrying around Junior in there isn't exercise enough?" There was a hint of affection in his voice and an endearing softness in his gaze as it settled on her pregnant belly.

"I'll need my strength when it comes time to give birth."

He came closer, almost close enough to touch, though he kept his hands at his sides. "Have you been preparing for it?"

"Childbirth?"

He nodded.

"Some, yeah."

"Have you taken Lamaze classes?" His tone was uncomfortable, as if he'd brought up a particularly delicate subject.

She stifled a smile. "No, it's not really something that's popular in the Kaziri community. But there's a Kaziri midwife in the neighborhood—I consulted her along with my doctor. And I've done some reading and practicing on my own."

"On your own," he echoed faintly, turning away to look out the window at the snowy side yard.

She joined him at the window. "I didn't know I was pregnant when this all went into motion. By the time I realized it, it was too late to back out."

He inhaled deeply, releasing his breath in a slow whoosh. "How did we get here?"

She didn't have to ask what he meant.

He turned to look at her. "I thought we were happy."

"We were."

"Then how could you have just walked away?"

"Dal convinced me you would be in grave danger if the people trying to kill me had any inkling I was still alive."

"Dal." He growled the word with disdain. "Now Dal's

dead and you can't even be sure he was telling you the truth, can you?"

"No," she admitted. "But you know there were things I did in Kaziristan that would have made me a pretty valuable target to al Adar."

"Which means you're still a target. If Dal was telling the truth."

"Yeah." The heat of his body beside hers was both a comfort and a source of intense frustration. Every instinct was screaming at her to put her arms around him and bury her face in his chest, to let him wrap his strong arms around her and remind her that she wasn't alone anymore.

But the "don't touch" vibes he was giving off kept her at arm's length. And reminded her that, in all the ways that mattered, she was still alone.

THEY HAD MET on one of the coldest days of the year in Kaziristan, shivering in the icy wind pouring through the mountain gap to whip through their layers of clothing like a hot knife slicing butter. For the first hour, Connor had thought she was a Kaziri informant, there to guide his unit through the treacherous pass on their way to a top-secret, gravely important meeting between the Marines and one of the most powerful tribal leaders in the country.

American efforts to quell the uprising that once again put the troubled republic at risk of another long, deadly civil war had come down to gaining the support of the tribes. Gulan Mohar's good will could potentially save hundreds, even thousands, of lives.

Connor wasn't a politician. He was a warrior, and it had been his job to stay outside the tribal leader's home with the woman while the brain trust talked to Mohar. As they'd waited, she'd started slanting looks at him around the edges of her *roosari*, curious, sultry glances that had set his heart racing.

Then she'd said something in Kaziri he couldn't understand.

"I don't speak the language," he'd told her in Kaziri, some of the only words he'd known at the time.

"No, you really don't," she'd answered in perfect, Georgia-accented English, her broad grin making her hazel eyes sparkle like jewels.

He'd been halfway in love with her before they left Mohar's compound and headed back down the mountain to the operating base.

It had taken a while longer, he remembered with a faint smile, to convince her she was in love with him as well.

She sat at the breakfast bar with her laptop, surfing the internet for information, while he searched the refrigerator for something to turn into lunch. They'd found where the cable modem and wireless router were stored, along with written instructions for setting it up and using the equipment. After appeasing Connor's worries by making a list of obstetricians within a thirty-mile radius, Risa had started looking for information on Martin Dalrymple's death.

"There's no public record of exactly how he died," she'd told him after an hour of searches. "I mean, yes, the reports all say he was shot, but the police seem to be treating it as a robbery gone wrong, not an execution."

"You know the cops aren't going to tell the press everything they know. Especially if they suspect a professional hit."

She'd fallen silent but kept searching the web while he went outside to scout their surroundings.

The snow was soft and wet and would probably melt

before nightfall, as long as the temperature rose into the forties as the forecast predicted. A melt-off would certainly make it easier to make a fast escape if they needed to. But it would also make it that much easier for someone on their tail to find their way up the mountain to this safe house.

At least they were well armed. Both he and Risa had personal weapons, and the set of keys Quinn had given him included a key to a closet down the hall that contained a couple of rifles, a Mossberg shotgun, and hundreds of rounds of ammunition including .45 ammo he could use in his Ruger and .40 rounds that would fit Risa's Glock 23.

"Why did you join Campbell Cove Security?"

Connor looked up from his refrigerator search to find Risa looking at him from her perch at the breakfast bar. Her head was cocked slightly to one side, her eyes bright with curiosity.

"Since I was already planning to leave the Marine Corps before...the plane crash, I went through with it. But then I needed a job. We'd talked about both of us doing something in security consultation, so when Maddox Heller contacted me to see how I was holding up, I guess he realized I needed something to occupy my mind. He, Quinn and a woman named Rebecca Cameron had started the security company a few months earlier. They had also started an academy for ordinary citizens and civilian law enforcement—teaching them skills and tactics for combatting terrorism in their own communities."

"That's a great idea," she said.

"I know. So when he offered the job. I took it."

"I'm glad you had someone looking out for you."

He wondered if he was ever going to reach the point

where talking about the plane crash and the nightmare afterward, knowing the truth about what had really happened, wouldn't make him angry.

He hadn't reached that point yet.

"Just say it, Connor."

"Say what?"

"Say something. Anything. Tell me you hate me for what I did. Tell me you don't even want to look at me. Just say something, because I know you're furious and it's making me crazy to watch you try to hide it."

Something snapped inside him, and as hard as he tried to hold on to his calm, it slipped like water through his fingers, leaving him shaking. "You left me, Risa!"

"Not willingly."

"How can you say that?" He strode away from her, needing distance, needing to breathe. "You let me think you were dead, Risa. One phone call could have fixed that. One stupid phone call!"

Her face showed signs of starting to crumple, but she fought it off, her chin coming up even as her lips trembled. "I know."

Somehow, her strength of will only infuriated him. "*What* do you know, Risa? Do you know that I used to dream every single night for weeks that you'd shown up, safe and sound? That you showed up on the doorstep of our apartment with a smile, telling me that it was all a mistake, that you never got on the plane in the first place?"

He saw her throat bob as she swallowed hard, but she didn't speak.

"I had that dream for weeks. Months. After a while, I lost track. It was the same thing, over and over. I'd wake up, elated, thrilled that you were alive, that you were with me again, and then I'd turn over and look at that empty, cold space on my bed where you used to lie. And it was like losing you all over again."

Her face had gone pale, and she looked as if she were going to be sick. "I'm sorry, Connor. I made a terrible mistake in judgment."

He couldn't stay in this house a moment longer. Grabbing his jacket from the back of the sofa, he headed for the front door.

"Where are you going?" she called after him.

He didn't answer.

SHE WASN'T GOING to cry. She'd done enough crying a few months ago, when she'd made the decision to become another person and leave her old life behind. There wasn't much point in second-guessing the decision at this point. It was done. She couldn't change it.

But maybe she could change the future. Starting with whatever danger might still be hanging over her head.

And Connor's.

So far, all the online articles she'd found regarding Martin Dalrymple's death had been cursory at best. His body had been found in Rock Creek Park early in the afternoon on the previous day. She tried to remember when she'd last spoken to him in person. Three weeks ago? They'd met at a diner in Covington, Kentucky, so he could give her a photograph of a couple of people of interest he wanted her to watch for.

After that, everything she'd received from Dal had come by encrypted email.

He hadn't responded to the last message she'd sent, which made sense, given that he'd been lying dead in Rock Creek Park.

God, Dal was dead. She didn't even know how to feel about that news. Sad? Of course. But she hadn't really been friends with her old boss, had she? Friendships between colleagues could be a liability in the kind of work she'd done for the past decade. She'd learned that from Martin Dalrymple himself.

Had he ever seen her as anything but a useful implement in his espionage toolbox? Had she ever thought of him as something more than a puppeteer, pulling her strings and positioning her exactly where he needed her?

She rubbed her gritty eyes and refreshed the search engine page, hoping a new article had been added to the queue. Because she couldn't shake the growing certainty that whoever had killed Dalrymple was the real danger hanging over her head.

And if she didn't figure out who'd put a price on her head, and soon, she might not get out of this mess alive.

A WATERY SUN had finally begun to break through the clouds overhead, adding an additional layer of warmth to the rising temperatures that had turned the snow underfoot into slush. In the woods surrounding the safe house, snow slid off pine boughs at regular intervals, hitting the ground with soft whooshing plops. Birds sang in the treetops, and somewhere in the distance, he heard the faint rumble of traffic moving along a nearby highway. But otherwise, the world around Connor remained quiet and still, a stark contrast to the maelstrom of disquiet inside his head.

He had to get his feelings under control. Giving in to his anger only gave the situation power over him.

Gave *her* power over him. And he couldn't afford to let that happen. He'd fought damned hard to escape the abyss of grief and despair he'd fallen into after the plane crash. He couldn't go back to that dark place again, even if it was now awash with anger instead of grief.

Maybe especially because of that.

She had made a mistake. They both had. Thinking they could have any sort of real relationship, being the people they were. He was a warrior. She was a spy. They could, at times, be colleagues of a sort, people who shared the same overarching goal, at least, if not the same tactics.

But they never should have tried to be more than that. Never let a few nights of physical release turn into a reckless, hopeless desire for happily-ever-after. It was doomed to disaster from the start. He understood that now.

Maybe she'd done him a favor, proving it sooner rather than later, before their lives became all tangled up with mortgages and—

And what, McGinnis? And kids?

He rubbed his tired eyes. He was going to be a father. With a woman he didn't trust.

And did he even love her now, knowing how she'd hurt him? Would he ever love her again?

That certainly qualified as a whopper of a tangle, didn't it?

He heard the sound of the door opening behind him and turned to find Risa standing in the open doorway, her arms wrapped around her pregnant belly as if she could protect herself—and the baby—from the cold. "Connor?" she called.

He crossed the crusty yard and headed up the porch steps, nodding for her to get back inside. He shook the snow off his boots and followed her into the house, closing the door behind her. "Is something wrong?"

She turned to look at him, her brow furrowed and a

jittery look in her warm hazel eyes. "I found an article online a few minutes ago. With a little more detail about Dal's murder. You know he was found late yesterday afternoon at Rock Creek Park, right?"

Connor nodded.

"Well, the latest article had a quote from the police detective in charge. He said they believed Dal had been dead for at least twenty-four hours before he was found. Maybe even as much as forty-eight."

"So?"

"So, who was it who sent me an email yesterday morning, asking for an update on my mission?"

Chapter Seven

"What do you think it means?"

Risa stopped her pacing to look at Connor, who was watching her from his perch at the breakfast bar. Compared to her own agitation, his calm was preternatural—and downright annoying. "I think it means someone pretending to be Dal has been corresponding with me for at least the past day. Or maybe two."

"How many messages are we talking about?"

"At least two if it was the past twenty-four hours. Five if it's as much as forty-eight."

He nodded at her laptop, still sitting open on the breakfast bar. "Can you show me?"

She crossed to the computer and pulled up her emails. "The most recent one was from yesterday morning. It came in just before I had to leave for my ob-gyn appointment."

He looked over her shoulder. The email program was set up to decrypt the incoming emails from Dal, but even without encryption, Dal used a letter-substitution cipher on all the messages he sent to her. She translated for Connor. "He's asking if I've located the Hawk."

"Who's the Hawk?"

"That is the big question." She sat on the stool beside him. "One of the reasons Dal hid me in Cincinnati was to find the Hawk. According to some of our intelligence sources, the Hawk is in the US, setting up some sort of terrorist attack that will rival that of the attacks of 9/11."

"Never heard that boast before." His tone was dry.

"I know. Every Mohamed Atta wannabe talks up his big plot as if it's the next coming of the attack on the Twin Towers. But Dal seemed to think this latest intel was legit and needed to be investigated."

"So he sent you? A pregnant dead woman?"

She worried her lower lip between her teeth, wondering if she should tell him what she suspected about Dal's operation. There wasn't any reason to keep it secret at this point, was there? Dal was dead and she was nearly five hours away from Cincinnati and unlikely to go back there any time soon.

"What aren't you telling me?" Connor's tone was neutral, even relaxed, but she saw a wariness in his blue eyes that made her heart ache.

She'd put that wariness there. Earned it fair and square.

"I don't think Dal was running this operation with official sanction," she said.

"Meaning?"

She wished she didn't have to admit this to Connor, on top of all the other reasons he had to hate what she'd done to him. But if she ever wanted to find her way back into Connor's heart, she had to stop lying to him.

She took a deep breath and said, "I think the CIA believes I'm dead, too. I don't think they know what Dal was doing."

BRIGHT DAYLIGHT POURED through the window of Alexander Quinn's office, the afternoon sun glinting off the melting snow. Campbell Cove Security might be a high-tech government-contracted security facility on the inside, but the outside looked like the sprawling brick and concrete high school it had once been, nestled in the little town of Campbell Cove just a few miles east of Cumberland, Kentucky—and about a fifteen-minute drive from the safe house where he'd sent Connor and Risa McGinnis.

He wondered if they were feeling as tired as he was. He was getting a little too old to run these overnight covert operations without feeling the consequences.

The door to his office opened without a warning knock, and two people entered without hesitation or preamble. One was a sandy-haired man in his early forties, with blue eyes and a golden tan that seemed to have lingered from the years he spent bumming around the Caribbean. The other was a slender, handsome woman in her midforties, with golden-brown skin that showed little of her age, black hair worn in a short, neat cut and sharp brown eyes that missed nothing. They were Maddox Heller and Rebecca Cameron, the closest thing he had to partners.

Over the years, Quinn had learned that he wasn't really partner material.

"We need to talk, Quinn," Cameron said.

"About what, Becky?" He was taking his life in his hands, using her nickname without being asked to do so. Only her close friends called her Becky, and along with being a lousy partner, he wasn't exactly great at being a friend, either.

"What's this about you going to Cincinnati last night?" Heller asked flatly, pulling up one of the chairs in front of Quinn's desk.

Quinn arched one eyebrow. "Have a seat."

"Are you running an op without consulting us?" Cameron asked.

"No," he said. "It's not my op."

"Then whose?" Heller asked.

"Martin Dalrymple's."

"The dead spook?"

Quinn slanted a hard look at Heller. "Martin Dalrymple served this country with honor and distinction, at great sacrifice to himself. A little respect for a fallen hero, please."

Heller looked suitably repentant. "Was he in contact with you?"

"Not exactly." Quinn unlocked the lap drawer of his desk and withdrew a phone he kept locked away most of the time. It was a burner, a phone not even his partners had the number for. It was for old contacts from his days in the agency. Martin Dalrymple had been one of those contacts. "I got a text message from Martin two days ago. It was a code we'd used years ago on another op. He knew I'd remember it."

Cameron's shapely brows lowered, carving a couple of small lines in the smooth skin over her nose. "What kind of message?"

"It said, 'Get her out.'"

"And you knew he was talking about Risa?"

"I'd contacted Dal when we spotted Risa in that surveillance photo," Quinn said. "I asked if he was running an op with her."

"What did he say?"

"He never replied—until that text message."

"So you have no idea what he was up to?" Cameron

asked, her curiosity apparently beginning to overcome her irritation with Quinn.

"I'm hoping Risa McGinnis can fill in some of the blanks," Quinn answered calmly. "But I imagine she's skittish at the moment, so we're going to let her calm down and feel safe again before we approach her."

"She won't talk to you," Heller warned. "She ain't stupid."

Quinn looked across the desk at Heller, then turned his gaze to Cameron, taking in her neat-as-a-pin blue business suit, immaculately manicured nails and tasteful, barely-there makeup. Unlike Quinn, the spy, and Heller, the former marine, Rebecca Cameron was all diplomat, which was the role she'd filled for nearly twenty years before a personal loss had driven her out of Foreign Service and into academia. When Quinn had been asked by an old friend to create Campbell Cove Security and the in-house academy as a resource for the government's war on terrorism, Rebecca Cameron had been one of the first people he'd thought of to bring on board.

She looked like a person who could be trusted. She *was* a person who could be trusted.

"Did you ever meet Risa McGinnis?" he asked Cameron. "Did your paths ever cross while you were in the Foreign Service?"

"No, though I heard about her later, of course. After the plane crash."

Quinn nodded. "She's eight months pregnant. She could probably use another woman to talk to."

Cameron's dark eyes narrowed. "What are you up to, Quinn?"

"Dal's been murdered. Risa may be a target. And meanwhile, we're hearing sporadic chatter from known and suspected terror groups suggesting there's something in the works for the US." Quinn leaned forward, folding his hands in front of him and gazing at his partners across the desk. "If we can stop it, we'll get more assignments in the future."

"This is about money?" Heller stared at Quinn with a look of disgusted disbelief, but Cameron, Quinn noted, had a more thoughtful look on her face.

"I have all the money I need," Quinn said simply. "This is about protecting the people of the United States. That's what it's always been about for me. Are we clear?"

Cameron inclined her head in answer. Heller just pressed his lips together and gave a gruff nod.

"Cameron, I want you to make contact with McGinnis after lunch. Use a burner phone, just in case. See if there's anything they need." Quinn looked at Heller. "I want you to go to Cincinnati, Mad Dog," using the former marine's old service nickname. "Ask about renting a room in the building where Risa was living. And visit The Jewel of Tablis for lunch. Keep your ears open. I want to know if people are talking about her sudden disappearance."

"Will do."

Quinn waited until his partners left the office before he picked up his own burner phone and made a call to an old friend. "It's me."

On the other end of the line, a smooth baritone answered him with a mixture of pleasure and wariness. "What's up this time, Quinn?"

"I need to know everything you can tell me about Martin Dalrymple."

THE WANING COLORS of sunset clung to the western sky as if unwilling to let go of the day, but what heat the sun had offered was long gone, and to ward off the cold, Risa curled up with her laptop in one of the armchairs next to the fireplace, leaving Connor to come up with something for dinner.

Risa had always been an indifferent cook, happy to let him claim the kitchen in exchange for handling the cleaning and laundry duties. She'd already washed a load of clothes earlier that afternoon, returning from the small laundry room off the kitchen to inform him she was in the mood for eggs and toast for dinner.

He scrambled eggs for their evening meal, adding cheese and onions for a little extra flavor, and toasted the bread in the oven so he could melt butter on top while it was browning. He'd found some frozen strawberries in the freezer and thawed them so that she could get a serving of fruit to go with the carbs and protein.

"Tomorrow," he told her when he brought her plate of food into the living room and set it on the table by her chair, "I need to go into town and find a grocery store. We need better food choices."

She set aside her laptop and picked up the plate. "Cheesy eggs with onion. Do you know how many times I tried to replicate this dish over the past few months?"

"No. How many times?"

"At least two dozen before I gave up. I'm a complete loss in the kitchen."

"You're too impatient," he said, allowing himself a smile as he remembered her whirlwind style of cooking. "Good food requires patience."

She scooped up a forkful of eggs and took a bite. Her eyes rolled back and she gave a moan of pleasure that seemed to rumble through Connor's body like an earthquake, finally settling in a low hum of desire in the pit of his belly. He hadn't let go of his anger at her, or his

frustration and pain, but he was nowhere near to im-
mune from the passion he'd always felt when she was
within reach.

He set his plate on the fireplace mantel, moving a
short distance away to regain control of his hormones.
"What do you want to drink? We have water, milk and
orange juice."

"Milk, please," she said around another mouthful of
eggs.

He poured milk for her and water for himself, then
returned to the living room. As he sat in the chair beside
her, resting his plate on his lap, he congratulated himself
on recovering his lost equilibrium.

Mostly.

"So, any progress?" He nodded at the laptop computer
lying on the floor at her feet.

"I've started a timeline of Dal's emails to me, trying
to see if there's a pattern to them. I was hoping maybe
they'll tell me more specifically what he was actually
looking for in Cincinnati."

He frowned. "Why didn't he just tell you what he was
looking for?"

She cocked her head, her brow furrowed. "You know
Dal. That's not how he worked."

"Quinn's the same way." He poked a fork into his
eggs, the corner of his mouth quirking. "You know, that
explains so much about the CIA."

"There was a method to his madness," she said with
a touch of defensiveness. "Sometimes, on an undercover
op where there are a lot of unknowns, you try to go in
with no preconceptions. Or at least, as few as you can
manage. Dal didn't want me to assume anything about
the Kaziris I'd be living with. He wanted me to assess

them on my own, make my own judgments about them and then write up my observations."

"Do you have copies of those written observations?" Connor asked. Maybe some of the things she had observed could add to some of the incomplete findings of their surveillance operation in Cincinnati.

"Of course. I'll have to decrypt them for you."

He nodded, uncomfortably aware that if she'd been any other operative, he might not have been willing to leave the decryption to her. Instead, he might have taken advantage of their forced proximity to sneak a copy of her notes to Quinn for Spear to decrypt.

But he couldn't seem to function as an operative with Risa, no matter how much she'd hurt him by letting him believe she was dead. She was a lot of things, but she wasn't a traitor to her country.

If she knew anything that could protect the US against a terrorist attack of any sort, she'd share it. He was utterly certain of that.

"Why did your company decide to do surveillance on the Kaziri community in Ohio in the first place?" Having finished off her dinner, she set her plate aside, tucked her legs under her and turned to look at him. Her left hand settled on her belly as if by habit, gently rubbing it the way she might soothe a fussy child. He couldn't seem to drag his gaze away from her hand and the swell of her abdomen.

His child was in there, growing and getting ready to greet the world. A week ago, he'd been all alone without any real hope of having a family again, and now he was about to be a father.

Emotion rose in his throat, choking him. He forced himself to look away and struggled to remember what she'd just asked. "Quinn and Cameron—she's the other partner at Campbell Cove Security— both had contacts in the government who believed that there might be al Adar operatives hiding in the migrant community. The only Kaziri groups seeking work visas in the US in any numbers were the non-Muslims being driven out of the southern part of the country by terrorist attacks on their churches and homes, and the Mahalabi tribe from north of Tablis. We didn't think al Adar spies could easily hide among the Kaziris who settled in the Research Triangle in North Carolina."

"Which left the Mahalabi Muslims who settled in Cincinnati."

"Exactly."

"I think that was probably Dal's reasoning as well," she said with a nod. "He told me I would have to behave as a practicing Muslim in order to fit in."

Her mother's family were Muslims from the Mahalabi tribe, Connor knew, though Nazina DeVille had converted to Christianity a few years before she met Risa's father. It had been her change of faith that had put her and her family in danger in the first place. But Nazina had educated her daughter about Islam so that she would understand the world from which her grandparents, aunts and uncles came.

"You've done it before," Connor said. "In Kaziristan, anyway. Was it harder this time?"

"A little." She shrugged. "It would have been easier if the refugees had come from a different tribe, maybe. The Mahalabis are patriarchal in ways that don't have much to do with religious beliefs, to be honest."

"Most of al Adar come from that tribe, don't they?"

She nodded. "Most. Not all."

"You were in Cincinnati the whole time I thought you were dead?"

"The first month, I stayed with Dal at his hunting lodge in West Virginia."

A flicker of jealousy darted through him. "Just the two of you?"

She flashed him a look of disbelief. "Dal? You're jealous of Dal?"

"I'm not jealous."

"Right." Her lips twitched as if she were going to smile, but the expression died away before it ever really started. "Poor Dal."

"A double tap doesn't really sound like an al Adar style of murder," Connor murmured. "Way too businesslike and not nearly symbolic enough."

"Dal probably had other enemies, as many years as he was in the CIA," Risa said. "It might not have had anything to do with what I was doing in Cincinnati."

"Or maybe what you were doing in Cincinnati had nothing to do with al Adar at all."

Her shapely eyebrows notched upward. "Interesting thought. I suppose it could be a branch of al Qaeda. Or ISIL."

"Maybe. Maybe not." He set his plate on the table on top of hers and turned his chair to face her. "When Quinn recruited me, before I agreed to anything, I did a little research on him and his partners in the company. And something I thought was pretty interesting is that most of his expertise, at least when he was running The Gates, was in domestic terrorism. Specifically, he spent a lot of time and money dismantling a militia group called the Blue Ridge Infantry. Ever heard of them?"

She shook her head. "No, but most of my career has

been dealing with foreign threats, not internal ones. It's one reason I've been assuming that whatever I was investigating in Cincinnati had an overseas provenance."

"I'm not saying the Blue Ridge Infantry or any group like them is behind whatever you were investigating in Cincinnati," Connor added quickly. "I'm just saying, we can't assume we're looking at a foreign threat just because both Dal and Quinn are interested in whatever is going on there. They have—had—their fingers in other pots."

"Hmm." Risa leaned toward him, the sweet smell of herbal shampoo wafting toward him, filling his head with potent memories. "Know what I think?"

"What?" he asked, trying to clear his suddenly befuddled mind.

"I think we need to have a long talk with your bosses."

He smiled. "That's good. Because while you were taking a shower earlier, I got a call from one of my bosses. She's coming here to talk to us in the morning."

Chapter Eight

So this is Parisa McGinnis. Rebecca Cameron entered the small safe house shortly after nine the following morning, her gaze taking in everything—the cozy fire, the way Connor McGinnis stood slightly in front of his back-from-the-dead wife as if to protect her, and the sharp-eyed gaze of the woman herself, who seemed to be studying Cameron with the same animal wariness with which Cameron was assessing her.

Parisa was smaller, somehow, than she had anticipated, even pregnant. She was only average height, several inches shorter than her tall, broad-shouldered husband. She looked almost delicate, though the unclassified information she'd been able to access about the woman's career suggested she was much tougher than she looked.

"I've heard a great deal about you," she said aloud as she shook the other woman's hand and nodded a greeting to Connor.

"I've heard a few things about you as well," Parisa said with a smile that didn't quite reach her eyes. She had a lovely voice, warm and low, with a drawl that was pure South Georgia. It reminded Cameron of a year she'd spent in Savannah, working on a master's thesis in military history.

She'd met Mitch Cranston there as well, although it had been many more years before she thought of him as anything other than a cocky young marine in town on shore leave who could promise nothing but trouble.

She pushed away the memory of Mitch before it distracted her and took in the look of wary concern in Connor McGinnis's blue eyes. She let her own Alabama accent make an appearance, sensing it might put Parisa at ease. "I hope everything you heard was, if not good, at least interesting."

"I was surprised to hear from you last night. I figured we'd be getting another visit from Quinn," Connor said with his characteristic bluntness.

Unhurriedly, she turned her gaze to him. "Quinn asked me to stand in for him, since he was unable to get away."

"Are you here to appease us or to answer our questions?" Parisa asked.

"May I call you Parisa?"

"Risa," the other woman answered shortly.

"Risa," Cameron said with a smile. "It's a lovely name. I should tell you we were all very pleased to learn you had not died in the plane crash."

"Two hundred and twelve other people did," Risa replied bleakly, waving her hand toward the sitting area of the small living room. There were two armchairs near the fire and a small sofa angled opposite. Risa and Connor took the chairs, leaving her to sit on the sofa alone.

Clearly she was the one in the hot seat.

She sat, crossing her legs casually and folding her hands on her lap, waiting for one of them to speak.

For a moment, they simply looked her over, as if trying to discern her hidden motives. For once, her motives were exactly what she'd told them. She was here to help them, no matter what their dealings with Alexander Quinn might have otherwise suggested. And she was here to find out what they'd learned, pick their brains about what they might be up against, and figure out how Campbell Cove Security could help them.

Connor was the one who finally broke the increasingly uncomfortable silence. "Why did Quinn send you and not Maddox Heller?"

"Heller is on another assignment. Besides, he's our tactics and training guy. Foreign relations and diplomacy are my areas of expertise," she answered with a smoothness born of years in embassies and consulates around the world, dealing with people even more suspicious than the pair sitting in matching armchairs in front of her. "Quinn suspects, and I concur, that whatever trouble you've become embroiled in probably has its basis in a foreign threat."

"Probably," Risa murmured.

"That doesn't mean we shouldn't consider other possibilities, however." Cameron knew that in a government of a country the size of the US, corruption was inevitable. And the higher the stakes, the greater the risks—and rewards—of playing dirty.

She was doing a little investigation into the Cincinnati situation herself, from a different direction. But that wasn't something Risa and Connor McGinnis needed to know, for the moment at least.

"Would you like a cup of coffee? Or I can probably brew a cup of tea." Risa stood, color rising in her cheeks as if she had suddenly realized she was being a bad hostess. Cameron nearly smiled, recognizing the inbred guilt of a fellow Southerner caught in a moment of bad manners.

"Coffee would be lovely," she said with a smile, belatedly observing the proprieties. "One sugar and a splash of milk if you have it."

While Risa disappeared into the kitchen, Connor leaned closer to her, lowering his voice. "What kind of game is Quinn playing here?"

"I don't think he is," she answered, keeping her voice down as well. "He seems to sincerely want to help your wife uncover and eliminate the threats that drove her to fake her own death."

"Does he have any idea what Martin Dalrymple was trying to uncover in Cincinnati?"

"Beyond the stated desire to stop a terrorist attack? No."

"Not as far as you know," Connor corrected.

Cameron inclined her head in agreement. They both knew that Quinn might have motives on his own that he wasn't willing to share with others. "Not as far as I know."

"What about you? Any thoughts on what Risa's actually up against?"

Rather than reply to a question to which she had no good answer, she smiled at Connor. "We'll get to that when your lovely wife returns. Meanwhile, I've brought supplies for you—groceries, for the most part, and a few first aid supplies and other things you might need. They're in my car in the backseat." She handed him her key fob and nodded toward the door.

His eyebrows arching, Connor took the key fob and

headed out the door, just as footsteps coming down the hall signaled the return of his wife.

Risa entered the room with a tray on which sat two steaming cups of coffee. She paused a moment when she saw that Connor wasn't there.

"He's gone outside to fetch some supplies I brought," Cameron explained with a smile. "He'll be right back."

Risa set the tray on the coffee table in front of Cameron, sliding one of the cups toward her. She set the other one in front of the chair Connor had vacated. "I don't believe we've ever met before, have we?" she asked, her tone polite.

Cameron smiled. "No, I believe our paths never crossed during my time in the Foreign Service. But you spent a bit of time in Tablis, didn't you?"

"Yes." Risa settled in her chair, one hand smoothing over her round belly. Cameron tried not to let her gaze linger, but emotion overcame her wisdom for a brief moment, allowing her to look a bit longer than she should, her imagination conjuring up the phantom of an old dream. Motherhood. Marriage. Two things she'd once desired with great intensity.

Two things she no longer considered an option.

"I discussed the matter of your pregnancy with Quinn and Heller," she said aloud, dragging her gaze back up to Risa's face. "We have access to an obstetrician in Lexington who has been vetted and cleared to handle sensitive cases. Our company will cover your medical costs if you need treatment before we figure out how to neutralize the threats against you."

"That's very generous."

Cameron smiled. "Your husband is a valued member of our company. Technically, you'd be covered under his insurance policy anyway. We're just cutting through the red tape."

The door opened and Connor entered carrying two large canvas bags full of groceries. He angled a quick look at Risa. "She brought more ice cream. Including Rocky Road."

"Put it in the freezer before it melts," Cameron suggested.

Connor sighed and headed for the kitchen.

"My sister craved ice cream when she was pregnant. I told her she was a walking cliché, which didn't amuse her." Cameron laughed. "But I thought even if your cravings were different, everybody likes ice cream. So I bought three flavors. I take it you like Rocky Road?"

"Who doesn't?" Risa offered the first genuine smile Cameron had seen since her arrival at the safe house. "Thank you."

"This is all very polite and civilized," Connor interrupted, returning from the kitchen, "but I'd like to know how long we're supposed to hide here in the mountains. Shouldn't we be doing something constructive?"

"Such as?" Cameron asked.

"Maybe someone should go have a talk with Risa's boss at the restaurant in Cincy. Find out why he thought it was okay to let a stranger in her apartment to have a look around."

"Someone is," Cameron said, leaving it at that.

"Farid is a chameleon," Risa said with a grimace. "He's not really religious at all, but he plays the game around some of the true believers so that his business doesn't suffer. With others, he's about as American as they come. He's happy to bow to the tribal pecking order if he thinks it'll win him some approval, but I don't think he'd have been helping that man find me if he thought it was about a terrorist attack."

"So you don't think he's driven by any religious or political beliefs?" Cameron asked.

"He believes in money and power. Period." Risa sighed. "Although, in truth, that's what most of the brains behind al Adar believe in, too. They're not like ISIS, trying to establish a worldwide caliphate. Al Adar uses people's beliefs to manipulate them, but it's not about religion for them. It's about getting control over Kaziristan's oil and mineral resources."

"So Farid could be aligned with al Adar?"

Risa thought about it for a moment, then shook her head. "No, I don't think so. The kind of power he wants is much smaller in scale. He likes being the top dog at the restaurant, but I don't think he'd appreciate the responsibilities of being the top dog in a bigger organization. When someone of real power or import comes into the restaurant, Farid's quick to curry favor. That's not the way of al Adar."

"What about other people in the community? Did you have much interaction with them?"

"Ninety-nine percent of the Kaziris living in Cincinnati are wonderful people. Devout, peaceful people who are horrified by what radicals do in their name."

"We know that," Cameron assured her. "But the one percent—"

"Can do a lot of damage," Risa finished for her. "I know."

"Is it possible that the threat against Risa has nothing to do with any of the terrorist groups normally associated with the Middle East and Central Asia?" Connor asked.

"What do you have in mind?" Cameron asked.

He looked at her, wariness in his blue eyes. Analysis wasn't Connor McGinnis's area of expertise, Cameron knew. He'd joined Campbell Cove Security as an expert in weapons and tactics.

But he would never have been on the company's radar if he hadn't also possessed the intelligence to make smart choices and work out tricky puzzles. Quinn, Heller and Cameron had been tasked with hiring only the best people. They'd taken that calling to heart.

"I'm wondering if there could be another reason why someone wants Risa dead."

"Such as?" Cameron directed the question to Risa.

"I was involved in several delicate operations," Risa admitted, looking uncomfortable. "Some of which are still classified and I can't really talk about."

"Was your cover ever blown?"

"Not that I know of, but maybe it happened without my realizing it. Or maybe someone in the government has loose lips. Wouldn't be the first time."

"What was your role in these operations? Were they personal?"

"Do you mean was I a honey trap?" Risa glanced at Connor, as if gauging his reaction. "Early in my career, yes. A couple of times. But not for the past few years."

"So a man you…charmed as a part of your job isn't likely to be the one who put a hit out on you?"

"No," Risa said firmly. "I know the results of both of those operations, and the men involved aren't in any position to seek revenge."

Connor's eyes slanted toward his wife, but he didn't speak.

"So you tell me then, Risa. Who would want you dead

badly enough to kill over two hundred innocent people to make it happen?"

A look of realization flickered across her expression briefly before her brow furrowed. "Oh my God."

"What?" Connor asked.

She turned to look at her husband, her eyes wide. "Remember when I told you that man at the restaurant looked familiar?"

"Yeah. You said you thought you saw his face on Dal's corkboard."

"I did, but I think I know why his face made an impression." Risa looked at Cameron. "I mean, I can't really be sure. The last time I saw this guy's face, it was a decade ago, at least. He wouldn't look exactly the same."

"Who was he?" Connor asked.

"He was one of the terrorists who was part of the siege on the American Embassy in Tablis about a decade ago. I was assigned to track his movements shortly after the siege ended and he escaped. I managed to discover his whereabouts and alert the Kaziri government of his new identity. He was exiled from Kaziristan after that."

"That sounds like a pretty good motive for revenge," Cameron murmured.

"But see, the thing is, he popped back up a few years ago. In fact, you might want to ask your friend Maddox Heller about him."

"Why's that?" Connor asked.

"Because if I'm not mistaken, Maddox Heller watched him die almost eight years ago."

MADDOX HELLER'S DRAWL rumbled over Rebecca Cameron's cell phone, slightly distorted by the speaker. "At the time, Quinn told me they'd found the body. But you know Quinn's relationship with the truth is distant at best. I talked to him about it before I called you back. Turns out that, technically, the authorities never found his body. There were parts of that building that sank into the ground in a geologically unstable area. The government of Mariposa didn't have the money to do an excavation just to recover a missing body."

"And there's no way Tahir Mahmoud could have survived the explosion?" Connor asked, his stomach muscles tightening as he awaited the response.

Heller took longer to answer than Connor liked. "Since nobody recovered his body, I don't know that I could say there's no way he could have escaped," he said finally. "But it's highly unlikely. And since we haven't had any further sightings of the man…"

Something in Heller's tone made Connor sit up straighter. "Why don't you sound more certain?"

"It's just—remember that photo you sent me last night? From the restaurant?"

Connor glanced at Risa. She sat with her legs curled under her, smoothing both hands rhythmically over the curve of her belly. She looked at him, her brow furrowed.

"Yes," Connor answered. "You said you weren't sure it looked familiar."

"I wasn't. I'm still not. It would almost be impossible."

"What would be impossible?" Risa asked, her tone tight with impatience.

"If I hadn't seen that lab in Mariposa blow up myself, I'd have thought the man you saw at the restaurant was an older Tahir Mahmoud."

Connor looked at Risa. "You said you were part of getting him exiled from the country after the embassy siege. Wouldn't he remember what you looked like?"

"I tracked him anonymously. My cover was a junior-grade pencil pusher at the embassy. He wouldn't have known what I looked like."

"What about the surveillance photos from Cincy?" Connor asked Heller. "Have you looked at all of them?"

"I'm just getting up to speed on this case," Heller admitted. "I'll take a look."

"Do that." Connor looked at Cameron. "Can we get our hands on all the surveillance photos from Cincinnati, too? We've seen the man most recently, so we might be able to spot him more easily."

Her eyes narrowed, but she nodded. "I can arrange that."

"Today?"

She shook her head. "It'll take a while to digitize everything. But I can have them all to you by tomorrow morning. Will that do?"

"Yes. Thank you," Risa said.

"I'll make some calls to some old friends in Mariposa, too," Heller said, sounding subdued. "I'd like to be damn certain Tahir Mahmoud hasn't escaped the grim reaper myself." He hung up.

"I remember the name Tahir Mahmoud from the siege on the embassy in Kaziristan," Connor said as he and Risa walked Cameron to the door. "But I never heard about what happened in Mariposa."

"Because of Mahmoud, Heller's wife, Iris, nearly died," Cameron told him. "Mahmoud died—allegedly— during an attempt on their lives. Iris barely escaped."

"Eight years is a long time to go to ground without a trace." Risa wrapped her arms around herself, shivering a little as a blast of icy air came through the open door.

"He could very well be dead, you know." Rebecca

Cameron put her hand on Risa's arm. "Let me know if you need anything. Anything at all."

"Thank you again."

Cameron took a step back and smiled at them both. "I know things are tense and difficult right now, for a lot of reasons. But remember, this was a Christmas you thought you were both going to spend without each other. And now you're not. That's a blessing, regardless of the circumstances."

She flashed another smile and walked down the porch steps to her car.

Connor gave Risa's elbow a light tug, pulling her back inside the warm house. He closed and locked the door behind them before turning to face her.

"She's right about one thing," Risa said, a faint smile tugging at her lips. "I thought I was going to spend Christmas alone. No tree, no decorations, no Santa down the chimney. It was a lonely prospect."

"You remember last Christmas? When we bought that real tree and spent most of January vacuuming up the needles it shed?" Connor's smile faded when he remembered the rest of the story. How he'd found needles in the carpet for months after the plane crash as well, when they'd served to remind him poignantly of all he'd lost.

Risa put her hand on his arm. "I know you're still angry, and I don't blame you. Not a bit. But can't you at least be happy I'm alive?"

He stared at her, feeling as if she'd just slapped him. "My God, Risa. You know I'm so very grateful that you're alive. No matter what else has happened, you have to know that."

"Then can we just hold on to that for a while? Try not to dwell on the rest of it?" She stepped closer to him, her hand sliding up to his shoulder. "I missed you every single day."

He felt a flutter of anger but pushed it down. Not now. He could be angry later.

Now, he just wanted to be grateful she was here, alive, with him.

"I missed you every single day, too," he admitted.

She rested her cheek against his shoulder. Her belly pressed against his, the sensation strange but somehow perfect. He lifted his hands up her back, letting them settle just above her butt. The pregnancy had given her unexpected curves; he let his hands roam over them lightly, taking in the new shape of her body.

She leaned her head back, looking up at him. "A little more junk in the trunk than you remembered?"

He grinned at her. "I have to admit, your breasts are a delightful surprise, too."

She gave her chest a self-conscious glance. "Not too much?"

He shook his head. "Definitely not."

She reached behind her back and brought his hands around to her belly. "Sweet Pea's kicking again."

He curved his palms over the swell of her belly, feeling the flutter of movement against his hands. "Sweet Pea?"

"I'm trying out nicknames."

"Based on the way Sweet Pea's kicking, Bruiser might be the better name." He ran his fingers lightly over the curve of her belly, feeling her shiver under his touch. She looked up at him, her hazel eyes wide and dark.

He knew that look. He'd loved that look, reveled in the way he could make her long for him with just a touch or the sound of his voice. He'd dreamed of that look after the plane crash, deep in his loneliest nights.

She rose to her toes, lifting her face toward his. It would be the easiest, most natural thing in the world to bend his head and meet her halfway.

If only she hadn't lied.

Risa pulled back. "I'm sorry."

"No, I am," he said, reaching for her. He pulled her into his arms, holding her tightly. "I'm sorry that I've let my hurt feelings get in the way of telling you how damn glad I am you're alive." He pressed his lips to her forehead. "No matter what."

Chapter Nine

"I think I should go back to Cincinnati."

Connor's head shot up, his gaze disbelieving. "Are you insane?"

"I lived there for months, Connor, and nobody bothered me."

"That doesn't mean you could go back now without consequences."

"My rent is paid through the end of the month and I didn't send in a request to end my lease, so it's not like my landlord is going to have rented my room to someone else. My job at The Jewel of Tablis wasn't that great. I could get a different job. Or I could go without a job for a few weeks. It would leave me open to do more snooping around that way."

"Quinn wouldn't have pulled you out of there if he didn't think there was a real threat to your life."

"I think he's proceeding with an overabundance of caution."

"You make it sound like that's a bad thing."

"If it gets in the way of finding out who brought down that flight out of Kaziristan, it *is* a bad thing."

"Risa—" He stopped with a sigh and rose from his crouch by the fire, which he'd been trying to stoke back to life. He crossed to where she lay curled up on the sofa, tucked beneath a warm quilt. Sitting on the coffee table, he took her hand between his. "Your hands are cold."

"Please don't try to talk me out of this, Connor."

"I don't want you to go back to Cincinnati. The thought terrifies me."

"I feel as if I'm walking away from the first real break I had in the case."

"It's not your case anymore. Cameron, Quinn and Heller are on it."

"No, listen, Connor." She squeezed his hand. "I've been thinking about this ever since Cameron left this morning. Dal wouldn't have put me in Cincinnati if he didn't think I was uniquely suited for the investigation."

"But you were there for months and didn't discover a damn thing, did you?" He twined his fingers with hers, leaning closer. He smelled good, crisp and clean with just a hint of wood smoke from the fire, and she felt as if her insides were melting into a gooey mess.

"It was a delicate operation," she protested, annoyed that she couldn't seem to drag her gaze above his mouth. Connor was an amazing kisser, she remembered. Instinctive, knowing when she wanted a soft wooing and when she wanted unbridled passion.

Either would do very nicely at the moment.

But he'd been right to slow things down between them earlier. She wanted him as much as she ever had, and the way his blue eyes dilated with desire when he looked at her told her he felt the same raw longing that she did. But what they both wanted was what they'd had before the plane crash. Before her lies. Before his grief.

Until they could want something else, something built

on the future rather than trapped in the past, then it was best to move carefully.

"You know what I think?" he murmured, a smile curving his lips.

"What do you think?"

"I think you're getting stir-crazy." His smile widened. "I think maybe we could risk getting out of this place for a little while, don't you think?"

She sat up, intrigued. "What do you have in mind?"

"Just go get dressed." He tugged at the quilt. "And bundle up!"

For the first twenty minutes, they seemed to be driving through endless woodland, broken here and there by the striated rock that revealed where the road had been cut through the mountains. Then, as the last of the day's sunlight painted the western sky in hues of amber, rose and purple, the trees thinned out, revealing a picturesque town nestled in a small valley.

"Welcome to Laurel Hollow, Kentucky," Connor said with a smile in his voice. "Population, hmm, somewhere around 250, I think."

"How did you know how to find this place?" she asked, charmed. The town looked like something out of a postcard, a quintessential small Southern town, complete with a tiny white church on the corner with a tall white spire rising into the twilight sky.

"I might have made a call to Quinn while you were napping this afternoon," he said with a smile.

"Just to find a quaint little mountain town to drive through?"

"Not exactly." There was a secret behind his smile, reminding her of the old days, when they were happy and in love. He'd loved to surprise her, something that hadn't always been easy to do, considering her career as an intelligence operative.

He had that same look now.

"What are you up to?" she asked, further intrigued.

His smile grew more mysterious. "You'll see."

Within a couple of miles, the town of Laurel Hollow was a faint glow in the rearview mirror, the scenery replaced by rolling farmland and sporadic lights of houses dotting the landscape here and there. Then they rounded a curve and ahead lay a brightly lit copse of evergreen trees.

Not a copse, she realized as Connor slowed the SUV and turned off the road onto a narrow dirt lane.

It was a tree lot.

"Rebecca Cameron was right," Connor said as he cut the engine and turned to look at her. "No matter what else is going on, we're getting to spend Christmas together this year. And it wasn't very long ago that I didn't think I'd ever get the chance to do that again. So let's do it right."

Tears pricking her eyes, she reached across the space between them and touched his face. "This is a wonderful surprise."

"Yeah?" He looked so pleased, she thought, struggling against a fresh sting of tears.

Why had she let Dal talk her into walking away from her life? How could she have even contemplated it? If the circumstances had been reversed, she'd have been furious. And deeply, perhaps irrevocably, hurt.

"What are you thinking?" Connor asked, covering her hand with his own, holding her palm in place against his cheek.

"How incredibly unfair I was to you," she admitted.

"You always did undervalue yourself." He released her hand but held her gaze, his eyes sad.

"What can I help y'all with?" The booming voice so close behind her made Risa jump. She turned to find a short, burly man in overalls and a thick fleece-lined denim jacket standing behind them, his weathered face creased with a big smile. "We've got big trees, small trees, fat ones and skinny ones. You just tell ol' Ray what you need and I'll get you just the right tree."

"How about medium-sized?" Connor suggested. "Not too fat, not too thin." He winked at Risa, making her heart turn a little flip.

"That sounds perfect," she agreed with a smile.

"You just head over there to the right side of the lot and you'll find exactly what you want," Ray said, still grinning at them.

Connor reached out and took Risa's hand, giving a light tug. "Let's go find us a Christmas tree."

"WE'VE GOT VISUAL contact with McGinnis." The voice over the phone line was a growly bass, with just a touch of a Boston accent. Adam Lovell was a Harvard washout who had developed an obsequious style early on, perhaps hoping he could make up in sycophancy what he lacked in brainpower.

It hardly made his boss respect the young toady any more, but it did make Adam very, very useful.

"What about the woman?" he asked.

"She's there with him. But she's not wearing a hijab."

Of course she wasn't. She wasn't really a Kaziri widow, after all, no matter how well she'd played the part. She was Georgia born and bred, the daughter of a tough old leatherneck who'd parlayed her mother's Kaziri blood into a career in the CIA.

Damn Martin Dalrymple's wily old hide.

"If you can get your hands on the woman, do it."

"She doesn't seem to be getting very far from Mc-Ginnis."

"So find a way to separate them."

Adam was silent so long he began to wonder if he'd lost the connection to the young man. But finally, Adam spoke, his tone tentative. "May I ask why we're trying to bring this woman into custody?"

"No, you may not," he answered, and ended the call.

He sat back against the buttery leather of his desk chair, staring out the window at the lights of the National Mall, blurred by the foggy drizzle that had enveloped the capital in a dreary haze. In retrospect, he should have guessed that Dalrymple would have had a few tricks up his sleeve. He should have anticipated that Parisa McGinnis might have survived the explosion. That after years of blending in with the Kaziri natives in their homeland, she could have found a way to blend in with the Kaziris who'd fled to the US.

He had looked for her in North Carolina among the Christians, thinking she'd have fit in better with them, given her personal background. But that hadn't been smart thinking. He was rather embarrassed at how short-sighted he'd been.

But that was water under the bridge. He'd found her. She was still alive.

That reality had to be remedied as soon as possible.

"WHAT DO YOU THINK?" Risa asked, cocking her head as she considered the fir tree that sat in the middle of the maze of conical-shaped evergreens that filled the Christmas-tree lot.

Connor seemed to give it some thought, although she could tell from his expression that he knew this was the tree for her. Still, he made her wait a few seconds as he stroked his chin and surveyed all sides of the tree, giving the limbs a few light tugs before he finally turned his head to look at her.

"I love it," he said.

"Yay!" She wrapped her arms around him and gave him a hug before she realized she had thrown away her right to touch him whenever she wanted to. She looked up at him, feeling uncertain and not liking it.

"Remind you of anything?" he asked, smiling as if to put her at ease.

She looked at the tree again, suddenly realizing why she'd liked it on sight. "Our first Christmas tree."

"Yep." Connor touched the fir's thick needles with one finger. "It was almost bigger than your apartment in Germany. Remember?"

She smiled at the image his words conjured in her mind, of a fat little Christmas tree, decked to the hilt with garland and ornaments, taking up half of her tiny economy flat in Günzberg, halfway between her assignment at the US Consulate in Munich and Connor's temporary duty at the Marine Corps' Camp Panzer Kaserne in Böblingen. "I remember."

"Remember that night we had some of the guys at the base over for a party and we could barely move around because of that bloody tree?" He laughed softly.

"And then you proposed after they left. Because you said they all told you if you didn't, one of them would."

His smile broadened, and he looked as if the memory

made him genuinely happy. Risa felt her throat tightening, waiting for him to realize the past was truly past and the present was full of lies and regrets.

But before his expression had a chance to change, the tree lot proprietor, Ray, appeared as if out of the ether. "Found one you like?"

"Yes, sir," Connor said. "We'll take this one."

Ray gave them a price that seemed fair. Connor pulled out his wallet and paid in cash. "Don't suppose you have a wheelbarrow or something I can use to cart it to my truck."

"Of course I do." He flashed Connor a smile of pure delight. "Anything else I can help y'all with tonight?"

"Do you know any place where we can find some reasonably priced decorations?" Risa asked. "Doesn't have to be anything fancy."

"As a matter of fact, you're already in the right place." Ray turned his grin toward her and waved his hand to one side. "Back yonder, you'll find a shed where we have all sorts of genuine handmade ornaments made by some of Kentucky's most gifted local artisans."

Those artisans were probably Ray's wife and kids, Risa thought, but she wasn't in any position to be picky. "Just back that way?"

"Yes, ma'am." Ray turned to help Connor pick up the tree.

"I'll catch up," she told Connor, giving his arm a pat and heading in the direction Ray had indicated.

"Back yonder" was farther away than she'd realized, as she weaved her way through the maze of evergreen trees. Night had fallen completely during the time she and Connor had been selecting their tree, the darkness broken only by a string of bare bulbs hung along a series of garden stakes planted in the soft ground of the tree lot. They were apparently powered by a generator, as she could hear the equipment humming somewhere nearby.

A light wind had begun to pick up, making the light-bulbs sway, casting eerie, dancing shadows across the ground. Risa tugged her coat more tightly around her, trying to ignore the sudden prickle of unease that rippled its way down her spine.

It's just the wind, she reminded herself. She wasn't back in Cincinnati anymore. She was in nowhere, Kentucky, where nobody knew her from Adam or Eve. Connor was just a few short yards away.

She turned around to reassure herself that he was within sight.

But she saw nothing but trees.

For a second, she felt a frisson of panic. But she calmed herself quickly. The road was nearby. All she had to do was follow the string of lights back to where Connor waited with their lovely new tree.

Meanwhile, they had ornaments to select.

She kept heading toward the back of the lot, following the string of lights, until she thought she spotted the edge of a wooden shed peeking through the gaps in the trees. She started to relax.

Then, with shocking suddenness, the lights went out.

As CONNOR FINISHED securing the fir tree in the back of the Tahoe, the night went suddenly dark. Only the dome light inside the truck relieved the bottomless gloom that fell over the tree lot behind him.

"What the hell?" Ray's voice carried through the darkness.

There was a flashlight in the SUV's glove box. Connor retrieved it and turned it on, a strong beam of light slashing through the blackness. It played across Ray's weathered features, making the man squint and hold up his hand against the glare.

Connor moved the light away from Ray's face as he walked closer. "What happened?"

"Not sure," Ray answered, frowning. "The generator's back this way." He waved for Connor to follow him with the flashlight as he turned and entered the tree maze.

Connor followed, not liking the sudden darkness. As a retired marine, he was used to making the dark work for him, but he wasn't equipped to handle the loss of easy visibility, especially when he was separated from Risa. The light outage was probably a coincidence.

But he didn't like coincidences. Especially not now.

"What the hell?" Ray said again, sounding even more confounded than before.

"What?" Connor asked.

Ray held out his hand. "Can I borrow that?"

Reluctantly, Connor handed over the flashlight. Ray played the light across a small open area in the middle of the tree lot. Connor could see what looked like a generator wheel kit, but there was no generator contained within the frame.

"Well, hell," Ray said, sounding annoyed. "Who the hell took my damn generator?"

Connor's heart skipping a beat, he grabbed the flashlight back from Ray and started to play the beam of light across the trees ahead of him. "Risa?" he called.

But Risa didn't answer.

Chapter Ten

Risa's pulse hammered loudly in her ears as she tried to orient herself in the darkness. There was a furtive sounding rustle nearby, as if someone were moving through the densely packed trees in an attempt at stealth.

Or was she just imagining things? There was any number of reasons the lights of the tree lot could have gone out, starting with a generator failure.

"Risa!" Connor's voice carried across the tree lot.

And the furtive rustling stopped.

Someone was definitely out there. And if she responded to Connor's call, that someone would know exactly where she was.

She eased backward, wincing when she bumped into one of the trees, setting its limbs rattling softly against one another. She heard the sound of movement again, coming her way.

"Risa?" Connor's voice was closer now, and she realized she was seeing flashes of light moving toward her through the trees. A flashlight?

She remained quiet, letting Connor do all the moving. He was getting closer, although he was a few rows of trees away from where she was crouched.

Suddenly, the sound of movement in the trees nearby picked up, moving away from the light.

She risked edging closer to where Connor was weaving his way through the trees, calling his name when, finally, she could see him only a few feet away. "Connor!"

He pushed through the trees, sending a couple of them toppling, stands and all, to reach her. "Why didn't you answer?" he asked breathlessly, wrapping one strong arm around her waist and pulling her to him.

"There's someone out there," she whispered. "I think they might have been following me."

His only answer was to take her hand and lead her back to the roadside, where the SUV was still parked, a big black shadow in the unrelenting gloom. In a rustle of tree limbs, Ray emerged as well, stepping into the small circle of light cast by Connor's flashlight beam.

"I found the generator," he told Connor. "Someone had dragged it a few dozen yards away and emptied out all the gas."

Connor slanted a look at Risa. "Must have been some kids, pulling a stupid prank."

Ray's lips curved in a grimace of a smile. "Or some of my competitors, out to screw up my night's worth of sales."

Connor rubbed Risa's back, his touch warm and comforting. "You have a lot of trouble with your competitors?"

"Christmas is a cutthroat business."

"What are you going to do now?" Risa asked, trying to settle her jangling nerves. It was possible Ray was right, that one of his competitors had tried to sabotage his business.

Possible. But not likely.

Ray pulled out his phone. "I'll call my wife to bring me some more gas. Get the lights up and running again, and then the kids and me can clean up that mess where those jerks poured out the gas." He nodded at their truck. "Go on, I'll be fine. Maybe y'all can come back out tomorrow when it's light and buy your decorations. I'll give you half price on 'em for your trouble."

Risa looked up at Connor, not sure she wanted to leave Ray alone, under the circumstances. He read her expression and gave a slight nod before he turned to Ray. "Actually, if it's no problem, we'll wait here with you. I'd like to go ahead and get the decorations tonight."

"If you're sure?"

"Positive," Risa agreed.

Ray flashed them a quick grin. "Mighty friendly of you." He pulled his cell phone from the pocket of his jacket and walked a few yards away to make his call.

"I don't think it was his competition," Connor murmured, his lips so close to her ear she felt his breath stir her hair.

"I don't, either."

"Whoever it was, I don't think he went far. He's probably out there somewhere, waiting for a chance to follow us wherever we go next."

"Which can't be back to the safe house," Risa murmured. "At least, not tonight. Agreed?"

"Agreed."

"Who do we think it is?"

"I think the more pressing question is, how did they find us?"

Down the road, headlights appeared in the gloom. Seconds later, Risa heard the rumble of a vehicle engine. Instinctively, she edged closer to Connor, who tucked her under his arm and turned so that his body was between her and the advancing vehicle.

"It's Carla." Ray moved past them toward the roadside as the vehicle, an older-model Chevrolet truck, slowed to a stop.

A short, plump woman with faded red hair and a round, pretty face stepped out of the driver's seat and glanced at Risa and Connor before she turned to look at her husband, who had retrieved a plastic gas container from the bed of the pickup. "What happened?" she asked as she handed him the flashlight she held in her right hand.

"Must've been a kid pulling a prank," Ray told her. "Thanks for gettin' here so quick, hon."

Carla slanted another curious look at Risa and Connor.

Ray nodded in their direction. "Sorry, didn't get your names."

"Mac and Marisa," Connor said before Risa could speak. "Nice to meet you. We were about to look at some decorations out back when the lights went out."

"Well, I can help you out with that," Carla said with a smile as Ray turned on the flashlight and headed into the maze of trees. "I brought a couple more boxes of ornaments and garlands the girls put together—the local girls' clubs in town make money for their activities by doing arts and crafts. Both of our girls are involved, so we sell 'em here at the tree lot every Christmas. Want to take a look and see if there's anything you like?" She reached into the back of the truck, hauled out a large cardboard box and set it on the ground by the truck.

Risa glanced at Connor, wondering if they dared stay there any longer. It wasn't like she could be sure they'd get a chance to use that tree they'd just bought, not if they were about to go on the run. Plus, money was about to become a real problem for them.

"We'll take a look," Connor said, meeting her gaze with steel in his blue eyes. He pointed the beam of his flashlight toward the box.

Carla opened the box to reveal several small ornaments, individually sealed in clear plastic zip-top bags. Some had been carved from wood and painted, the quality surprisingly sophisticated. Others were made of needlework or handwoven, in homey colors that reminded Risa of some of the craft work she'd seen in the small villages of Kaziristan when she'd been living there undercover.

"They're beautiful," she said.

"Thank you. I'll be sure to pass along the compliments to the girls. Anything you like? They're fifty cents an ornament, and the beaded and woven garland strands are two dollars apiece."

Risa selected three wood-beaded garlands, two frosty blue and the other a weathered gold. She also selected a couple dozen ornaments in complementary colors. Connor pulled fifteen dollars from his wallet and handed it over just as the generator roared to life somewhere in the middle of the tree lot. The string of bulbs flickered on, lighting up the darkness.

"Thank you for everything," Connor told Ray when he emerged from the thicket. "Hope you have a merry Christmas!"

"Enjoy your tree and decorations!" Ray gave a wave as they packed their decorations in the back of the truck with the tree. Risa waved back as they drove away from the brightness of the tree lot.

Ahead, the winding road seemed to disappear into

inky blackness beyond the beams of the truck's head-lights. Risa quelled a shiver and turned to look at Connor. "How the hell did someone find us?"

In Cumberland, Connor found what he was looking for—a public establishment still open at 8:00 p.m., with enough cars in the parking lot that an open ambush would be hard to accomplish. In this case, it was a pizza restaurant with a parking lot almost full on this cold Friday night.

"You're hungry?" Risa asked, her tone dry, as Connor pulled into the parking lot and angled the truck into a place near the back.

"It's dinnertime," he murmured as he cut the engine.

"Seriously, what are we doing here?"

"Getting dinner," he answered, lifting one finger to his lips.

Risa's eyes narrowed, but she understood the unspoken order.

Connor reached into the glove compartment and pulled out a small rectangular box. Inside was an RF detector, designed to pick up signals from wireless transmitters, such as listening devices. He switched it on and waited for it to scan for a signal. It detected a GPS signal—Quinn put GPS trackers on all of the company's fleet vehicles—but nothing else.

"No bugs," he told her. "You can speak freely."

"What's that picking up?" she asked, pointing to the flashing green light.

"GPS—this is a company vehicle, so they'll be tracking it."

"What if someone at Campbell Cove Security is the

one who's following us? Maybe they needed to make covert contact."

Connor shook his head. "Someone would have found a way to let me know he or she was there. No reason to disable the generator and make such a production."

"So nobody's bugging the car, or us. How did they find us? We need to figure that out, because they may be following us right now."

"I don't know," he admitted. "I know we weren't directly followed this time—as dark as it was on the road driving here, nobody could've followed without my knowing it."

"Does that make any sense?" Risa tugged her coat more tightly around her, looking spooked. "They risked following me around that tree lot with you and Ray there, but they don't even try to follow us when we leave the place?"

She was right. It didn't make any sense. Unless—

"Damn it," he growled, snapping open the driver's door. He grabbed the flashlight from the console compartment and started examining the underside of the Tahoe.

Risa came around the truck to stand beside him. "You said the RF detector picked up the GPS signal. What if—"

"Exactly." He spotted the tracker that Campbell Cove Security placed on all the fleet vehicles, as expected.

But a few inches farther down the underside of the chassis, he found another small tracker, almost invisible against the mud-spattered undercarriage. He checked to make sure it wasn't connected to anything that could damage the car if he removed it, then plucked it from the undercarriage.

"If we could put it on another vehicle…" Risa looked up at him, her eyes dark and unreadable.

"We'd be putting the driver of that vehicle in danger."

She nodded. "I guess we can just throw it away."

He looked around the parking lot, trying to come up with an option besides leaving it sitting, static, in the parking lot of the pizza restaurant. It wasn't a terrible option, he supposed, but for their purposes, it would help if the tracker could be on the move for a while, maybe drawing the people following them on a wild goose chase.

"The river," Risa said.

He looked at her. "The river?"

"We crossed a river on the way here," Risa said. "We could throw it in the river."

"The electronics would short out. It wouldn't give us any lead time."

She grinned at him, and for a second, he felt transported back to the early days of their relationship, when just being together was enough to make them both feel giddy and light. "Luckily for us, we just bought a whole lot of plastic-wrapped ornaments from the crafty girls of eastern Kentucky."

"Brilliant," he said, opening the back of the Tahoe to retrieve one of the bags. "Which way is the river?

"Something isn't right." Risa stared out the windshield at the darkness, unease rising in her chest. They'd dumped the GPS tracker in the Poor Fork tributary fifteen minutes ago and gotten rid of the Campbell Cove Security tracker as well. Now they were driving west toward Harlan, but she didn't feel any safer. "How did they connect the Tahoe to me? I don't have any relationship to Campbell Cove Security. And this is a fleet vehicle."

"You have a relationship to me," Connor said grimly. "And I was using my real name and my real credit cards in Cincinnati."

"But that only works if…"

"If they made you." Connor glanced at her. In the light from the dashboard, his face was a road map of shadows, but she could see enough of his expression to know it was grim.

"That has to be it. They made me. And they connected me to you."

"So they're tracking me, not you."

"Not anymore," she said. "We don't use your credit cards anymore. Throw away your phone if it can be connected to you."

"I have a burner phone that should be safe."

"Stick with that. How much cash do you have?"

"About a thousand in a lockbox under your seat. Another five hundred back at the safe house."

"We can't go back there."

"No," he agreed. "Do you have any cash?"

"Three hundred in a hidden pocket in my backpack."

"Also back at the safe house?"

"Actually, no. I stashed my backpack under the backseat before we left. After the close call in Cincinnati, I didn't think it was a good idea to let my laptop get too far out of my sight."

"We can't use your phone to connect to the web."

"No, but maybe we can spare a couple hundred dollars to buy a new burner we can use instead," she said, her sense of equilibrium beginning to return. "Also, I don't think we can risk getting in touch with Campbell Cove Security. At least not for a few days, until we can figure out if they've linked you directly to the company. It's possible they put the tracker on the Tahoe after we left Cincinnati, maybe at that gas station where we stopped outside Lexington."

"Quinn will start looking for us if we don't check in. And if he sends someone to the safe house to check on us and finds us missing—"

"I know," she interrupted, "but it's a risk we have to take. At least until we get some distance from where our last tracking coordinates show up. Let's just look for a low-rent motel that'll take cash and ask no questions. Get a good night's sleep and then we can worry about what comes tomorrow."

Connor was silent for a long moment, long enough that she was beginning to fear he was going to argue. But finally, he nodded. "Okay. You're right. We're cold, we're exhausted, and I don't know about you, but I'm starving. Maybe we can find a late-night drive-through on the way."

Her stomach rumbled in response, making them both laugh. She rubbed her stomach, where the baby was kicking up a storm. "Junior votes yes to the food, too."

Connor reached across the space between them, resting his hand on hers where it lay on her stomach. "We never talked about kids before."

"We hadn't been married that long." She took his hand and pressed it against her belly. "We thought we had time."

Connor's fingers flexed against her stomach. "Time. Everybody think there's time. Until there's not."

The baby kicked against her belly, and she heard Connor's soft gasp of surprise. She suppressed a smile. "And sometimes, you just have to figure out how to make more time for what's important."

"Like Junior."

Exactly, she thought, blinking back the sting of tears.

THE REST STOP Motor Lodge a few miles west of Harlan was two stories of shabby brick and mortar, held together, the best Connor could tell, primarily by years' worth of grime. The bedding on the double bed in the room they rented for the night looked relatively clean, but just in case, Connor retrieved the emergency camping kit from the SUV and spread the two sleeping bags over the bedding for them.

"Resourceful," Risa said, her tone approving as she sat down on one side of the bed, her legs crossed beneath her rounded belly. Digging in the bags they'd picked up at a burger joint on the way out of Cumberland, she retrieved a small box of French fries and started nibbling.

She grinned at him as she passed him the bag, feeling a strange sort of exhilaration as the food hit her empty stomach. Or maybe it was just the feeling that she was, finally, herself again, after months of being someone else. She was Risa McGinnis, she was with the man she loved, and she was weeks away from giving birth to their child.

Even the threat of ever-present danger didn't seem to quell her sense that she was finally where she was supposed to be.

But the sight of Connor's sober face took a little edge off her sudden sense of well-being. He ate his hamburger slowly, methodically, as if his mind was somewhere far away.

Back at Campbell Cove Security? Or somewhere else altogether?

Something Dal had told her a couple of weeks ago, when she'd asked if he knew anything about what Connor was doing now, flashed through her mind, chilling her mood further.

Seven months is a long time when you think your wife is dead.

Chapter Eleven

The Friday night crowd at The Jewel of Tablis was larger than Maddox Heller had anticipated. For cover, he'd brought along his wife, Iris, for this trip, leaving their two children with Iris's sister Rose and her husband, Daniel, who'd been nearby in Lexington for the week doing research for Daniel's latest book on criminal profiling. They'd agreed to take the kids through the weekend.

"That's Farid," he murmured to Iris, glancing toward the emailed photo saved on his phone. "Quinn and Cameron said he might be the weak link. If we can convince him it's worth his while to tell us why the man wanted to look around inside Risa's apartment."

"Do you think it was really Tahir Mahmoud?" Iris was trying to appear unfazed, but he knew the thought that Mahmoud might still be alive disturbed her. The man had nearly killed her eight years ago. She'd had nightmares about him for a couple of years before she'd finally managed to conquer the residual fears of that encounter.

"You saw the photo," he said, wishing he could give her a definitive no. But he and Iris didn't lie to each other. It was one of the cardinal rules of their marriage.

"I did."

"What did *you* think?"

"It looked a lot like him," she said after a brief pause. "Damn Alexander Quinn for telling you they'd found the body when they hadn't."

He reached across the table and took her hand. As always, he felt a light quiver of energy where their fingers touched. "Are you afraid he'll come after us?"

"I don't know." Her fingers tightened under his. "I guess it's a plus that he hasn't bothered us in eight years. Assuming he's still alive."

"That's how I'm choosing to look at it," he admitted. "But I've asked Quinn to harden the security at our new house, just in case."

"What about the kids? Daisy rides a bus to a public school every day. Jacob is about to start school next year. How do we protect them?"

"By finding out if this guy really is Tahir Mahmoud," Maddox said quietly, glancing across the restaurant at a pretty young woman wearing a bright green scarf over her lustrous dark hair. Darya Nahir. Risa McGinnis had identified the young waitress as a person to interview, since she had waited on the table of the men in question and might have gleaned a little information about them. "There's Darya. You ready?"

Iris nodded. "Showtime."

Darya approached their table, a friendly smile on her face and a pair of menus in her hands. "Welcome to The Jewel of Tablis. Would you like something to drink while you're looking at your menus?"

"I'll take a mint tea, iced," Maddox said. "Sweetheart?"

"The same, only I want mine hot." Iris smiled up at Darya. "That is a gorgeous *roosari*. It looks handmade."

Darya smiled. "It was. My mother made it."

"The embroidery work is exquisite."

"Thank you." Darya looked pleased by the compliment.

"Oh, I bet you're the girl Con was telling us about."

Darya's dark eyebrows lifted as she finished jotting down their drink orders. "Con?"

"Connor. A friend of ours who was in town earlier this week. He's the one who recommended the restaurant to us. I think he was here the other night—maybe Tuesday or Wednesday? He couldn't stop talking about the pretty waitress he saw—he said she was beautiful, like a bright flower."

"Wow, I don't know if he was talking about me."

"Well, you're definitely not the other waitress he mentioned," Iris said with a laugh. "That woman was about nine months pregnant."

"Yasmin," Darya said, her smile fading. "Yes."

"Is something wrong?" Iris put her hand on the young woman's arm. Her fingers trembled, and Darya gave her a curious look.

"I'm a little worried," Darya admitted. "Yasmin was supposed to work the past two nights but she didn't show, and she's not answering her phone."

"Do you think she had her baby?" Iris asked, dropping her hand away from the young waitress's arm. She slanted a look at Maddox, her light brown eyes dark with meaning.

Darya gave Iris a troubled look. "I don't know. Farid— our boss—tells me not to worry, but it hasn't really made me feel any better. I wish I knew what happened to her." She cleared her expression deliberately, flashing them a smile that wasn't quite convincing. "I'll be back in a few minutes for your order."

Maddox waited until Darya was out of earshot before he leaned across the table toward his wife. "Well?"

"She's tense. Definitely worried about Risa. If there's a terrorist plot cooking in this town, she's not part of it."

"Then maybe she could be an ally," he murmured.

"Maybe," Iris agreed. "But I think the person who can really tell us the most about what happened here Wednesday night is her boss."

Maddox glanced across the room, where Farid Rahimi stood talking to a couple sitting at a table in the corner. From this angle, he looked vaguely familiar.

Where had he seen him before?

As WEARY AS he was, after the past two eventful days, Connor found that sleep was elusive. Beside him, Risa had fallen into an occasionally restless slumber, lying on her side, her body curled up around her pregnant belly as if she were protecting her child, even in slumber.

He lay on his back, gazing up at the ceiling, where the faint thread of light seeping in through the motel room curtains cast odd shadows on the water-stained Sheetrock.

Something wasn't right. Actually, a lot wasn't right, but the one thing that continued to bug him was how quickly their pursuers had found them at the Christmas-tree lot.

They'd guessed that the tracker might have been added to the car when they stopped in Lexington. But how had anyone found them in Lexington if they didn't already know where to look for them? He was pretty sure he hadn't been followed out of town, at least once they hit the long stretch of highway between Cincinnati and Lexington. So either someone had spotted them leaving together in Cincinnati, seen the direction they were going and made a calculated guess about their route, or…

That's where he hit a wall. What was the "or"? Was there any other way someone could have put a tracker on the car before they arrived at the safe house?

"You're still awake, aren't you?" Risa's sleepy voice rasped softly in the dark.

"How did someone put a tracker on the Tahoe?"

She rolled over, propping her head on her hand and looking at him. "You said you thought it was when we stopped in Lexington."

"But how did someone find us in Lexington that fast? Yes, I know I used my credit card, but we were gone within a few minutes after that transaction was processed. No way did anyone have time to reach our location and put the GPS tracker on the Tahoe that quickly."

"You're right," she said, her voice sober. "So someone was either expecting us to be in Lexington, at that place we stopped, or…"

"Or someone had already put the tracker on the Tahoe in Cincinnati."

"But it's Quinn's car."

"I know." He rolled over to face her, a light shiver running down his spine as he studied her features in the dim light. She was so familiar to him, and yet, somehow after these seven months apart, she seemed like a stranger. A beautiful, intoxicating, very pregnant stranger.

"Maybe someone was tracking Quinn."

Possible, he supposed, though his new boss was known for his fanatical security measures. "I don't think they would have been able to put the tracker on the Tahoe until Cincinnati," he murmured. "Quinn would have had the vehicle checked before he left Campbell Cove. But someone could have spotted him when he arrived and put the tracker on his vehicle then."

"So maybe it's really someone after Quinn?" she asked hopefully.

"Maybe." But he didn't think so. Whoever had disabled the generator at the tree lot had to have known that Connor and Risa were the people in the SUV. He growled. "I can't make this make sense. Even well-organized terrorist groups don't have the resources to be so Johnny-on-the-spot with surveillance. Do they?"

"No," she agreed. "They're more and more technologically savvy these days, yes, but what you're suggesting would have to be…" She frowned, shadows falling over her eyes as her brow furrowed.

"It would have to be a government," he finished for her. "And Kaziristan sure as hell doesn't have that sort of capability."

"No. But people in our own country do," she said soberly.

"You think our own government could be behind this?" It seemed to physically hurt to say those words aloud. He'd dedicated the better part of his adult life to serving the government of the United States. And while he certainly didn't trust every member of the bureaucratic behemoth that was the federal government, he couldn't believe his country would target a woman who had given most of her own adult life in government service.

"I don't know," she said. "I don't want to believe it, but it wouldn't exactly be the first time someone in government went rogue, would it? Barton Reid's treason wasn't that long ago, after all. Ask Maddox Heller."

Barton Reid had been a State Department official who'd played terrorists and other enemy elements against the US government for his own financial gain. A lot of damage had been done before the man was taken down and sentenced to life in prison for his treachery.

Could the attempt on Risa's life have been ordered by another government official gone rogue?

"But why would you have been targeted?" he asked. "What were you working on last? Is it something you can tell me about?"

"The last thing I was working on was pretty mundane. And kind of gross." She rolled over onto her back, gazing up at the ceiling, a smile playing at her lips. "I was tasked with doing basic background analysis and surveillance on a group of Kaziri entrepreneurs who were planning to start an agri-tech company. Their goal was to research and implement the best agricultural practices for Kaziristan's climate and ecosystem. You know, selecting drought-resistant crops and livestock that have the best chance of thriving in Kaziristan. They were looking for UN grants as well as grants from the US and the government of Kaziristan."

"That sounds…fun." Connor's tone sounded skeptical.

"Actually, they were nice guys. Young, forward-thinking. Well-educated and hoping to pull even the rural parts of Kaziristan kicking and screaming into the twenty-first century. They wanted to improve the chances of profitable agriculture in Kaziristan that didn't include growing poppies for warlords to turn into drugs to fund their turf battles."

"Did you turn in your final report before the crash?"

"If things had gone smoothly, I would have been able to give them a green light, but something came up at the last minute that was going to require more investigation.

I was supposed to meet with another agent when I got back to DC, but…"

"But you didn't get there." He nodded. "So, what was the holdup?"

"One of the big things the guys wanted to do was harvest bat guano from the caves in the mountains. From a chemistry standpoint, it was showing great promise as an affordable, effective fertilizer for some of the crops that needed extra nutrients not available in the soil. But the guys discovered that some of the bats in the area they were targeting had started coming down with a hemorrhagic disease. At the time of my investigation, the disease hadn't jumped into another species as far as we could tell, but there was a very strong concern that the disease might spread to livestock or even humans through the guano."

"That doesn't seem as if it should have put a stop to the project," Connor said. "It was just one source of fertilizer, right?"

"Yes, but it was a pretty significant part of the cost-control aspect of their plan. Other sources of fertilizer, like cow and goat manure, weren't naturally occurring the way the bat guano was."

"That's what you were coming back to DC to discuss?"

"Yes. I was supposed to meet with someone in the CDC to determine if there was a way to test the guano on-site to ascertain whether the bats in the area were diseased, and what kind of costs that might incur. Also, I was hoping to meet with some people in the Department of Agriculture to see what protocols for food safety might be involved."

"And they say a career in the CIA is mostly a big bore."

She smiled. "I know it sounds kind of dull, but if these guys were able to accomplish their goals, it could mean that hundreds of thousands of people in rural Kaziristan could live vastly improved lives."

"Well, it certainly doesn't sound like anything that would put you on a hit list," Connor agreed. "But I guess it's something we should look into."

"How do you propose we do that? How do we look into anything at this point?" Her voice was tight with frustration. "Do we dare risk trying to contact Quinn if someone's out there tracking your electronic trail?"

"I have enough cash to buy a burner phone. Nobody will know to track it, and we can reach Quinn that way."

"Unless they're tracking Quinn's electronic trail, too."

"Quinn is pretty savvy. It would be hard to track him without his knowing it."

"It's still a risk," she warned. "But since we don't have internet access at the moment, he may be our only option to do a little digging into that possibility."

He turned over, facing her. "We can't do anything before morning. So why don't you try to stop those wheels in your head from turning and get some sleep?"

Her lips twitched up at the corners.

"What?" he asked.

"Remember how you used to help me go to sleep when my mind wouldn't stop running in circles?"

He did. Vividly. "I could give it a try."

Her eyes widened. "You're serious?"

"Turn over."

She stared at him, her dark eyes gleaming in the low

light. Then she rolled over to her other side and went very still.

He shifted until her body was spooned against his. She felt small and deliciously warm, tucked against him beneath the blankets. He could feel the tension in her body, as tangible as a low-level electric current running through her muscles.

Starting with her neck, he pressed his thumb against the taut muscles, rubbing firmly but gently, trying to work loose some of the tension. Moving relentlessly downward, he followed the curve of her arm, down to her hand, where he massaged each finger. Then he traced the curve of her hip, gently massaging the muscles of her outer thigh.

"Helping?" he murmured, struggling to hold his own body in check.

"Mmm," she answered with a guttural groan of pleasure.

So not what he needed.

His fingers trembled as he sat up and worked his way down her calves, kneading the knotted muscles.

"Don't," she whispered as he reached her ankle. She turned onto her back and sat up, turning to look at him. She was breathing hard, her chest rising and falling beneath her thin T-shirt. "You forgot how these moments always ended."

He curled his hand behind the back of her head, tangling his fingers in her hair. He tugged her closer, whispering against her lips. "I didn't forget."

Her lips parted, her breath hot on his mouth as he kissed her.

He'd kissed her hundreds, thousands of times before, but this felt strangely new somehow, as if it was the first time. She darted her tongue lightly across his lower lip, tasting. Testing.

He ran his hands down her sides, letting them settle lightly over the bulge of her belly. He kissed her again, more deeply. With more intensity. Reacquainting himself with the taste of her, with the sweet headiness of her scent. She responded with eagerness, curling her fingers in his hair as she rose to her knees and took control of the kiss with a fierce passion that made his head spin.

"I missed you. Every day." She kissed her way across his jaw and down the side of his neck, nipping lightly at his skin. "Every night."

He was losing all control. Had this been what he'd been hoping for when he offered to help her get to sleep?

She lowered herself until she was straddling his hips, the heat of her body enveloping his. Claiming him all over again.

Branding him with her need.

He had lost all restraint now, his body surging with desire as she pressed herself harder against his erection.

"It's okay," she whispered against his throat. "This doesn't have to mean anything beyond this moment."

Her words worked like an ice bath, cooling his runaway ardor. He found the strength to pull away from her grasp, to put distance between them on the bed until he was able to recapture his breath.

"I'm not ready for this," he admitted. "I can't just pretend it doesn't mean anything. I can't act as if everything between us is okay now."

She sank back against the pillows, her breaths coming fast and harsh. "I know." Her hands moved to her belly, stroking, soothing, as she struggled to get her breathing back under control.

"I'm not saying never," he added, even though a part of him wished he could. The raw, vulnerable part that wanted to pretend that if he didn't let her back in his heart, he'd never be hurt again. But he knew better now. There was no escaping what he felt for her.

He was just going to have to find some way to deal with it.

"I understand," she murmured, her hands playing over her round belly.

He rolled over on his side, his back to her. Needing what little space, what little distance, he could put between them in this tiny motel room.

FARID RAHIMI LEFT his apartment building around seven the next morning, dressed in sweats and a thick fleece jacket. The North Face, Maddox noticed. High end, top quality. The restaurant business must be doing well for him. Or he had another source of income.

He couldn't shake the sense that he'd seen the man before. But it hadn't been in Kaziristan, when Maddox was working as a Marine Security Guard at the US Embassy in Tablis.

It was somewhere else, more recently.

"Still can't remember where you know him from?" Iris sat beside him in the passenger seat of the truck, wrapped up against the cold and sipping a hot coffee.

"No. It's not from my time in Kaziristan, I'm pretty sure."

"Any word on the background check?"

Maddox gave himself a mental kick and checked his phone. There was a new email from Kyra Sanchez at the office. The subject line read Background.

He opened the email and scanned the contents. "Hmm."

"Hmm?"

"Rahimi held a job in Mariposa at the American Consulate for a couple of years."

"Maybe that's where you know him from?"

"Maybe." He started the truck and began following Rahimi, who was now jogging up the street toward Washington Park. He found a place to park the truck on the street and kept an eye on Rahimi as the man started running a brisk circuit of the park.

"Interesting that a Kaziri man ends up working in the US Consulate on a tiny Caribbean island," Iris murmured. "And Quinn worked there, too, didn't he?"

Maddox dragged his gaze away from Rahimi long enough to look at his wife. "What are you thinking?"

She took another sip of coffee, her dark eyes meeting his over the rim of the cup. "Wouldn't be the first time Alexander Quinn was running an op without telling you about it."

He looked back at Rahimi, taking in the trim physique and strong running form. Not the kind of fitness he'd normally associate with your average middle-aged restaurateur.

He picked up his phone and dialed a number. Quinn answered on the first ring. "Quinn."

"Heller," he snapped back. "When were you going to tell me that Farid Rahimi is on our payroll?"

"Need to know, Heller." Quinn's voice tightened. "We've got a bigger problem. The McGinnises have dumped the tracker on the Tahoe. They've gone rogue."

Chapter Twelve

"I've been thinking about the Tahoe," Risa said over their breakfast of cheese crackers and sodas from the vending machines next to the motel office.

"You think we need to ditch it somewhere."

She nodded. "If there's any possibility we're being tracked by someone with access to government resources, we need to take measures to thwart them."

"You're right. We're lucky they haven't tracked us already."

"If we'd stayed in a normal motel room, management might well have asked for our license plate number when we registered." Risa finished the last of her crackers and downed the rest of the Sprite he'd bought.

"That's why I went for a place where nobody would ask any questions."

"Do you think Quinn has figured out we're not at the safe house yet?"

"Probably," Connor conceded. "Someone will have noticed that the GPS tracker was disabled. We didn't put it in a plastic bag the way we did with the rogue tracker. The next step is to check the safe house."

"So they must know we've gone."

He nodded. "If we ditch the Tahoe, how are we going

to get around? I don't want to steal a car, and we don't have enough money to buy one, even a piece-of-garbage car."

She bit her lip, thinking. She wasn't nearly as certain as Connor that Alexander Quinn was playing things straight with them, but Connor was right about one thing—if they wanted to have the mobility to stay on the run, they needed transportation. And she wasn't any more inclined to grand theft auto than he was.

"Who do you trust the most at Campbell Cove Security?" she asked him.

"Heller," he answered immediately.

"Any way to get in touch with him without anyone else at Spear knowing about it?"

He gave it a moment's thought before he smiled. "As a matter of fact, yes."

TEN MINUTES LATER, they stood outside a small gas station on the main road, huddling together against the frigid cold and praying that the pay phone hanging on the front of the attached food mart was in service.

Connor breathed a sigh of relief at the dial tone. He punched in the number jotted in his address book and waited for a response. "Please answer," he muttered.

Next to him, Risa edged closer, as if seeking his warmth. He put his arm around her shoulders, tugging her closer.

On the fourth ring, as he was starting to lose hope, a woman's voice replied, "Hello?"

"Iris, it's Connor McGinnis. I need to talk to Maddox. Is he with you?"

A moment later, Maddox's gravelly drawl answered. "Where the hell are you, Connor?"

"We had to run. Someone put a tracker on the SUV—besides the Campbell Cove Security tracker. Whoever it was tried to get his hands on Risa last night at a place we stopped. We didn't think it was smart to return to the safe house."

"Good call," Maddox said. "Why'd you call Iris's number?"

"We don't know who might be trying to find us or how they're doing it. I didn't think it would be wise to call a company-connected phone, but I hoped I might catch you with Iris."

"You lucked out. What do you need?"

Connor glanced at Risa. They had discussed what they'd ask for on the way to find a pay phone, but now that it was time to make their demands, he was beginning to wonder if they weren't being a little too paranoid.

"Connor?" Maddox asked.

"I'm here," he said, looking at Risa. He covered the mouthpiece of the phone. "Are you sure this is how you want to do it?"

She nodded.

"We need a car that can't be connected to Campbell Cove Security. And I don't want Quinn to know I contacted you. Can you do that?"

Maddox was quiet for a moment. "Yeah. I can do that. But I want to see you. I need to talk to you face-to-face. Do you trust me to do that?"

"He wants to meet with us," Connor told Risa.

Her brow furrowed, but after a moment, she nodded. "Tell him not to use a vehicle that could be easily connected to him."

Connor relayed the request.

"I'll make it happen," Maddox agreed. "Where and when?"

Connor thought fast. "You know that sandwich shop next to the dollar store in Cumberland? Think you can get there by lunchtime?"

"It'll be cutting it close, but yeah. I should be able to."

"See you at twelve thirty." Connor hung up the phone and looked at Risa. "We're set."

She looked tense. "You think I'm paranoid."

"Maybe a little. But we have to keep you and the munchkin safe, don't we?"

She rubbed her stomach. "So what do we do while we're waiting?"

"There's a public library in Cumberland. Why don't we see if we can find a free internet connection?"

THE PUBLIC LIBRARY was doing a brisk business that Saturday morning, mostly parents with young children who were there for a special reading of Clement Moore's famous poem, "A Visit from St. Nicholas." They passed the group of rapt children listening to the tale of the night before Christmas on their way to the computer terminals.

"We'll be reading that poem to Junior next Christmas," Connor murmured.

Risa slanted a glance at him, noting the faint look of amazement in his blue eyes and wondering if he realized he'd used the word *we*. Deciding not to push, she followed him to the computer area, where they found that three of the terminals were open. He went to the one that was the farthest away from other library patrons and pulled up a second chair for Risa.

"Okay, what should we look for first?" he asked.

"I can't stop thinking about the project I was supposed

to report on before the plane crash, ever since we discussed it last night." She pulled up a search engine and typed in the name of the upstart company.

The first hit came as a shock. "Agri-Tech Entrepreneurs Killed in IED Attack."

"Oh. That's not good," Connor murmured.

She clicked the link, which took her to an English-language paper from Qatar, which reported the death of the two Kaziri businessmen, the owners of the agricultural start-up called Akwat, which loosely translated to "sustenance" in Kaziri. The date of the article was the day after the plane crash.

"Why didn't Dal tell me about this?" Risa wondered.

"I don't know. Maybe he didn't think there was a connection?"

"The day after the plane crash? Isn't that a bit too much of a coincidence?"

Connor frowned. "Maybe not."

She searched deeper in the article for more details. The attack had actually happened the same day as the plane crash, a few hours after the first report of the crash. "It's almost like they waited to be sure I was dead before they struck the agri-tech business."

"But why? Why try to kill all of you?"

"I don't know!" Her voice rose higher than she intended, and a nearby patron gave her a disapproving look. She quickly lowered her voice. "I think we need to get out of here, in case somebody is tracking web searches about Akwat."

"You really think that's possible?"

"It's absolutely possible, if someone has access to national-security internet resources."

Connor lowered his voice to a whisper. "You're talking about someone inside our own government."

"Or China's or Russia's or any number of countries in Europe." She glanced around her, making sure nobody was watching them. "Or hackers, for that matter, if someone was paying them for the information."

"But why? Why would anyone care about an agri-tech start-up business in Kaziristan?"

"Why did anyone want me dead? I don't know. But I need to find out." She rose from her chair and started to reach for the straps of her backpack. Connor beat her to it, swinging the heavy pack over his shoulder.

They made their way back through the library, trying to blend in with the rest of the patrons. They emerged into bright sunlight and a hint of warmth that took the edge off the cold breeze flapping the American flag hanging on a pole outside the library. It was already noon, close to the time they were supposed to meet Maddox Heller at the sandwich shop.

Inside the Tahoe, Connor turned to look at her, his gaze intense. "Whatever this is you're up against, I'm in it with you. You know that, don't you? What I said to you last night—it doesn't change that fact. We're going to figure this out together. We're going to get your life back for you."

She held his gaze, afraid to read too much into what he was saying, especially since he'd said *your life* instead of *our life*. But she found his words heartening anyway. "Okay."

"And then we'll have the time and space to figure out what happens next." He softened his words by reaching out to touch her face, his callused fingers deliciously rough against her cheek.

She closed her fingers over his. *I know what I want already*, she thought, intensely aware of the quivering sensation of the child wriggling in her womb. *I want us to be a family.*

BY HABIT, CONNOR sat with his back to the wall, facing the door of the sandwich shop, acutely aware of the store's glass-front facade. It wasn't the most secure of meeting places to have chosen, but at least nobody else in the shop seemed to think there was anything amiss about the man and pregnant woman sitting alone at a table for four. They had gone through the buffet line to select their sandwiches—beef and Swiss with tomatoes and peppers for Connor, and chicken salad with spinach and tomatoes for Risa. They had barely unwrapped their sandwiches before Maddox Heller and his wife, Iris, entered the sandwich shop.

Maddox spotted them and gave a wave before he and Iris went through the line for their own sandwiches. Carrying their trays, they joined Connor and Risa at the table.

"Did you know there's a tree in the back of the Tahoe?" Maddox sat across from Connor with a grin that carved deep dimples in his lean cheeks. He'd been a favorite with the female embassy employees during his time with the Marine Security Guards, and he'd not been afraid to take advantage of that popularity during his off hours.

But Maddox was clearly smitten with his pretty brunette wife, Iris, a slim woman with eyes the color of pecan hulls, an odd hue somewhere between brown and gray.

She smiled across the table at Connor before turning her attention to Risa. "Welcome back from the dead."

"Thank you." Risa managed a smile in return before

turning her attention to Maddox and his opening statement. "Yes, we're aware we have a tree in the SUV. It's Christmas."

Connor quickly caught them up on the details of what had happened to them the night before. "We don't think we're safe in the Tahoe. They have our tag number and the make and model of the vehicle."

"Yeah, I can see how you'd be worried." Maddox leaned closer across the table, lowering his voice. "We drove here in a Dodge Durango. Rented by my brother-in-law, and there shouldn't be any easy way to connect it to you. He just asks that you don't do anything crazy in it."

"I'm not sure it's safe for you two if you're in the Tahoe, either."

"No worries. We've already called to have the Tahoe towed back to the office. We've also booked a week at one of the lodges near Sunset Mountain, in the names of Daniel and Rose Hartman. You roughly match their descriptions. Well, except for..." Iris waved at Risa's pregnant belly. "They're waiting for us at the lodge. You'll drop us off and they'll drive us back home. Then you stay in the lodge in their names."

"The lodge has free Wi-Fi, so you can get online if you need to do any research. And here." Maddox reached into his pocket and pulled out a phone, which he slid across the table to Connor. "No trackers, no connection to Campbell Cove Security or anyone else. Daniel bought it earlier this morning. It's got an app that lets you change your phone number as often as you like, so if you have to make calls, use the app and keep switching out the numbers. That will make you very hard to track."

So far, they hadn't told Maddox about their suspicions regarding the agri-tech firm Risa had been vetting shortly before the plane crash. Connor glanced at Risa and saw the wariness in her hazel eyes. He decided to let her make the decision about what else to tell Maddox.

Apparently she decided to keep those facts to herself for the time being, for she remained quiet through lunch and made only small talk as they exited the sandwich shop into the warming afternoon sunlight.

"Since y'all will be at the lodge through New Year's Eve, if everything goes well, why don't we put the tree on top of the Durango?" Iris suggested. "Most people who stay in the lodges at this time of year are there celebrating the holidays, so it'll add a touch of authenticity."

Connor looked at Risa. Looking genuinely pleased by the idea, she gave a quick nod. "Good idea," he told Iris, and he and Maddox got to work transferring the tree to the Durango's roof rack, while Iris helped Risa pack the rest of their supplies in the back.

"We packed some clothes for y'all," Maddox told Connor when they had finished transferring everything to the Durango.

"I had some maternity clothes left over from my last pregnancy," Iris told Risa. "I'm a little taller than you, but I think they'll fit well enough."

Risa looked up at Connor, her eyes shiny with emotion. She turned back to Maddox and Iris. "I don't know how to thank y'all for everything."

"You'll probably get a chance to return the favor sooner or later, if I know my husband and his history of attracting trouble," Iris said, flashing her husband a look of exasperated affection.

"Here's the wrecker," Maddox said, nodding toward the large tow truck that pulled into the sandwich shop parking lot. While Maddox and Iris took charge of getting the Tahoe loaded onto the tow truck's flatbed, Connor helped Risa into the front passenger seat of the Durango, then took his place behind the steering wheel.

"Maybe this will buy us enough time to figure out what's really going on," he murmured.

"Maybe." Risa leaned her head against the back of the seat. "I feel as if I'm standing in the middle of a highway with no way to escape. Vehicles flying toward me in both directions, and I don't know which way to turn."

He reached over and took her hand, bringing her knuckles to his lips. He gave them a quick brush of a kiss. "You're not alone in this. We'll figure it out. I promise."

She turned her gaze to meet his, giving his hand a light squeeze. "Don't make promises you can't keep."

"Come on, Risa, have a little faith in me."

The look she gave him was sharp and intense. "I do. I made a big mistake not telling you everything that was happening. I won't make that mistake again."

He wanted to believe her. More than anything in the world.

Iris and Maddox climbed into the backseat of the Durango, snapping the sudden tension that filled the SUV's quiet interior. "All taken care of. You know how to get to the lodges?"

Connor gave a nod, and they were quickly on the road.

"Listen, there's something you need to know." Maddox broke the comfortable silence that had fallen inside the SUV as they neared the turnoff to Sunset Mountain. "Farid Rahimi is one of ours."

Risa turned around to look at him. "What?"

"Rahimi is one of ours. Working for Campbell Cove Security undercover."

"Since when?" Connor asked, glancing at Maddox's reflection in the Durango's rearview mirror.

"Since the beginning of the company, it seems. He's former CIA. Worked with Quinn for a while at the consulate in Mariposa, under a different name—Malcolm Faris. He's not even Kaziri. He's Iranian. But he spent several years in Kaziristan with Central Intelligence, so…"

Risa shook her head. "Unbelievable. What did Quinn task him to do, act like a complete ass?"

"More or less. He wanted someone in a position to know who's got the power in the Kaziri community in Cincinnati. So they set up the identity of Farid Rahimi and let him play the role from there. He quickly picked up the fact that The Jewel of Tablis was becoming the center of the community, so he and Quinn manufactured him a background and résumé that made him perfect for the management job."

"Did he know who I was?"

"No. Quinn didn't tell him, and apparently you look different enough from your official photos from your previous cover jobs that nobody made the connection."

"Thank God for that," Connor murmured.

"I don't know if it matters now, knowing the truth about Rahimi. But I thought you had the right to know."

The large wooden sign proclaiming that they'd reached the entrance to Sunset Lodges appeared as they took a sharp curve into a straightaway. Connor slowed the Durango and made the turn through the entrance gates.

"Your cabin is the Big Bear," Maddox told them as they neared the lodge office. He nodded toward a dark blue sedan parked in a space at the side of the building.

"That's Daniel and Rose. No need to stop and chat—just drop us off here and keep going."

Connor slowed to a stop to let Maddox and Iris get out of the Durango. He met Maddox's gaze. "Thank you for everything."

"Be safe." Maddox joined his wife and headed for the parked sedan.

Connor drove on, up the gravel-paved road marked "Big Bear Cabin." The road wound up the mountain, ending at a two-story chalet-style cabin nestled in the woods.

"Beats the hell out of the Rest Stop Motor Lodge," Risa said.

With a fervent nod of agreement, Connor parked the Durango and started unloading their things.

Chapter Thirteen

The Christmas tree filled most of the large picture window that, during daylight, offered a splendid view of the fog-veiled Appalachian Mountains spreading east into Virginia. The homemade ornaments and garland went well with the open-beam walls and ceiling of the cabin, Risa decided, and made herself stop wishing they'd been able to purchase twinkling lights to complete the festive picture.

"I can't believe Christmas is less than a week away," she said as she sank onto the sofa next to Connor, who sat with his socked feet propped up on the coffee table while he used her laptop to surf the web.

Connor set aside the laptop and turned to look at her, lifting one hand to touch her cheek. "I can't believe we're actually going to spend another Christmas together."

She leaned closer, and he wrapped one arm around her shoulder, tugging her against his side. They sat quietly for a while, looking at the tree, content not to speak.

"I called Quinn on the burner phone while you were taking a shower," he said a few minutes later.

She looked up at him. "Did you change the number with the app afterward?"

"Yeah."

"What did Quinn have to say?"

"He said we made the right choice, but I could tell he wasn't that happy about it."

"Do you care?" she asked.

He grinned. "Not really."

"Does he have any new information for us?"

"I didn't bring up some of the things we discovered," Connor admitted. "I didn't know if you'd want me to."

"I'd really like to know why Farid—or Malcolm, or whoever he is—took the chance of blowing my cover when he talked my landlord into letting that guy in my apartment. What if it really was Tahir Mahmoud? What if he'd killed me right there in front of Malcolm? Would he have let Tahir kill me in order to protect his own cover?"

"I don't know. But the first chance I get to talk to Quinn face-to-face, you'd better believe I'm going to ask him."

Risa nestled closer to Connor. "I can't shake the feeling that whoever wants me dead is somehow connected to Akwat."

"How could it be connected? All you were doing was a background check."

She rubbed her belly, where the baby was kicking lightly against her womb. "Well, yeah, it was just a background check at first. But I did start to make a few deeper inquiries."

He looked down at her. "What kind of deeper inquiries?"

"Honestly, it was probably just my paranoid nature, but it occurred to me that if the hemorrhagic fever the bats were incubating in those caves could somehow be coaxed into jumping species, it might turn out to have—strategic implications."

"Coaxed? You mean, on purpose?"

"Maybe."

He frowned, his gaze moving toward the window. He stared at the Christmas tree in silence for a moment. She had a feeling his mind was nowhere near this cozy little living room.

He finally spoke again. "But if the disease jumped species, the bad guys couldn't be sure that they could control the infection."

"That's kind of what I was looking into," she said. "I wanted to see if the disease DNA was close enough to the hemorrhagic fevers we're already familiar with. Maybe something that could be controlled before the effects became pandemic. Bad guys wouldn't necessarily want to wipe out the world's population. In fact, an epidemic wouldn't be necessary to spread terror. You know the kind of hype that accompanied that Ebola outbreak in the US a few years ago, and those cases amounted to almost nothing."

"But imagine if someone were able to spread a new, unknown virus in a deliberate, controlled way." Connor shook his head, a light shiver rippling through him. "The panic alone could be devastating."

"Exactly the sort of panic terrorism is intended to create."

He turned to face her. "But we're going on the premise that someone in our own government is gunning for you. The US isn't in the terror business."

"No, but what if someone inside the government wants to get their hands on this pathogen first? To weaponize it for his own purposes?"

"What purposes?"

"Any number of things—manipulate the stock market? Undermine trust in public health services? Or private health services, for that matter. Or maybe target a particular population to foment racial unrest."

"God."

"Yeah. Exactly."

Connor laid his head back against the sofa cushions, gazing up at the ceiling. He looked as shaken as she felt. "And you really think it's possible?"

"I was in the CIA long enough to realize that most of our worst-case scenarios weren't nearly bad enough. Look at what happened with Barton Reid. The man was making backroom deals with terrorists in order to manipulate public opinion and legislation that would suit his personal desires. Don't you think he'd have done something just this ruthless if it had served his purposes?"

"But Barton Reid is in jail."

"He wasn't the only person involved in that mess. We know that much from the post-arrest Senate hearings."

Connor rubbed his chin. "You know who we really need to talk to? The people who took Barton Reid down."

"The Coopers," Risa murmured.

Connor nodded. "The Coopers."

CARA COOPER WAS the world's most adorable six-month-old. Wavy dark hair like her mother's and her father's bright blue eyes made her impossible to resist, even on a bad day.

And today had been a very bad day, thanks to the first baby tooth trying to make its way into her toothless little mouth.

Jesse Cooper's cell phone ringing was barely audible over Cara's fretful wails. Evie patted the baby's back soothingly and nodded for her husband to go take the call.

He didn't recognize the number displayed on his phone, but after an hour of trying to help his wife soothe their little darling, even a crank call would provide a welcome distraction. He closed the door behind him, muting the baby's cries, and answered the phone. "Jesse Cooper."

"Mr. Cooper, my name is Connor McGinnis. I work for Maddox Heller."

Ah, Jesse thought. His former partner strikes again. "How's Heller these days?"

"Seems well," McGinnis answered, his tone suggesting he was running low on patience.

So Jesse cut to the chase. "What do you need?"

There was a brief pause, as if Jesse's blunt question had caught McGinnis by surprise. Then the other man outlined the reason for his call in the sort of quick, organized spiel that told Jesse that Connor McGinnis was, like Jesse himself, a product of the US military.

"So, you want to know if any of Barton Reid's associates could still be pulling strings inside the government?" Jesse summed up.

"Yes."

"Short answer, yes. It's possible." He and his family had done a lot to limit the damage Barton Reid did to American influence in the Middle East and Central Asia, and to thwart his group's domestic terrorism ambitions. They had helped authorities apprehend and convict the worst offenders, but Jesse had never lost sight of the fact that there were probably others like Barton Reid out there, lying low, waiting for a chance to make another move.

"Possible," McGinnis repeated. "But you don't have a handy list of suspects, I take it?"

"No. But if you think that's what you're up against, I

might be interested in looking into the matter." He had a few resources inside the government he could turn to. Plus, his gruff father-in-law, retired US Marine Corps General Baxter Marsh, knew where a whole lot of bodies were buried at the Pentagon.

If someone was planning to use a position high in the US government for his or her own benefit, it would give Jesse a great deal of pleasure to put a permanent stop to the plot.

"I'm not really able to come down there and discuss it with you." For the first time in the phone call, McGinnis sounded tentative, even wary.

"Are you the person with a target on your back?" Jesse asked.

"No."

But maybe it was someone he cared about, Jesse thought. "Why haven't you taken this to Heller? Isn't he working for some government security contractor now?"

"He is. So am I."

"But contacting the company could be dangerous to you?"

McGinnis didn't respond. It was all the answer Jesse needed.

"Okay. I can come to you," Jesse said finally. "But I'll have to talk to Heller first. Make sure you're on the level."

"Are you sure you want to get that involved in this situation? Maybe this is something we could just discuss over the phone. It would be safer that way. For you, at least." From McGinnis's tone, Jesse could tell that the situation might be even more dire than he thought.

But he'd been in some grim tangles before and lived to tell about it.

"I spent over a decade in uniform risking my life to

protect the citizens of the United States," Jesse said. "I didn't stop doing that when I finally took the uniform off."

"Neither did I."

"Then you know what I mean. You're talking about a plot to deliberately infect people with a deadly disease in order to create panic and terror. I can't let that stand if I can do something about it."

"I know," McGinnis said grimly. "But all I'm working with right now is suppositions. What-ifs."

"So let's try to find something a little more concrete," Jesse said.

DEEP NIGHT HAD fallen over the mountains, and with it, the first flutterings of new snowfall. Just flurries at the moment, but even inside the cabin, warmed by central heat and a crackling fire, Risa felt the unmistakable chilled, damp promise of more snow.

"I don't know if this is a good idea." She turned to look at Connor, who was crouched by the hearth, stoking the fire as if he, too, felt the gathering fury of winter.

"I don't, either." He stood and crossed to where she stood at the big picture window, gazing past her own faint reflection to the dusting of snow starting to gather on the wooden deck outside. "But we can't just hunker down here forever. You're—we're—about to have a baby. I don't want Junior to come into the world with a target on his own little back."

"Or hers," Risa murmured, turning toward him as he moved closer.

He pulled her into an embrace as if it were the most natural thing in the world. And it had been, once. As natural as breathing.

She nuzzled closer. "When's he supposed to arrive?"

"If the weather cooperates, tomorrow afternoon. Apparently Cooper Security has their own chopper."

"Unfortunately, I think we're getting more snow sooner or later."

"Hopefully later." He tangled his fingers in her hair, gently tugging until she looked up at him. "Meanwhile, let's think about something pleasant, okay?"

She flattened her palm over his chest, enjoying the feel of his heartbeat beneath her fingers. "Like what?"

"Like, have you thought about names for Junior?"

She hadn't, she realized. Was that strange? She'd tried out numerous nicknames over the past few months, as her pregnancy went from little more than a notion and slight thickening of her lower belly to the reality of stretch marks, cravings, weight gain, and something alive and kicking inside her.

"No," she admitted. "I haven't."

"Why not?"

She looked up at him and blurted the truth she hadn't even realized herself. "I think I was hoping we could choose a name together."

For a second, she thought he was going to pull away from her at the stark reminder of the way she'd failed him. But his expression shifted, a smile flirting with his lips. "Knew you couldn't stay away from me forever, huh? That old McGinnis mojo in overdrive."

She gave a surprised laugh and punched his shoulder. "Conceited ass."

He lowered his head, resting his forehead against hers. "That's half my charm, darlin'."

She rose to her toes and kissed him, just a delicate brush of her lips on his, but sparks seemed to crackle between them on contact, and Connor sucked in a swift breath.

Then he kissed her back, and there was nothing delicate about it. She met his fierce passion with equal fervor, curling her fingers through his hair and pressing her body against his, straining to get closer. Each caress seemed born of storm and fury, as if months of need and longing, pent up to the point of bursting, had breached a dam and spilled over, swamping them with need.

He took her hand and began moving toward the bedrooms. They stopped at the nearest one, the one she'd chosen as her own. Tripping over one of her discarded shoes, they stumbled into the bed, laughing as they almost slid into the floor.

In a way, stripping his shirt over his head and reaching to unzip his jeans seemed like the most natural thing in the world to Risa. She knew his body almost as well as she knew her own. The scar on his shoulder, thick beneath her fingers, was a near miss from the Battle of Fallujah. The thin scar on the back of his hand was from a Taliban soldier's knife, wielded in hand-to-hand combat in the Helmand province of Afghanistan.

And the bullet furrow just over his hip had come nearly a decade ago when al Adar rebels took the US Embassy in Tablis, Kaziristan, in a three-day siege.

He caught her face between his hands, gazing into her eyes as if he was seeing her for the first time. Maybe, in a way, he was. He'd never seen her face filled out the way it was from her pregnancy. And there were new marks on her body as well, stretch marks around her hips and belly. Her breasts had grown a cup size, and her bottom was a lot curvier than he would remember.

Slowly, he tugged her sweater over her head and

dropped it over the side of the bed, taking a moment to simply look at her. His gaze dropped to her breasts, straining against the too-small bra that Iris Heller had lent her. Downward, taking in the round swell of her pregnant belly, the road map of stretch marks and the button of her navel.

She felt suddenly self-conscious in a way she had never felt with him, nearly overcome with the urge to cover herself, to hide the changes in her body from his too-sharp eyes.

As she reached for the blanket, he caught her hand. "Don't."

She waited, heart pounding, as he smoothed his hand across her belly, his fingertips tracing a shivery path over the curves. The baby gave a sharp kick against Connor's palm, making him grin.

"You are so beautiful," he said, bending to kiss her belly. Then, his beard stubble rasping against her stomach, he lifted his gaze to her and grinned. "You, too."

God, she loved him. More than she had ever realized.

RISA CURLED UP like a kitten in her sleep, her naked backside tucked in the curve of his body, soft and deliciously warm. Connor pulled her against him, feeling a powerful need to shelter her from the world outside the walls of the cabin, a concept she would laugh at if he ever spoke it aloud.

She was, as he knew, supremely capable of protecting herself. She'd managed to stay alive with very little protection for seven months with a price on her head, after all.

But she was his wife. The other, vital part of his heart. He'd thought she was lost to him forever, and now that he'd had time to work through all the reasons she'd hidden the truth from him for as long as she had, he knew whatever mistakes she'd made weren't significant compared with the possibility of losing her again.

He had to find out who had targeted her. Find a way to put an end to the threat, once and for all.

And that meant finding out why there was a price on her head in the first place.

"You still awake?" Risa's sleepy voice was a soft murmur in the quiet darkness.

"Mmm-hmm," he answered.

"Do you think I'm fat?"

He laughed softly. "You don't really expect me to answer that question, do you?"

"Does that mean you do think I'm fat?"

He gave her backside a light slap. "I think you're perfect."

She made a soft, purring noise. "That's such a good answer."

He grinned. "I missed you so damn much."

She was silent for so long, he thought maybe she'd drifted back to sleep. Then she rolled over to face him, cupping his jaw with her palm. "I missed you, too. Every single minute of every single day."

He kissed her brow. "We've got to figure out who's trying to kill you."

"First we have to figure out why. That'll tell us who." A soft grumbling noise rose between them, and she grinned. "The kid and I are hungry."

He wrapped a piece of her dark hair around his finger. "We never got around to dinner, did we?"

She sat up and started scooping up clothing. "Beat you to the kitchen!"

By the time he pulled on a pair of jeans and padded barefoot into the kitchen, Risa was bending to look inside the refrigerator. "It was very sweet of Rose and Daniel to buy some groceries for us."

"We need to start adding up all the money we're going to owe people when this is over," he said.

"I know." She pulled out a package of sliced roast beef and a small jar of mayonnaise. "Roast beef sandwiches?"

"Sounds good to me." He found the loaf of bread in the box by the refrigerator and pulled out a few slices. He started to put two pieces in the toaster for her before he remembered that pregnancy could change a woman's food preferences. "Toasted or not?"

"Toasted," she said with a quick grin. "You had to ask?"

"Didn't know if Junior in there preferred it a different way."

"Ah." She smiled. "I've been lucky. Junior hasn't really changed any of my tastes."

"No cravings?"

"Oh, I've had cravings. But I just crave stuff I already like. Chocolate. Salt-and-vinegar chips." She nodded at the toaster. "And toast."

They lowered the lights and ate at the coffee table in the den, with a view of both the homey Christmas tree and the snow flurries falling in light showers outside, illuminated by the floodlights on the outside of the cabin. Afterward, they curled up on the sofa and flipped channels on the television until they found an old Cary Grant movie they hadn't seen in years.

It was such a normal way to spend an evening, Connor thought as he draped his arm around his wife's shoulder and nuzzled her hair while Cary Grant hid in a dried-out cornfield, chased by a crop duster. Just an ordinary married couple, baby on the way, watching a movie in front of the Christmas tree. It was the life they'd been planning, he realized, before everything had gone so very wrong.

As the movie wound to its exciting end, Risa stirred in his arms to ask, "Have you ever visited Mount Rushmore?"

He looked at Cary Grant clinging to the rock face between George Washington and Thomas Jefferson. "No. Definitely not like that."

"My dad used to take my mom and me on what he called our America trips," she said with a smile in her voice. "Did I ever tell you about those?"

"I don't think so."

"After we spent those years in Kaziristan while he was on duty, I think he wanted to be sure I remembered I was an American."

"Do you think he's ever suspected you were a CIA agent?" One thing he and Risa hadn't done as a married couple was spend much time with the in-laws, thanks to jobs that kept them overseas so much of the time.

"I think he probably did, but he was always pretty big on the concept of loose lips sinking ships. So he'd never say it out loud, even if he was pretty sure all my trips across the world weren't really about diplomacy."

Maybe once they got clear of this hit-list mess, he and Risa would finally have a chance to get to know each other's families, like real married couples did. His mother would be thrilled that one of her three sons had finally given her a grandchild, he knew. And he had long suspected that beneath crusty old Benton DeVille's drill-sergeant exterior, there lived an old softy who'd spoil the hell out of his grandchild.

But to have any of those things, they first had to survive.

Whatever it took.

Chapter Fourteen

The list was growing longer than Risa had anticipated. She'd been working for the CIA since the year after she'd graduated from college, plucked out of a Foreign Service fellowship program by Martin Dalrymple himself. Her fluency in Kaziri, Farsi and Arabic had made her a valuable asset put to use quickly.

Now, ten years later, she was beginning to realize just how many contacts she'd made during her time in the agency.

"That many, huh?" Connor set a glass of apple juice on the table in front of her and pulled up a chair next to her.

"I really thought it might be easier to figure out who I might have ticked off enough to earn a price on my head." She put the pen down on the table and picked up the coffee mug, curling her cold hands around the warm stoneware. "But apparently there are dozens of people who could want me dead."

"Not everybody on that list has a reason to want you dead, surely."

"That's the real problem," she said. "I could be on a hit list for reasons I know nothing about. What if someone thinks I saw or heard something that could someday cause a problem? It wouldn't even have to be something obvious to me. It could be something that, eventually, will make sense to me once it all unfolds. And maybe someone doesn't want me to be around when that happens."

"Oh, well. That certainly narrows it down." His tone was dirt-dry.

"I wish we could find out what Dal was thinking."

"A little late for that."

She rubbed her gritty eyes. "Yeah, I know."

His fingers brushed her cheek, making her look at him. His expression was both tender and anxious. "We'll figure this out. Or we'll figure out a way to disappear. I won't let anyone get to you. You know that."

She nodded. "It's just—I don't want to disappear. I've already done it once, and I hated it."

"You won't be alone." His thumb caressed her chin. "Junior and I will be there."

She held his hand against her face. "I know. But I'm going to have a baby. Our parents are going to have their first grandchild. Do you really want Junior to grow up not knowing them?"

She could see the answer in his troubled gaze, before he said the words. "No. I don't."

"I don't, either. So we're going to have to find the answer, not just run away again."

She leaned in and kissed him lightly before pulling away and picking up the pen again. "What did Heller have to say this morning?"

"Not much. He's looking into the death of the agritech guys, to see if there's any chance their deaths were anything other than random terrorism, but it can be hard to get information from that part of the world, especially when he's trying to do it anonymously."

"The last thing he needs to do is ping anybody's radar," Risa warned.

"Believe me, I don't want him and his family to be on anybody's hit list, either. But we need information. We can't hide out forever." He reached over and touched her stomach, grinning as the baby gave a sharp kick against his palm. "We've got a kid to raise."

Risa patted his hand. "I wonder if maybe we should be talking to Rebecca Cameron instead of Heller. She's the one who has all the contacts in the State Department. Maybe she might have an idea or two about who might be running something on the side."

"She hasn't been in government in almost five years."

"But she knows a lot of people who are still there."

"I could call Heller back. Suggest he talk to her, tell her what we're looking for."

Good idea, Risa thought. Better to let Heller ask the questions, at least for now. She wasn't sure how well the burner app Connor had downloaded to the phone was going to work if he kept calling people on it.

While Connor wandered off to make the call, Risa looked at the list of names she'd written down. The problem, she realized, was that almost everyone on the list had people they had to report to in some way. And most of those people had bosses as well. Even covert operations had layers of bureaucracy involved, and anyone on any level of the operation could be the person who had put her on the hit list.

And that was assuming she was dealing with someone in the government in the first place, and not al Adar or one of the other terrorist groups she'd gotten crosswise with over the course of her covert career.

Connor returned and sat beside her. "Heller said he'll

get Cameron involved. He wants me to call every eight hours to get an update, since he can't call me because I'll be changing the phone number after every call."

"Okay. Good idea," she said, barely listening.

"You're distracted."

She sighed, looking up from the paper. "What if we're chasing shadows here? Dal seemed to think al Adar was who put the hit on me. Maybe we're trying too hard to complicate things when we should be focused on our original belief."

He didn't look happy. "Is this you telling me you want to go back to Cincy?"

"It's where Dal thought I should be."

"And Dal is dead now."

"We could find Farid—Malcolm—whoever he is. Find out what he knows about those men."

"I'm sure Quinn already knows everything he knows about those men," Connor said firmly. "If it's something we need to know—"

"We need to know!" she said sharply. "And Quinn has no right to keep information from us that way. If Heller hadn't figured it out, we still wouldn't know Farid was on your company's payroll. This is our lives, Connor, not just one of Quinn's operations. I don't trust him to tell us what we need to know. Do you?"

"No," Connor said although Risa could tell he didn't like admitting it.

"For the record, I don't think we should go back to Cincinnati," she said with a sigh. "But I do want to talk to Malcolm. If nothing else, I think we need to find out if the man who tried to talk his way into my apartment was really Tahir Mahmoud."

"I can guarantee you, Maddox Heller will be on top of that question."

Risa supposed he was right. If there was anyone in the world who had a better incentive to find out if Tahir Mahmoud was still alive, it was Heller. Not only had he witnessed Mahmoud killing an embassy translator in cold blood during the US Embassy siege a decade ago, he'd also nearly lost his wife to Mahmoud's murderous plot.

"Okay. So we leave that to Maddox Heller."

"I did some digging on the murder of Martin Dalrymple," Connor added. "Still no idea who killed him, but the postmortem results suggest he was killed forty-eight hours before his body was found."

"Which means whoever tried to contact me Wednesday morning wasn't Dal." She frowned. "Do you think that means he was killed because he was trying to protect me?"

"You're not blaming yourself, are you?"

"No," she lied.

He caught her hands in his, making her look at him. "Dal is the person who put you in this situation, which means he knew the score. He made his choices knowing the potential consequences."

"I wish he'd told me more about what he was investigating. I should have asked more questions." The problem was, she'd been taught not to ask questions. Dal had always told her just what she had needed to know. No more, no less.

Without his direction, she felt as if she were stumbling around, blind.

A good way to end up dead.

JESSE COOPER ENTERED the Sunset Mountain Grille at three on the dot and went to stand near the restrooms, as Connor had suggested. He wasn't a particularly large man, which somehow caught Connor by surprise. Though it shouldn't have—some of the toughest marines he knew had been average-sized. What he lacked in size, Jesse made up in sheer presence. He was lean and fit, his dark hair cut high and tight, as if he hadn't really left the Marine Corps behind when he retired.

Connor approached him slowly, giving the man time to see him coming. Jesse's dark eyes followed him in, his gaze assessing. "McGinnis?"

"Cooper." Connor extended his hand.

Jesse shook it with a firm grip. "Good to meet you."

Connor nodded for Jesse to follow him to the table near the back where Risa waited. Jesse gave her a nod of greeting and took the seat across from her, while Connor sat beside her.

"I was intrigued by what you told me on the phone," Jesse said as soon as a waiter took their drink orders. "I had some of my people do some digging, and it seems that your thoughts about a potential bioweapon aren't out of the question. Terrorists, whether foreign or domestic, would love nothing more than to use diseases to spread terror. We saw it after 9/11 with the anthrax letters. There's some fear that terrorists might be looking for ways to get their hands on the Ebola and Marburg viruses to use to spread fear."

"So, this hemorrhagic fever in the bats that Akwat found could be a potential weapon in the hands of terrorists?"

"Only if it jumps species," Jesse answered. "Which could potentially be hurried along if infected bats were harvested and induced to bite animals like goats and pigs, increasing the likelihood that the disease could jump into those animals. And that would increase the likelihood that humans could eventually be infected, since they're exposed to livestock far more regularly than bats in a cave."

"Right," Risa said with a nod. "Akwat had been considering applying for a UN research grant to isolate the infected bat colonies and provide them to scientists for research, while separating them from the healthy bat populations that they planned to use to harvest guano for fertilizer."

"Except, now Akwat is no more," Jesse said.

"Right." Risa looked grim. "The question we're considering is, could their deaths be connected to the attempt on my life?"

"Potentially, yes." Jesse lowered his voice and looked at Connor. "A former employee of mine is working at Campbell Cove Security now. Eric Brannon. Do you know him?"

"Not well," Connor admitted. "He's a former navy doctor, right?"

"Right. One of his interests is infectious diseases. I think it's the main reason he joined your company—access to a research grant studying the potential use of infectious diseases as weapons of terror."

Risa looked at Connor. "Did you know about this?"

He shook his head. "It's not my area of expertise."

"But Quinn would know, wouldn't he?"

"Yes," Connor admitted. "He would."

"Quinn and his 'need to know' garbage," she growled.

"Listen—I'll vouch for Eric Brannon. He's a good guy. A man of integrity." Jesse reached into his jacket and pulled out a card. "I wrote his home number on the back of my card. Call him. You can trust him. Heller will vouch for him, too."

Connor glanced at Risa. She was wearing her best poker face, but he could feel the tension in her leg where it rested against his. "Thank you," she said aloud, taking the card.

The waiter brought their drinks—coffee for Connor and Jesse Cooper, and water for Risa—and asked if they were ready to order. Connor told him they needed a few more minutes and the waiter headed for another table.

"I'm up here for a couple more days. My wife and I needed a little alone time, so we left the baby with my sister and her husband." Jesse grinned. "Meggie just found out she's pregnant, so I thought they should get a sneak preview."

Risa smiled. "I could use one of those. Get ready for Junior."

Connor tamped down a sudden rush of sheer panic. In a month, he was going to be a father.

What the hell did he know about being a father? His own father had only recently retired from the Navy. He'd been away from home as much as he was there, and while he'd loved his children dearly, he hadn't exactly given Connor a hands-on example of how to be a dad.

"It's a lot of work. Not much sleep. But I wouldn't trade it for anything." Jesse smiled. "And believe me, I never thought I'd say something like that."

Connor felt Risa's fingers curl around his beneath the table, her touch comforting. Calming.

"If you want me to be there when you talk to Brannon, let me know. Don't feel obligated to do so, though." Jesse picked up his menu. "Let's eat, shall we?"

DESPITE THE VOUCHING of both Jesse Cooper and Maddox Heller, Connor and Risa agreed that it was wiser to meet Eric Brannon in a public place rather than letting him come to them. Connor made the call and set up a meeting for the next morning at a park a few miles outside of Cumberland.

"I think Quinn just wants us to hunker down somewhere and stay out of his way." Connor tugged her closer under the covers.

Risa flattened her back against his front, enjoying the light rasp of his chest hair against her skin. "I'm beginning to think that's what Dal wanted, too."

"Maybe they're both right. Maybe you should just concentrate on staying safe. You're weeks away from giving birth—this isn't the time to put your life in danger."

"I won't stop being in danger if I lie low." She rolled over to face him. "I want our child to be born in a hospital under his or her real name. I don't want to try to raise a baby while we're constantly on the run."

"I don't want that, either." He brushed her hair away from her eyes, letting his fingers trail across her cheek. Sheer pleasure raced through her where he touched her, and she had to struggle to focus on his words. "But I don't know how to make the danger go away. We don't even know where the danger is coming from."

"I don't think it's from Tahir Mahmoud or whoever that guy at the restaurant was," she said.

"Even after he tried to get inside your apartment?"

"He did that because I followed him. Before that, I don't think I was on his radar at all. Which means he's not the person who wanted me dead."

"But someone was tracking us, and that tracking started the night we left Cincinnati."

"Exactly. I think the men in the restaurant were coincidences. I think whoever was looking for me had probably been keeping an eye on you while you were in Cincinnati. In fact, they might have been tracking Quinn and other people at Campbell Cove Security as well. You're on the government payroll, which means there are ways for people in the government to track what y'all do."

"So, technically, someone might have already known we spotted you in Cincinnati, and they just waited for me to find you before they made their move." Connor shook his head. "If you're right about that, then whoever's gunning for you is someone inside our own government."

"I can't live like this. I've spent over a decade living my life as someone else. I quit the CIA so I could just be me again." She touched his cheek. "So we could finally be us."

Connor caught her hand and pressed a light kiss to her palm, then rolled onto his back and gazed up at the ceiling. He remained quiet so long that Risa thought he might have fallen asleep.

But a moment later, his voice rumbled in the darkness. "We can't meet with Brannon tomorrow. Not if someone in the government is following employees of Campbell Cove Security."

Risa sat up suddenly. "Maddox Heller met with us in Cumberland. And drove us here. He's one of your company's management team."

"But he drove us here in his brother-in-law's SUV."

"What if someone connects Iris's brother-in-law to Maddox?"

"I think we'd already be under siege if that were so."

Risa lay in the dark, her skin tingling. Suddenly every moan of the wind in the eaves, every rattle of winter-bare tree limbs brushing against one another, sounded like an invasion waiting to happen.

"What if they're out there right now, preparing to make their move?" she asked in a whisper, waiting for him to tell her she was crazy.

But his only answer was to roll out of the bed and pick up his Ruger from the bedside table.

IF THERE WAS anyone outside the cabin, they were extremely well-hidden, Connor decided after going from room to room in the dark, checking their surroundings through the window. Without night-vision gear and thermal imaging, he couldn't be absolutely sure, but he didn't think they were in immediate danger.

But Risa was right about one thing. If the person who was looking for her was in the government, with access to some of the government's resources and secrets, it would be only a matter of time before they figured out where Risa was hiding.

There was only one option to keep her totally safe. They had to cut all ties to their pasts.

"No," Risa said flatly when he brought up the topic when he returned to the bedroom. She was standing at the window, gazing out into the darkness, her arms wrapped around her body as if she were cold. "That's not a life I want to live. It's not a life I want for my child."

"Our child," he said. "I don't want you or Junior dead, and if this is the only way to be sure you stay alive—"

"It's not. You know it's not. It's not any kind of life to live, looking over your shoulder all the time. I spent the past seven months doing just that, Connor. I don't want to spend the rest of my life that way."

"Then what the hell are we supposed to do?"

She turned to look at him. "We meet with Brannon tomorrow, as planned. Pick his brain about Akwat."

"Even though he's connected to Campbell Cove Security?"

"Your people know they have to be circumspect when they meet with us. I'm sure Heller probably spent hours drumming that fact into Eric Brannon's head." She turned back to the window. "We just have to keep taking precautions. We'll be okay."

He wrapped his arms around her from behind, resting his palms against her belly. The baby wasn't kicking, exactly, just sort of rolling, but the feel of that small life beneath his hands was reassuring. He thought he could stay here, just like this, for the rest of the night.

Until Risa's body went stiff against his, and she uttered a soft profanity.

"What?" he asked, his own nerves instantly on alert.

"There's somebody out there in the woods," she whispered.

Chapter Fifteen

In the darkness, there was a flash of movement. A shape, fractionally darker than the shrouded woods surrounding it, moved laterally from one tree to another. Then there was a second shadow gliding through the dark. And a third.

"Three," he murmured, his brain already going through a checklist of defensive actions. The doors and windows were all locked—he and Risa had made almost a ritual of the lock-checking process.

"Four," she corrected as another shape slipped briefly into view.

"And that's just one side of the cabin."

"So maybe as many as sixteen?" Risa's voice shook a little.

"Maybe. Check the window over the deck. I'll take the bathroom." Connor headed for the roomy bathroom with its enormous tub and separate shower. The window there was set higher on the wall, forcing Connor to pull up the dainty chair that went with the vanity table next to the sink. He peered out the window, looking for more signs of movement. He spotted only one dark-clad figure out this window after watching for several minutes.

He went back into the hall and found Risa returning

from the room at the back of the house that overlooked the back deck. "Two," she said quietly. "They seem to be taking position just beyond the clearing."

"I guess we should check the front."

"Let's get dressed first. And armed."

Neither of them needed prodding to dress for warmth. They chose their sturdiest shoes—hiking boots for Connor and a pair of trainers for Risa—and armed themselves with the weapons they had—the Ruger and a folding combat knife from his Marine Corps days for Connor, and the Glock and a canister of pepper spray for Risa. Connor tucked extra ammo for them both in the inner pocket of his fleece jacket as they edged quietly toward the front windows of the cabin.

They had almost reached the front when Connor's cell phone hummed against his hip. Adrenaline spiked through him as he eased back into the middle of the cabin, pulling Risa with him.

He didn't recognize the number on the phone display. Warily, he answered. "Hello."

"Mr. McGinnis?" It was a vaguely familiar male voice. Connor couldn't place it immediately.

"You must have the wrong number."

"It's Jesse Cooper," the other voice said quickly, stopping Connor as he reached for the End Call button.

Connor placed the voice now, but he remained wary. "Jesse who?" Risa leaned closer to listen, and he lowered his head to hers so she could hear.

"Cooper. We met this afternoon. After our discussion, we received intel from some of our sources in the US government that your location may already be compromised."

"I really have no idea what you're talking about."

"We contacted Maddox Heller by way of a secure channel and he agreed it was time for an extraction."

"Extraction?" Connor eyed the front door. Though it was made of reinforced wood and had a sturdy dead-bolt lock, there was also a four-pane window in the upper half of the solid wood, covered on the inside by simple plaid curtains that blocked their view of the other side of the door, though the curtains were thin enough that light from the outdoor spotlights seeped through the fabric.

Suddenly, he thought he saw a shadow move across the squares of light. Was that a footfall on the wooden porch?

A second later, there was a brisk knock on the front door. Beside Connor, Risa gave a start, and Connor's own heart rate rocketed upward.

"I'm outside your front door right now." Jesse's voice filtered through the whooshing pulse in Connor's ear. "I have assets surrounding the perimeter of the cabin in case something happens before we can extract you safely to a new location."

Connor found his voice. "Extract us? Extract us where?"

"Please answer the door, Mr. McGinnis. I'll explain everything." The call ended abruptly.

"This is insane," Risa whispered.

There was another knock at the door, a little more forceful this time.

Risa looked up at Connor, her eyes wide and glittering in the low light. "What do we do?"

"Cover me," he said, and moved to the front door. Edging to one side, he flicked the curtains and took a quick look outside.

Jesse Cooper stood in the doorway, dressed all in black. A grim smile curved his lips as he spotted Connor.

Connor leaned against the wall and took a couple of bracing breaths, then opened the door. "What the hell, Cooper?"

Jesse shrugged off his heavy jacket as Connor locked the door behind him. Beneath the jacket, Jesse was armed for combat, Connor saw—a Glock in a shoulder holster, and a combat knife similar to the one strapped to Connor's leg. "Sorry for the cloak-and-dagger. I didn't want to risk a call until my people were in place."

"Your people?"

"Heller agreed it was too risky to bring company assets into the mix, since it looks as if Campbell Cove Security has been compromised." Jesse nodded at Risa. "Sorry to handle things this way, without giving you any warning, but we thought the fewer communications flying through the atmosphere, the safer it would be for everyone."

"How many people are outside?"

"I brought a force of ten agents. They're all trained for close combat and asset protection. We know how to get you out of here safely."

"This is moving really fast." Risa's voice was soft but intense. "We met you for the first time this afternoon and now you expect us to just go with you to God knows where on your say-so?"

"I wish I had time to give you the full Cooper Security sales spiel, but I left my PowerPoint files at home," Jesse drawled. "Meanwhile, there may very well be some very dangerous people headed your way."

"How could they have found us?"

"Your vehicle is registered to a rental company, who gave me the name Daniel Hartman as the person who rented the SUV. Got his billing information in the same call, and it took little effort to discover he's married to a woman named Rose Browning Hartman. Rose Browning's name came up on a news search, connecting her to a woman named Iris Browning. Who's married to Maddox Heller, co-owner of Campbell Cove Security."

"You knew all that already."

"That's why I gave the task to one of my researchers, who knows nothing about Heller or the Brownings or anyone else. She came up with the information pretty quickly."

"But you had to know my car tag number to begin."

"You think that information couldn't be reversed? Start with Maddox Heller and start making connections until you found a Daniel Hartman who'd rented an SUV and a cabin in the Kentucky mountains?" Jesse shook his head. "They know about Campbell Cove Security. So anyone connected to your company or the people there is a liability at the moment. Heller agrees."

"Aren't *you* connected to Heller?" Connor pointed out.

"Not anymore. Not for over a year now. It was worth the risk, but we're still using burner phones and vehicles that can't be directly connected to Cooper Security."

"Why are you doing this?" Risa asked. "We can't pay you."

"Let's just say this is personal and leave it at that."

"Because you think it might be connected to Barton Reid?"

"If it is, my company needs to know. We have a long history dealing with Barton Reid and his happy clan of lunatics." Jesse's voice darkened. "I really hate loose ends."

A MALE VOICE crackled over the handheld radio in response to Jesse Cooper's terse query. "East quadrant clear."

"So far, so good," Jesse said as he hooked the radio

onto his belt again and leaned his hips against the dresser. "Can I help you with anything?"

"Tell us where we're going, for one thing," Risa suggested, stuffing the last of her borrowed clothes into a rucksack Jesse had supplied, apparently at Maddox Heller's suggestion.

"My brother-in-law and sister are acquaintances of a family who runs a small motel and tavern not far from here," Jesse said, checking his watch. "But there's not a known connection between them, so it should be perfectly safe. They've agreed to rent us a block of rooms for the next few days, no names given, no questions asked. We'll be paying in cash. We'll be traveling in cars rented by people with only the loosest of connections to my family and no connection at all to Maddox Heller or Alexander Quinn."

"You think of everything," Risa muttered.

"I know you two aren't sure you can trust me," he said quietly. "I wish I had time to prove you can. But time is something we just don't have."

Connor zipped up his bag. "I'm done."

Risa closed her bag as well. "Me, too."

"Okay, good. Now, here's where it gets a little harder."

Risa exchanged glances with Connor. "Harder in what way?"

"For this next short trip, we're going to have to separate you."

"No," Risa and Connor said in unison.

"We don't want to go in a full motorcade out of here. It'll be too obvious. I want to split you up so that you'll both have a lead vehicle and a vehicle in the rear. If something goes wrong with one package—the package being each of you—we can still whisk the other package to safety."

"With all due respect to your obvious planning and preparation," Connor said, "Risa and I just spent the past seven months apart. I'm not letting her out of my sight that long again. Not even for an hour."

"I agree with Connor," Risa said firmly.

Jesse pressed his lips into a thin line. "And you won't budge?"

Again they spoke in unison. "No."

A faint smile curved Jesse's lips. "I now owe my wife fifty dollars. She said you'd never go for the splitting up idea."

"Wise woman," Connor said.

"So, there's a plan B, I hope," Risa said.

"Well, it's basically plan A, but instead of there being two packages, there'll be one real package and one decoy," Jesse told them. "My sister Isabel has a similar build and coloring to you, so she was going to play the role of you anyway, if we'd split you up from Connor. Under a coat, with some extra padding, she'll pass for pregnant. Her husband, Ben, looks enough like Connor to make a decent decoy, too. So they'll be the other package."

Risa looked at Connor, not sure she was happy about so many people being in harm's way just to protect her. Dal was already dead. Malcolm Faris might already be in danger because she'd chosen to work at the restaurant where he was already undercover.

Now Jesse Cooper and ten other agents were about to put their lives on the line to protect Risa.

But why? Did they know something they weren't telling her?

"Wait," she said as they reached the front door. "I need to know something."

Both Connor and Jesse turned to her with questioning looks. "We're already running out of time," Jesse warned.

"You know why I've been targeted, don't you?" she asked. "You must know, or you wouldn't have put your people on the line this way. What have you found out? Where are we really going?"

Jesse sighed. "I was going to explain it all when we got there, but yes. I do think I know why you've been targeted. I just don't know who's pulling the strings." He nodded toward the door. "Let's get on the road. I'm your driver anyway, so I'll tell you everything on the way."

Risa looked at Connor, trying to gauge what he was thinking. Were they crazy to trust their lives to a man who was, despite his reputation as a security expert, a stranger to them?

Connor flashed her a smile that she suspected he meant to be reassuring. It might have worked if he'd looked a little less queasy.

But she steeled her spine, took his hand and fell into step with him as they followed Jesse Cooper to the big black Explorer parked outside the cabin.

SUNSET MOUNTAIN WAS one of the few towns in the county with its own police department, a holdover from a time decades ago when it had been one of the larger towns in the area. The Sunset Mountain PD had slowly downsized over the years to its current staff of eight uniformed officers, four detectives, an assistant chief and Chief Kenneth Halsey.

Halsey was a big man, tall and broad-shouldered, his steel-gray buzz cut giving him the air of an aging but still-fit drill sergeant. He knew his time at the head of the police department was limited; already the town council was making a lot of noise about disbanding the department to save money. Sooner or later, they'd vote to turn over policing duties to the county sheriff's department, and Halsey would either have to go to the county boys, hat in hand, in search of a job that probably wouldn't be there, or retire.

But he'd worry about that when the time came. Meanwhile, he had a whole other kind of headache that had just landed on his desk.

"What kind of terrorists are we talking about?" he asked the well-dressed stranger who'd barged into his office a few minutes earlier, asking for help in setting up a roadblock.

"We believe the woman is planning to set off a bomb at Kingdom Come Park as soon as it opens this spring. She's one of those immigrants causing all that trouble up in Cincy."

"Ah." Halsey had heard about the protests. "But weren't those people up there the ones protesting against the terrorists in their country?"

The man, who'd identified himself as Garrett Leland, flashing Department of Homeland Security credentials to prove it, arched his eyebrows as if surprised the police chief knew even that much about the immigrant protests.

What, he thought Halsey was some sort of inbred hillbilly cop who hissed and spat at the mere thought of foreigners in his neck of the woods? Halsey's wife was from Nigeria. His kids were half-black. Ol' Garrett Leland had picked the wrong yokel if he thought he could play the foreigner card.

"She was involved with four terrorist bombings in Ka-

ziristan, and another in France. We believe she's radical-
ized the father of her unborn child and they should both
be considered armed and extremely dangerous." Leland
placed a photograph on Halsey's desk. It looked like a
security camera image, a little grainy, showing a very
pregnant woman wearing a shabby overcoat and a gauzy
scarf over her dark hair.

Pretty girl, Halsey thought. Didn't look like a terrorist, but looks could be deceiving. And if there was any
chance the woman was up to no good in his neck of the
woods...

He released a sigh. "Okay, tell me what you need."

He didn't like the smile that flashed across Garrett
Leland's face.

"His name is Garrett Leland," Jesse Cooper said. "He's
an agent with Homeland Security."

"You're kidding me," Connor said.

"I wish I were."

"We haven't made a direct link between him and Barton Reid." The speaker was a dark-haired woman with
intelligent blue eyes and a quirky smile. Evie Cooper,
Jesse's wife. Like Jesse, she was dressed in dark clothes
and well-armed, though she confessed, as she buckled
herself into the passenger seat, that she worked in Cooper Security's accounting office.

"I train all of my people to handle dangerous situations," Cooper had explained, slanting a proud look at
his wife. "Evie can hold her own."

"But you obviously have a reason to think there might
have been a link," Risa said.

"He's been on our watch list for a while, but we
hadn't really seen any signs that he's working a personal

agenda," Evie explained. "But our analysts did some poking around this afternoon after Jesse called in the details of your suspicions about Akwat and the deaths of the two founders. Like I said, he's on our watch list, and you two seemed to think you might be under surveillance by someone with government ties."

"And they found something?" Connor asked.

"About eight months ago, shortly after you filed your preliminary report on Akwat, he requested and received permission to open an investigation into the company's American investors."

Next to Connor, Risa made a skeptical noise in the back of her throat. He couldn't blame her. "That sounds like a fairly reasonable thing for Homeland Security to investigate," he said.

"Which is probably why it didn't ping our radar before now," Jesse said. "But the thing is, he was given carte blanche to form his own investigation team from State, Homeland Security and the Pentagon. And guess what all of the people he tapped had in common?"

A sinking sensation roiled through Connor's stomach. "They were all on your Barton Reid–related watch list?"

"Bingo," Jesse said.

"How did you get this information so quickly?"

"Having the Akwat part of the puzzle speeded everything up. Everything we'd gleaned about the activities of the people on the watch list had been entered into a searchable database. Once we searched for 'Akwat,' the pattern became clear."

Connor rubbed his forehead, where a tension headache throbbed. "That's a lot of manpower for something you're not getting paid to do."

Jesse met Connor's gaze in the rearview mirror. "Who says we're not getting paid?"

"So what makes you think we're in imminent danger?" Risa asked.

"Two hours ago, I made a call to a friend I served with during my Marine Corps days," Jesse answered. "Gunnery Sergeant Ken Halsey, Gunny for short. He's now the chief of police with the Sunset Mountain Police Department. I thought I'd see if he and his wife could meet us for dinner somewhere. But he had to work—some suit from Homeland Security believes there's a terrorist on her way to Kingdom Come Park to scout the place for a terrorist attack once the park opens this spring."

"On *her* way?" Connor echoed.

"Yeah. Seems this woman is a Kaziri. Pregnant and probably traveling with her American lover she's helped radicalize. Ring any bells?"

"Son of a bitch," Connor muttered. "They've come out of the shadows with their search."

"Yeah. And want to take a stab at the name of the Homeland Security suit Gunny was talking about?"

"Garrett Leland," Connor and Risa answered in quiet unison.

"I told him he was looking for the wrong person, and it was important that we got out of town without running into Homeland Security," Jesse said quickly.

"And that was good enough for him?" Risa asked.

"Marine's word," Connor murmured.

"Gunny trusts me, and I trust him—" Jesse's voice cut off abruptly, his body going tense.

"Oh no," Evie murmured, gazing forward through the windshield.

Connor leaned to the center of the SUV and saw the

red glow of a string of taillights on the road ahead. Beyond the backed-up traffic, a bank of flashing blue-and-red lights illuminated the scene about a mile away, blocking both lanes.

They'd run into a police roadblock.

Chapter Sixteen

As he tapped the brakes to slow the SUV, Jesse's cell phone rang. Evie answered and listened for a moment, then looked at him. "It's for you." She held the phone to his ear.

Gunny Halsey's gravelly voice rumbled like distant thunder in his ear. He was obviously trying to speak quietly. "We've set up roadblocks on the major arteries in and out of town. Where are you?"

"About to run into one of those roadblocks on Bald Eagle Road."

"How far out?"

"A mile?"

"Anybody behind you?"

Jesse checked the rearview mirror. "No."

"Kill your lights. The taillights ahead should be enough light for you to see Black Creek Road turnoff on the right. Spot it yet?"

Jesse turned off his headlights manually, slowing as he neared the traffic snarl ahead. As his eyes adjusted to the lower light, he spotted the sign to his right. "Got it."

"Take it. It'll be dark as an Afghan cave, but you'll be blocked by trees almost immediately. Put on your parking lights until you think you can risk headlights again."

Jesse slowed into the turn. The glow from the tail-lights on Bald Eagle Road disappeared almost immediately, blocked out by the thick evergreen canopy that closed in Black Creek Road. He decided he could risk the parking lights, which offered a little illumination of the gravel track ahead of him. "Okay, I'm on Black Creek Road. What now?"

"Go until you hit Mill Hollow Road. Take a left and follow it until you hit a T intersection on Grassley Road. From there, take a left and you should be able to get to Cumberland without hitting any of the major roads. Gotta go." Gunny hung up.

Jesse told Evie and the McGinnises where they were going.

"And you trust this Chief Halsey?"

"With my life. Several times, as a matter of fact."

He was far enough into the woods to hit the headlights. They lit up the road ahead, almost painfully bright until his eyes adjusted again.

They drove in silence until an intersection appeared in the gloom ahead, four-way stop signs bringing them to a brief halt. The words *Mill Hollow Road* gleamed in fading fluorescent paint at the corner of the crossroad. Jesse took a left, as Gunny had directed.

Risa broke the silence. "You haven't told us what's waiting when we get to the motel. Something about a second plan of action?"

"Are you familiar with Senator Gerald Blackledge?" Jesse asked.

"Of course," Risa answered. "He's been a senator since the Lincoln administration, right?"

"He may be a politician down to his bone marrow, but he gives a damn about national security and nothing pisses him off more than corruption in the government. He knows where a lot of the bodies are buried, and he's been instrumental in protecting many of the key witnesses against Barton Reid and his cronies. He's setting up a satellite feed so you can testify to everything you learned about Akwat. You don't have to name names or anything else—just report what you were going to report before your plans were cut short by the plane crash."

"It's going to catch some people by surprise, since your name was on the list of casualties in that crash," Connor said.

"This is good," Risa said. "I think the only reason I've been targeted is because of my unfinished report on Akwat, right? It's the only thing that makes sense, given all the rest of the things we know."

"It seems likely," Jesse agreed.

"It took almost seven months for them to figure out you were still alive and where you might be," Connor said thoughtfully. "I wonder if that's because they managed to get information out of Dalrymple before he was murdered."

"We believe he was working this case off the CIA's radar, so yeah. If somebody found out I was still alive, it was probably through Dal in some way. Or dumb luck, the way Connor did."

"Do you have the original report somewhere you can access it?" Evie asked, turning around in the seat to look at the McGinnises.

"Yes," Risa answered, the hint of a smile tinting her voice. "I do."

"NO SIGN OF them at either checkpoint?" Garrett Leland's accent reminded Ken Halsey of a greenhorn captain he'd been burdened with during a tour of duty in Iraq during the first Gulf War. Complete ass who thought his master's degree in logistics made him God's gift to the Corps. He'd been from somewhere in Massachusetts. Somewhere rich and privileged. His accent was a lot like Leland's. Same attitude, too.

"Afraid not," Halsey answered in the same careful tone he'd used when talking to the idiot captain of yore.

"We've confirmed they've vacated their last known whereabouts," Leland growled, his brow creasing as he started to pace. "We've got the two ways out of town covered. Where the hell could they have gone?"

Another voice piped up. "There's another way out of town, sir."

Alarm rippled down Halsey's spine. He turned to look at the deputy who'd spoken, Josh Phelps, sending him a warning look.

But Phelps was looking at Garrett Leland with a mixture of awe and eagerness to please. Stupid damn pup.

"What way?" Leland asked.

"There's a back road—Black Creek Road, just off Bald Eagle Road. They coulda seen our roadblock and taken the detour. Black Creek Road takes you to Mill Hollow Road, and from there you can get out of Sunset Mountain without going through either of the roadblocks."

Leland turned to look at Halsey. "You didn't tell me about the detour."

"Nobody except locals know anything about it." Halsey tried not to grit his teeth with frustration. "You said they're not locals."

Leland's expression darkened, and his voice sharpened to a diamond edge. "I said, I wanted to block off every road out of town." He pulled his cell phone out of his pocket and made a call. "It's me. I need a chopper in the air now. Grab a map and find Mill Hollow Road. Make sure every exit off that road is covered. Now!"

Halsey swallowed a profanity. "I'll get you some extra bodies out there to help you," he told the Homeland Security agent, pulling his phone from his pocket. He texted his assistant deputy and gave the order, then pulled up Jesse Cooper's number and typed in a quick message.

Before hitting Send, he glanced up and found Leland watching him, his dark eyes suspicious. Halsey faked a smile. "Should have four more deputies on board in ten minutes. They'll meet your folks at the T intersection off Mill Hollow Road."

He pocketed his cell phone again, but as he slipped it in his pocket, he hit Send.

"OH, HELL."

Evie Cooper's voice roused Risa from a light doze. She looked up to find the woman peering at her husband's cell phone, the light from the display casting blue light across her face.

"Text from Gunny. Leland's ordered a roadblock at the end of Mill Hollow Road."

Risa went from drowsiness to instant alertness. "Can we get there before the roadblock's set up?"

"Unlikely," Jesse answered. "We haven't even reached Grassley Road."

"How big a net are they throwing?" Connor asked. He was on his phone, Risa saw, looking at a map program. "Just the roads?"

"What are you thinking?" she asked.

"We could go on foot," he answered. "Just the two of us, through the woods. Jesse and Evie stay in the SUV and get through the checkpoint. Then we meet back up on the highway past the checkpoint and go the rest of the way to the motel."

Risa saw Jesse and his wife exchange a quick look before he gave a nod. "That could work."

"It's really cold out there." Evie looked worried.

Risa glanced at Connor, smiling. "We've trekked ten miles up a mountain in Kaziristan in winter. We know about dealing with the cold."

"We'll bundle up. Plus, we'll be moving, so that'll keep our body heat up." He was still looking at the map on the phone. "About a quarter mile from the intersection with the highway back to Cumberland, Mill Hollow Road crosses a large creek. If we get out there and start hiking, we can follow the creek to the highway, bypassing the roadblock."

"I'm not sure I like being out of contact that long," Jesse said.

"Do you have another one of those handheld radios?" Risa asked. "We'll have the phone and if we had a radio, we'd have two ways to stay in touch. Then, if something went wrong, we'd know we'd have to come up with a plan C."

"I think this *is* plan C," Jesse murmured. But he waved his hand toward the glove box, and Evie opened it to retrieve an extra radio. She checked the radio's channel setting and handed it to Connor.

THEY CROSSED THE creek and stopped on the other side of the small bridge, pulled over onto the sandy shoulder. There were no headlights visible behind them on the curvy road, but that could change quickly, so Risa and Connor didn't drag their heels. They left Risa's laptop with the Coopers—they'd have no use for it in the woods.

Evie had directed them to stow it away in a hidden lock-box tucked under the middle row of seats for just such a purpose. It wouldn't be found in a cursory search, and if the search went any deeper than that, the laptop would be the least of their worries.

Instead, they stashed a change of clothes in a large rucksack Jesse provided. "There's a first-aid kit, some protein bars and a liter of water in there," he told them as he helped Connor strap the sack to his shoulders. "There are night-vision goggles in there if you need them."

By the time Risa and Connor climbed down the shallow incline to the rocky creek bank, the Coopers were back on the road, their taillights casting a faint red glow over the area for a few brief seconds before they disappeared, leaving them in utter darkness.

Connor retrieved the night-vision goggles and slid them onto his head, adjusting the straps until they fit snugly but comfortably. He was well-accustomed to using the goggles, so adjusting to the green glow of the landscape stretching out ahead of him took only a couple of seconds.

"Just follow me," he told Risa. "I'll let you know if there's an obstacle to worry about, trust me."

"I do," she said with quiet confidence.

He swallowed a smile and started walking.

For a while, they stuck close to the creek bank, avoiding the tangled underbrush of the woods in favor of the clearer, if rockier, path the bank provided. But within a half mile, the creek narrowed considerably, the woods encroaching on the bank until there was no clearing left.

There was no choice but to venture into the underbrush, and their forward progress slowed.

"How're you holding up?" Connor asked Risa as he

picked his way around a half-hidden stump in the middle of a tangle of vines.

"I'm okay," she answered, but there was a tightness in her voice that made him turn and look at her.

She smiled at him, her teeth bright through the goggles. But her brow was slightly furrowed, and she had both gloved hands pressed over her stomach.

"Are you sure?" he asked. "You having pains?"

"Just twinges. I've had them before. I'm okay. Let's keep going."

Stopping to argue, he decided, would just prolong their time in the woods. What she needed was a clean bed and full night's sleep. The sooner they rendezvoused with the Coopers, the sooner she'd get what she needed.

They were coming to a part of the creek where the trees and underbrush receded, leaving the bank relatively clear for a long stretch. There was also a fallen tree near the edge of the clearing that offered a tempting place to rest for a few moments. "Let's take a load off for a minute. Get some water."

Risa followed him to the fallen tree trunk and sat, gratefully accepting a drink from the liter bottle of water. "How far are we?" she asked as he flipped up the night goggles and pulled out his phone.

He checked for reception. One bar, but it might be enough to check the map. He pulled up the GPS app and got their current coordinates, then plugged it into the map. "A little over halfway there."

Risa swallowed a sound that sounded a lot like a groan. "Any messages from the Coopers?"

He checked. There was a text message, posted about five minutes ago: Do you want pizza?

"They're at the checkpoint." With any luck, the Coopers would be allowed to pass through the checkpoint unmolested, especially since, during the quick stop to let Risa and Connor out to start their hike, they'd packed away their weapons and firearms—all legally owned and licensed to possess even in Kentucky, Jesse had assured him—in hopes that they wouldn't raise any suspicions. "Hopefully the name Cooper won't trip any alarms."

"I don't know." Risa was rubbing her stomach rhythmically, as if trying to calm both herself and the baby. "If Garrett Leland really is part of the old Barton Reid network of corrupt government employees, I'm guessing he'd be pretty wary of anyone named Cooper."

Connor pulled off his glove and touched her face. Despite the cold, she looked and felt a little flushed. "Are you sure you're okay?"

"I'm okay. Let's just keep going. The sooner we reach the rendezvous point, the better."

He stashed everything back in his rucksack and pulled the goggles down over his eyes, letting them readjust to the night-vision glow. He stood and reached out for Risa's hand, helping her to her feet. "You sure you don't need to rest a little longer?"

"Positive." Her voice sounded stronger. "Let's go."

Over eight months pregnant, he thought. Almost thirty-eight weeks.

Most airlines stopped letting pregnant women fly at thirty-six weeks, didn't they? But here he was, dragging his pregnant wife through the woods in the middle of December.

What the hell was he thinking?

JESSE COOPER'S HEADLIGHTS illuminated the brown-and-tan uniforms of the county sheriff's department, but the man who came to the window, flashlight in hand, was a tall, slim man in a Sunset Mountain Police Department uniform. Lifting his flashlight, he checked Jesse's driver's license, then Evie's. "Alabama, huh? You're a ways from home."

"We're driving north to see my sister for Christmas," Evie said with a friendly smile. "She lives in New York. We decided to make a fun trip of it. Go antiquing, visit some of the sights."

"What's the roadblock for?" Jesse asked, because it was a logical question to ask.

"Just routine," the police officer answered with a polite smile. He handed their licenses back. "Can you lower all your windows?"

"Sure." Jesse depressed the power window buttons, lowering the front and back passenger windows.

The policeman ran the beam of the flashlight through the car, taking in the luggage in the back and the small plastic trash bag hanging on the back of Evie's seat. Jesse knew they'd look like normal travelers. He'd made sure they looked that way.

"All right," the policeman said with a smile. He leaned a little closer and lowered his voice. "Chief Halsey says hi."

Then he stepped back and waved for the others to let them through.

Jesse drove slowly past the small phalanx of deputies and police officers, his pulse pounding like a drum in his ears.

THEY WERE GETTING closer to the highway. Sound carried well in the cold night air, and now and then, Risa heard a vehicle motor, which meant the highway couldn't be that far away now.

The odd sensations in her belly were starting to come more frequently. It wasn't pain, exactly, more a tight rippling sensation in the lower part of her abdomen. It might be muscle spasms, she thought, from the stress of hiking through the woods.

"I think I'm starting to see car lights," Connor said as he pushed his way forward through the undergrowth. They'd had to abandon the creek bank again, slowing their pace as they struggled against the pull of the vines and the constant threat of hidden obstacles under the tangled carpet beneath their feet.

Risa's legs had begun to feel rubbery, and the odd sensation in her stomach was starting to feel less like twinges and more like pain.

Don't think the word, she told herself firmly.

"Definitely seeing lights now," Connor said, excitement and relief coloring his voice. He started to push ahead more quickly now, no doubt spurred on by the prospect of reaching the end of their journey.

Risa followed, struggling to keep up as she refused to dwell on the swelling pain that had started to feel like hard cramps in her lower back and belly. *Don't think the word. Don't think the word.*

Connor slowed to a sudden halt, reaching into his pocket for his phone. He flipped up the goggles and checked his messages. "They got through the checkpoint. They're waiting off the road near the creek crossing."

Relief swamped her, sending a rush of heat pouring down her spine. "Good. Let's go." She put her hand on Connor's shoulder to nudge him forward.

But as she started to take a step forward, a hard cramp

shuddered through her stomach, sucking the air from her lungs in a harsh gasp. She grabbed for Connor's arm, doubling over as the pain started to crescendo.

"Risa?" Connor turned to look at her, flipping the goggles up again. His eyes were wide and dark in the gloom.

The pain subsided to a light ache, and she loosened her death grip on his arm. "It's okay. I'm okay."

"No, you're not." His voice was low and shaky. "Are you?"

She could no longer lie to herself. Or to him.

Rubbing her trembling belly, she took a deep breath and said the words she wouldn't even let herself think a few minutes earlier.

"I'm having contractions."

Chapter Seventeen

Do not panic.

Connor's heart had started to race the second Risa uttered the word *contractions* but he hadn't been through years of Marine Corps training and combat experience for nothing. It wasn't even the first time he'd dealt with a pregnant woman, was it? He'd been there when an Iraqi woman gave birth to her fourth child in the back of an armored Humvee. Granted, he'd mostly guarded the vehicle while the team medic handled the push-and-pull stuff, but hadn't he been pleasantly surprised by how smoothly things had gone?

Of course, there was a difference between a fourth baby and a first one, wasn't there? And Risa wasn't some anonymous woman giving birth on the side of the road with the help of a trained medical professional.

She was his wife. Carrying his baby. And depending utterly on him to get her through the next half mile of woods and safely to the waiting SUV.

He had stopped only long enough to pull out his phone and text a heads-up to Jesse Cooper, then started pulling her through the woods as quickly as they could go.

She had her next hard contraction as they were nearing the highway. As he helped her ride it out, he spotted bits of the blacktop highway through the trees. Less than two hundred yards away.

"Okay," she breathed as the pain ebbed again. "Let's go."

The last hundred yards felt like a nightmare. The hard contraction had passed, but smaller, lighter spasms had Risa panting and groaning as they threaded their way through the thinning underbrush. Finally, they broke through the trees and onto the shoulder of the highway, winter-brown grass crunching beneath their feet.

The SUV was parked about twenty yards from where they emerged, across the highway. Connor ripped off the goggles and waved his arm. The SUV growled to life, the headlights piercing the darkness, and rolled forward to meet them as they hurried across the highway.

Connor lifted Risa into the backseat and climbed in behind her, buckling her in as he gave Jesse an urgent look. "She's had two contractions. About ten minutes apart. How close is the nearest hospital?"

"We can't," Risa said, her voice coming out in soft pants. "I don't have any identification, no insurance—"

"Already taken care of. There's an ob-gyn waiting at the motel," Jesse said, reaching back to give Risa's hand a quick pat. "We'll be there before you know it."

He might have oversold how quickly they'd arrive at the Meade Motor Inn; Risa rode out a third contraction before they reached the motel, but soon the SUV's headlights illuminated the shabby facade of the motel, giving Connor a brand-new problem to worry about.

"This is where you're proposing that my wife have our baby?" he asked in disbelief. It was a long, one-story building with a boxy office at one end and about twenty small rooms in a row, fronted by a concrete walkway covered by corrugated metal awning held up by rusty steel poles. The place looked as if it had probably been shabby twenty years ago.

"Looks can be deceiving," Jesse said, parking in front of one of the rooms on the far end of the building.

"There's a helicopter in the side lot," Risa said. "Why is there a helicopter?"

"It's for you." Evie turned in her seat and reached for Risa's hand. "The doctor will evaluate your condition and if she feels it's necessary, we'll chopper you to the nearest hospital with a labor-and-delivery unit."

When he entered the room Jesse led them to, Connor saw what Jesse meant when he'd said looks could be deceiving. The room's carpet was a little worn but very clean, the bedclothes neat and spotless. What little he saw of the bathroom before Risa closed herself inside it was also clean and bright.

He turned to Jesse, who had brought their belongings into the bedroom. "Where's the doctor you promised? And who is he?"

"She. And she's in the room next door, with the senator."

Connor stared a moment. "The senator?"

Jesse smiled. "I didn't tell you about the congressional hearing? Senator Blackledge agreed to meet us here and bring some video equipment. We were hoping to have her testify by video to a special panel about her experiences with Akwat and everything that happened after the plane crash." He nodded toward the bathroom. "We didn't count on your wife going into labor."

Risa came out of the bathroom, looking tired and pale. "I can still testify."

Connor put his arm around her and helped her to the

edge of the bed, where she sat, bending forward with her hands on her knees. "We can worry about that later. Let's get the doctor in here to take a look at you."

THE OB-GYN WAS an attractive woman in her early fifties named Dr. Andrea Bolling. Besides a pleasant smile and a gentle touch, she possessed a calm competence that went a long way toward easing some of Risa's nervousness. "You're in active labor, and since this is your first, I think we need to get you to a hospital sooner rather than later."

Connor let go of Risa's hand. "I'll go tell Jesse to get the chopper ready to move."

Risa waited until Connor had left the room to ask the doctor, "Are you sure everything is okay?"

"As sure as I can be until we get to a hospital and get an ultrasound done. But from what I can tell, the baby seems to be in the right position, your contractions seem normal, and other than being tired from your recent ordeals, you appear to be healthy. We'll get you through this."

The contractions were getting closer. Only seven minutes between the last couple she'd had. But her dilation was only around five centimeters. From the books she'd read about childbirth, she should still be a few hours away from giving birth.

She went through one more hard contraction before the helicopter was ready to go. Connor and Evie helped Risa out to the black Bell 407 and settled her in one of the five passenger seats. Connor and Dr. Bolling took the seats nearest her, joined by Evie, while Jesse sat in the cockpit with the pilot, a tall, rangy man in his late forties Jesse introduced as his cousin J. D. Cooper.

"We've contacted the Eastern Kentucky Regional Medical Center and arranged for a labor-delivery room to be on standby," Evie told them as they buckled in for the flight. "Courtesy of Senator Gerald Blackledge."

Then the helicopter engine roared to life and it was too loud in the cockpit to hear what anyone had to say.

Connor and Dr. Bolling coached Risa through two more contractions before the helicopter finally came to a landing on the helipad atop the medical center. An attendant and a nurse were waiting with a gurney to whisk Risa down to the labor-delivery floor. The nurse helped her change into a hospital gown and settled her in a wood-paneled area that strived to look like an ordinary room in someone's home, except for all the medical equipment and the narrow adjustable bed in the center of the space.

Connor entered dressed in a blue coverall gown, a mask hanging around his neck. He took her hand in his. "Ready to get this mission started, Mrs. McGinnis?"

She managed a tired grin. "Ooh rah, Major."

He stroked her hair and looked at Dr. Bolling, who had donned a gown and protective goggles, her hair tucked under what looked like a blue paper shower cap. "I just found out about this a few days ago, so I haven't had time to prep for my part of this job," he told her. "So tell me what to do."

Dr. Bolling's smile crinkled the skin around her soft gray eyes. "In my experience, your best bet is to treat your wife as a queen. She's in charge. Do whatever she tells you she needs."

The look Connor gave Risa made her heart contract. "It'll be my privilege."

"TROUBLE INCOMING."

Evie's voice drew Jesse's attention away from his phone, which he'd been using for the past hour to coordinate with the senator's team as well as his own assets still in Kentucky. Everyone from Cooper Security had made it through the roadblocks unaccosted to reach the motel.

Following his wife's gaze down the hallway outside the delivery suite, Jesse released a gusty sigh.

He should have known everything was going too smoothly.

A tall, officious-looking man in a neat charcoal suit strode down the corridor as if he owned the place, flanked by a small army of uniformed officers and a couple of men who reeked of "federal law enforcement agent."

Wearily, Jesse rose to stand in front of the delivery suite door.

"Who are you?" the officious man asked in an impatient, imperious tone. Garrett Leland, Jesse guessed a moment before the man reached into his jacket and pulled out a small wallet containing his Homeland Security credentials.

"Jesse Cooper," Jesse answered.

"Why are you here?"

Jesse felt his anger rise. "Why are *you*?"

"That's none of your business."

"Exactly."

Leland's mouth flattened to a thin, angry line. He nodded toward the two men who stood at his sides. "These gentlemen are with the FBI."

Jesse nodded at them. "Nice to meet you."

One of the two men shot Jesse a look of mild amusement, but the other continued to look grim and imposing.

"Where is Parisa McGinnis?" Leland asked.

There was no point in lying. "In the delivery suite, having her baby."

Leland nodded toward the door. "Get out of the way."

"You never did say why you were here," Jesse said,

keeping his tone conversational, even as he refused to budge.

"This is a federal investigation."

The door behind Jesse opened, and Connor nudged him aside, taking Jesse's place. He closed the door behind him and gave Garrett Leland a glowering look. "This is a hospital. My wife is in labor. I don't care who you are or why you're here, you will remove yourselves from this corridor until after she's delivered. Do you understand?"

Behind Jesse, Evie cleared her throat deliberately. He looked at her, and she nodded toward the nurse's desk, where a silver-haired man dressed in a dark gray suit and crimson tie stood with his own entourage. One of the men beside him was holding a large brown teddy bear, while another was carrying a small potted plant.

Jesse grinned as the silver-haired man spotted the clump of uniforms down the hall. The old man began to walk with a strong, purposeful stride toward them, his entourage following in his wake.

"Major McGinnis!" The man's bombastic drawl carried down the hall. "How is your lovely wife?"

A look of pure loathing twisted Garrett Leland's face, but he schooled his features quickly as he turned to face the newcomer. "Senator Blackledge. How unexpected."

Gerald Blackledge pulled up short of the man from Homeland Security, his thick silver eyebrows notching upward with mild disdain. "Well, of course it was. I took great care to keep my trip here under wraps." He turned his attention to Connor. "I hope all is well with Mrs. McGinnis?"

"So far, so good, Senator."

"Wonderful. My committee so looks forward to hearing from her as soon as she's well enough to speak to us."

"Senator, I'm afraid Mrs. McGinnis is under arrest."

"Nonsense." Blackledge waved off the notion with one hand. "Mrs. McGinnis is a national hero. I believe if you'll check in with the secretary of Homeland Security, you'll find that your precipitous trip to the lovely state of Kentucky was for naught. The warrant for Mrs. McGinnis's apprehension was a dreadful misunderstanding. She is, in fact, a vital part of the Senate's investigation into governmental corruption."

Leland didn't hide his fury. "You're overstepping your bounds, sir."

Blackledge took two strides forward, until he stood directly in front of the man from Homeland Security. "And you, Mr. Leland, have dug your own grave."

Leland was half a head taller than Blackledge, and at least three decades younger, and for a moment, Jesse thought the man from Homeland Security was about to take a swing at the senator. But when the two FBI agents who'd accompanied him to the hospital stepped away and joined the ranks of the senator's entourage, leaving Leland standing in the midst of several confused-looking Kentucky lawmen, the younger man soon realized he'd been beaten.

He started to leave, then stopped and slowly turned to look at Connor. "This is not over."

Connor's lips curved into a feral smile that gave even Jesse a chill. "You're right. It's not."

As Leland began to walk away, a growl of pain erupted inside the delivery suite. Connor hurried back through the door, shutting out all the drama behind him.

Evie sidled closer to Jesse, slipping her hand into his. "I can't believe I'm about to say this, given what a whiny little pain in the backside she's been for the past week, but I can't wait to get back home to Cara."

Jesse pictured his little daughter's scrunched-up, reddened face—Cara Cooper at her imperious worst—and smiled. "Me, either."

"SHE'S BEAUTIFUL," CONNOR BREATHED, one large finger brushing delicately over the newborn's wrinkled red forehead.

Risa took in the slightly misshapen head, the toothless maw opened wide and emitting soft bleats, the reddened skin and squinty eyes, and murmured her agreement. "The most beautiful thing I've ever seen."

Connor met her tired gaze. "I wouldn't go that far. Her mother's just as beautiful."

Risa laughed. "This must be that post-childbirth temporary euphoria thing I've heard about."

The nurse approached with a rueful smile. "Dr. Sankar, our neonatal specialist, wants to give her a full examination since she's a couple of weeks early, so I need to take her to the neonatal unit for a bit. Why don't you try to sleep, Mrs. McGinnis? If everything is okay, I'll bring her back before you know it."

With reluctance, Risa released the infant into the nurse's care, reaching for Connor's hand. "Do you think you could go with her? After everything we've just gone through, I don't like letting her out of our sight."

He gave her hand a squeeze. "I'll see what I can do."

Risa tried to relax, her body aching with overall weariness, beyond the physical ordeal of giving birth. She knew she was probably being overly anxious—the hospital was one of the best in the state, and everyone she'd talked to during her labor had assured her there was ample security in the neonatal unit as well as the nursery.

Connor was back a minute later. "Quinn is here."

Risa frowned. "Why aren't you with the baby?"

"They wouldn't let me go into the neonatal unit, but Quinn brought Eric Brannon, so he suited up and went to stand guard. He has a license to practice medicine in Kentucky, so it's sort of a professional courtesy thing, apparently."

"Are you sure we can trust him?"

"Maddox Heller says yes, and I trust Heller."

She caught Connor's hand, tugging it up to her chest. "And I trust you."

Connor pulled up a chair and sat by the bed, leaning closer. "I love you."

"I love you." She touched his face, relished the rasp of his beard growth against her fingers. "We have a daughter."

His smile was like sunlight. "We do."

"What do you want to name her?"

"I haven't given it much thought," he admitted with a soft chuckle. "I didn't know I was going to be a father until a few days ago, and I was a little preoccupied with other issues."

"I have to admit, I really thought she was going to be a boy." She sighed. "So most of my best name ideas were boy names."

"We could name her after your mother."

She made a face. "Nazina? My mother doesn't even like her name that much."

"My mother?"

"You know I love Shirley, but..."

Connor grinned. "It's a little dated."

"One of the boy names I liked was Kyle," she said, stifling a yawn. "Maybe we could feminize it. How does Kylie sound?"

He tried it out. "Kylie McGinnis."

"Flows well."

He smiled. "It does. Kylie Parisa McGinnis."

Risa wrinkled her nose. "We'll work on the middle name."

He bent and kissed her forehead. "Get some sleep. Kylie will be back in here, looking for an early breakfast before you know it."

Sinking a little deeper into her pillows, Risa closed her eyes and dreamed.

Epilogue

Christmas morning came complete with a light dusting of snow outside the Sunset Lodges cabin where Connor and Risa had returned after she and tiny Kylie were released from the hospital. She'd given two hours of testimony by video feed from the Meade Motor Inn to Senator Blackledge's panel shortly after she and the baby had been cleared to leave the hospital, then joined a convoy of both Cooper Security and Campbell Cove Security Services agents back to the mountain cabin still booked through New Year's Eve.

"Your apartment isn't set up for a new baby," Maddox had told Connor when he bundled them into the Durango for the trip back to Sunset Mountain. "Iris is going to go shopping for the things you'll need back home. I think Evie Cooper's got you covered until New Year's Eve at the cabin. Just relax. Enjoy Christmas with your family."

By family, it turned out, Maddox had meant more than just Risa and their newborn. Connor's parents as well as Risa's were waiting for them at the cabin. Nazina and Benton DeVille were in tears at their first sight of the daughter they thought they'd lost, but it didn't take long for them to transfer a large chunk of their joy to their introduction to their first grandchild.

The past few days had been chaotic, if full of joy, but Connor was happy that he and little Kylie were the first ones up on Christmas morning.

He soothed the mewling infant as he carried her into the large living room, where the first glow of sunrise tinted the eastern sky. The Coopers had gifted them with more than just the baby gear they needed for Kylie while they were staying in the cabin. They'd also trimmed the tree with small, sparkling lights that glowed like stars in the gray morning light when he flicked the power switch.

"I don't think you can see the twinkles yet, baby girl, but one day, when you see a big tree like this, decorated with lights and garland, you're going to be overcome with happiness." He kissed the fuzzy crown of her head. "And greed. But we'll deal with that when it happens."

"Life lessons with Daddy?" Risa's raspy voice made him turn toward the doorway, where he found her mussed and sleepy-eyed, leaning against the wooden frame.

"Something like that." He watched with sympathy as she hobbled toward him, still a little sore from the birth. "Did you get any sleep?"

"Yeah, I got some. You?"

"Some." He rubbed his cheek against Kylie's head. "I guess it's Mommy time, baby girl. She's the one with the milk."

Risa settled in the padded rocking chair near the window and reached for Kylie. Connor handed her over and perched on the window seat beside the rocker while she unbuttoned the front of her nightshirt and guided Kylie to her breast.

With greedy grunts, the baby began to feed, and Risa lifted her gaze to Connor's. "I'm trying really hard to relax, but it's difficult to shake the feeling that I need to be running and hiding."

"I know. You've been at it a long time. But everyone we talked to agreed that you should be safe, now that you've given your testimony. And Campbell Cove Security is going to give us protection for a few weeks, just to be sure."

"I wonder if my testimony is enough to stop whatever Garrett Leland and his cohort were planning for Kaziristan." Risa frowned. "Every time things seem to be going the way of the democratic reformers, something always happens to set them back."

"Rebecca Cameron told me she's going to be heading a task force at Campbell Cove Security to look a little deeper into what happened with Akwat. She asked me if I thought you'd like to be part of that task force."

"You mean work for them?"

"It's a good place to work. We're doing important things there."

She looked down at Kylie. "I can't make that decision right now. All I can think about is our little family."

"There's time."

She looked up at him, her eyes sparkling with tears. "I'm really happy our families are here to share this Christmas with us, but I sort of wish it was just us. We have so much to talk through."

He didn't pretend he didn't know what she meant. "You know, I think we could get ourselves tangled up in all the mistakes and all the choices we made, right or wrong. We could turn this whole thing into a bigger mess without much trouble."

Risa made a face. "I don't want that."

"So let's not. I just need to know one thing. Do you love me?"

She touched his hand where it lay on his knee. "God, yes."

"And I love you."

She gave his hand a squeeze. "I know."

"We want to be together as a family. You, me, Kylie and whatever children we might have in the future, yes?"

She smiled, tears sparkling in her eyes. "Yes."

"Then let's make it happen. Whatever it takes." He leaned over and kissed her, then brushed his lips across Kylie's head. "It's always been how we do things, isn't it?"

She touched his face, her fingers soft but strong. "Yes." Then she pulled him toward her for a longer, deeper kiss.

The sound of stirring down the hall filtered through Connor's haze of happiness. The rumble of his father's voice made him smile and groan at the same time. "Grandparent alert."

Risa laughed softly. "Don't complain. We might be glad to have them hovering around once the sleep deprivation starts to kick in."

Giving Risa one more swift kiss, Connor turned to wish his parents happy Christmas.

The best Christmas ever.

* * * * *

Campbell Cove Academy is just heating up!
Look for THE GIRL WHO CRIED MURDER,
the newest book in award-winning author
Paula Graves's series
CAMPBELL COVE ACADEMY,
available next month.

You'll find it wherever
Intrigue books are sold!

MILLS & BOON®

INTRIGUE
Romantic Suspense

A SEDUCTIVE COMBINATION OF DANGER AND DESIRE

A sneak peek at next month's titles...

In stores from 20th October 2016:

- **Landon** – Delores Fossen *and*
  Navy SEAL Six Pack – Elle James
- **The Girl Who Cried Murder** – Paula Graves *and*
  In the Arms of the Enemy – Carol Ericson
- **Scene of the Crime: Means and Motive** –
  Carla Cassidy *and* **Christmas Kidnapping** –
  Cindi Myers

Romantic Suspense

- **Runaway Colton** – Karen Whiddon
- **Operation Soldier Next Door** – Justine Davis

Just can't wait?
Buy our books online a month before they hit the shops!
www.millsandboon.co.uk

Also available as eBooks.

MILLS & BOON®

Why shop at millsandboon.co.uk?

Each year, thousands of romance readers find their perfect read at millsandboon.co.uk. That's because we're passionate about bringing you the very best romantic fiction. Here are some of the advantages of shopping at www.millsandboon.co.uk:

* **Get new books first**—you'll be able to buy your favourite books one month before they hit the shops

* **Get exclusive discounts**—you'll also be able to buy our specially created monthly collections, with up to 50% off the RRP

* **Find your favourite authors**—latest news, interviews and new releases for all your favourite authors and series on our website, plus ideas for what to try next

* **Join in**—once you've bought your favourite books, don't forget to register with us to rate, review and join in the discussions

Visit **www.millsandboon.co.uk**
for all this and more today!

ILLS_WEB

Former naval intelligence officer and US Naval Academy graduate **Geri Krotow** draws inspiration from the global situations she's experienced. Geri loves to hear from her readers. You can email her via her website and blog, gerikrotow.com.

Also by Geri Krotow

Her Christmas Protector
Wedding Takedown
Her Secret Christmas Agent
Secret Agent Under Fire
The Fugitive's Secret Child
Reunion Under Fire
The Pregnant Colton Bride
The Billionaire's Colton Threat

Discover more at millsandboon.co.uk